Perfect Daughter

Amanda Prowse

W F HOWES LTD

This large print edition published in 2015 by
W F Howes Ltd
Unit 4, Rearsby Business Park, Gaddesby Lane,
Rearsby, Leicester LE7 4YH

1 3 5 7 9 10 8 6 4 2

First published in the United Kingdom in 2015
by Head of Zeus Ltd.

A CIP catalogue record for this book is available
from the British Library

ISBN 978 1 51000 979 0

Typeset by Palimpsest Book Production Limited,
Falkirk, Stirlingshire

P.   ritain
by TJ   Cornwall

I am so lucky to have the Perfect Niece! Amelie Beth Smith, you are beautiful inside and out. We are all so very, very proud of you. You are kind, patient, smart and funny and I can't wait to watch your journey unfold. Never forget how much you are loved.

PROLOGUE

When the last of the guests had left and Jacks had wrapped the leftover sausage rolls in clingfilm, the newlyweds kicked off their shoes and lay on their donated double bed, looking up at the ceiling.

'That all went well, didn't it?'

It had been a small, low-key wedding at the Register Office on the Boulevard. The registrar had mumbled and Pete's mum had cried. And then everyone had piled back to their new home in Sunnyside Road, bought with the help of both sets of parents. Pete scooted round putting coasters under cans of beer, Jacks passed around plates of sandwiches and cakes, and her best friend Gina teased her for acting like a grown-up married woman. Jacks had looked around the small, square kitchen of their little Weston-super-Mare terrace, trying to stop her mind flying to the vast kitchen in the seafront villa where she had not so long ago lain on a daybed and succumbed to the charms of a boy who had told her about the big wide world beyond her doorstep and had made her believe that one day, she might see it.

1

Then she had spied her dad, Don, with his arm around Pete's shoulder, and felt a strange sort of contentment. She sidled up between them.

'I was just saying to young Pete here, the best advice I can give you is never go to bed on a cross word. And if you can smile through the bad times, just imagine how much you will laugh in the good.'

'And the best advice I can give is don't take advice from him!' Jacks' mum jerked her thumb in her husband's direction. She spoke a little louder than she would normally – but normally she wouldn't have polished off three glasses of Asti and four Martini-and-lemonades.

'Thank you, Don.' Pete had beamed at his new wife. 'I'll look after her, I promise,' he'd said, as if she wasn't present.

Pete stroked Jacks' shoulder and brought her back to the present. 'Feels weird having all these rooms to wander around in and only us to live in them. Three bedrooms, the bathroom and two rooms downstairs – I'm still used to being in my little bedroom at my mum's!'

'I know, me too. It'll be great, Pete, all this space.'

She scratched the itching skin, stretched taut across her stomach. 'There'll be one more occupant before we know it!'

'Yep. Can't wait. Shall we decorate the littlest room, make it cosy?'

'What with? Don't think we've got any spare cash for decorating right now.' She hated having to point out the practicalities and quash his enthusiasm.

'I know, and I don't mean anything flash, but we can manage a lick of paint. And Gina's arty, couldn't we get her to draw something on the walls?'

'Blimey, I've seen her artwork. No thanks! Poor baby would be waking up to the Take That logo every morning.'

They both laughed. Pete reached for her hand. 'I've got a wife.'

'Yes, you have.' She smiled.

'Do you feel like a wife?' he asked.

'I suppose I do. What are wives supposed to feel like?'

She felt him shrug. 'Don't know. I guess like they are part of a pair, and no longer having to face the world on their own.'

'Oh, Pete, you old softie! That's lovely, and yes, in that case I do feel like a wife.' She leant across and kissed him.

'I wonder how long we'll live here.' Jacks let her words float out into the darkness.

'I reckon a couple of years, just till we are on our feet. We should get this place shipshape, replace the windows, get the garden nice, put a new kitchen in and then move up.'

She smiled into the darkness, loving the idea of a new kitchen and a lovely garden. 'Poor house, we've only been in it for three weeks and already we are planning on moving!'

'It's good to plan, Jacks, set our path and find a way. That's how you get on in life, isn't it. You work hard and you fight for better.'

'I like that, Pete. Work hard and fight for better – it sounds like a plan.' She squeezed his hand. 'I wouldn't want much more than this, mind. Maybe an en-suite bathroom and room in the kitchen for one of them big fridges.'

'I'd love a garage. I could have a workbench and a place to store all my tools and I could make things.'

She could tell he was smiling. 'What would you make?'

'Dunno. Things from wood and I could do repairs, fix things. I'd love to be out there tinkering.'

Jacks chuckled. 'You sound like my dad!'

'I'll take that as a compliment.'

'I tell you what I would love, a conservatory, with wicker furniture in it. I'd sit in it and read a magazine and have a coffee, somewhere to put my feet up.'

'That sounds like a plan.'

She nestled up to him and laid her head on his chest.

'Funny how things work out, isn't it, Mrs Davies?'

Jacks smiled at the unfamiliar title. 'It sure is.'

CHAPTER 1

S
he supposed it was a talent of sorts, her ability
to wake a couple of minutes before her alarm
roused her every single morning. It didn't
seem like a big deal – who worried about a measly
two minutes here or there? But when she multi-
plied them over a year, it amounted to an extra
seven hundred and thirty minutes of sleep that
she was missing out on. And when you were as
tired as she was, those extra twelve hours over the
course of a year would have been most welcome.
She wished she could take them all at once, literally just lie in bed, in silence and drift off without
fear of disturbance. Bliss.

She lay back and stared at the ceiling with its
fringed blue paisley lampshade housing a single
dull bulb hanging from the centre. They had meant
to change the shade for something yellow to match
the wallpaper, that had been the plan, they might
even have had a look at a few in British Home
Stores, she couldn't remember, but fifteen years
later it still hadn't happened. Like everything else
in the house that was defunct, mismatched or
ageing, they had got used to it, lived with it, until

5

it was just how things were. This even applied to the cardboard boxes full of clothes and bits and bobs that had been packaged up and stacked in the front hallway. They were intended for the loft. What had he said? 'Pop 'em there, love, and I'll shove them up in the loft next time I bring the ladder in.' But three years later, they had taken root in the hallway, become furniture. She hoovered around them and stacked clean laundry on the top, and the kids threw their school bags on to them rather than take them upstairs. In fact she wasn't even sure what was in a couple of them.

Opening her eyes wide, she tried to force herself into a greater state of wakefulness. Her nightie was twisted in an uncomfortable ring around her midriff; she lifted her bottom and in her crab-like pose pulled the fabric until it lay flat beneath her. She had got into the habit of wearing both a nightie and pyjama bottoms, whether for warmth, comfort or an added obstacle for Pete to navigate should the mood take him, she wasn't sure. Although she had to admit the mood hadn't taken him for quite some time and, if she was being honest, that was something of a relief.

She glanced across at her husband, who slept without a pillow, his head tipped back, mouth open, his dark stubble poking like little sticks through skin that could do with a good dollop of moisturiser. Chance would be a fine thing – he considered owning hair gel a statement of questionable sexuality. Unaware of her scrutiny, he raised his arm and scratched his nose. Then he turned and breathed open mouthed in her direction. She looked away; anything his body emitted at that time of the morning was less than fragrant. He was still a young man, still good-looking when he was spruced up, but there was something about him in the early-morning light, with the sweat of a warm night clinging to his skin and his breath laced with spices, that made her shrink from him.

She smiled at the irony as she flexed her toes inside his old sports socks that she slept in. Hardly sexy. He still on occasion had the ability to elicit a longing deep inside her, especially when he smelt good and was confident, reminding her of the self-assured banter of their youth. She remembered when they left school, eighteen years ago. She had been a beauty then, with her long, slim legs, blonde hair and a tan that seemed to last year round. Her nose was freckled and her long eyelashes framed her green eyes without the need for mascara. Whenever she stumbled across photographs from that era, it always shocked her how lovely she had been and how unaware of it she was. She recalled her many insecurities and how she had worried about the slight cleft to her chin, her gangly limbs.

They had married soon after they had started dating and in those days slept skin to skin, her face pressed into his chest, arms and legs entwined. Any time separated was considered a waste. They would wake in the early hours to make love before falling asleep again. Not that she had needed much sleep, not then. Neither sleep nor food sustained her, all she needed was him, him and her new baby. The sight of him, the thought of him, the feel of him against her, he was everything.

Jacks crept from their bed and looked back at him as he screwed his eyes shut, wrinkled his nose and farted. She rolled her eyes. 'Those were the days,' she whispered as she collected her towel from the back of the old dining chair in the corner of the room and headed for the shower.

'Mum?'

'What?' Jacks answered without lifting her head from the newspaper. It was 7.15. She had shoved on some clothes, run a brush through her hair, turned on the lights, flicked on the heating, placed the breakfast cereal on the table and made a hot drink. She now sat at the kitchen table. This was her one small window of opportunity at the beginning of every day when she was able to read the local news. A brief moment before the world came rushing up to meet her and she had to run to keep up, like a lady she'd once seen balancing on a glittery ball in the circus. Her smile had been fixed, but under her elaborate false eyelashes Jacks had seen the terror in her eyes. One wrong step and she would fall off. Jacks knew exactly how she felt.

'Mum?' The shout was louder this time.

She closed her eyes. 'For God's sake, Martha, you know I hate this shouting up and down the stairs.' She tapped her palm on the kitchen table, liking the sound of her wedding band on the wooden surface. 'How many times have I told you, if you want to ask me something, come down here!' She shook her head and returned to the article in the *Weston Mercury*, interested in how to get a smear-free shine on your conservatory windows with nothing more than warm water and a squirt of vinegar.

Her daughter's footsteps thundered down the uncarpeted stairs. Jacks drew breath: how many times *had* she told her? Too many to count, but Martha, aged seventeen, who had lived in this house since she was born, still hadn't mastered conversing face to face, preferring to holler from room to room. Neither, it would seem, had she learnt how to walk down the stairs without shaking the rafters.

'Have I got a shirt for school?' She practically bounced on the spot, her tone was urgent. It amazed Jacks that despite the fact that they left the house at 7.45 every morning and had done so for the last six years, time always seemed to sneak up on Martha like it was a shock or a deviation from the norm, each and every morning.

Jacks looked at her daughter in her tight black school skirt, thick woolly tights and pyjama top, reeking of perfume and trying to tease her roots with her fingers as she loitered in the doorway. She decided not to comment on the dark ring of black kohl that masked her daughter's pretty blue eyes and made her heart-shaped face look top-heavy. There were only so many times she could have that conversation. Besides, when she was a lawyer, rushing up the court steps in a crisp white shirt with her briefcase full of important notes, she would surely rethink her knotty hair and over-the-top eye make-up. She would want to emulate her colleagues. Jacks smiled at the thought. Her brilliant girl, soon to take her A levels, which would put her on the path to a university education and then a dazzling career. Jacks would never forget Mrs Fentiman, the woman who had come into Martha's school and given a talk, extolling the virtues of doing law and painting a picture so vivid, Jacks could taste the champagne with which they toasted their wins and could smell the leather-topped desk at which she sat and enjoyed a perfect view of St Paul's Cathedral. Her suit was elegantly tailored and she wore Chanel earrings. Jacks wanted that life for Martha, all of it. She wanted Martha to go into schools and inspire girls to strive for better, she wanted her to drink flutes of champagne in chambers instead of pints of cider-and-black under the pier.

'So have I got a shirt?' Martha prompted.

Jacks nodded. 'In the airing cupboard.'

'The airing cupboard on the landing I just came from?' Martha pointed to the ceiling.

'That's the one.' Jacks traced the words of the newspaper article with her finger, ignoring her daughter's sarcasm.

'If you don't mind me asking, what is it you're reading?' Martha was chewing gum, which Jacks found inexplicable before breakfast. It must make everything taste of mint and what if she accidentally swallowed it? That didn't bear thinking about.

'It's an article about conservatory windows and how to clean them.' She looked at her daughter as her tortoiseshell-framed glasses slipped down her nose.

'But we haven't even got a conservatory!' Martha rolled her eyes.

Jacks removed her specs and looked at the back wall of the kitchen that ran the width of their house. 'Yet. I don't have a conservatory yet.'

Martha rolled her eyes again. 'Instead of a conservatory, can't you just build an extra bedroom in the loft so I don't have to share with Jonty? I hate sharing with him. It's not fair!'

'Really, Martha? Funny how you've not mentioned it.' She gave a wry smile as her daughter thumped back up the stairs. Jacks felt a familiar flicker of guilt. Martha was right; she shouldn't have to share with her little brother. Jonty had been moved into his big sister's room with a set of open bookshelves dividing the space when Jacks' mum had come to live with them. It was Martha's favourite topic of conversation. Jacks had hoped the complaints about just how hard done by she was might have waned. They hadn't.

For the first time that day she considered the seven thousand, four hundred and eighty-two pounds that sat in their savings account and had done so for a little over a year. It was the sum that remained from the sale of her parents' house, a couple of streets away in Addicott Road, once they had paid for the hoist to be installed in the bathroom. A hoist her mum never used because it scared her and anyway, as it turned out, it was so much easier to pop her in the shower, less palaver. The hoist, however, hadn't cost as much as the stair lift that had been fitted. A stair lift on which Jacks bashed her shins in the dark of night and about which she had to continually reprimand Jonty, who liked using it as a ride and to ferry his Transformers up and down.

'I'll be late tonight. City are playing at home, Tuesday-night friendly, so don't worry about tea, I'll get a pie at Ashton Gate.' This her husband Pete yelled excitedly from the landing. She shook her head; no wonder Martha thought shouting was okay.

'Righto.' She sighed, reaching for her mug and draining the contents. The best cup of tea in the whole day was undoubtedly this first one.

'Mu–um?' Jonty hollered from behind the bedroom door.

'I give up.' Jacks closed the paper and placed her empty mug and toast plate in the sink. 'Yes, love?'

'I need to take in some things to make a model of a famous building!'

'What?' Jacks spun round and marched from the kitchen into their narrow hallway, avoiding the sports bag that blocked her path and the stack of boxes, hoping she had misheard.

'Mrs Palmer says we need to take in things from our household rubbish and recycling that we can use to build a model of a famous building.' He was precise, probably reading from whatever scrap of paper he had discovered bearing this information.

'When do you need it by?' *Not today, please not today . . .*

'Today!' he answered.

'God, Jonty! And you are telling me *now*?' Jacks snapped. Placing her hands on her slender hips, she tried to think of a solution: what had they thrown away recently that might resemble a building?

'Thought we weren't supposed to shout up the stairs?' Martha poked her head around the bathroom door, her hand gripping the straightening irons that were plugged in on the landing.

'Don't be sarky to your mum,' Pete interjected as he thundered down the stairs in his baggy sweatpants, thick socks, long-sleeved T-shirt and body warmer, the uniform of a man who worked outside.

'I would have told you before, but I forgot!' Jonty explained.

'We out of milk?' Pete called.

Jacks turned her head towards the kitchen. 'No, it's on the side, near the kettle!' Then she trod the first stair. 'Forgetting is no good, Jonty. I've told you to let me have any notes or pieces of paper as soon as you bring them out of school. That way we can make sure we have a bit of notice for things like this.'

'Yeah, we don't want a repeat of the Harvest Festival embarrassment!' Martha laughed.

'Thank you for that, Martha! Just get yourself ready.' Jacks felt her cheeks flame as she remembered sending him off for the grand Harvest Festival service with an offering of a tin of pinto beans and a Cadbury's Creme Egg. It was all she could lay her hands on at the last minute as they had walked out of the front door. Apparently Mrs Palmer had sniffed at the items and asked what pinto beans were. To which Jonty had replied, 'They're for making pinto.' Jacks had grabbed them in error from the supermarket shelf and was secretly quite glad not to have them lurking in the cupboard, taunting her with their fancy label, confirming her lack of culinary knowhow.

'Sorry, Mum,' Jonty offered.

'That's okay.' She smiled, the sound of his eight-year-old baby voice and his contrition twisting her heart. He was a good boy, her baby. 'Can you both come down and have your breakfast as soon as you're ready, I don't want to be late today!'

'*I* gave you a piece of paper a week ago, about that art trip to Paris and you still haven't said if I can go or not!' Martha said.

'Your dad and I are still discussing it.' Jacks nodded. She placed her hand on her forehead, simultaneously trying to think about what Jonty could take in and how to explain to Martha that there just weren't the funds for a trip to Paris. The savings-account money was for a rainy day or any expenses her mum might have. Her own conservatory was a pipe dream and so, sadly, was her daughter's desire to go to Paris. Paris indeed! It made her chuckle. In her day they'd had a trip to Oldbury Power Station, with a packed lunch thrown in.

'What are we still discussing?' Pete asked from the kitchen.

'Martha's trip to Paris!' Jacks replied.

'So I *can* go?' Martha said.

Jacks shook her head. 'No, we are still discussing it!'

'I don't know why anyone would want to go to Paris!' Pete joined in from the kitchen table. 'Dirty, 'orrible place where you'll get mugged and you need a mortgage just to buy a cup of tea!'

'Dad, you think I'm going to get mugged everywhere! You said I'd get mugged if I went to Worle on my own on the bus, and I didn't!'

'You was just lucky, girl. And just cos you survived Worle, doesn't mean you'll have the same luck in Paris.'

'And anyway, how do you know what Paris is like, you've never even been!' Martha pointed out.

'No interest in it, love, that's why.'

'God, Dad, you think going up to Bristol is a big day out!'

''Tis when the mighty City are playing.' Pete clapped his hands together, making a big noise.

'Can I come with you tonight, Dad, to see the mighty City?' Jonty asked.

'No, mate. No midweek games till you can stand a round at The Robins, them's the rules.'

'I think you make up the rules as you go along.' Martha jumped to her little brother's defence. 'It's not up to Dad if I go to France or not, is it, Mum? You know what he's like!'

'I *can* hear you, Miss Martha!' Pete yelled.

'What building am I making, Mum?' Jonty asked.

'Errmm . . .' Jacks was trying to think of something when the bell rang out, loud and clear above the chatter and accusations flying back and forth up and down the stairs.

'Nan's ringing!' Jonty and Martha shouted in unison.

I know. I heard it.

When Jacks' mum, Ida Morgan, had first come to live with them eighteen months ago, she had seemed disorientated, uncomfortable and confused, so Jacks had given her a small hand bell, to be rung whenever she needed tending to. Turned out she needed tending to quite a lot.

When Ida's dementia had first become apparent, several years ago now, it was ignored. Jacks' dad, Don, had trivialised it and they had all just gone along with it, joining in the banter of distraction. What did it matter if Ida forgot where she lived and served frozen oven chips without cooking them first? Called everybody by the wrong name, put eggs in the tumble dryer and the car keys in a jar of coffee? Jacks' dad had made light of it as he tried to keep things ticking along, not wanting to frighten his wife or distress their only daughter. But after he died, Ida declined rapidly; or maybe it was that Jacks' dad had shielded her from the extent of her mum's condition. Either way, it was a shock.

To begin with, Jacks would go round to Addicott Road and sit with her mum during the day and Pete would pop in on her every night, checking up on her and locking the doors and windows for bedtime. One night he found her in the garden, wearing nothing but her nightie as she placed food on the small patch of lawn. He watched as she piled up uncooked potatoes, scattered cereal from boxes and threw down an old chicken carcass and some cheese on to the grass.

'What are you doing, Ida?' he had asked gently.

She looked at him without recognition. 'I'm putting food out for the rabbits,' she replied. 'They don't feed themselves, you know!'

'You really shouldn't do that, Ida. It will attract rats,' he said softly, racking his brain, trying to recall if they had ever had a pet rabbit.

'Don't be stupid!' she snapped. 'This isn't food for the rats, it's for the rabbits!'

He had guided her inside the house, where she made a cup of tea as though nothing had happened.

Not long after that, Jacks and Pete decided she

should move in with them, to Sunnyside Road. Eighteen months on and her mum was now frail. She was quiet mostly, with the odd burst of lucidity, preferring to be in bed than on the sofa and favouring things that were familiar and routine. Sometimes she recognised her family and at other times not. For Ida it was a dark, difficult and lonely way to live. And, awful though it was to admit, for Jacks, Pete and the kids it was as if a ghoulish spectre lurked in the rooms Ida occupied, visible and scary; given the choice, they avoided sitting in its shadow. They loved her of course, but the kids could find little to recognise in the old lady who yelled and whistled; she was quite unlike the nan who used to make the best apple pie in the world and who would sneak them sweets before bedtime when their mum wasn't looking.

Jacks placed her cupped hands at her mouth and hollered, 'Shan't be a minute, Mum!' before dashing into the kitchen. 'Mum's ringing, Pete. Do me a favour, try and find Jonty something he can make a building out of. You'll need to sort through the recycling in the boxes out back.' She disappeared into the hallway.

Pete stopped shovelling his cornflakes and stared after his wife. 'What?' he called, but it was too late, she was already running up the stairs.

Jacks stood on the small square landing and gripped the door handle. She inhaled and painted on a smile.

Holding her breath, as she did every morning, unwilling to breathe in the claustrophobic fug of ammonia, wind and something akin to rotting, she marched over to the curtains and pulled them wide as she opened the window a little, welcoming the cold blast that hit her face. It was a decent-sized bedroom, with built-in wardrobes along one wall and a double bed facing the window. The floral rugs were from her parents' house, as were the pictures on the walls and the cluster of photographs dotted along the windowsill showing Jacks through the ages.

She turned to the wizened figure in the middle of the bed. Ida was shrinking month on month, slipping further and further down the mattress each night, to the point that Jacks imagined she might one day turn to dust and disappear altogether. At least then Jonty could have his room back. She swallowed the wicked thought. This was her mum after all.

'Morning, Mum!' she chirped, not expecting a response. Jacks adopted a note of false joviality for when she addressed her mother. It made it easier somehow to smile and be jolly, just as it did with any boring job or tricky customer. 'How did you sleep? Good? Come on, let's get you up.'

She pulled back the pink candlewick bedspread that had graced her parents' marital bed for as long as she could remember. She had a vivid memory of being scolded by her mum for picking off the pattern, pulling the tiny threads between

19

her fingernails until there was a square inch of missing ripple and a bald spot in its place. This treasured cover was one of the few things that had travelled with her across town.

'It's a lovely brand-new day!' Jacks beamed as she pulled her mum's pale lilac nightie up above her nappy. She was no longer embarrassed or even noticed the sodden bulk that sat between Ida's emaciated limbs. Her actions were purposeful, matter of fact, focused. This hadn't always been the case. The first few months had been a steep learning curve. Jacks had felt very uncomfortable and, shocked by her mother's body, her hesitancy and reluctance to touch her had served only to heighten the grim reality for them both. They had never been over-demonstrative, not the kind to hug or kiss, and nudity had been a big no-no. Prior to the monumental shift in their relationship, she had seen her mum in a bathing costume maybe once or twice and that was the extent of their intimacy. Yet all of a sudden she was forced to clean under the flat, sagging, triangular-shaped breasts with their long nipples pointing towards the floor; to touch the ancient, leathery skin that was almost translucent, stretched over brittle bones and peppered with protruding, purple veins; and to clothe her private parts, now hairless and defunct. At first this was repellent, shocking, but it soon became just another area that needed soaping and drying before being eased into the demeaning adult nappy that reduced her mother to the status of a helpless baby.

'Let's get you comfy.' Jacks smiled as she turned her mother gently on the mattress until she was lying on her back. The crackle of the plastic under-sheet provided the familiar background noise. Jacks pulled a clean nappy from the basket on top of the chest of drawers and grabbed the wet wipes that sat next to them. 'I'll get you shipshape, Mum, then I'll bring you a nice cup of tea, how about that? I'll drop the kids at school and then I'll do your breakfast when I get back. I shan't be too long and Pete will be here for a bit. You'll only be on your own for a few minutes.' It was similar to what she repeated every morning, with no idea how much of it went in, offered more to reassure herself than relay information.

'I . . . I'm waiting for that letter,' her mum stated, clearly, eloquently.

'Oh, right. Well, the postman's not been yet, but I'll keep an eye out for him and if he brings you a letter, I'll pop it straight up to you.' She kept a singsong note to her words, as though addressing a petulant child. Waiting for letters that never came was one of Ida's more recent obsessions. It had started one Sunday lunch, when she'd suddenly burst into tears and shouted, 'I've lost them! I've lost them all! They were in a bundle, all my letters. I tried to keep them safe, but now they've gone!' No one had any idea what she meant, but they soon found that humouring her was the best response.

'I've had an idea!' Pete shouted up the stairs.

21

'What about the Leaning Tower of Pisa? I can do that with four beer cans and an empty Cornetto.'

'I don't want to do a tower! That's rubbish. It's just beer cans!' Jonty replied. 'Mu-um? Mum? Tell Dad I can't just do a tower, that's just rubbish!'

'It's supposed to be rubbish, you wally.' Martha laughed.

'Just one second, Mum.' Jacks pulled the blankets and bedspread over Ida's semi-naked form. She thrust the soiled nappy into an empty carrier bag and tied it with a double knot. Popping her head out on to the landing, she spoke quietly but firmly.

'Martha, don't call your brother a wally. And Jonty, you don't have much choice at this stage in the game, love. Dad is doing his best to find stuff for you to take in at very short notice. Now go and eat your breakfast, both of you.' She smiled at her little boy, who stood with his arms folded across his chest.

'But I don't want to do a tower, it'll be pants.' His eyes brimmed with tears.

'What do you want to do then?' Jacks spoke quickly, encouraging her son to match her pace. She had her mum to see to, the breakfast things to tidy away and only sixteen, no, fifteen minutes in which to get both kids in the car.

'I want to make the Clifton Suspension Bridge.' He rallied, eyes bright at the idea.

'Clifton Suspension Bridge?' Pete guffawed. 'You'll be lucky, son. I'm afraid it's the Leaning

Tower of Pisa, or the Angel of the North if you bend these three coat hangers.' He held them up.

'The Angel of the North isn't even a building!' Martha shouted as she bolted down the stairs with her jacket and bag over her shoulder.

'Well, excuse me! We can't all be clever, can we, Jacks?' He winked at his wife from the bottom of the stairs.

Jacks bent low and mussed her son's hair. 'Your tower will be fine, Jonty. You can paint it and cover it with foil and bits and bobs. It'll look lovely. And I think it's your best bet in the circumstances.'

'Okaaay,' he mumbled, finally heading downstairs for his breakfast.

Jacks straightened up and returned to her mum's room. As she opened the door, the smell of faeces hit her in the face, offending her nose and making her retch. 'Oh God!' she whispered as she placed her hand over her nose and mouth.

'I have passed water,' Ida stated nonchalantly, as if she was announcing the day of the week.

Jacks nodded and drew back the covers, trying not to inhale through her nose. 'That's okay, Mum. Quick change of plan: we need to get you into the shower for a quick once-over before I take the kids to school. Okay?' Pulling the sheet from the bed, she wrapped it around her mum and manoeuvred her into a sitting position.

'I'm expecting a letter.'

'Yes.' Jacks nodded as she helped her mum to stand, supporting her feather-like weight as she leant against her. 'When it comes, I'll bring it up to you, don't worry.'

With the bathroom now thankfully empty, she used her elbow to open the door, then switched on the shower and removed the sheet and her mother's nightie, bed socks and vest, rolling them into a ball in the corner of the room. 'Here we go.' She guided her mum under the deluge.

'Oooooooh! It's too hot! You are burning me! Help! Someone help me!' Ida shrieked.

Jacks smiled and thrust her own hands into the running water. 'Look, Mum! Look! If it was too hot, it would be burning me too and it's not. It's fine. I checked it. I promise you it's not too hot.' She reached for the shower gel that hung from its natty little plastic hook on the shower bar. 'It's fine, Mum, just the right temperature. See? It's fine.'

She no longer panicked when her mother yelled that she was getting scalded, even though her heart still leapt at the tone of Ida's shrieks. She was used to it, even expected it. And now that she'd explained to their next-door neighbours Angela and Ivor that they might hear this on a regular basis, she no longer felt the lurch of fear that she might get into trouble. She tried not to look at the dark clots of waste that gathered in the plug-hole of the shower cubicle where her children stood. Instead, she concentrated on building a lather between her palms and covering every inch of her mother's skin as quickly as possible.

With four minutes to spare, her mum was

returned to a clean bed, smelling of talc and wrapped in her fleecy bed jacket with Radio 4 on for company.

Pete knocked and entered, carrying a tray with a cup of tea and three Rich Tea biscuits on a saucer. 'Morning, Ida. Here we go, a nice cuppa for you.' He placed the tray on the bedside cabinet.

'Thank you, Toto. So very good to me.' Ida patted her thin hair into place.

'Thanks, love.' Jacks smiled at her husband, whose small acts of kindness when time was at a premium made all the difference.

'Toto?' Ida called from the nest of pillows on which she was propped.

'Yes?' Pete stopped in the doorway and turned. He didn't mind being confused with Ida's long-dead brother. Toto had been in the RAF and, truth be told, Pete quite liked her thinking he had a more dashing career than laying patios up on the new estates that were springing up all over the place.

'I need to see that letter.' She looked at him, concerned.

'Ah, don't you worry. If it turns up today, we'll be sure to run it straight up to you.'

'Mu-um?' Jonty shouted.

'Yes, love, coming! I'll be back in a little while, Mum, to get your breakfast. Okay?'

Ida reached for her tea, made with chilled milk, and ignored her daughter.

It was a day like any other.

CHAPTER 2

Nineteen Years Earlier

Her dad was outside, as if waiting to greet her. 'What time do you call this then?' His voice was stern, but his smiling eyes gave him away.

Jacks laughed at him as he stood in the middle of the grass, his shirtsleeves rolled high above the elbows, leaning on the handle of the lawnmower and pulling his serious face. The smell of cut grass was intoxicating, reminding her of sunshine and lazy, school-free days. The grass as ever looked immaculate, as did the straight, weedless borders. He never tired from telling her that, like a good haircut, his lawn required regular attention.

The summer holidays were right around the corner and she couldn't wait! Six whole weeks when she would never be out of shorts and wouldn't have to wake to the dreaded alarm clock. It was when Weston-super-Mare sprang to life, tourists filling the B&Bs and unfamiliar faces adding variety and excitement as they strolled along the Marine Parade. It was the time of year when everyone seemed to breathe a sigh of relief. Money came in as people queued for ice cream, chips and donkey rides. Laughter and the scent of suntan oil floated in a pungent cloud that settled in even the grimmest of corners, lightening the mood all round.

She looked at her watch. 'Nearly 5.30!'

'Good day at school?' he asked as he lit a cigarette and drew heavily on it, inhaling deeply like it was fresh air and flicking the match twice to make sure it was extinguished, as was his habit.

She nodded; it had in fact been an exceptional day. A bubble of excitement floated from her stomach up into her throat.

'How did netball go?'

'We won! Despite the umpire being really rubbish. She was totally on their side. I was trying to shoot and their goal attack made contact, loads of times! She just overlooked it! And it was right in front of her. I wanted to go mad, but I knew I'd get into trouble so I didn't say anything.'

'But you won anyway?'

'Yes.'

'Well, there's a lesson there then.' He nodded sagely.

'What lesson?' Jacks pushed up the sleeves of her cardigan.

Her dad scratched his chin. 'I'm damned if I know, probably something like, it's good to think before you act, keep a calm head, that kind of thing. But you won anyway, so who cares!'

He trotted over and placed his cigarette-free hand around her shoulders, pulling her towards him and kissing her scalp. He then showered her with a handful of cut grass he'd gathered for the purpose.

Jacks shrieked and jumped backwards, shaking her long hair as she patted her shirt and skirt. 'Da-ad!' She instinctively looked towards the kitchen window, where her mum stood at the sink with pursed lips and a straight back. Jacks felt the disapproval dripping off her.

'Ooh, look, the fun police are on patrol.' Her dad jerked his head towards the house and pulled a wide mouth. 'No spontaneous laughter, you have been warned!' He winked at her.

She wanted to laugh, to come back with a retort, but the feeling that she was being disloyal to her mum kept her silent. It had always been that way. As an only child she regularly felt like a referee, caught in the middle of their daily, long-drawn-out battle.

'Got any homework?' he asked.

'A bit. I've got to read a scene from Oscar Wilde's *An Ideal Husband*. And I have to draw a graph for business studies.'

'An ideal husband? Well, I can help with that. It was probably written about me!' He leant back and laughed loudly.

'Not sure Mum would agree.' Jacks pulled her bag up on to her shoulder and made towards the house.

'Love, if I said black, your mother would say white. She doesn't agree with anything I say.'

Jacks ignored him and pushed open the back door. Not wanting the seesaw of emotions to spoil this wonderful day.

'Tea's nearly ready.' Her mum spoke quietly as she poured a steady stream of salt into a pan of boiling water, into which she would tip the carrots she had peeled and sliced. 'You've got a few minutes if you want to take your stuff upstairs and get settled. I'm just going to lay the table.'

Jacks nodded, her eyes wandering over the mess that her mum always created when she prepared the evening meal.

'What were you and Dad laughing about? I saw you larking about in the garden.' Ida smiled briefly as she gathered the knives and forks and the tomato ketchup bottle.

'Nothing.' Jacks shrugged, feeling her cheeks flame as though laughing with her dad was not allowed.

She climbed the stairs, kicked off her shoes and pushed her over-the-knee socks down, rubbing where the tight elastic had cut into her thigh, before flopping down on her bed. She stared up at her poster of Take That before pulling her notepad from her bag. She wrote the word for the first time, encircling it in a heart. *Sven. Sven.* This was the word that danced in her mind and sat on her tongue. *Sven.* He had been at school for the last six months, but apart from her having noticed his

29

shock of blonde hair and rather nifty home-knitted jumpers, they had had little contact. He was one of the clever kids and was in some of her classes, and she had listened and smirked with her mates at his pronunciation of certain words, which often left a lot to be desired. She had watched in the dinner queue as some of the boys in the football team had asked if he was a member of Abba and if his mum and dad owned a Volvo. He had responded quickly that they were being ridiculous, of course his parents didn't own a Volvo, but, yes, he was in fact Agnetha, from Abba. *Sven.* She wrote it again and then wrote *Jackie Lundgren* by the side.

'Tea's ready!' her mum called up the stairs. Jacks shut her notebook and placed it under her pillow, ready for further doodling in later.

She slunk down the stairs, pausing at the hallway mirror to push up under her boobs, which she wished were bigger. Her friend Gina had massive boobs, although comparison was probably stupid as she and Gina were about as opposite-looking as they came. From the side they gave a slight bump to her shirt, but head on, she looked flat.

'What you looking so glum about Missus?'

She looked up at her mum. 'Nothing. Just wishing I looked a bit more like Gina.'

'Gina?' Her dad laughed. 'You're kidding! I'm not being mean, but if ever there was a girl that had to rely on her brains, it's her. You, on the other hand, can do like the rest of the family and use your good looks to get you far.' He batted his eyelashes.

30

'Don't flatter yourself. Your side of the family maybe, but my dad was very clever.' Ida muttered as she put the plate in front of her daughter. 'He was quite high up at the Gas Board. A very astute man, had a small fortune in Premium Bonds.'

Her dad pulled a funny face. 'Oh yes, the mysterious Premium Bonds! Tell you what, Ida, if they really existed, we'd have cashed them in years ago and had a couple of weeks in Tenerife! But until I see evidence of their existence, it'll be a week in the caravan as usual.' He laughed.

Jacks studied the carrots, peas, boiled spuds and individual chicken pie that had puffed up on top, just the way she liked it.

'Cor, this is lovely!' She watched as her dad, with his mouth full, winked at his wife and she saw the way her mum's face split with joy at the compliment he gave. As if she couldn't help it. Jacks chased the peas around the plate and wondered what Swedish people ate for tea.

'Penny for them, Dolly Daydream?' Her dad reloaded his fork with gravy-rich pastry and a couple of carrots.

'Huh?' Jacks hadn't been listening.

'You're miles away, not still brooding over your biased umpire?'

She shook her head. 'No. I was just wondering what Swedish people have for their tea.'

'Ryvita probably. That's Swedish.' Her mum nodded, certain of the fact.

'And fermented herring,' her dad added. 'I

remember a bloke I worked with on the rigs telling me about it. They let the fish go off in a tin and then eat it the next year, or something like that.'

'God, that sounds horrible!' Jacks grimaced.

'Why the interest in Swedish food all of a sudden?' Her dad spoke with his mouth full and a couple of peas nearly made a quick getaway; he pushed them back in with his tongue.

'No reason, it's just a boy in my year is Swedish, he's called Sven.' She was delighted to have the opportunity to mention him, to say his name out loud.

'Sven, eh? Isn't he one of the blokes from Abba?' Don smiled at his daughter.

Jacks laughed loudly. 'No! He's very clever and funny and . . .' She once again pictured his face, his thick hair, his intense stare. 'His dad's an architect, works in Bristol, lots of kids take the p . . . mick out of him, but I think he's just quirky, a bit different.'

She saw the look her parents exchanged. 'Thought you liked Peter Davies?' her mum asked as she squashed peas on to the back of her fork.

'I do. But we're just mates.' Jacks concentrated on her plate of food, trying to erase the memory of their snog on the dancefloor of Mr B's nightclub.

'His mum thinks you're more than mates, she told me you were going out with him. And he's quite smitten apparently,' Ida commented innocuously.

Jacks cringed. She had moved on from Pete and to be reminded of their connection irritated her.

'Pete's a plonker. Walks around like he's Gary Lineker.'

'He's got a trial with Bristol City,' her mum added, passing on more snippets of gossip.

'Yes and don't we know it, it's all he talks about. Sven isn't sporty, he's going to go to university.'

'Sven, Sven, Sven! I think I know someone else who's a bit smitten.' Her mum spoke to her dad over the table as if she wasn't present.

'I'm not!' Jacks shouted. 'He's just a boy in my year, that's all!'

'Good,' her dad said. 'Peter's a nice boy and we know his mum.'

'What's that got to do with anything?' Jacks shouted back.

'Stop yelling!' Ida said. 'There's no need for dramatics.'

'Dramatics? I don't think I'm being dramatic, there's you both telling me I practically have to marry Peter Davies just cos you know his mum!'

'We never said anything of the sort!' Ida tutted. 'Honestly, Jackie!'

'Good, cos I think I can do a bit better than a footballer who's going to leave school with just enough qualifications to work in Maccy D's.'

'Don't be so mean,' Ida said.

'I'm not, just truthful. Pete's all right, but he's not really my type. He's staying in Weston, close to a football field, and I want to go to college and travel.'

'To Sweden?' her mum asked.

'She can go anywhere she likes, can't you, love?' Her dad, ever supportive, smiled at her.

Ida placed her cutlery on the plate. 'Of course she can. I didn't say she couldn't!'

'No, but your face implied otherwise.' Don shook his head.

'Well, we all know you'd rather not have to look at my face.'

'Oh, here we go . . .'

Jacks slipped from the table and up the stairs. She lay on her bed and could hear the burble of their row rising up through the floor. Flipping open her notebook, she ran the nib of her pen over the heart in which sat the name of the object of her affection. *Sven.*

CHAPTER 3

Jacks opened the cupboard under the stairs, unhooked her pale linen duster coat with over-sized wooden buttons from the back of the door and slipped her slender frame into it. She pulled on her battered brown cowboy boots and picked up her car keys and the box of recycling that Pete had sorted for Jonty.

'Oh, Jacks, can you pick up some razor blades? And we need cornflakes, kids have just polished off the last.' This Pete shouted with his head poking over the banister from upstairs.

Jacks nodded. 'Will do. See you later. Kids, come on! We are leaving now!'

Out on the pavement in Sunnyside Road, she shoved the box into the boot. 'Morning, Ivor!' She raised her hand to wave at the young man who lived next door with his wife; he was loading up his van ready for the day.

'All right, Jacks! Bit nippy, innit?' He rubbed his big hands together, a labouring man like Pete.

This made her smile. He, like her husband, seemed constantly surprised by the cold weather. She wanted to remind him that this was September and they lived in Weston-super-Mare, not the Bahamas. 'Baba okay?' she shouted back as she walked to the driver's side – he and his wife Angela had an eight-week-old boy, Jayden.

'Sound as a pound!' He grinned. 'Keeping us up all hours, screaming and shouting to be fed.' He tutted.

'Ah, sounds like mine and she's eighty-one.' She laughed.

'Could be worse, Jacks.' He laughed and she laughed too, although she wasn't sure why. 'Hope he doesn't keep you awake,' he said sheepishly.

'Mate, don't forget I've got two, been there done that. You have to not worry about him, he's part of our little neighbourhood and that's his way of letting us all know he's here. He's just chatting.'

Ivor picked up his toolbox and stowed it in the back. Jacks noted a flask and sandwich box and thought how lovely that Angela found time to make her man his lunch. Poor old Pete, who now had to make do with a quick drive-through when time allowed.

'I just wish he'd chat between the hours of nine and five and the rest of the time keep quiet!' Ivor chuckled.

'Ah, if only it were that simple.' She smiled as the kids ran from the front door, leaving it open for their dad to shut behind them as they jumped in the car.

'*I* heard that baby last night. Drives me nuts.' Martha tutted.

'Oh, he's a sweet little thing,' Jacks said.

'He's a squirmy pink little thing that shouts a lot, very loudly. He just poos, sleeps and shouts. Don't see what's sweet about that.'

'It's different when it's your own, you'll see.' Jacks laughed.

'It'd have to be.'

'All buckled up?' Jacks asked.

They ignored her as usual, as the idea of not buckling up had never occurred to them.

Jacks parked in the lay-by and waved Jonty first and then Martha into their adjoining schools. She watched as her son wrestled with his school bag and the shallow box full of beer cans, the exercise hampered somewhat by his hands that were, as ever, covered by at least three inches of sleeve on his too-big sweatshirt that had to last the year.

'Bless him. Clifton bloody Suspension Bridge!' And she laughed, before letting the window roll down an inch and breathing deeply.

There was a bus that practically went door to door on the four-mile round-trip to school. In fact, she allowed the kids to travel home under their own steam as long as they were together or with friends. Pete had offered on more than one occasion to take them in, but Jacks always refused the help. This daily venture out in the car meant so much more to her than simply dropping the kids off. It was the only twenty minutes in the entire day that she was completely alone, where no one could get to her, and she needed it.

Sitting back in the seat, with her head on the headrest, she took another deep breath. The faintest scent of her dad still lingered in the fabric and she welcomed it, letting this small fragment of him envelop her in a hug. A vast black 4x4 pulled in behind her, dispensed three blonde children of various ages from the back seat and quickly pulled out again. Jacks looked into the car as it passed and caught sight of the occupants: the female passenger had a large pair of sunglasses on, despite the chilly morning, and pouted into the vanity mirror of the sun visor as she applied a coat of lipstick, pressing her lips together against a tissue to blot and spread.

Jacks closed her eyes and pictured herself in the passenger seat of one of those huge flashy cars. Her mind wandered further and suddenly she was no longer alone. Sven was in the driver's seat. 'Where to?' he asked. 'My meeting's been cancelled and we've got the whole day.'

She threw her head back and sighed, running her hand over her tailored designer jeans. 'I don't mind as long as I'm with you. How about lunch in Bristol? Somewhere with a view.'

'I know just the place.' Sven reached over for her hand and brought it up to his lips, grazing her knuckles with a kiss. 'I think a nice walk and then lunch, with champagne.'

'What are we celebrating?' she asked.

'Another day together.' He smiled.

'You spoil me,' she simpered, placing her hand on his thigh.

'That's because I love you.' He grinned as he put his foot down and headed for the motorway. She pictured the two of them travelling along the motorway with the windows down and the wind whipping through her hair. They had no responsibilities and no timeframe on their day. Jacks chortled and indicated to pull out of the lay-by. The dream dissolved, but although fleeting, it had lifted her spirits.

Sitting in the traffic, she beamed as she cleaned the dash with a spare bit of tissue that she had found in her pocket. The car in front moved forwards and Jacks followed suit in her dad's old Skoda Fabia, waving and smiling at her various neighbours, whom she knew by sight if not by name.

Turning on to the Marine Parade, with the seafront to her left, her eye was drawn as it always was to the Weston Wheel. 'Like the London Eye,' as Pete always said, 'but better, cos it's in the West Country!' She smiled at the big sky and the outline of the pier on the horizon, a beautiful sight to gladden any heart on such a bright blue autumn day. She ignored the druggies and dispossessed who gathered in the shelters dotted along the front. The season had finished and so they lay undisturbed on the benches, whiling away the day with nothing to stand up for. She passed the parade of shops, her attention caught only when yet another one had changed hands or been boarded up, which happened with regularity in Weston, especially when the grim reality of winter in a seaside town hit home.

Jacks thought about what she might make for tea, noting the students who clutched A4 files to their chests as they waited for buses in skinny jeans and silly woolly hats that made it look like they had animals or puddings on their heads. They stood next to young professionals who commuted to Bristol and Portishead and who were fast buying up Weston's vast Victorian villas, extending them, improving them and pushing up the prices. She had admired those houses for as long as she could remember: beautiful, spacious buildings with grand fireplaces, wide staircases, tiled hall floors, boot scrapers by the heavy front doors and the odd turret perched whimsically above an attic corner. When she was younger she used to dream of sleeping in one of those round rooms, like a princess. They were now and always had been beyond her wildest dreams.

Sven and his family had lived in one of those villas and with hindsight she supposed that had been part of his appeal. Until she met Sven, Jacks had thought her own family were quite worldly: unlike her mates' families, her mum and dad took her to the pub, where they would eat scampi and chips or, in the summer, give her the choice of KP cheese-and-onion crisps or nuts while they sat outside. Her dad would always have a pint, her mum a Martini-and-lemonade with a slice of lemon on the side of the glass, and she would have Pepsi in a bottle, which she drank through a straw. To her, Pepsi meant America, and she coveted all things American. But Sven made her realise that her family was anything but worldly. Their occasional holiday in a Devon caravan park and the odd day trip to London were nothing compared to his globetrotting childhood. She listened in awe to his tales of aeroplanes, mountains, deserts and palm-fringed tropical beaches. Another world entirely. The more she learnt of exotic destinations far and wide, the less enamoured she became with the familiar streets of Weston-super-Mare.

'Ah, Sven . . .'

She pictured her dad's disapproving stare. 'Don't look at me like that! I can remember him, can't I? There's no harm in that, Dad.'

Ever since he'd passed away, she'd carried a little image of him inside her head. Not the sort of snapshot that might materialise when she visited a place they used to go to together or heard a piece of music he'd liked. No, this was literally a mini picture of him, a younger and happier version, his hair still dark and lustrous, his eyes crinkling with humour and a twist about his mouth as though he was about to laugh. An image of him from the days before the gauze of sickness had muted every part of him. And this image sat at the centre of her mind, always.

41

So much so that if she wanted to read a page or look at a picture, she almost had to duck around him.

The lights in the town centre were in her favour and she got through the one-way system in a haze of green. She thought that she was probably the only person who hoped for red lights, wanting to enjoy the solitude a little longer.

Turning the key in the front-door lock, she shouted, 'I'm back, Mum!' She climbed the stairs, opened the bedroom and was unsurprised to see her mother sitting upright, her fingers fidgeting with the bow of her bed jacket.

'Have you got my letter?' Ida asked anxiously. 'I need it.'

'No. Postman hasn't been yet.' Jacks walked to the open window and closed it a little. The place smelt fresher, better now that the bed had been stripped and the air had had a chance to circulate. 'How about I make you some porridge? Or would you prefer toast today?'

'When's Don coming?' she asked.

'I'm not sure.' Jacks smiled, still uncertain how best to respond to the request for her father.

'I didn't want it all written down and now I don't know where the letter has got to.'

Jacks sighed and sat on the side of the bed. She pushed her mother's bed jacket up her arm, watching it gather in little folds under her elbow. She then squeezed out a blob of hand cream and massaged it into her bony fingers, slender wrists and pale palms.

'Smell that, Mum, it's lavender. Isn't it lovely?' She lifted her mum's hand and placed it under her nose.

'Smells like France.' And just like that, a moment of comprehension, a memory from another time and place that floated clear and acute to the top of the cloudy soup of her thoughts.

'That's right! You and Dad had a lovely trip to France, didn't you? Do you remember going to the lavender fields? You went on a coach and you brought me back a dried bunch. It kept its scent for ages. I had it hanging in the kitchen, it was gorgeous. Everyone commented on it.' She smiled, remembering her parents' big adventure for their golden wedding anniversary. Her dad had packed three packets of Rich Tea biscuits and enough fish-paste sandwiches to last the whole four days, just in case they didn't like the food.

'I need my letter.' And just like that, they were back to square one.

Jacks nodded. 'I'll go get your breakfast.'

She tucked the blanket under her mother's legs and closed the door behind her. After retrieving the bundle of soiled laundry from behind the bathroom door, she doused the shower with a liberal slosh of bleach, then made her way downstairs. Stopping halfway at the sound of the bell that rang for her attention, Jacks sighed. She thought of her dad and how much she had loved him.

His last day played like a movie inside her head. His eyes wide, grasping the oxygen mask with difficulty, fingers slipping and missing as they struggled with the flimsy elastic that held the plastic cup over his nose and mouth. She hadn't helped him, didn't want to acknowledge his weakness, tried to keep up the charade. She had instead smiled, as though he could manage and was still the strong, capable man who cut the grass and drove the car. She had picked at her nails, bitten them, anything but become his carer, aiding where his gnarled knuckles refused to yield. She had tried for nonchalant. 'Take your time . . . I've got three hours on the car.' Her flippant practicality hiding a heart that was splitting like a ripe tomato, spilling and overflowing with desperate sorrow. *Don't leave me, Dad, please don't leave me, I'm not ready . . .* The truth was she would never be ready.

'I need you to promise me something.' His words coasted on stuttered breaths, his voice a failing whisper. 'Promise me . . .'

'Promise you what, Dad?' She attempted a jolly tone through her steady stream of tears.

'Promise me . . . that you will look after your mum. Please . . . Try . . .' He held her gaze, hanging on, waiting for reassurance.

She nodded. 'I promise.' And as soon as the words had left her mouth, he let out a long, laboured breath as his fingers unfurled.

She often replayed those last minutes. Her face, inches from his, breathing in the last breaths that he exhaled, sharing the tiny space in which life lingered till the end. She kissed his fragile head and stroked his papery cheek and he left her. Finally, slowly, he left her alone in that room and she felt a large part of her capacity for joy leave with him. Her dad died. Her dad! She had to keep saying it to herself because even after a month, a year, eighteen months, it still felt like a lie in her mouth. How could he have left her? She needed him. But of course she didn't say that. Jacks was a grown woman with a family of her own and as everyone said to her, 'It's the natural order of things . . . He had a good life . . . It's the end of his suffering . . .' That may have been the case, but it still felt like shit. He used to say that one man couldn't change the world, but he was wrong, he changed her world, made it a better place. And she loved him very much. That was why she had made the promise. He had never asked anything of her before and she wanted to make him happy. The trouble was, she found it very hard to love her mum. In fact, as painful as it was to admit, she didn't always like her.

CHAPTER 4

Nineteen Years Earlier

'Is this seat taken?'

Jacks laughed. Sven spoke as though he were old and they were in the middle of a grand restaurant and not on a bench in the school canteen.

'Help yourself.' She gestured towards the empty space opposite her at the table, hating the way she cast her eye behind him to see if anyone was watching. She liked him but didn't want her friends laughing at her as she ate her lunch with the foreign weirdo kid.

'What do you eat in Sweden?' she asked.

'What?' He smiled.

'What food? I was just wondering.'

'Same as here: meat, potatoes, vegetables. Probably more fish than here – cured fish, like smoked salmon, my favourite. The usual.' He concentrated on removing the top layer of his sandwich and scraping the mayonnaise from the lettuce.

She grinned. She'd never had smoked salmon. Her fish came in breadcrumbs and was shaped into a rectangle even though it was called a finger, or it was breadcrumb-free and covered in parsley sauce that you boiled in a bag.

'So what's the best thing your mum makes?' She bit delicately into her roll, wanting to look ladylike and feeling suddenly self-conscious about eating in front of him.

Sven replaced the bread and wiped his fingers on his trousers as he considered this. 'Pizza – she's not the best cook! But if you mean traditional food, I guess meatballs, mashed potatoes and pickled gherkin with sweet jam on the side. And your mum?'

'Oh . . .' She was taken aback by the question, it wasn't as if anything her family did was of interest. 'My mum and dad are older, boring really, well, not my dad so much, but my mum, she's boring. But food . . .' She swallowed, conscious of rambling. 'Things like roast dinners, pies, boring.' She sipped her squash.

'Have you always lived in Weston?' He held his chin as though in deep thought, waiting for her answer.

'Yes, worse luck. But I'm not staying here. I think it's shit. I want to travel, go to New York, probably work there for a bit.' She blushed, hoping her admission sounded as sincere as she had meant it.

'I like New York.' He smiled.

'Have you been?' She sat forward, the questions piling up inside her head. *Did you walk up Fifth Avenue? Did you go to Times Square? Does everyone eat hotdogs?*

'Yes. We lived there for a while – my father's an architect, that's why we're here. He's working on a project in Bristol.'

'Cool.' She bit her lip, wishing she could rewind and ask her questions; then she blurted out, 'I don't know why I said "cool", that's a word you use when you can't be bothered to think of a good reply or don't know how to say something without making a tit of yourself.'

Sven looked across at her. 'Do you like astronomy?'

'I don't know.' She got confused between astronomy and astrology but wasn't about to tell him that.

'You don't know?' He held his sandwich in mid air. 'That's like saying you don't know if you like poetry or art. You must know if you like it or not!' He gave his easy laugh.

Jacks stared at the boy who was different to every other boy in the school; in fact different to every other boy she had ever met. He was confident and seemed to care little about what anyone thought of him. He wore hand-knitted jumpers that the other boys mocked, but still he smiled at their straight-faced compliments as though they were his friends.

'So, poetry, is that something you like?'

'Well, here we are.' Jacks hadn't seen Pete and his mates arrive, not until they sat on the bench either side of Sven and opposite her. 'How you doing, Abba-boy?'

'Good, thanks.' Sven beamed, as though Pete had asked without a trace of sarcasm. 'And you?'

48

'Ah, you know.' Pete flexed his linked knuckles in front of him. 'Busy training for my trial. I'm going for a try-out with Bristol City.'

'Cool.' Sven caught Jacks' eye, twinkled, and nodded at Pete. 'What is your position?' he asked.

A couple of Pete's friends laughed. 'Vat is your position?' they repeated with a Germanic accent.

Sven held up his palms. 'Oh, I'm sorry. I know my inflection is far from perfect. Would it be easier for you guys if we switched to Swedish or French? I can hold my own in German, but I warn you, it's worse than my terrible English!' He laughed.

Pete's friends shut up.

'You coming up the pier tonight, Jacks?' Pete asked, cutting to the chase.

She felt her cheeks flame. 'No.'

Pete stared at her for a second, unsure of where to go next. 'I'd better get on. Got to go to the gym, push a few weights.'

'Enjoy!' She waved before he had left.

'You must know if you like poetry?' Sven pressed, carrying on as if they hadn't been interrupted, and she was grateful, unwilling to comment on the rumour that she'd snogged Peter Davies at Mr B's.

'I like some,' she whispered.

'Some is good.' He smiled.

'Jacks!' Gina shouted from the other side of the canteen. 'Come on! I've been looking all over for you. I need a fag.' She lifted her fingers and mimed smoking.

Two teachers on the middle table turned to tut

their disapproval in Gina's direction. She placed her hand over her mouth theatrically, as though she had spoken in error. Everyone loved Gina; she was short, rotund, confident and daring. A blatant rule breaker, but her lack of guile made her incredibly appealing. She was also Jacks' very best friend.

'I'd better go.' Jacks piled her plate and empty juice carton on to the brown plastic tray.

Sven placed his hand over hers. 'Some say the beginning is the most exciting part.'

She swallowed and stared at him, her body shaking, her eyes fixed.

'Jacks! Come on, you div, this is my fag time you are wasting!' Gina's words hit her like shards of glass and broke the spell.

CHAPTER 5

Jacks heard the thump of discarded work boots hitting the bedroom floor and then felt the sag of the mattress as Pete, fresh from watching his beloved Bristol City, climbed under the duvet beside her. There they lay, back to back. She glanced at the alarm clock; it was quarter past eleven. He carried with him the faint odour of beer and fried food.

'Did we win?' she mumbled through the fog of sleep.

'Course we did!' He chuckled, delighted. 'Boys were on form tonight, girl.'

She closed her eyes and drifted back to sleep, ready for another busy day tomorrow.

'Two nil! Two nil! Come on, you mighty Cider Army!' Pete clapped out a rhythm and sang loudly from the landing.

Jacks filled the kettle for her first cuppa and pulled her blonde hair into a ponytail. She did this every other day, to avoid having to wash her hair. It gave her an extra twenty minutes that she didn't have to spend with her head bent over the kitchen sink, rinsing her hair with a plastic jug so as not to eat up precious shower time first thing.

'How did the other ones get on?' Jonty shouted from the bedroom.

'What other ones?' Pete laughed.

'The ones the mighty Cider Army were playing.'

The bathroom door opened and Martha popped her head out. 'That's what "nil" means, you doughnut! It means zero. That's what the other ones scored – nothing, zip!'

'Don't call your brother a doughnut, Martha,' Jacks shouted up the stairs. And there it was, the clear ringing of the bell.

'Nan's ringing!' the kids shouted.

'On my way!' Jacks gathered Pete's jacket and football scarf from the bottom of the stairs. Never a wasted trip – that was her motto.

'It's a lovely brand-new day!' She beamed as she drew Ida's curtains wide.

'I've passed water,' her mother announced with a smile.

'Yep, that's fine, Mum. We'll get you cleaned up and I thought, when I get back from school, we might go for a stroll into town, you can go in your chair. We can pick up something nice for tea and have a walk along the seafront. Do you fancy that?' She cracked the window open.

'I am waiting for a letter.'

Jacks swallowed and turned to her mother, ready

with her reassurance that, when it arrived, she would bring it straight upstairs.

'Did you get my razors, Jacks?' Pete yelled.

'Yep, in the bathroom cabinet.'

'I can't find them!' he wailed.

'On my way.' She waltzed from the room.

Martha grabbed her arm on the landing, sending her mum into a twirl, as though the two were engaged in an elaborate dance. 'Have I got a shirt?'

'Yes, ironed and in your wardrobe.'

'Cheers.'

Jacks smiled, that was almost a thank you.

'Mum?'

'Yes, Jonty?'

'How do you know we are not all living in a computer game and that there is someone controlling us with a controller?'

Jacks paused and looked at her skinny son, naked from the waist up and still in his Spiderman pyjama bottoms. 'That's a good question, and I don't know the answer, but all I can say is that if they are, Jont, I wish there'd be a power cut so I could have a sodding rest.'

'Mum said "sodding"!' Jonty giggled.

The lights were red; Jacks pulled up the handbrake and waited. Jonty was ensconced in a comic that he held two inches from his face. Martha pushed a button on the radio and the car filled with a booming sound with no discernible beat. She nodded her head.

'I don't know how you can listen to this.'

Martha laughed. 'You always say that! You hate nearly all my music.'

'Apart from 1D.' Jacks winked at her daughter.

'Fancying them and liking their music are two completely different things.'

Jacks laughed loudly. 'I don't fancy them, for goodness' sake. I'm old enough to be their mum! I just think they're cute. They seem like nice boys. I wouldn't mind you going out with one of them.'

Martha looked at her mum. 'Well, thank you for your blessing. And it is very likely that I will go out with one of them. I mean, I often see them queuing ahead of me and my mates in the chippy or hanging around the precinct!'

'I like their music because I can sing along, I can pick out the words, not like this.' Jacks pointed at the stereo. 'This boom boom boom just gives me a headache!'

'It's because you are old. And uncool.'

Jacks snorted her laughter. 'Christ! I am not uncool! I'm a very cool mum. You have no idea. Your nan would never have offered me her clothes to wear or let me nick her make-up – not that I'd have wanted to, she always wore granny clothes, unlike my trendy self. I always thought she was a bit of an old fogey.'

'Yeah, that's right, Mum, my friends think you are practically Alexa Chung, you're such a trendsetter!'

'Who?'

Martha gave a derisory laugh in reply. Jacks opened her mouth to respond but couldn't think of what to say. She didn't want to give her daughter another chance to raise her eyebrows and remind her once again that she had just landed from Planet Stupid. She recalled having a similar conversation with her dad when she was young, but in her case it was true. Her parents had had her when they were forty-five. Not considered quite so exceptional for a first baby nowadays, but in 1979 it was practically unheard of. From what Jacks could gather, they had assumed they were unable to have children. Her mum's pregnancy came as a massive shock to her mum and brought with it a huge sense of embarrassment, but for her dad it was nothing but a cause for celebration. And that was how he'd made her feel his whole life, like she was a gift to be treasured.

'I'm not that old, Martha. I'm thirty-six, that means I'm not even halfway through my life!'

'You hope!' her daughter quipped.

'Yes, good point.' Jacks laughed.

'What's the worst thing about being old, Mum?' Martha twisted the end of her bleached braid between her fingers.

Jacks chuckled, remembering how when she was seventeen, anyone over the age of twenty-five had indeed been considered ancient. Jonty had more of an older mum, granted. Nearly ten years was a big gap between the two. It was ironic that as soon as she and Pete had given up trying to conceive, having put it out of their minds after years of trying, including one failed IVF attempt, she had fallen pregnant almost immediately with their darling boy, *their* little bonus gift.

'Well, as I said, I'm actually rather young and you will realise that one day. But I suppose the worst thing about getting old-*er*, is having to listen to this horrible boom-boom music!' She grimaced. 'That and not being able to eat like I used to. When I was young, I could shovel in chips and chocolate and not put on an ounce. Now, if I so much as look at a bit of cheese, my hips swell.' She winked at her daughter.

'Sounds horrible!' Martha squirmed.

Jacks laughed. This was best. Keep it light. What was the alternative? Tell her the truth? Hardly.

Martha sang along loudly to the remorseless racket.

Jacks pushed Ida's wheelchair along the Marine Parade, stopping and bending forward every so often to check her mum was warm enough or to turn the chair to face the sea. At this time of year, though, the sea was nothing more than a distant grey foaming flutter over the vast expanse of mud that tourists optimistically called the beach. Seagulls swooped and swirled, hovering on the breeze, cackling overhead as they hunted for abandoned chips and specks of burger bun that lay in tantalising trails, as if a modern-day Hansel and Gretel needed to find their way back to McDonald's.

She paused to nod to other walkers and wheelers, all taking the air. She wondered if they too were escaping from homes that were too small to contain their occupants and all their belongings. Whether they too had cupboards crammed full of things deemed too precious to discard and whether they also felt the slow suffocation of living in a house that oozed disappointment, a temporary house, just until . . . Sunnyside Road had been temporary since they had married eighteen years ago. The improvements they had promised had simply become dreams: the conservatory, loft conversion, hand-built shiny kitchen. She thought about the money in their savings account, the first time it had ever been in credit. Money for a rainy day, it felt nice.

Jacks had lied to Martha earlier. Having to listen to crappy music? Ha! That wasn't the worst thing about getting older, oh no. The worst thing was knowing she would never achieve all the things she'd once thought she might. She no longer saw a glowing window of opportunity ahead of her that she could jump through. She was stuck. She was Pete's wife, the kids' mum and Ida's carer. This was the sum total of her life. She was the finished article and what she saw when she looked in the mirror didn't come close to what she had imagined. 'The worst thing about getting older is knowing that my life is ordinary but wanting so badly for it to be extraordinary and realising that I might be running out of time to change it.' This she whispered into the air above her mother's head.

'It's marching on. Can only ever make the most of what you've got. It's not a trick, it's the truth. Contentment in what you've got. That's it.' Ida's voice was strong and clear.

Jacks bent down and looked into her mum's face, acknowledging the truth in her words. Ida stared out to sea, silent once again, like she was looking at a painting. It was as if Jacks had imagined her mum's words.

'For goodness' sake, hold him, Polly!' The man's voice echoed along the pavement as his wife raced towards them, in pursuit of a beardy-faced Border terrier that was now taking an interest in Ida's wheelchair.

'I am trying, Paz! Jeez, do you think I'd let him go on purpose?' The woman giggled, trying to catch her breath as she ran along the Marine Parade in ridiculously inappropriate heels. 'God! I'm so sorry! He's new to us and we're still getting the hang of being dog parents. I think the actual kids are easier, but possibly less cute!' She smiled.

Ida reached down. 'Hello, Rexy!' she cooed. 'Good boy.' To her, it was the dog of her child-hood, even if he had died when Ida was six. If he were alive today, Jacks thought, he'd be in his late seventies – off the scale in doggy years! He looked pretty good on it.

'Come on, Bert! I'm so sorry, we're only here for a little holiday, he's a London dog, not used to this sea air. That and so many stationary birds are sending him a little bit crazy!' The woman waved apologetically as she ran back along the prom towards her long-haired husband, who laughed good-naturedly at her inept dog handling.

Jacks resumed their walk, watching with a rueful smile as the woman fell into her husband's embrace. She hadn't wanted to trouble Martha with the mundane reality of her life. Her daughter was going to take the world by storm; she was a clever girl who worked hard and was well liked. Jacks pictured her all grown up, a lawyer, living in a swanky flat somewhere far away, like Paris or New York! Imagine that. She would do it all. And Jacks couldn't wait! She'd miss her, of course, but had decided that she would visit her every birthday and they would go for a posh lunch and have pudding and then coffee after their main course. What was it her tutor had said? *The sky is the limit for a girl like Martha. With hard work and application, she can pick her path.* A bubble of excitement filled her throat. *Pick her path* . . . how wonderful. *And you can do it for us both, Martha. You can make the most of all the chances I didn't have.*

Jacks regularly listened to Gina and other mates from school recounting tales of the girls who'd got away, girls who had escaped from Weston-super-Mare and made something of themselves. There was Rosie Barnes, who had married a banker and now lived in Monaco with a swimming pool in her basement and a tennis court on her roof.

Which Jacks thought sounded ridiculous; it seemed like a hell of a long way to go to retrieve lost balls. And then there was Martine Braithwaite, who had gone to Oxford; this wasn't something you could forget, not with her mother telling anyone that would listen every time you bumped into her in the street, whether it was relevant or not.

'Hello, Mrs Braithwaite. Bit windy!'

'Ah yes, probably windy in Oxford too, where my Martine went to university!'

'Tell me, Mrs Braithwaite, how are your haemorrhoids?'

'Oh, fine. I've been to see the pharmacist, a smart man, but not as smart as my Martine, who went to Oxford, you know!'

Jacks chuckled at this imaginary exchange. Martine was now a successful doctor working in London and gave the odd interview to the BBC about her various triumphs. It wasn't that she was outright jealous of girls like Rosie and Martine – that would be ridiculous, knowing that Martha was all set to be the Martine of her year – but she had to confess to a certain touchiness that flickered within her and flared at different times in her life, sometimes turning to anger, which she swallowed. It wasn't that she wanted to *be* them, not at all, but rather that she wanted more out of the life she had. Sometimes, when she was exhausted and miserable, she would contemplate Rosie's life in the sunshine, away from her parents, away from the seafront, the monotony and the relentless pull of duty. With her arms deep in foul, tepid water, trying to scrub away the evidence of her old and unable Mum, she would visualise Rosie waking late each day, wandering down a sweeping staircase and ambling off to retrieve her tennis balls from the street below. Other times, as she answered the bell yet again – for a drink, an extra pillow, a change of bed linen – she would imagine Martine's life and how, after a day of doctoring, she must be spending her evenings laughing and having fun in the capital.

Sometimes, roused from the deepest sleep, Jacks would jump up, thinking she had heard the bell. Tumbling into her mother's room she would find Ida sleeping peacefully, slack mouthed and snoring in blissful oblivion. It was as though a cruel joker waited until 4 a.m. to ding-a-ling her from her rest, knowing she could not return to it once she was up and about.

She looked out across Beach Lawns towards the house in which Sven and his family had lived, picturing her teenage self with a curly perm and backcombed fringe, trotting up the path with a tummy full of nerves and a heart that fluttered. She had rather liked it. She wondered what it would be like now if Sven had stayed, if they had both moved into one of those conservatory houses. She saw herself waking and staring across a pristine white sheet towards his sleeping form. As the sunlight poured through the large sash window, she would sit up, stretch and take in the vast room with the white carpet, neat dressing table and carefully positioned silver-framed photos of them on holiday in far-flung places.

'I've passed water.' Her mother reached backwards, gripping Jacks' arm and pulling her from her dreams.

'Oh, okay, Mum. Not to worry. Shall we get you back then?' She smiled and slowly turned the wheelchair in the direction of home.

Jacks sometimes wondered how she had ended up with the life she had. What was it Sven had said? *'You are not like these sheep-girls. You're different. You will have an amazing journey.'* And where had that amazing journey taken her? Three streets away from where he had uttered those words as they lay flat on the grass in the dark. Some journey! Glad she hadn't bothered buying a return ticket. She quickened her pace. They would have to forgo a trip to the supermarket; instead, she'd dig something out of the freezer for tea. She was glad that the wind was quite fierce as it carried the odour away from her and out to sea.

CHAPTER 6

Nineteen Years Earlier

It was the first day of term, a brand-new school year and her last ever. She was in the upper sixth! She sat at the breakfast table and ate her bowl of Frosties. Steve Wright's breakfast show was playing Whigfield's 'Saturday Night'. Fish-and-chip wrappers from last night's tea sat scrunched into a greasy ball on the draining board. Jacks drummed her fingers in time to the music.

Her mum stood by the table. 'Got everything you need, Jackie?'

'Yes, thanks.'

Ida hovered, twisting the tea towel in her hands. 'Did . . . did you hear Dad come in last night?'

'From work? No. I was asleep, plus I had my Walkman on as I dropped off.' Her dad was working later and later, she loved him for it. He wasn't getting any younger and yet was still a grafter.

'Upper sixth, can you believe it? You're growing up so quickly.' Ida looked close to tears.

'I'm not leaving home, Mum, just going to school. I'll be home by four.'

63

Ida patted her arm. 'I know, love. I know.' She returned to the kitchen to busy herself at the sink.

Jacks walked to school with an air of superiority as the reality of her now being at the top of the school hierarchy began to sink in. Once in school, it took only a matter of minutes for her to feel the absence of Gina, who had taken different options to her and was going to be in fewer of her classes than ever before. She arranged her new locker as she considered her lessons for the morning: English and business studies. She loved the look and feel of her immaculate folders, newly sharpened pencils and pristine notepads, all ready to go, and she felt the excitement of a new term in the air. Just one more year, one more year of school and then her dad had agreed she could go to college. These were the stepping-stones to getting out of this place. She would go somewhere exciting, somewhere that wasn't Weston-super-Mare, anywhere!

Suddenly there he was, walking towards her. She felt a warm blush, as though the lingering scent of summer followed him on this frosty morning. Her heart beat so quickly she felt like she might fall over. *I love you. I love you!* The words danced in her throat before whooshing straight up the back of her nose and exploding inside her head like fireworks. She was sure that if he looked into her eyes he'd see the glittering cascade as it rained down on everything she glanced at. She would never tell him, because if he didn't feel the same way, she was sure she would die. Actually die.

Just a single glimpse of him across the corridor and she couldn't speak and couldn't breathe. She was just as enamoured of her beautiful blonde Swedish boyfriend as she had been when they had first started seeing each other, and every time he sought her out, ordinary Jackie Morgan, she felt like a very special thing. It made her feel like one of the smart girls, the girls who discussed future careers, knowing they would be going on to university, or the girls who went abroad during the holidays to practise their second language. At all other times, she was as far from these girls as you could imagine, lurking at the back and aiming for a junior administrative role at a firm within walking distance of home – that was, until she found her career path, and then whoosh! There'd be no stopping her. And she had to admit, she liked being one of those girls, even if it was only for the few minutes that she was in his company.

Gina thought he was a nerd. 'Have you seen Brains?' she'd ask and Jacks would beam because even if Gina was calling him names, sneering and failing to see the attraction, at least they were talking about him and he was her favourite topic.

She had seen him eight times over the six-week holiday. They had walked barefoot together down to the chilly edge of the sea and as her toes had touched his on the shoreline, she'd felt a thrill like a thunderbolt jolt right through her body. She wouldn't ever forget it. It was the same when he held her hand. They had been for glorious bike rides along Poets' Walk and stopped for picnics at the Sugar Lookout with a wonderful view of the Bristol Channel. It was while they'd lain staring at the sky, using their raised arms as pillows, that Jacks had learnt his mum was called Stina and came from Stockholm. She spent hours before falling asleep wondering about his mum's foreignness. Did she grow up in the snow? Did they celebrate Christmas? As someone who craved travel and who woke with a yearning to jump on a plane, eat food under a foreign sun and paddle in a warm sea, his family fascinated her. Stina had a fat twist of blonde plait that sat over her left shoulder and pale blue eyes in a heart-shaped face. Strangely, despite being blonde and rangy, her perfect parts did not add up to a beautiful whole; in fact she was quite manly, boxy and plain, with a soft down covering her cheeks and chin.

Jacks heard her speak once, pulling up outside school in her car. She had rolled down the window of their chunky Volvo estate and shouted in Swedish at Sven. Jacks of course had no idea what she was saying – it was simply a rapid staccato of V- and Y-sounds followed by a volley of long Os. But judging from Sven's face and the slope of his shoulders, it was the same things being shouted in Swedish as in English: 'Hurry up, Sven! I haven't got all day! Your brother's got to get to Cubs and your dad needs his tea cooking!' At least that's what Jacks imagined.

Now, on the first day back at school, Sven stared at her as he approached, concentrating on her alone, as was his way, and speaking unabashedly as though there was no one else around. 'I dreamt about you last night.'

'You did?' She shrank backwards and looked left to right to make sure no one was listening.

He nodded. 'We were running on sand, across a wide, pale beach with palm trees, and the sun was hot. It was wonderful. I stopped and said to you, "Where shall we go next?" and you said, "Anywhere, as long as it's with you."' He walked forward and stood close to her so they were almost touching. 'And you would say that, wouldn't you?'

His lips brushed her cheek. She nodded and stared at him. Yes. Yes, she would.

CHAPTER 7

Jacks prodded the rice with a fork to check on its progress. Still unsure, she burnt her fingers as she dipped them into the murky boiling water, pulled out a couple of grains and bit; they were still gritty and firm.

She listened as Martha chatted to her mate Stephanie in the hallway by the front room, a room Jacks hardly ever entered, not because the house was so vast, but because it was where the family congregated to socialise and watch TV, neither of which she had much time for. With its sagging couch and two comfy old armchairs, the room was already mismatched and cramped before her mum had moved in, and now some of Ida's clutter, items too precious to be discarded or stored in Gina's garage had been assimilated into the mix. The shelf above the gas fire held a clutch of ornaments, including china birds that her dad had lovingly collected over the years and a couple of badly hand-painted Harry Potter figures that Martha had made at primary school.

Sometimes, while waiting at the supermarket checkout, Jacks browsed the pictures in interior magazines. Flicking through the glossy pages, she marvelled at the sleek coordination of matching fabrics, shiny, dust-free surfaces and not a cardboard box in sight. She wondered how you got a house like that, deciding that the answer was probably to remain childless and not to allow your design influences to be whatever Pete fancied the look of in a skip, supplemented by a biannual trip up the motorway to Ikea.

'Come on, Martha! Don't be so boring! It's nearly Halloween and it's a right laugh out! Let's just go and hang out on the pier and if we see them, great, and if we don't, we can just come back and chill out.'

'I can't, Steph, I've got to write these notes up for Mr Greene's essay.'

'You're such a swot. Can't you just give it a rest for one night?' Steph tutted.

'Not if I want As and to get into Warwick.' Jacks beamed.

'It doesn't matter what uni you go to. Uni is uni and I don't think I could be arsed if it meant having to revise every minute of every day.'

Martha gave a small laugh. 'I think it is important. I want to start off right, get the grades, get on my course, study business and law and be a millionaire by the time I'm thirty.'

'Money's not everything, Martha!' Stephanie's tone was indignant.

'True. But imagine earning so much that you can do anything you want. Anything! Money gives you choices and that's freedom, isn't it? You know, like, oh, I'm cold, think I'll go get some sunshine, and so you just make a call and jump on a plane! Or you get invited to some snazzy do and you go to your big walk-in wardrobe and there are three or four things that you could wear, because you have clothes for all occasions. Or knowing you don't have to do something you don't want to because you can afford not to. And never having to share a bedroom again – unless you want to of course!' Martha giggled.

'Of course!' Stephanie replied.

They had the excited air of girls who had so much yet to experience and Jacks felt a flicker of envy.

'Wouldn't it be incredible, though, to be in control of your own life like that, to be so comfortable and for things to be that easy?'

Jacks braced her arms against the sink and looked out into the long, narrow garden, invaded in places by Angela and Ivor's overzealous planting. She remembered a conversation about living in a place so huge she wouldn't be able to see the boundaries. Wouldn't that be something. Her daughter's words swam in her head and danced on her tongue like a sweet-flavoured prayer that Jacks sent straight up to heaven. *Hear that, Dad? That's my girl!*

'Well, I'm going to see if I can find the boys. Sure you don't want to come?' Stephanie pleaded.

'No, I'll stay here. Text me later, though, tell me what happened!'

'Course. Bye, Jacks!' Stephanie called from the front door.

'Bye, love. Take care!' Jacks walked into the front room and leant on the doorframe, wiping her wet hands on a tea towel, watching as Martha sank down on to the sofa and opened her notebook before picking a pen from a stash in the front pocket of her backpack. 'When did you get to be so smart?' She smiled at her beautiful girl.

Martha shrugged. 'Dunno. Guess I take after my mum.'

Jacks pulled back her shoulders. 'I don't know about that.'

The bell rang from the upstairs landing, followed by Ida's call. 'Someone, please! I need some help!'

'Sounds like you're needed,' Martha said sympathetically.

Jacks sighed and headed for the stairs.

'Someone! Toto?' Her voice was louder this time.

'I'm coming, Mum!' Jacks shouted as she took the stairs two at a time.

Hurrying, she pushed the door open wide and found Ida crying. Big fat tears fell down her mum's cheeks, turning her eyes blood red and making her nose run.

'Oh, Mum!' Jacks sat on the side of the bed and plucked a tissue from the man-size box on the windowsill. 'What's this all about? Come on, let's dry those tears.' She pushed the thin wisps of grey hair from her mother's forehead and gently mopped at her face. 'There, there, it's okay. Nothing can be that bad!' She smiled, feeling slightly repulsed by the proximity of her mum's face to her own, and then instantly guilty because of that.

'I need my letter,' Ida wailed. 'I need it. He promised. Being here on my own is no fun, none at all and he promised me! I don't know where he is. He went to dig up oil.'

'It takes a long time for letters to get back. And if he promised, then I'm sure it'll be on its way.' Jacks swallowed the lump in her throat, wishing her dad *were* the man of his youth. Before her arrival, he'd worked on an oilrig somewhere foreign, making his way home across Europe, writing the odd letter as he went.

'I miss him.' Her mum sobbed once again.

Me too . . . Jacks tentatively placed her arms around the thin shoulders and pulled her mum towards her. Cuddling this woman, even in her hour of need, still felt alien and awkward and was in some ways harder than giving her more practical attention, cleaning and tending, which could be classed as medical, necessary. 'Sssshhh . . .' she cooed as her mum clung to her arm. It would twist the heart of any onlooker, seeing this frail old lady so broken and confused. But Jacks was not any onlooker. She had a filter of memories to wade through, memories that were hard to remove and that complicated every interaction with her mum.

She remembered being small and listening to her dad come home from work, followed by the sound of her mum shouting and then crying. It made her tummy flip, not wanting her mummy to cry, not wanting to feel frightened just before she fell asleep. Her dad would come into her room to tuck her in as he always did, always putting her first. He'd bend low and kiss her forehead, Jacks smelling his familiar scent of beer, cigarettes and his favoured musk-based aftershave.

'Sweet dreams, my little Dolly Daydream.' He'd then creep backwards from the room and she'd hear the creak of the stairs as he went downstairs.

The odd word of her parents' rows used to float up the stairs. 'This is unbearable . . . I just can't cope . . . You have made this situation and it's unfair. I've never met anyone so selfish!' She wished they would stop.

Jacks rocked her mum back and forth, trying to put the memories from her mind. She often wondered why her mum had felt the need to be so sharp, judgemental. Her anger seemed to come in bursts, often followed by bright smiles and acts of kindness intended to wipe the slate clean. A sneering laugh at what she considered to be a minor achievement of her husband's could be countered by an apple pie, freshly baked for tea. A sharp dig in the ribs as Don leant in for a cuddle or a kiss was made better by the knitting of a scarf and matching hat, delivered with a wide smile. And as far as Jacks could see, these peace offerings did the trick. Her dad would beam and nod, as if grateful for his wife's benevolence, the status quo restored. If only Jacks could find it that easy to forget.

The front doorbell rang. 'Back in a sec, Mum. There's someone at the door.'

Jacks released her gently and trod the stairs, only to see that Martha had abandoned her studies and beaten her to it. She was standing at the open front door. Jacks hovered halfway down and stared at her daughter, watching her in profile. She felt her stomach sink. Call it a mother's intuition, but though Jacks observed her for no more than five seconds, what she saw filled her with fear.

'Steph said you weren't coming out?' The boy spoke with a strong Weston accent. He was gripping a motorbike helmet in his hand and let it bounce against his thigh. He was broad and tall, taller than Pete, slim, wearing jeans and a fitted grey T-shirt that hugged his toned physique. His glossy straight hair sat on his shoulders, his fringe partially obscuring his right eye. He sounded assured, comfortable. This clearly wasn't the first time they had met.

'S'right.' Martha twisted her legs as she nodded with her head tilted to one side and her mouth breaking into a smile. They stared at each other during the silent pauses as if they carried a secret.

Jacks heard his easy laugh from the other side of the step, a laugh full of meaning, anticipation and happiness. She didn't know who he was, but she instantly hated the way Martha looked at him, disliked the shy, coquettish slant to her daughter's head as her eyes gazed up at him through voluminous lashes, her lips pouting and her gentle blush screaming out, *'Like me! Love me!'* Jacks wanted to slam the door shut, take her daughter's head in her hands and twist her face away from him, screaming, *'Not him! No! Not anyone from here! You need to wait! Wait for that boy you will meet at university who will be smart and well read, someone who will become a professional and who will take you to the south of France on a camping holiday and who will buy you a conservatory!'* Instead, she smiled, tripped down the stairs and stared at the boy in the leather jacket with the long hair and perfect teeth who stood on the front-door mat.

'Hello there!'

The boy raised his hand in a confident wave and Martha rolled her eyes as if apologising to him.

Jacks ignored her daughter and stepped closer to them. 'Nice to meet you, but I'm afraid we're all about to have tea, otherwise I'd invite you in.'

'Oh, no worries, Mrs D, I was off now anyway, just wanted to see Martha.'

'And now you have.'

Martha smiled as she bit her bottom lip.

Jacks wasn't sure she liked being called Mrs D, but she had to admit the boy had charm.

'Later,' Martha mumbled as a blush rose up her cheek. When the door closed behind him, Martha threw a pointed look at her mum, as if daring her to say anything as she flounced up the stairs, a small smile playing around her mouth.

★   ★   ★

Jacks placed the bowl of chilli in the middle of the table and the saucepan of disgustingly over-cooked rice next to that.

'Let me get you some tea.' She lifted Ida's plate and placed a small mound of rice on it with a scoop of chilli, not too much. 'There we go, Mum. Don't worry, it's not too hot.' She smiled, trying to pre-empt any shouts about being scalded.

'Do you want to hear my joke?' Jonty sat up straight, wiggling his bottom on the chair in anticipation.

'Oh yes, I love a joke!' Jacks nodded as she dished up for Pete and placed his food in front of him.

'I don't like kidney beans!' Martha commented as she gripped her fork.

'Just pick them out.' Jacks sighed as she put the plate of chilli in front of her daughter.

'Are you ready for my joke, Mum?'

'Yes, sorry, Jonty. Go ahead. I'm listening.' She loaded up her mum's spoon and helped her guide it to her mouth.

'There's too many to pick out, they make me feel sick. Can I just eat the rice?' Martha prodded the gelatinous lumps with her lip curled.

'For God's sake, Martha!' Pete shouted as flecks of rice fell from his lips. 'Firstly, your mother's cooked it for you, so just eat it. And secondly, your brother's trying to speak!'

'Can't I just have some toast?' Martha whined.

'No!' Jacks and Pete shouted in unison.

'Can I become a vegetarian? Then you can't make me eat this!'

They ignored her.

'Go ahead, Jont.' Jacks nodded. She watched as her little boy took a deep breath.

'What happens in space when they want to have a party?' He beamed.

'Don't know!' she and Pete chorused.

'They planet!' he shouted.

'Ah, very good!' Jacks chortled.

Martha winced and placed her head in her hands. 'That's bad, Jonty. You are talking out of Uranus!' She grinned.

'Oh, please!' Pete sighed. 'Eat your chilli, Martha. I can tell the moon has eaten all his tea up tonight because he's full!'

'Oh, Dad!' Both kids groaned.

'And you're certainly not getting pudding,' Jacks added sternly. 'Although if you are good, I might fetch you a Mars Bar!'

All four laughed, eagerly trying to think of the next joke.

It was Martha who came up trumps as Jacks fed her mum her next mouthful. 'I might not eat my chilli actually. In fact I'm thinking of trying that new restaurant they've built on the moon, but I've heard it lacks atmosphere!'

Jonty wheezed with laughter and Pete laughed to see his son so happy.

'Cracking!' Jacks guffawed loudly. 'Brilliant, you lot!'

All four were brought back down to earth by Ida's sudden loud sniffing. Her distress was evident.

'Oh, Nan! What's the matter?' Martha was sweet, leaning towards her nan, her voice soft.

'What's up, Mum?' Jacks placed her hand on Ida's arm.

'I need to find something, but I don't know where to start. I need some help!'

And just like that the joy was sucked from the room and everyone finished their meals in silence, broken only by the sound of Ida's sobbing between mouthfuls of brown chilli that dribbled down her chin.

Jacks kissed Jonty's forehead and snapped off his bedside lamp.

'Why does Nan get so upset?' he whispered.

'Because she's confused, love. She feels sad and she doesn't really know why. Sometimes she thinks she's young again, waiting for Grandad to come home. Other times I think she's sad because she realises he's gone and she misses him.'

'I miss him.' Jonty pulled the duvet up to his nose.

'Me too.'

'He'd have liked my jokes, wouldn't he?'

'Oh!' Jacks shook her head. 'He would have loved them!' She watched as Jonty turned onto his side and pushed his face against the wall, cocooned in his Batman duvet, snug as a bug.

She made her way over to Martha's side of the

room and ran her palm over her daughter's beautiful thick blonde hair, which in a certain light had a glint of ginger streaked through it. 'Night night, love.'

'Night, Mum.'

Jacks stood, hesitantly, and pointed at the book in Martha's hand. 'Not too late, now.' She knew Martha sometimes read until the early hours.

Martha nodded.

'He seemed like a nice boy, the one that knocked for you earlier?'

'Mmm . . .' Martha's face split into a grin. It was almost automatic.

'Do you know him from school?'

'No. He left a couple of years ago. He works with cars and stuff.'

'Oh, right. And is he a friend of Steph's?' She tried to sound casual.

'No, he's a friend of mine.' Martha raised her arms over her head on the pillow and sighed.

'What's his name?'

'God, Mum, what is this, twenty questions?'

'No, no. Just haven't seen him before and I'm interested in your mates – which is a good thing, some parents take no interest at all.' Jacks tried to appear nonchalant as she folded a T-shirt, retrieved from the floor.

'How do I get parents like that? Sounds quite nice!'

'Ha ha!' Jacks threw the T-shirt at her daughter. 'His name is Gideon Parks. He's twenty. And he is really nice and clever. He works with cars, but he's very artistic too. He's got great plans.' Martha blushed.

'Well, it's nice to have friends to hang out with before you go off to uni and make new ones. Definitely.' Jacks couldn't help but reinforce the idea that this wasn't her life; her life was what would happen when she left this place. Like him, like Sven, who went away and never came back.

'Sweet dreams, darlings,' Jacks whispered as she backed out of the room and closed the bedroom door.

Jacks tidied the kitchen, wiped down the surfaces and washed up the remaining pots and plates, then popped a wash load into the machine before climbing the stairs to bed. Pete was already propped up on his pillows, reading a tatty motorbike magazine in his vest and pyjama bottoms.

'Tell you what, Jacks, seven grand buys you a very nice bike.' He winked.

'That's a great idea – let's blow our savings on a motorbike. It'll give us the space we need and solve all our problems. Maybe we can balance on its saddle at meal times, or Jonty can sleep on the petrol tank and give Martha her room back!' She added a jokey brightness to her voice but couldn't avoid noticing the twist of disappointment to his mouth.

Jacks climbed beneath the duvet and let her tired muscles sink into their old mattress. Her eyes roved over the yellow roses on the wallpaper that she had liked when it went up over fifteen years ago. Martha had been a toddler and she and Pete had laughed as they got to grips with the wallpaper paste and long, fiddly strips of paper in the confined space. Everything had made them laugh back then.

'You going to read for a bit, love?' Pete asked over the top of his magazine.

'No. I've left my glasses downstairs and I can't be bothered to go and get them.'

'Do you want me to go?'

She smiled at her husband. 'No. But thank you. I quite like the fuzzy world without my goggles. It definitely has its advantages. When I see my face without glasses, I don't look too bad, not exactly dewy and glowing, but, you know, not as bad as some. The thing is I sometimes forget I'm not sixteen any more. I look in the mirror and get the shock of my life at the face staring back at me. I've definitely got the beginnings of a tash and when I crinkle up my eyes, they look really liney.'

Pete snorted his laughter. 'When anyone crinkles up their eyes they look really liney! You look lovely to me, Jacks. I don't know why you worry about what you look like or why you bother with that face cream and stuff.'

'It's to try and turn back the clock!' She jutted her chin and stroked upwards.

'Don't know why you'd want to turn back the clock and anyway, cream's not the answer, you'd need plastic surgery.'

'Well, thanks for that! Are you saying I should go under the knife?' She sat up, resting on her elbows.

'No!' He laughed. 'I'm just saying that all those potions are a waste of time.'

'Why would I go to the trouble of plastic surgery, Pete, even if I could afford it, when all I have to do to look better is remove my glasses and I'm back to fuzzy perfection!'

'You're mad, you are.' He leant over and kissed her head before straightening quickly. 'Ooh, my bloody back! I'll tell you what, I'm getting a bit old for this landscaping lark. I try to keep up with the young lads on the site, but I get slower every year.'

'Blimey, you're only thirty-six, you're in your prime!' She laughed.

'Yep, that's what they tell me. Just wish someone would tell my back.' He paused. 'I am going to have a think about things though, Jacks, going to look at our options.'

'What's the plan, Pete? What can we do?' She swallowed.

He shook his head. 'Don't know yet. Something'll come up. You'll see. Things have a funny way of working out.'

She nodded sadly. He'd been saying that since they were in their teens.

Jacks placed her head on the pillow and closed her eyes. She thought about how she lay next to her man night after night largely without feeling the slightest flicker of desire. She liked him, loved him of course, but it was as if they had turned a corner, waved goodbye to that aspect of life, become so comfortable in their routine that anything spontaneous, sex included, didn't even figure. She occasionally considered how she might initiate it, assuming she could summon the energy, and couldn't. If anything, she was embarrassed to touch him sexually, it had been so long. It saddened her. An image of Sven filled her head. She wondered whether, if it were him she lay next to every night, she would have been happy to wave goodbye to her libido without putting up a fight. She squashed the thought instantly.

'I love you, Pete.' She did that regularly – uttered this cure-all to dampen disloyal thoughts.

'I know.' He patted her hip under the covers.

Jacks sighed and felt her shoulders sink into the mattress. She was tired. Her eyelids fell in slow blinks that lasted longer and longer until finally they closed. One, two, three seconds later, her breath was even, her mouth slightly open. And then the bell rang from across the hall, rousing her from sleep and pulling her from the warm dip in the mattress where she yearned to stay.

Jacks fumbled with her dressing gown. 'Coming, Mum,' she said, trying to get the volume right, loud enough to reassure her mum but not so loud as to wake the kids. Her fist hit a wall of fabric as her arm struggled to find the armhole on the dark landing.

She creaked open her mum's bedroom door. The nightlight picked out her silhouette against the headboard.

'You'd better put the shower on!' Ida spoke firmly, lucidly issuing her instruction.

Jacks approached the bed and her nose wrinkled. Pulling the bedspread down, she blinked away the tears. 'Come on, let's get you cleaned up.' She eased her mum into a sitting position.

'Mu-um? Can you get me a drink of water?' Jonty's voice growled in the darkness.

'Yes, love. One second!' she called over her shoulder.

Without warning, the sob built in her chest and her tears came in a torrent. *Come on, Jacks, you're just tired. Just tired. It'll be okay. Pete's right, things have a funny way of working out.*

CHAPTER 8

Nineteen Years Earlier

Sven marched ahead as they tramped across the playing field, tripping in the dips and stumbling over the uneven tufts. Their clumsiness, along with their nerves, made them laugh. Jacks tried to ignore the tremble in her limbs as Sven quickened his pace heading into the encroaching darkness. She didn't dare look at the large trees that edged the field. At that time of night they conjured a myriad of shapes, all sinister. The wet grass soaked through the gaps in her school shoes and drenched her white over-the-knee socks.

'This is it,' he announced matter-of-factly, as though there were something scientific to his decision. He stopped in the middle of the field and placed his hands on his hips, then promptly lay down on the ground. 'You need to lie flat on the grass and look up at the sky!' Sven urged, pulling her down on to the damp ground.

'My uniform will get soaked!' she protested as her knees buckled in submission.

'Come on, don't be such a baby! What does it

matter if your clothes get wet? They'll dry. I don't think you ever heard Vasco da Gama say, "Oh no! I can't cross the ocean in my quest for knowledge because I don't want my cloak to get wet!"'

She stared down at him. 'I never heard him say anything actually and the difference is, he didn't have to go home to my mum and explain why his cloak was soggy.' She laughed, knowing she would do his bidding.

Tucking her skirt under the backs of her legs, she slowly sank down, positioning herself next to him in the darkness, her body centimetres from his. As the evening dew seeped through her cardigan and shirt, cooling her skin, she regretted declining the earlier offer of her dad's cagoule. But it took only a few seconds for her to stop thinking about the ruinous mud and grass stains on her clothes or the fact that her hair was curling against her neck; instead, she felt her head grow heavy as she relaxed and looked upwards as instructed into the night sky. It looked vast and beautiful. And the more she stared, the more she saw. It had never looked so clear or so close.

Sven reached across and took her hand in his. She smiled, happy to have her palm coiled inside his like a warm secret. He raised his free hand. 'If you look straight up at three o'clock you can see the Plough. It's a constellation of seven stars and you will always be able to make it out by the shape . . .' He traced the edge with his fingers. 'Because you can see the seven stars quite distinctly. Some people call it the Big Dipper because it looks a bit like a ladle. Can you see?'

She nodded. Yes! Yes, she could.

'And even more amazing, if you follow a line from the two stars on the right of the Plough and look upwards, about five times the length from those two, you'll see the Pole Star, part of what's known as Ursa Minor. It's one of the brightest stars in the sky and my absolute favourite. Can you see?'

'Yes!' Jacks squinted as she stared at the inky sky, where stars punched pockets of light in the most intricate pattern. The silver moon looked huge, hanging on the edge of the sky. They were silent for some seconds, breathing clouds from warm mouths.

'Okay, now do this. Make a fist and then lift your thumb and close one eye – you can fit the whole moon behind your thumbnail.' They both did just as he described. 'Amazing, isn't it? The moon is about a quarter of a million miles away and it's just over two thousand miles wide and yet you can fit it behind the nail of your thumb! That one fact alone makes me realise how very mysterious our little universe is and how our understanding of things can be dramatically altered, depending on how you look at them.'

They both stayed like that for some seconds, with one eye closed and an arm sticking up into the air.

'How do you know so much about everything?' Jacks asked, hoping not to sound too much in awe of him.

Sven laughed. 'I don't. I only know a little bit about a few things, but I figure if I keep impressing you then I'm in with a chance.'

More than a chance. I think I love you. I really do . . .

'You know more than a little bit,' she gushed. 'Don't forget, I'm in nearly all your classes. You never seem to get stuck like I do.'

'The secret is to read ahead. You only need to know a bit more than what they're teaching you at any one time – it's not about being clever, just good planning. I try to stay one chapter ahead.' He laughed again.

'I don't know if I could be bothered to plan like that, it's bad enough having to do homework.'

'You are lucky. You don't need planning or homework, you are special. You are unique, not like those sheep-girls who all look the same and chase the same sheep-boys and listen to the same sheep-music and waste their miserable lives. You're different. And you are beautiful, beautiful inside and out. And as unfair as it is, your beauty will take you places. You will have an amazing journey. I, on the other hand, I need clever. It's all I have.'

She squeezed his hand. *I'd swap it all for a small slice of clever. That would be my ticket and I'd take you with me.*

'What do you think you'll do when you leave?' She tried to sound nonchalant. *Less than a year from now and you will be gone, I know it. University and travel . . . Even the thought of you leaving makes my heart flip.*

'I suppose architecture, same as my dad. That will make my family happy. But if I could do anything . . .' He paused.

'Go on, tell me. If you could do anything . . .?' She heard him exhale and watched the plume of breath spiral upwards.

'If I could do anything, I would like to be a sailor.'

'A sailor? What, like the navy?' She pictured grey gunships, jaunty hats and shared bunks.

'No, not exactly.' He paused again. 'I'd like to get a big boat and sail round the world, hopping from one place to the next and speaking to as many different people as I could find. I'd like to try everything, see everything and fill in the detail in my head where at the moment there are just shapes and outlines.' The enthusiasm spilled from him.

'Wouldn't you get homesick?' She hated the naivety of her question, regretting it the moment it had left her mouth.

'No. I've moved around so much that now I don't think of home as a place, I think of it as a state, a feeling. I am home right now, here with you.'

She felt her gut churn with a warm longing for this clever boy who sounded like a poet and looked at the world like no one else she knew. He was quite unlike the other boys, who lived for football and pooled their money for chips and a battered sausage after school.

'Maybe I'll come with you!' Jacks laughed, to give her suggestion an edge of frivolity, masking the neediness.

'You can always come to where I am.'

'Oh yeah?' She was curious, wondering how that might be possible with her meagre savings and the fact that she always had to be home for her tea.

She felt him shift on to his side until he was blocking the silver light of the moon. His shadowy outline sat against the star-riddled sky. 'It's easy.' He laced his fingers against her own. 'Every night when you go to sleep, look at the moon and let yourself drift to the Lake of Dreams.'

'Is it a real place?' she whispered.

'Yes. It's right there on the nearside of the moon and it's where I'll be waiting. We can sail away together, far away from all the sheep-people, and nothing and no one can get to you, ever. It'll just be you and me with all the time in the world to go wherever we want.'

'It sounds lovely.'

'It is lovely. Meet me there tonight. It'll be the beginning of our adventure!'

She nodded as he bent forward and kissed her on the mouth, his full lips soft and warm. She reached up and pulled him down on to her. 'The beginning of our adventure . . .' she sighed as he leant in for a second kiss. His hands travelled up under her shirt to where her skin bristled with goose bumps under the lightness of his touch. She closed her eyes and wished they could stay right there on the damp ground forever.

CHAPTER 9

It was a cold November day. A biting wind and driving rain meant Weston town centre was virtually visitor-free. Jacks always thought that a seaside town in the cold and rain felt like one of the saddest places on earth. Elderly local residents in plastic macs congregated behind the rain-lashed windows of the coffee shops and tea rooms, staring out across the bleak, windswept seafront, mirroring the seagulls who huddled together on the beach looking equally miserable.

'Chilli?' Jacks muttered under her breath as she perused the supermarket shelves. 'No, I did that quite recently.' She pushed her hair from her eyes. 'Chicken? Possibly. Oh, I know, something Mexican with wraps. They like that.' She placed a few items in the basket on her mum's lap. 'Guacamole, is that Mexican? Not sure.'

'Jacks?'

She turned to see Lynne Gilgeddy, who lived on the Bourneville Estate. She was a few years older and Jacks had known her for as long as she could remember. They had danced in the same sticky-floored nightclubs in their youth and strolled the Grand Pier in their crop tops and shorts, giggling whenever they caught the eye of a good-looking Midlander of a similar age. Later they'd organised play dates for their girls when they were at nursery. That was a long time ago now and Lynne bore the marks of someone who'd had it tough – her hair was brittle, her eyebrows were beginning to thin and she had deep furrows either side of her mouth from the constant drawing on a cigarette. Jacks noticed this matter-of-factly: she was fond of Lynne and knew she was probably having similar thoughts about her. But Jacks at least tried to keep her few grey hairs at bay through the regular application of cheap highlights and, despite her thickening waist and sagging bust line, she still had the slim legs of her younger days.

'How are you?'

'All right, Lynne. Yeah, not bad.' Jacks knew people didn't want the truth; it wasn't an invitation to list all that was wrong. 'You?'

'Good, yeah. Ashley's doing great, still dancing. She's got a spot on a cruise. She's gonna see the world, Jacks. Amazing, isn't it?' Lynne shook her head. 'But the biggest news is, I'm going to be a grandma. Caitlin-Marie's having a baby!' She beamed and her whole face changed, as though even the thought of the child lifted her spirits.

'Oh!' Jacks concentrated on fixing her smile. 'Well, congratulations! Is the dad around?' It just slipped out.

'No. Just a bit of a fling, you know what these blokes can be like.' She tutted.

Jacks nodded as an image of Gideon Parks floated in front of her eyes.

'But what can you do, Jacks? We either get on with it or sink, right?'

Jacks nodded again. *Not my girl. There'll be no dancing on cruise ships for her, no walking the seafront with a secondhand pram and a baby clad in her second cousin's cast-offs. She is going to be a professional woman, a lawyer. She will go to meetings all over the world, she'll have a little black case on wheels that she trails behind her and people will see her confident walk and her beautiful face and they'll know she's a someone, a someone who is really going places . . . And it all starts with university. Her applications are in and now we just need to wait for the offers.*

'How are you, Mrs Morgan?' Lynne spoke directly to Jacks' mum, for which Jacks was grateful.

'She's fine,' Jacks answered. Ida stared blankly ahead, her mouth opening and closing, her fingers fidgeting in her lap.

'Do you still see Gina?'

'Yes, we're still good mates.' Jacks smiled, thankful for Gina's friendship.

'Give her my love, won't you. I haven't seen her for ages.'

'I will. And good luck. When's the baby due?'

Lynne beamed again. 'Ten weeks. I can't wait!' She clapped with joy.

★　　★　　★

93

Home safe and sound, Jacks propped her mum up with some pillows. Ida's bedroom was the one room in the house that was warm all day. Economising meant all other radiators were off while the kids were at school, but her mum's room was always toasty.

'It was nice to see Lynne today, wasn't it? Fancy her going to be a grandma! I remember her eighteenth birthday and that feels like a couple of years ago.' She spoke with a singsong tone as she changed her mum and ran a wet wipe around her mouth. 'Do you want to come downstairs or would you like to sit up here for a bit, Mum? I think *Bargain Hunt* is on, you like that, don't you?'

'I need to find this letter!' she shouted. 'It's just not good enough!'

'Well, as soon as it comes, I'll run it up to you, okay? Tell you what, sit here for a bit. I'll pop your little telly on and then you can come down for lunch and a change of scenery, how about that?'

Jacks tucked the cover over her mum's legs, gathered up the soiled nappy and knotted it into a carrier bag. She cleaned the bathroom, finishing up yet another bottle of bleach. *I should buy shares in bloody Domestos*, she sighed to herself. She made the kids' beds, then headed into her own bedroom to retrieve the nest of dirty laundry that Pete left at the foot of the bed each night. As she smoothed the creases from the duvet, the telephone on the bedside table rang.

'Gina! That's funny, I was just talking about you earlier. I bumped into Lynne Gilgeddy.'

'Ah, bless. She's had a bit of a life, that one.'

'Yes, and she's going to be a grandma!'

'Oh God, don't! She's not that much older than us! Don't tell me her Kyle is reproducing? That's all we need, the next generation of graffiti artists!'

'No, well, not as far as I know. But Caitlin-Marie is having a baby.'

'Ah, lovely. Well, I hope it works out for them. Listen, I've got something funny to tell you.' Gina giggled.

Jacks sat back on the bed and set her bundle of laundry and waste to one side. 'I'm all ears.'

'Well, you know I took Rob up to London for the Boat Show earlier in the year?'

'Uh-huh.' Jacks wondered where this was going.

'Well, they sent us a brochure through in case we want to go again next year – fat chance, we argued all the way home. Anyway, I was just having a flick through and guess who is on the bloody cover, the star exhibitor with some mega pricey, flashy yacht thing?'

'Don't know,' Jacks replied flatly. She was thinking of all the chores she had to do before she picked up the kids – she didn't want them coming home on foot in this horrible weather. And she was wondering how to make the Mexican chicken spicy but not too hot as her mum wouldn't like that.

'You've got to guess!' Gina insisted.

'I don't know . . . Gary Barlow? The Pope?'

'One and the same, but no, not even close. It's Brains! Your mate Sven!'

All other thoughts disappeared. Jacks felt her pulse race and her heart quicken.

Gina continued. 'There's a picture and everything. I mean, he's got older, but it's definitely him! It even says, "Sven Lundgren world-renowned yacht designer is launching his new blah blah boaty thing at this year's Boat Show" and there he is, larger than life, stood on the bloody deck! "World-renowned", can you believe it?'

Jacks remembered that night all those years ago, his words indelibly etched on her memory. *I would like to be a sailor . . . I'd like to get a big boat and sail round the world, hopping from one place to the next . . .'* She remembered the weeks after he had gone without saying goodbye, the way her heart had felt like the heaviest weight, trying hard not to burst with all that it contained. Crying herself to sleep every night as hot tears soaked her pillow and her thoughts churned: *What am I going to do? What on earth am I going to do?* And then Pete popping up quite unexpectedly, the solution she had been looking for. Dear, kind Pete. It was as if she had simply transferred her relationship with Sven over to Pete, without thinking about or questioning it, not then.

'Jacks? You still there?' Gina shouted.

'Yes! Sorry, mate. Wow! There's a turn-up for the books!' She swallowed the many questions. *Does he look happy? Is he married? Is his hair still blonde? Where does he live?*

'Do you want to see it?' Gina asked casually.

Yes! I want to see it! Right now! Bring it over, please!
'If you like, G.' She tried to sound equally casual. 'Drop it in, but only if you're passing.'

'Will do. See you soon, lots of love.'

'You too.'

Jacks replaced the phone and sat back against the headboard. She looked at the flattened pillow where Pete Davies laid his head every night. She placed her palm in the dent, closing her eyes and picturing his kind, hopeful face on the day he had proposed. Things had been so good then, so full of possibility. But now it felt like her life had become one long treadmill, running around looking after everyone else, wiping her mother's arse at a moment's notice. Peeling wallpaper and chipped paint everywhere, cardboard boxes full of crap stuffed into every available corner. Watching as she and Pete slid further into mediocrity with everything in short supply: money, heat, space and physical affection.

Sven . . . I can't believe it! She shook her head. 'Come on, Jacks. Get a grip, woman,' she muttered, sighing heavily. She stood, gathering the bundle of laundry and the stinking carrier bag into her hands.

As she tiptoed down the stairs, trying not to snag her socks on the gripper rods that remained firmly glued to the treads despite having long since lost the carpet they were meant to be holding down, she reminded herself that Pete was not to blame for how they lived. It wasn't as if she had married David Beckham or Pierce Brosnan and he had morphed into Mr Average. She'd known what she was taking on, kind of.

Opening the front door, Jacks placed the carrier bag in the wheelie bin and let the lid bang shut. She was about to go back inside when she heard Martha calling from the end of the street.

'Mum! Mum!' Uncharacteristically she was running, her hair flying loose in the rain and her school bag in her hand, decorum and poise thrown out of the window.

'Slow down! Whatever's the matter? Why are you home at lunchtime?' Jacks watched as Martha bent over and rested on the wall.

'Oh my God, Mum!' she managed between breaths.

'What is it, love? Take deep breaths and tell me.' Jacks was starting to feel the slight swell of panic. 'Is Jonty all right? Where is he?' Jacks scanned the street as her heart pounded.

'He's fine.' Martha pointed to the street behind her. 'I told him you'd collect him like we agreed at the usual time.'

'Right, good. So what's going on, Martha?'

'I got a text this morning to say that something had changed on my UCAS application!'

'Okay.' Jacks stared at her daughter. She didn't have a clue what that meant, but at least it sounded like something administrative and not an emergency. Her muscles relaxed.

'I've been going nuts. I couldn't log on until

after my lessons finished, so I spent the whole morning just wondering what had happened. Then I managed to go online just now and . . .' She swallowed and exhaled.

'What? Tell me?' *Please be good news, please . . .*

Martha stood straight and looked her mum in the eye. 'I got an offer from Warwick! Three As!'

'Oh, Martha! Oh God! That's amazing! I'm so proud of you.' Jacks couldn't hide her delight. This was happening, this was really happening!

'And you know what, Mum? I can so get three As!'

'Of course you can, you can do anything you set your mind to.' Jacks screamed and jumped up and down. She grabbed her daughter by the shoulders and the two pogoed on the spot together.

'I got an offer, Mum! I can't believe it! Some people haven't even got their applications in yet and I've already got an offer!'

'That's because you are brilliant and they all want you.' She hugged her girl. 'This is wonderful, wonderful!'

'Everything all right, Jacks?' Ivor opened his gate and searched in his pocket for his key. It wasn't unusual for him or Pete to come home when the weather was this awful. Pete called it a cricket day – rain stopped play.

'Yes! Oh yes, Ivor. Martha's just got an offer from Warwick University. She's going to be a lawyer.' As she spoke the words out loud, her tears sprang.

'Well, I've got to get the grades first!' Martha laughed.

'Oh, she will.' Jacks wiped her tears. 'I'm so proud!'

'You should be! Well done, Martha.' Ivor smiled.

Martha shrugged her shoulders as they made their way inside, a little awkward at receiving so much praise.

'What do you fancy for tea tonight? I was going to do chicken, but that'll keep. Anything you want, you name it and I'll go get it for you!'

'Pizza?' Martha didn't have to think twice.

'Pizza it is. Oooh, I know, we can have a little celebration drink with our food.' Jacks reached into the cupboard under the stairs and retrieved the bottle of Buck's Fizz that was left over from the previous Christmas. She wiped the dust from the neck. 'I'll stick this in the fridge for later!'

Martha ran up the stairs while Jacks made room in the fridge for the bottle. The bubble of excitement in her stomach filled her completely. This was it! Martha was on her way.

Pete coughed and banged the table with his fork. Ida jumped and clutched the front of her cardigan. Jacks patted her arm.

'Well, we have a lot to celebrate tonight.' Pete raised the glass of Buck's Fizz. 'Well done, Martha! You should be very pleased with yourself, my girl!'

Jacks nodded and sipped the drink, which tickled her nose. She gave a small giggle. This was a good day. Jonty took a large bite of his pizza and was trying to get a second bite in before he had finished chewing the last mouthful. Pizza was a rare treat. Jacks laughed again.

'You are such a lightweight.' Pete grinned at his wife. 'Couple of sips and you're anybody's!' He winked.

'When Martha goes to Warwick, can I move to her bed?' Jonty asked, trying to keep his food inside his mouth.

'Oi! I'm not gone yet!' Martha shouted in mock protest.

'I know, but can I?' Jonty asked again, wide eyed, swallowing, kicking his legs back and forth against the chair.

'You can do what you like, Jont. I'll have my own room in halls and I'll be able to shout and play my music loudly without fear of waking you up!'

'Blimey, girl, it would have to be pretty loud to wake him up all the way from there!' Pete laughed.

'And can I have a sleepover when she's gone?' Jonty shouted.

'Yes, you can.' Jacks smiled at her son, saddened by his simple request, which had been out of the question for the last couple of years.

'Yeeeeees!' he screamed, beyond excited.

'Hang on, everyone.' Martha raised her hands. 'I'd like you to miss me a little bit!'

'Oh, Martha!' Jacks shouted, as Pete simultaneously growled, 'Darlin', it'll break my heart to have you go away.'

'So noisy!' Ida yelled.

Jacks patted her arm again. 'It's okay, Mum, we are just having a little party. Martha has had some really great news today. She's going to be a lawyer!'

'Will you have a star-shaped badge and a gun?' Jonty asked.

'That's a sheriff not a lawyer, you doughnut!' Martha laughed.

'Don't call your brother a doughnut.' Jacks tutted through her giggles.

Ida pushed her plate away and tried to stand.

'What's the matter, Mum? You want to go upstairs?'

Ida nodded. Jacks placed her glass on the table and looked round at her family. 'You guys carry on without me. Don't let your tea go cold. I'll be back in a jiff.'

She walked around the table and, placing her arm under her mother's elbow, helped Ida stand before guiding her towards the stair lift.

As she tucked her mum under the covers in her bedroom, she thought about the momentous day.

'It's such great news, Mum. Martha's going to go to Warwick University! She's the first person in either family to go to university, isn't that something?'

Ida ignored her. Her mouth moved as though she was mid conversation, her eyes smiling at the imaginary person with whom she conversed. Jacks watched the changes in her expression and wondered who she was chatting to. She felt a wave of sorrow wash over her. Despite their fractured relationship, she was sad that her mum had disappeared and that in her place was this shell of a lady who seemed to exist in a parallel universe, dancing to her own tune. Jacks thought how lovely it would be to have one of those mums who got their hair done, went on cruises, read books and had a jolly old time with her ageing buddies. Although, truth be told, Ida had never been like that, even before she came under the icy grip of dementia. Jacks never saw herself as being in any way similar to her mum, couldn't imagine *becoming* her mother, and yet already she was aware that she sometimes caused her own children acute embarrassment, and phrases she had once sworn she'd never use now tripped from her mouth with alarming regularity.

'What do you think, Mum? Do you think that maybe history is on a loop? I bloody hope not. My girl, unlike yours, is heading for the top and that's really something, isn't it?'

'My . . . my . . .' Ida stuttered, tapping her fingers and frantically searching her memory bank for the word that evaded her.

'Letter?' Jacks helped her out. 'Not arrived yet. But don't worry, we are all keeping an eye out for it.'

By the time Jacks came back downstairs, tea was over. The kids were in the front room and Pete was reading the *Bristol Post* at the table. Jacks started to gather the dirty plates and empty glasses, her own included. Someone had necked the last of her drink.

'I was just saying to Mum, what about that girl of ours, eh?'

Pete closed the paper. 'I know. It's fantastic! Can you believe it, our little Martha, a lawyer?'

'Yes I can!' Jacks grinned as she scraped the leftover scraps of pizza into the food recycling bin. 'I bet she'll be tough, with a fearsome reputation. I always knew she'd do something amazing.'

Pete laughed. 'Yes you did.'

'How are we going to afford it, Pete?' She paused from her chores, hating being the one to raise the ugly topic.

'Well, her student loan will help out and I reckon we can kiss goodbye to our motorbike!'

'Our conservatory, you mean?'

'Ha!' He chuckled. 'You win! We will give up our imaginary conservatory instead of our make-believe motorbike.'

She lowered the dishes into the sink full of suds.

'I can always get a second job.' His face was suddenly serious.

'Or I could get a job.' Jacks was conscious of having not contributed financially since she gave up her shifts at the bank to look after her mum full time.

'That wouldn't really work, Jacks. What we'd have to pay for care for Ida would be more than you could earn. Plus remember what happened last time we had that home help.'

Ida had shrieked and thrashed as the stranger had tried to get her changed. Jacks had hated seeing her like that and had vowed never to put her mum through that again.

'Something'll come up,' Pete said. 'You'll see. Our little nest-egg will give us some breathing space.'

Jacks nodded, hoping he was right.

'Tell you what, why don't I get that bottle of Asti I've got hidden in the shed and you and me can have a glass or two? We can re-create the dancefloor at Mr B's. We are celebrating, after all. You can even light one of your stinky candles.' He smiled.

'They're scented, not stinky!' She laughed.

'Well, that's a matter of opinion!'

Jacks bent forward to kiss her man, both of them enjoying the rare moment of closeness, when the bell rang loudly.

'Nan's ringing!' the kids yelled from the front room.

Jacks wiped her hands on the tea towel and looked at her husband. 'See you in a bit,' she said and made her way upstairs.

After she finally got Ida off to sleep, she changed into her PJs and slipped under the duvet beside Pete, who was snoring lightly. She switched off her bedside lamp, which he had left on for her, and thought about Sven. As she drifted towards sleep, she wondered what he looked like now. She imagined herself arriving at a huge building in London.

It was the Boat Show and he was striding through the crowds, coming towards her as if she was the only person in the world. 'Look at you! Oh my God, you look so young! Come with me!' he'd say. 'I've been missing you since the day I left!' And off she'd go, her hand in his, towards a wooden boat which would take her far, far away to the Lake of Dreams, where they would look up at the stars as they fell asleep.

Jacks' eyelids fluttered open briefly and she sighed. She just had time to wonder idly whether she and Pete would ever get round to replacing their mismatched lampshade, before sleep overcame her for real.

CHAPTER 10

Nineteen Years Earlier

Jacks clipped the seatbelt together and pulled it slack, hating the way it bit across her shoulder. 'All buckled up?' her dad asked, as he did every time she got in their plum-coloured Ford Escort, his pride and joy. He adjusted the rear-view mirror.

Jacks nodded back at him, her expression sour. She did not want to be spending her precious Sunday with her parents, especially not going to visit Aunty Joan, who lived in Bristol and could only talk about what she had eaten and what she was planning on eating and how much all the said food cost.

'Would you like a sucking sweet?' Her mum opened the tin of hard-boiled sweets that sat in a delicate sweet mound of icing sugar and pushed it through the gap between the front seats.

Jacks shook her head. She looked at her mum and dad and thought, not for the first time, that they seemed old. She wondered what it must be like to have young, trendy parents who didn't wear driving gloves and carry sucking sweets in their

Maggie Thatcher-style handbag. Parents who didn't say, 'I don't know how you can listen to that horrible booming music!' and who knew the name of Take That's lead singer and didn't confuse it with Ken Barlow from *Coronation Street*.

Her dad, as ever, drove too slowly for her liking along the back roads, to avoid the motorway.

'I saw Mrs Davies in the week.' Ida tilted her head to the right so Jacks could hear without her having to turn all the way round. 'She's a nice lady, has a hard time with no husband.'

Jacks said nothing but reread the paragraph in her textbook about the difference between a limited company and a sole trader. *Boring*.

'Mind you, she's got Peter and he's a love.'

Jacks looked up. It had taken less than five minutes since getting into the car to get on to the subject of Peter Davies. 'Sven's dad has got us access to the Wills Tower in Bristol – we're getting a guided tour next Saturday. Should be a great view from the top.'

'Well, maybe we should invite Sven and his mum over for a bit of tea one night.' Ida gave her husband a sideways look.

Jacks felt her intestines shrink. Sven had called her mum and dad 'provincial'. She'd had to look it up and the definition now sat at the front of her mind: *small-town, uneducated, unsophisticated, narrow-minded*. He was right; they were all of those things.

'Oh no! Mum! Don't do that. I'd rather have Pete round!'

'But I thought you didn't like him?' her dad flashed.

'I just don't *like him* like him. And it's embarrassing. I have to see him at school and he'd only give people the wrong impression, when he's not going on about crappy football.' She slid further down the seat and threw her head back.

'You could do a lot worse than go out with a footballer, Jackie! They have big houses and lots of foreign holidays.'

Jacks sighed and closed her eyes. 'Sven has already had lots of foreign holidays and he's never kicked a ball in his life.' She smiled at the thought of him.

'Oh well, I might have guessed that Mr Been There Done That would be able to top-trump anything I might come up with! There's something about him, Jackie . . . I remember when he knocked for you and I invited him in and he said, "Thanks, but I'll be strolling around the grounds," and he went and stood on your dad's lawn! It was rude. Peter would have come in, had a cuppa.'

'Oh God! Enough with shining Pete Davies' halo! The main difference between him and Sven is that I really like Sven. Happy now?'

'It's all you talk about now, that boy,' her mum commented.

'Sven!' Jacks corrected. He was so much more than just 'that boy'.

'Why can't you do anything ordinary, Jackie?' Ida tutted. 'Why can't you just go with the flow and go out with a nice local boy and make life easy for yourself?'

'A local boy? So it's because he's foreign you don't like him? And how would that make life easier?'

'That's not what your mum means,' her dad interjected.

'Actually it is what I mean.' Ida now turned to look at her daughter full in the face. 'You always seem to pick the path that's hardest to navigate, the one that's most dangerous, unconventional . . .'

'That's me, choosing to go out with an unconventional foreigner!' Jacks smirked, thinking of Sven's love of astronomy and lack of street cred.

'Why can't you just accept that maybe we might know what's best for you? That maybe we have your best interests at heart?' Ida pushed.

Jacks laughed. They didn't even know her, not really, let alone what was best for her.

'It's not funny, Jackie! I mean it. It's like nothing we do or say is good enough. Peter Davies is a lovely boy, a lovely, lovely boy, but I know that as we've suggested him, he'll be off limits. It's like you do things just to spite me, to push me away. Sometimes you can be selfish and selfish people are very hard to love.' Ida threw a pointed look at her husband.

Jacks sat in stunned silence. Shocked by her mum's words, watching the shrubs pass by as her dad sped up a little. She swallowed the hard ball of tears that formed in her throat. She had no idea that her mum found it hard to love her.

CHAPTER 11

Jacks indicated and steered her little Skoda into the lay-by outside school.

'Have a great day, darling.' She smiled at her daughter, bundled up in her thick scarf, necessary on this frosty morning. They were all still buoyed up by her wonderful news.

Martha gripped the door handle but hesitated and turned towards her mum. 'Can I ask you something?'

'Of course.' Jacks twisted round to face her.

'Do you ever worry that you will end up like Nan?'

'With dementia, you mean?'

Martha nodded.

Jacks sighed. 'Well, my memory *is* shot – at least once a day I go upstairs, get to the top step and have absolutely no idea why I am up there. I pause, hang on to the wall and go through a list. Do I need the loo? Have I come to fetch laundry? Is it your nan? Often, after a minute, I walk back down, and I swear to God, the moment my foot touches the floor after the last step, it comes to me. "Bleach the loo!" Or, "Strip Jonty's bed!" I shout

111

it out like a bingo win, it makes me so happy that I've remembered.'

'I've heard you do that!' Martha shook her head.

Jacks laughed. 'I've talked about it with a few of my mates and they do it too. I don't let it worry me. I'm very different to Nan. I have a busy life and a busy family. I was thinking about it only last night. Before she got ill, Nan didn't really do anything apart from sit in her chair and watch telly. I don't think that helps. I think you can drive yourself nuts worrying about something that might never happen and, worse-case scenario, if it does, then I won't know too much about it anyway.'

'I'd hate to get like that – she's just like a big baby. It's like her life has been wiped out. I think it's cruel.' Martha's eyes brimmed.

Jacks sighed. 'You're right, it is just like she's a baby and it is cruel. But she doesn't worry about the sorts of things that you and I worry about. Her needs are more basic: she wants to be warm and fed and have a bit of company and that's enough for her.'

'I suppose so.' Martha clambered out of the car. 'I think you are amazing, Mum, the way you look after her. She's lucky to have you.'

Jacks replayed her daughter's words, letting them swirl around inside her head like a divine mantra. Martha never, ever said things like that. *And I'm lucky to have you, my amazing girl.*

✴ ✴ ✴

Pushing the front door with her foot, Jacks called up the stairs, 'I'm back, Mum. I'll just get your porridge and I'll be straight up!'

The doorbell behind her rang, making her jump. She opened the door and there stood Gina, stomping the cold from her boots, resplendent in a new razor-cut pixie hairdo and long, shaped fringe that had been dyed orange with the odd streak of pink.

'Good God, what have you done to your hair?' Jacks roared.

'As I said to Rob, it's bang on trend. Anyone that doesn't like it, just isn't with it.' Gina waltzed into the hallway.

'Blimey, G! If that's with it, then I think I'd rather be without it!' Jacks laughed.

'Anyway, I didn't come to discuss my new hair, I came to show you this!' Gina held the magazine up in front of her chest.

Jacks looked down and there on the front cover, staring back at her, was Sven. Older, different, but unmistakeably him. She felt the strength leave her legs as she tottered backwards and leant against the wall.

'You all right, mate?' Gina reached out and held her friend's arm.

Jacks nodded.

'Come on,' Gina coaxed, 'let's get you a cup of tea.' She guided her friend into the kitchen and pulled out a chair. 'Sit yourself down. You looked like you were going to faint!'

'I came over a bit woozy. That's the trouble – I rush around and if I don't grab breakfast and a drink first thing, it catches up with me. Cup of tea will do the trick.'

Jacks sat at the table and stared at the magazine, looking at the face of the boy she loved, a boy who in the intervening years had turned into a man. It was a shock to see the reality of him, a face that lived in her mind, altered by the passing of time.

Gina caught her eye as she filled the kettle. 'I thought it would make you laugh, seeing what Brains turned out like.'

Jacks rubbed her temples. 'I know! Seems like a lifetime ago that we had our thing.'

'I never did understand that, you nutter! He was hardly catch of the day.' Gina laughed. 'He was a bit of a weirdo.'

'Yep, bit of a weirdo.' She didn't confess to still taking daily trips down memory lane all these years later, nor to her frequent musings of *what if* . . .

'Well, that explains why you liked each other, two weirdoes together.' Gina smiled.

'Says you with the multi-coloured hair! You look like a Rhubarb & Custard.'

'I can't believe that both my best friend and my husband are so untrendy. My creativity is stifled here!' Gina shouted.

'You're right, you should probably move to Paris or Milan, where you can express yourself among other fashionistas.'

'Or I could stay here and put Weston-super-Mare on the fashion map!'

Jacks smiled. 'That's probably easier. Although think about all those Italian men you are denying yourself . . .'

'Ah, but I'd never trade in my Rob – though don't tell him that. Treat 'em mean and keep 'em keen and all that.'

'Treat 'em mean? You've been married forever and you are still all over each other!' Jacks hooted.

Gina smiled as she put the mug of tea in front of her friend. 'I know. We're lucky. He treats me like a princess, he really does. Plus he knows that if he so much as looked at another woman, I'd cut off his penis and feed it to the seagulls. I find the threat of that is quite an incentive.'

They both chuckled.

'Do you ever wonder what your life would have been like if things hadn't worked out with Rob? If you'd made a different choice, or if he had?'

'What do you mean?'

'You know, if things had worked out with that special someone who used to get your pulse racing but then slipped the net. The one that got away.'

'Jacks, you've known me my whole life, who are you on about? What one that got away? Do you think that weekend I said I was at my cousin's wedding in Crawley, I was really having it off with Jason Donovan?'

'No! But you know what I mean.'

'Actually I don't.' Gina stared at her friend.

Jacks closed her eyes and took a deep breath. 'Maybe it's just me, but don't you have anyone that you think about who makes you wonder, just for a minute, what your life would have been like if you had ended up with them?'

Gina bit her fingernail and thought about it. Her answer when it came was considered. 'Truthfully? No. No, I just have Rob.'

'Really? You only ever think about Rob?' Jacks was aware she sounded a little angry, wanting the reassurance from her friend that she wasn't the only one who had regrets. 'Are you saying there's never even the shadow of some bloke from your past who floats across the room or pops into your mind or who you imagine lying next to you on the mattress?'

Gina looked out of the window as if thinking about this for the first time. 'No, Jacks. I'm sorry but no. Not for me. I know it sounds boring, but I do only think of Rob, because he's enough. I love him. He's everything.' She shrugged. 'Why? Who have you got a crush on, you little devil? It's not that bloke on the fish counter, is it? The one with the dreadlocks that you said you'd like to take home?'

'For advice! I said I'd like to bring him home and have him cook me tea. I just wanted to know how to cook some cod. That's hardly a crush!' Jacks tutted.

'Hmmm, so you say.' Gina winked.

Jacks was weighing up her friend's words when

Ida's bell rang from upstairs. 'Shit, she hasn't had her breakfast.' She jumped up and glanced at the clock. 'Coming, Mum!' she shouted.

'I'll let you get on, mate, but see you soon?' Gina stood.

'Yes, great.' Jacks grabbed a breakfast bowl from the dirty pile on the draining board and rinsed it under the sink, slightly embarrassed by their discussion and wanting Gina to leave.

As soon as she'd waved goodbye to her mate, Jacks reached down with shaking fingers and pulled the magazine up to eye level. She clutched it to her chest, trying to feel him through the page and ridiculously wishing that she had brushed her hair and put on a bit of lippy.

Gina had stuck a Post-it note on the front – *Enjoy!* – presumably in case she hadn't been in. Jacks folded the note and placed it in her pocket. She laid the magazine flat on the kitchen table. He had aged, sure, but was still recognisable from the cover photo. The same bright, blue eyes, the same charming smile that caused his eyes to wrinkle, and that shock of thick hair, which had now turned sandy yellow.

Jacks traced his outline with her finger. He was wearing a navy linen shirt that showed off his tan and jeans. On his wrist sat a chunky metal watch. He had bare feet and was astride the deck of a vast, gleaming boat. It was a shiny, sleek design of chrome, glass and glossed wood with a bright white hull.

Jacks felt a little lightheaded and took a deep breath. She leafed through the pages and found the article. There was another photograph that showed him sitting on a leather sofa inside the boat, a more relaxed photo and one in which she could see the contours of his chest and the slight shadow of whiskers across his chin. The interior was luxurious and this was just a boat! It was grander than any house she had ever been in. She shot a glance at her own beige laminate kitchen cupboard door, which listed to the right, askew on its hinges, and at the work surfaces around her, cluttered with cereal boxes that were too tall to fit in the cupboards and plastic boxes that contained everything from pegs to pens. She grimaced at the tiled floor, chipped at the edges, her eye drawn to the too-bright slicks of mismatched white mastic where Pete had repaired the damaged grouting.

Ignoring the sink full of dishes, the pile of laundry waiting to be sorted and the layer of dust that coated the front room, she sat hunched forward, sneaking the time to read the article three times. Devouring the information, she swallowed the facts. He was 'currently single' – what did that mean? Divorced? Engaged? Widowed? She wished there was more detail. He was living in San Francisco and was a qualified pilot as well as a keen yachtsman. How could one person do so much and have so many opportunities?

Her mum's bell rang again and she jumped as though caught in the act. Quickly closing the

magazine, she shoved some porridge in the microwave, glancing back at the front cover while she
waited for the ping, before racing upstairs.

'Here we go, Mum, sorry about the delay. I got
a bit preoccupied. Gina dropped off a magazine
with a picture of an old friend of mine on it. Sven
– do you remember me talking about him? Feels
like a very long time ago now.'

She placed the porridge on the padded tray on
her mum's lap and went to open the window. The
room needed freshening.

'Funny, isn't it, how some people you know for
years and they barely affect you and yet there are
others who come into your life and breeze out
again and it's as if they leave a mark that no matter
how much you try, you just can't remove. Maybe
they're the ones we are meant to be with, the ones
that got away. I was thinking—'

There was a loud clatter and a bang. The bowl
of porridge had tumbled down the side of the bed,
leaving a trail of sticky, glue-like oats that clung
to the bedspread, the sheet and the carpet.

'No.' Ida said firmly. 'Bad.'

'No, no,' Jacks sighed, 'you aren't bad, Mum.
Don't worry, it was my fault. I should have made
sure it was steady.' She retrieved the bowl and
scraped what she could from the carpet with
the spoon. 'I'll come back with a sponge and some
hot soapy water.'

She pulled back the bedspread and couldn't stop
herself from retching. Her mum had managed to

remove her nappy and was sitting with it wrapped around her feet, mess streaked along her legs.

'I'll go put the shower on,' she said wearily.

It had been a long, tiring day.

Jacks allowed her mind to wander as, for the second time that day, she sprayed bleach around the shower tray, ran her hand under the showerhead and scrubbed the tiled walls. She wondered what it would be like if, instead of this cracked plastic cubicle, she had a huge power shower that took up the whole bathroom, in a big house with a glass deck and views of San Francisco Bay. She paused on the landing and held the banister. She didn't see the stack of boxes piled high in the hallway. Instead, she closed her eyes and saw herself bobbing around in the ocean on a boat that cost more than most people's houses. This was what it might have been like if she had chosen a different life, one where she had choices. 'I'll take ice with that!' She lowered her sunglasses and addressed the waiter who was proffering a tall white-wine spritzer that sparkled in the sunshine.

'Only me!' Pete called from the front door. 'You'll take what?' he asked as he removed his coat and dumped his keys on the windowsill.

'Nothing.' Jacks felt her face colour. She glanced at the clock on the landing: it was nearly six. 'I lost track of time.' She smiled weakly as she trotted down the stairs.

She filled and clicked the kettle to make him a

cup of tea, knowing that would help thaw him out after his day outside in the cold. Opening the oven door, she looked in on the roast potatoes, which were browning nicely.

'What on earth . . .?' Pete held the magazine up in the air.

Jacks felt the breath stop in her throat. *Oh God!* She had forgotten to hide it, so mesmerised by it that she hadn't wanted to put it out of sight.

Pete flicked through it and, much to her relief, chuckled, 'It's a motorbike I want, not a bloody boat! Although if this rain continues, a boat might be useful.'

'Oh, Gina left it here. Do you remember when she and Rob went to the Boat Show last year?'

'Do I ever. He's still going on about it. Reckons he was barred from going on all the really fancy boats cos he wasn't on the guest list. He tried to blag it apparently, but I told him he looks more pedalo than super-yacht to me!'

Pete casually threw the magazine down on to the table. Jacks resisted the temptation to retrieve it, hide it and smooth the pages to make sure they lay flat. She handed Pete his tea and watched, dry mouthed, with a twitch to her eye, as he placed the hot mug on Sven's picture. Her heart hammered loudly.

She grabbed a sheet of kitchen roll and swiftly picked up his mug and slipped the paper towel underneath. 'Better not get this wet in case Rob wants it back!' The little lie slipped easily from her mouth. She used her sleeve to wipe the residue of tea from Sven's image. Even holding his picture in front of Pete made her cheeks flush. She was beyond relieved that he hadn't recognised Sven.

The front doorbell rang.

'I'll get it!' Martha hammered down the stairs, making the glass in the kitchen windows rattle. 'See you later, Mum!'

'But your tea's nearly ready!' Jacks walked into the hallway and watched as Martha cringed.

'I'll have it when I get back.' Martha nodded towards the open front door, where Gideon stood, his hands in his jeans pockets, flicking his head to move his thick fringe from his eyes, the rest of his hair firmly in place under an Arran-wool beanie.

'Oh, hello, love!'

Gideon raised his palm and smiled. 'Martha, if you've got to eat, we can go out later.' He smiled again at Jacks.

'No!' Martha almost shouted. 'Come on.' She grabbed her parka with the fur-lined hood from the banister. 'Won't be late!' And she was gone, just like that.

'Where's she gone?' Pete asked.

'Out with her friends.' Jacks didn't want to elaborate, not until she had the situation a little more under control.

'Well, it's right she lets her hair down. It can't be all work and no play.'

'Mmmnn,' Jacks hummed, in semi-agreement.

After tea, she climbed the stairs to return her

mum to bed and as she did so she thought about the shine in her daughter's eyes. She knew exactly what that felt like. Nearly nineteen years later, she could still recall that night on the school playing field as if it was yesterday. The feel of her hand inside his, the way her heart jumped.

The phone in her bedroom rang. Jacks darted across the landing. 'Hey, Gina!'

'Well?' Gina's tone was keen.

'Well what?' Jacks whispered, hating having to be so conspiratorial.

'What did you think of Sven? Did you read the article? Weird seeing him all grown up and successful, isn't it?'

'S'pose so.'

'What do you mean, "s'pose so"? I got the feeling you were a bit unsettled by it earlier. I honestly felt like a gooseberry and that was just with his photo around!'

'Don't be so daft.' Jacks tutted as the blush crept up her neck. She was embarrassed and awkward at having this conversation while sitting on the bed she shared with her husband and with him on the floor below.

Gina laughed. 'I'm only teasing you! But don't tell me you haven't thought about jumping on a train and going to the Boat Show in January? Not after what I learnt today, that you still burn a little candle for him.'

'G! I do not!' Jacks remonstrated, unable to call her a liar. She could honestly say that she hadn't seriously considered going to the Boat Show, not until Gina had mentioned it.

'I mean, it's probably the only time in your life you are ever going to be in the same country. Plus you know exactly where he'll be. Unless you're planning to jet off to San Francisco any time soon?'

And there it was: the suggestion, the seed of an idea that would grow. 'I don't know why I'd go and see him. What would be the point?' Jacks asked.

'The point, Jacks, would be to see an old friend. Nothing more, nothing less.'

The bell rang in Ida's room.

'Gotta go. Mum's ringing. Speak soon.' Jacks replaced the phone in its cradle and raced across the hallway with a spring in her step and a flutter of excitement in the pit of her stomach.

As she tucked the bedspread over her mum's legs and went to draw the curtains, something along the street caught her eye. It was a couple standing under the streetlamp, encircled by the soft glow of yellow light, kissing in the rain. They had their arms wrapped tightly around each other and were clutching at each other's clothes, running fingers over each other's faces and clinging on as if their lives depended on it. She squinted into the darkness, confirming what the jump in her stomach had suspected. It was Martha and Gideon.

'For the love of God!' Jacks sighed and made her way downstairs.

She passed Pete in the hallway. 'Think I'll have an early night, Jacks. Shall I see you up there?'

She nodded as he kissed her gently on the fore-head. She hated the amicable formality of his gesture. When had they become so sexless? They never used to be like that, not when it came to the actual act. They had done it everywhere and anywhere at the beginning. It had been fun, exciting! Over the years, they had progressed to quiet, orderly sex, undertaken in the same posi-tion, only ever in their room, conducted under their duvet in silence and with the lights off. And after Jonty's arrival, even that was infrequent. Every movie, documentary and book seemed to harp on about sex in such detail that they only served to highlight what she was missing. She had become an expert at finding distractions when something a little bit risqué came on the telly. From getting up to make a cup of tea or picking up her knitting and getting lost in the rhythm to faking a coughing fit for which she had to dash to the kitchen for a glass of water. Anything rather than be forced to watch what she was missing, what they were missing. And miss it she did; it had been a big part of them.

And now Martha too had apparently entered this world of sex and was at that very moment prac-tising the art against the lamppost up the street.

Jacks sat on the stairs and waited.

It was half an hour that felt like a day before Martha placed her key in the door and came face to face with her mum.

'What are you doing? Why are you sitting on the stairs?' She looked bemused.

Jacks couldn't help but notice that her lips looked swollen. 'I'm waiting for you.'

'Okaaay.' Martha looked at her phone, her fingers red from the cold. 'It's not even ten o'clock.' She pulled off her coat and shook her hair.

'Come into the kitchen.' Jacks stood and followed her daughter along the dimly lit hallway. 'Sit down.' She pointed to a chair. They both sat.

'You like him, don't you?' Jacks watched as Martha's eyes lit up and she nodded, trying to keep the smile from her face. 'He seems like a nice boy.'

'He is, Mum. He's lovely.' She smiled again with a dreamy-eyed tilt to her head.

'I want you to be happy, Martha, I really do. And I want you to have adventures. But I'm worried.'

'Well, you can stop worrying, because I am happy and I'm having a great adventure, so that's all good.'

Jacks pulled her hair into a ponytail and fastened it with the band that lived on her wrist. 'That is good. But what I'm worried about is you being distracted from your studies. That offer from Warwick means nothing if you don't get the grades, and three As is going to take some work.'

'I know that and I'm not distracted. I don't see why I can't have both. I will get my grades, but I need Gideon too.' Martha looked close to tears.

'You *need* him?' Jacks was taken aback. This had clearly gone further than she thought.

'I do, Mum. He's makes me feel great. He's one

of the most interesting people I've ever met. I really like being with him.'

Jacks quashed her desire to scream. 'I'm sure he is, but your life is just beginning and you are on different paths.'

'You mean because he isn't heading off to uni and isn't desperate to leave Weston?'

'Kind of,' Jacks confessed. 'Who knows who you'll meet at Warwick.'

Martha rolled her eyes and pulled her sweatshirt sleeves over her hands. 'Maybe I don't want to meet anyone at Warwick, maybe I like what I've found here – a local boy.'

'No!'

'What do you mean, "no"?' Martha raised her voice to match her mother's.

'I mean you are too young to know what you want and I can see that this boy—'

'Gideon!' Martha corrected her.

'Gideon, or whatever his bloody name is, might be the thing that stands between you and your dream of becoming a lawyer!'

Martha sighed and ran her fingers through her hair, scratching her scalp. 'You don't know him, but you've made up your mind that you don't like him. I can tell you've decided you don't like who he is or what he does!'

'That's not true, I've nothing against him personally. But why can't you just accept that maybe I might know what's best for you? That maybe I have your best interests at heart?'

'Because *I* know what's best for me! And for the record, being a lawyer is *your* dream, Mum. It's not necessarily mine!'

Jacks sat in silence, as though she'd been struck. This was the worst thing that she could hear.

Martha wasn't finished. 'I think the problem is that you are living your life vicariously through me. And that feels like shit. It's unfair.'

'Watch your language, please.' It was all Jacks could say, because she didn't know exactly what 'vicariously' meant.

'You've got so many opportunities, Martha. I just don't want you to waste your life, not one day of it!' Jacks plucked a towel from the laundry pile on the chair and started folding it, using her chest and chin to assist.

Martha scraped her chair on the tiled floor. 'I'm not wasting one day of it! I'm spending the time I'm not studying with Gideon, and that's not a waste.' She looked at her mum, waiting for a response that didn't come. 'I'm going to bed, in the room I have to share with my little brother!' she snapped. And she flounced out of the room.

Jacks lowered herself to the floor and sat with her back against a kitchen cupboard as she scrunched the towel in her lap, giving way to the tears that had threatened. She sat for some minutes before managing to compose herself. Then she rose on shaky legs and rummaged through bundles of string, old tubes of superglue and a needle-and-thread kit before she pulled the pocket dictionary

128

from the back of the crowded bits-and-bobs drawer.

She ran her palm over the cover, which was slightly sticky in one corner. It had been her dad's crossword companion for more years than she could remember. She cracked the spine and let the flimsy pages flutter against each other. Her eyes crinkled in a smile as she noted the occasional little red dot marked against a word. If ever her dad had had to look up a word, he would place a little red dot next to it; if he looked it up twice, he wrote it out three times to make sure he learnt it properly. There were never three dots.

Jacks held the book at arm's length and there, nestling between *vicar* and *vice*, was *vicarious*. 'Vick-air-ee-uss.' She sounded it out and then read the definition: *Experienced in the imagination through the feelings or actions of another person.*

She closed the little book and stuffed it back in the drawer. Well, Martha was right, she did do that. But what mother didn't? She recalled the ballet class Martha had attended at primary school, full of slightly podgy mums lined up on chairs at the back of the church hall, every one of them picturing their precious daughter in an elaborate tutu as she stood with an arm full of flowers, taking a bow at the Royal Opera House. It was a world away from Miss Greenwood's shrill instruction to 'point and smile, point and smile!' And these mums weren't only thinking of their ungainly cygnets transforming into swans; they were imagining themselves in the audience, graciously accepting the smiles in recognition of their daughter's brilliance.

Jacks was no different, only her aspirations didn't lie in tutus and tiptoeing on pointes. She saw Martha travelling business class, with a Jaeger suit and a corporate credit card. They could keep the Royal Opera House. Her girl was heading for the city and no brooding teenager with an aptitude for snogging and a lovely set of teeth was going to keep her from that.

Jacks felt her tears rise again, and then, as if on cue, the bell rang. 'Fucking hell!' she whispered as she trod the stairs.

CHAPTER 12

Nineteen Years Earlier

It started out as a regular day, nothing to mark it as special. Jacks had walked to school and sat through double English followed by art, during which she tried her best to capture the bowl of fruit that sat on the table, while trying not to daydream.

She now stood tall in the lunch queue – being in the upper sixth afforded her a certain kudos in the school community. Her eyes darted to the doors every time they opened as she sought out Gina, preferring to be with her mate than without her during break times. Luckily she had a copy of *Marie Claire* rolled into the top of her school bag, should she find herself alone.

She waited for the slow queue to move along. The littler kids seemed to be taking an age, umm-ing and ah-ing over whether they wanted peas or beans and fumbling with cutlery, school bags and juice cartons. With her orange plastic tray resting on her hip, she sighed, trying to decide between a ham roll and the soup of the day. Two girls in the year below stood facing each other, close together as if colluding. Jacks tuned in to their conversation as soon as she heard Sven's name.

'Yeah, that Sven – the one with the funny jumpers who comes from Norway.'

This made Jacks smile. *Norway?* Stupid girls. But her smile soon evaporated.

'He's moving to America! I mean, that's really cool, isn't it? Even for a weirdo like him. My aunty went to America, said it was lush. I bet he'll go to Hollywood and everything . . .'

Jacks felt her legs shake. She walked backwards as if she were casually removing herself from the queue and not because she felt like she might throw up. As she replaced her unused tray in the stack, Gina came rushing over.

'Hiya! What we having? Go grab a chair and I'll come find you!' Gina shimmied her large frame as she broke into song, giving a heartfelt rendition of 'Baby, Come Back', quite oblivious of her friend's situation.

'I . . . I'll be back in a bit,' Jacks managed as she left the dining hall. She raced along the corridor and past the common room, where a quick scan told her he wasn't inside, then up to the physics lab, where he was sometimes allowed to hide out, being a star pupil. But that too was empty.

She ran down the stairs. Her heart hammered, tears gathered behind her eyes and something close to rage coursed through her veins. She readjusted her bag strap on her shoulder with trembling fingers and held the handrail to stop herself from tumbling. By the time she found him, skulking outside, sitting under the large oak tree at the side of the school field, her pulse was sky high.

He didn't need to confirm the news. One look at his face as he shifted his focus, unable to look her in the eye, told her all she needed to know. It was true. He was moving to America and he hadn't even bothered to tell her.

She dropped to her knees in front of him, both the adrenalin and her anger now subsiding, leaving her spent.

'I . . . I've got something to tell you.' He looked serious.

'Don't bother, I already know.' She plucked at the buckle on her school bag. 'Thanks for that. How do you think it felt, hearing it from some bloody lower-sixth kids in the dinner queue?' Her lip quivered despite her best efforts to stay calm and her tears spilled. She looked downwards, embarrassed and sad.

'I only just heard myself. I . . . I wanted to tell you in person, but Mr Quidgley asked me if I could head up the team for the Physics Olympiad next term and I told him I wouldn't be here and he asked why and . . . it just came out.' He snapped a dark twig between his fingers and shook his head as if searching for the words.

'Thanks a bunch, Sven.' She was angry for so many reasons; only one of them was hearing the news secondhand.

He leant forward until they were inches from each other, face to face. 'I didn't sleep last night. My parents made the decision: my dad's going to take up a lecture post at Harvard, we'll be living in Boston and that's that, I can't do anything about it. But I don't want to leave you. I want you to come with me!' His eyes sparkled as if this was the brilliant solution they had been searching for.

'How can I come with you? Don't be ridiculous! What, just pack up my school bag and follow you to Boston? This is real life, Sven, not one of your bloody poems with a romantic fairy-tale ending.'

'You're bigger than this place, Jacks; bigger than anyone in it. Don't let this postcode become your shackle. Come to America – you'll be eighteen in a few months and you can do what you want! We can travel, you can work, we can plan a future!'

He beamed and Jacks found herself smiling too. It felt possible, it felt like she could go and live with the boy she loved and see the country she had always wanted to go to.

'I don't know how . . .' She paused.

'We'll find a way!'

'But my mum and dad . . .'

'What about them? Are you going to tie yourself to them for the rest of your life? Stay here like a child, walking up and down the pier until you grow old? Or are you going to come with me and see the world?'

She looked at him, wondering how to explain that what she wanted and what she felt she was able to do were two very different things. He made it all sound so easy, so possible.

He took her hand and looked at her earnestly and in that moment she knew she would have to find a way. She would go to America!

CHAPTER 13

Jacks sloped into the kitchen with a plastic basket full of dirty bed linen. The first wash of the day but certainly not the last. She piled it into the machine. 'I'm going to make some bunting,' she announced.

'What, for breakfast?' Pete laughed. 'Why can't you do toast like everyone else?'

She ignored him. 'For Christmas. I was thinking it might be a way of brightening up this crappy kitchen, make it more homey. I saw some in a magazine.'

'How do you make bunting?' he asked.

'I'm not sure, but I'll figure it out. Can't be that hard.' She sat at the table.

'You look tired,' Pete observed as she took a quick sip from her first cuppa of the day. It had gone cold while she tended to her mum.

'I look tired because I am tired, so I guess that makes sense.' She shook out a cup full of detergent and poured it into the dispenser.

'What can I do to help you?' he asked. 'I could make the tea tonight?'

Jacks smiled. 'No, love, but thank you. You're out

working all day, least I can do is cook your tea. Plus it's just easier to get it done and get it all put away.'

'You saying I'm messy?' He grinned.

'Pete, you are beyond messy. It's like there's been an eruption at a food factory by the time you've finished.' She laughed in spite of herself. 'Has Martha told you she's got a boyfriend?'

She stuffed the sheets into the machine and kicked the temperamental door, then reached again for her cup and held it between both palms.

'Well, I know she's got a boy friend, but is he a *boyfriend*? Probably not, she's only young.' He shovelled a spoonful of cornflakes into his mouth.

'She's seventeen, eighteen in January and he is a *boyfriend* boyfriend, make no mistake.' She sighed. 'I saw them snogging last night. In the street.'

'No!' Pete smirked.

'Yes! And I don't find it funny.'

'Do we know him?'

'His name is Gideon.'

'Gideon?' He laughed. 'What kind of a name is that?'

'Pete, his name is not the issue here.' She sighed again, louder this time. 'He works at a garage in town.'

'He's not at school then?' Pete looked up.

'No, he's a couple of years older.'

'Well, as long as he looks after her and she's happy . . .'

Jacks shook her head. 'Are you nuts, Pete? We don't want her having a boyfriend!'

'We don't?' He looked confused.

'No! She needs to study, needs to get them As! Christ, am I the only one that can see that?' Jacks slammed her cup on to the table.

'She's not daft, Jacks. She knows what she needs to do. And the worst thing you can do is to object – you'll only make him more attractive.'

'Make who more attractive?' Martha asked as she came into the kitchen.

'Your boyfriend,' Pete answered honestly.

Martha smiled at her dad. He never lied to her.

'Why don't you bring him home for tea one night?' Pete asked, ignoring Jacks' glare, which bore into him from the sink.

'Do you think so?' Martha asked nervously.

'Yes!' Pete said. 'We'd like to meet him properly, wouldn't we, love?' he said, turning to Jacks.

'Mmmnn.' She nodded as enthusiastically as she could.

'Okay, I'll ask him. Have I got a shirt, Mum?'

'In the airing cupboard.'

'Mu-um, I can't go to school today!' Jonty yelled from the bedroom.

'Why not?' Jacks shouted from the bottom of the stairs.

'I've got period pain in my tummy!'

Jacks collapsed in a heap on the banister. Martha fell against the wall giggling and Pete guffawed loudly.

'Why are you all laughing?' Jonty shrieked. 'I have! Martha was allowed to stay off when she had it and I've got it!'

The three only laughed harder.

Ida started ringing her bell. 'I need help! I have passed water!'

Pete was still laughing as Jacks stepped back into the kitchen and ran the tap. 'We are the most bonkers family in the street! God knows what Giddyup or whatever 'is name is will think of it all!' He smiled with something close to pride. 'He'll probably run a mile!'

And even Martha chuckled.

We can only hope . . . Jacks thought as she ran up the stairs with her bucket of water, detergent, rubber gloves and sponge.

A few days later and Jacks' bunting was coming along nicely. She ran her fingers through the triangular pendants that she'd cut from a mishmash of charity-shop fabrics and threaded together on red ribbon. Still three weeks to go until Christmas Day, she thought, as she removed the growing pile from the kitchen table. She ran the hoover over the house, tidied the lounge as best she could, lit a scented candle on the mantelpiece and set places at the table.

Martha, meanwhile, split her time between checking her phone repeatedly and looking at her face in the hall mirror. 'I feel mean, Nan eating upstairs while we'll all be down here,' she offered as Jacks set Ida's tea tray.

'She likes eating up there, love. And it's only for one night. She might get a bit flustered with someone she doesn't know, and besides, there are only five chairs around the table and that's a squash. Where we would put her – on top of the fridge?'

Martha smiled.

'Or maybe we could put Jonty up there? He'd probably like it!' Jacks giggled.

The doorbell rang and Martha dashed to the front door, skidding in her socks along the hall floor and arriving before the bell had given its final chime.

Jacks noted her eagerness and took a deep breath. She looked at her own reflection in the window and saw her dad's face, 'Oh, Dad, I'm trying, I really am.' She turned, smiling, to greet Martha's boyfriend.

'Hello. Thanks for inviting me. I bought you these.' He handed her a bunch of tiny yellow roses.

It was the first time she had been given flowers in a very long time. 'Oh, Gideon, you shouldn't have done that! Thank you!' She was touched and immediately set them in the glass vase that lived in the cupboard under the sink.

'I was going to bring wine, but I don't really drink and I didn't know which one to pick. They all look the same – apart from red or white, obviously.'

Martha laughed as though it was the funniest joke ever told. Pete walked in and shook Gideon's hand: a hand with rings of black grease under its fingernails, working man's hands like his own.

'Blimey, you bought her flowers?' He indicated Jacks with his thumb. 'What are you trying to do, make me look bad?'

Gideon laughed.

'Sit down, love.' Jacks offered him a chair. 'Jonty, your tea's ready!' she shouted up the hallway.

Jonty thundered down the stairs and sat opposite their guest.

'How's your tummy now, Jont?' Pete asked.

'Have you been ill?' Gideon said.

'No.' Jonty sulked, not wanting to talk about his ailment of a few days ago, having been fully informed by his mum in the car on the way to school.

'So where do you live, Gideon?' Jacks asked as she cut a slice of steak-and-kidney pie and placed it on his plate.

'Thank you, that looks lovely,' he replied. 'Just up on Alfred Street. Not too far.'

'Have you always lived in Weston?' Pete asked, tucking into the crisp pastry, his favourite bit.

Gideon shook his head. 'No, we moved here when my mum and dad got divorced. I was ten. We'd been living in Bedminster in Bristol till then. But my mum got a job at Weston General – she's a nurse.'

'Ah, my mum was a nurse,' Pete said. 'She passed away a few years ago.'

Gideon looked a little ill at ease, unsure if it was fitting to offer condolences after this length of time. It led to an awkward silence, broken eventually by Pete.

'You a football man?' he asked.

'Yes. Love football.' Gideon smiled at Martha, as though he had given a correct answer.

'Who do you support?'

There was a moment of tension as everyone waited for the name of his team to fall from his lips.

'Rovers.' Gideon looked Pete in the eye, before collapsing in giggles. 'Nah, only kidding. City.'

Pete beamed. 'That's my boy!'

Martha laughed, clearly having briefed her man.

'Shocking season though,' Pete continued.

Gideon leant forward. 'No cohesion, that's the trouble. All going for individual glory, doesn't always feel like a team.'

Pete nodded. 'That's true, but that team spirit has to come from the top and it just hasn't been there. We should get Russell Osman back. Knew what he was talking about did Big Russ.' He winked his approval at his daughter.

Jacks groaned inwardly as she dished up her mum's food and trod the stairs with Ida's special padded tray. Her smile slipped the moment she left the kitchen. He was a nice enough lad – polite, and sweet to buy her flowers – but she had been hoping that he was going to be a disaster. With Pete now clearly smitten as well, it would only make it harder to keep him and Martha apart.

She pushed open the bedroom door with her foot. 'Here we go, Mum. Nice bit of steak-and-kidney pie with spuds and peas. It's not too hot.

Eat what you can – I've cut it into little bits. Let me get you started.'

She placed the spoon in her mum's hand and watched as Ida brought it up to her mouth, smacking the mashed food against her gums and letting most of it fall back on to the tray.

'Martha's brought a friend home for tea. A boyfriend, if you can believe that! I don't know, Mum, feels like five minutes ago she was starting school and now she's nearly finishing. Makes me feel old.'

Ida mashed more peas between her lips, some of which stuck to her chin in a gooey green streak. She had always been a messy eater, in fact messy in general and not overly fond of housework. In the latter years it had driven Don mad. He took control of the little things, fastidious almost in his quest for order. He was painstaking in his need to perfectly slice the bread – his ability to keep the loaf straight was an art. He was similarly obsessed with the patch of grass at the back of their house; no more than ten-foot square, it was never sullied by a weed or a stray leaf and was always lovingly referred to as 'the lawn'. Jacks could see now that he'd wanted to keep control of the little things because he could. He might not have been able to make his wife be kind to him, or stop her flinging dirty bras over the banisters for all to see, but he was happy as long as his toast was symmetrical and his grass immaculate. It made sense to Jacks now.

'I'm going away,' Ida announced through her mouthful.

'Oh, lovely. Be sure to eat all your tea before you go.'

'I'm going on a trip to find my letter.'

'Don't forget to send me a postcard and bring me back a nice stick of rock.' Jacks smiled and left the door ajar.

She trod the stairs and hovered in the hallway, listening to the boy holding court at the table.

'I've done a lot of research. No one is doing what I want to do at an affordable price. Usually body kits and pimp jobs for cars are only available at the high end of the spectrum, but I reckon there are loads of people with low- to mid-range cars who would love modifications that aren't too pricey. You know – lit-up dashes, neon subwoofers, fur roof-lining, you name it!'

'I can see you're really into this.' Pete was impressed.

'I am. I don't want to be relying on anyone else for my income, I want to be my own boss, work really hard and see where that takes me.'

She heard Pete sigh. 'Now you're talking – being your own boss, that's got to be the dream, hasn't it, to be able to manage yourself.'

Jacks took her seat at the kitchen table and watched Martha, who watched Gideon, taking in his every move, unable to tear her eyes away from the boy who sat at their table. Her heart sank. The girl loved him. Jacks recognised the looks of longing and admiration. And love, compared to a teenage crush, was a whole other story.

They waved Gideon off at the front door. Martha slunk up to her room with a dreamy-eyed expression on her face and Pete picked up the tea towel to wipe the dishes while Jacks washed.

'He seems like a nice boy. Polite, hard working and he's got some really good ideas, reckons this customised-car-interior business has a future. He seems to know what he's talking about.'

'What he's talking about is staying in Weston-super-Mare for the rest of his life, watching the shops close down one by one and living in a shitty house that he can barely afford until one day he wakes up and he is grey and old! And if left to his own devices, he will try and drag Martha along with him!' Jacks spat the words.

Pete was aghast. 'What, like I dragged you down, you mean?' His cheeks were red and Jacks could see the flash of hurt in his eyes. She felt a kick of shame.

'No!' She hesitated, unsure how much to share with him. 'It's not that. You know that I love you, and the kids. Things were different for us. But I just . . . I just want the best for Martha, and sometimes . . . sometimes I feel that I'm the only one who does. It's as if I can see what's going on and the rest of you have got your heads in the sand.' She shoved her hands back under the suds and scrubbed vigorously at the encrusted pie dish.

'Well, that's bloody charming. How to round off a perfectly nice evening. Thanks, Jacks.' Pete threw the tea towel on to the draining board and went upstairs.

'Are you and Dad arguing about me?' Martha asked from the doorway.

'Kind of.' Jacks dried her hands.

'I knew you wouldn't like him. I said that, didn't I?' Martha was almost pleading.

'Actually I did. I liked him very much. He's a nice boy . . .'

'He really is, Mum!' Martha gushed.

Jacks nodded. 'I just . . .'

'What?' Martha folded her arms across her chest, ready to defend whatever comments came her way.

'Nothing, love. Nothing. What do I bloody know?'

She walked past her daughter and headed for the bathroom, the one room in the house where she could lock the door and be alone.

She sat on the floor, letting the cold of the tiles seep up through her jeans and chill her bones. She glanced at the sink, where Martha had balanced a bottle of shampoo and conditioner upside down, trying to get one more wash out of them. The sight of this act of thrift was the final straw. She wanted so much more for her kids. She wanted them to luxuriate in a warm bath full of bubbles without worrying about how much hot water they were using, and to be able to wash their hair without eking liquid out of a cut-price bottle.

Jacks placed her head in her hands and cried. She wished things were different, and she wished she hadn't upset Pete, who had done his best and made Gideon welcome in their home. She sat on the floor and tried to get a grip. Taking two deep breaths, she rubbed her eyes.

She had been there a full five minutes when Jonty knocked on the door.

'Mu-um?'

'Yes, love?' She controlled her voice, pulled herself together.

'I need a poo!'

'Of course you do.' Jacks smiled, got up and opened the door, blotting her face with a towel as she did so.

Jonty rushed past her, colliding with her in the doorway, holding his trousers up with the button and zip undone to save time as he hopped from foot to foot.

That was it, her me-time was over. Back to the dishes. She shut the door behind Jonty and walked over to Ida's room. The door was shut. Jacks gently tapped, as she did on occasion, and opened it wide. She poked her head in and looked at the bed. The covers were in disarray and she was surprised to see it was empty.

'Mum?' She looked behind the door and on the floor on the other side of the bed in case Ida had fallen, as Jacks was always fearing she might. She leant over the banister. 'Pete? Is Mum down there?'

'No. Don't think so.'

'That's odd.' She knocked on Martha and Jonty's door. 'Nan's not in here, is she?' she asked Martha, who lay with her knees up and a book open on her thighs.

'No.' Martha rolled her eyes, irritated by the interruption.

She ran down the stairs. 'Pete?' she called, their previous ill-tempered exchange forgotten, as always, in the face of a potential crisis. She tried to keep the edge of panic from her voice as he emerged from the lounge to meet her in the hall. 'I can't find her!'

'Is she in the bathroom?'

'No, I was just in there. Jonty's in there now.'

'Kids' room?'

'No.' She shook her head.

'Our room?'

'Oh God!' She laughed nervously, feeling relieved. While there was somewhere she hadn't looked, there was still a possibility that it would all be fine. 'I didn't look in there.' She raced up the stairs, catching her toe on a tack. 'Shit!' she muttered as she stumbled into their bedroom and flipped on the light.

'Mum?' She stared at the empty bed and opened the wardrobe, whose cramped space, already full of boxes, suitcases and old clothes, would have difficulty accommodating another shoebox, let alone a person. *Where on earth . . .?*

Jacks made her way back downstairs as Pete came in from the garden shaking his head. 'I'll go

148

look out the front,' he said, grabbing his coat from the banister. Out in the street, Jacks saw him look left and right before knocking on their neighbours' doors.

'Where are you, Mum?' she whispered, trying to control the rising panic inside her. She did another full check of the house, looking under beds and inside cupboards, behind doors and even behind every curtain, as though it were a game of hide-and-seek. Ida was nowhere to be seen and definitely nowhere inside the house.

Hovering in the kitchen, she heard Pete in the hallway. His expression told her all she needed to know.

He shook his head. 'Ivor helped me. We did a quick scout of the road, knocked on doors and looked up the alley. Nothing. The kids are going around the block with a torch. Don't worry, I told them to stay together.'

'Where is she, Pete?' she asked, as though he might have the answer.

'I don't know, love. I mean, she can't have got very far, but I think we should call the police.'

'Really?' Jacks' breath came in shallow pants.

'Yep, they can look better than we can.'

'But, Pete, she can't walk far. What on earth . . .? She can't have just disappeared.' She sat on the stair and started to cry.

Pete squeezed her shoulder as he picked up the phone and dialled 999.

CHAPTER 14

Nineteen Years Earlier

Jacks was sitting on the stairs in her pyjamas with the curly telephone cord wrapped around her fingers and the receiver slotted between her chin and shoulder as she listened to Sven talk about what life would be like in Boston. She nodded and smiled in all the right places. Her feet rested in a basket of laundry that her mum had gathered from the line a couple of days earlier but still hadn't taken upstairs and put away.

'There are great theatres and museums, and the Franklin Park Zoo of course. We'll have a big day out and then go and eat clam chowder in some funky restaurant.'

Jacks wrinkled her nose at the idea of clams, wondering if they'd be anything like the ones they sold on the fish stall on the Marine Parade. 'Sounds good.' She smiled.

'Good? It sounds more than good, it'll be brilliant!' The enthusiasm spilled from him.

'Yes,' she agreed, 'it sounds brilliant!'

'Have you told them yet?' he asked.

Jacks shook her head. 'No,' she said, her voice no more than a whisper. She had no idea how to tell them she was leaving or how to ask them for the fare. 'I think I might this evening . . .' She bit her lip.

'Yes! Good! Do it! Ask them now, that gives us more planning time.' He sounded so assured, so certain, that it gave her the confidence that it might actually happen.

She ended the call and mentally rehearsed going into the lounge to talk to her mum, figuring that starting the conversation was going to be the hardest part. She was still sitting on the stairs, planning what to say, when Don arrived home.

Her dad came through the front door and gave her a small wave. He had an air of caution, as though he were sneaking in in the early hours. He had a dark smudge of tiredness beneath his eyes and his hair looked messy and dusty. He had explained to her a little while ago how he had taken on an extra job.

He stood by the front door and leant wearily against the frame in his big wool work coat with its leather panels across the back of the shoulders and two matching patches on the arms. She had asked him when she was little, 'Why's it called a donkey jacket?' and he'd stood ramrod straight, stroked the lapel and said, 'It's made of the finest donkey.' It was only when her lip wobbled at the thought that he'd let out his loud laugh and said, 'I don't know, my love, but if I had to guess, I'd say that it's because those of us that wear them work like donkeys, and I don't mean trotting up and down under the Grand Pier with a fat kid on our backs!'

Jacks returned his wave as he peeled off his thick socks, freeing his toes from the heavy work boots. He pinched her cheek through the banister and smiled at her. A long, slow smile, as if reminding himself why it was all worth it. She swallowed the guilt she felt, knowing she was going to abandon him for Boston's museums and clam chowder.

'Your dinner's on the table,' Ida snapped from the chair in front of the telly as the theme tune from *Kavanagh QC* wafted from the speaker.

Jacks stopped replaying Sven's words for a moment and listened to her dad.

'Ooh, smashing. Thanks. I'm starving.'

She heard him wash his dirty hands in the sink, using, as he always did, a squirt of Fairy Liquid to loosen the grime as he scrubbed their hairy backs and under his nails. Jacks hated the fact that he was starving, didn't like to think of her dad hungry as well as dirty. He pulled off his coat and hung it on the hook on the back of the cupboard under the stairs, the cupboard that always smelt of old carpet and mould.

She watched through the open lounge door as he was gripped by the scene on the telly, rolled up the sleeves of his long thermal vest and grabbed the knife and fork that Ida had laid ready. The plate was heaped high with shepherd's pie and diced carrots. He dug the fork into the mashed potato and placed it in his mouth.

'Oh, yuck!' He quickly spat it into his hand and walked over to the kitchen door, where a carrier bag hung off the handle, their makeshift bin. Lobbing it from his palm into the bag, he looked at his wife, whose gaze was fixed on the screen.

'It's icy cold, Ida!' He raised his voice.

Jacks gripped the receiver and held it under her chin, letting her parents think she was deep in conversation rather than following their every word and gesture. It didn't matter that she was on the verge of womanhood, she still craved domestic bliss, just as she had when she was seven. She wanted her home to be a happy one.

She watched as her mum unfurled her legs from beneath her and sloped to the table. 'That's easily fixed.' Ida hummed, a slight smile on her face. She was going to do the right thing, Jacks thought with relief. She was going to reheat her dad's tea like she usually did, by setting the foil-wrapped plate over a pan of boiling water.

Jacks stared, horrified, as her mum swiped the plate from the table, scattering carrots as she did so, walked over to the carrier bag and tipped the lot into it. 'If you want hot tea, you get here at teatime. Simple, really.' She let the plate clatter on the draining board. With that she sat back down on the chair and continued to stare at the screen.

Jacks felt her chest heaving. She wanted to wade in and explain to her mum that it wasn't her dad's fault; he'd been out working, working for them. But it wasn't her place to do that. Plus the set of her mum's chin and her dad's reluctance to speak up told her there was little point.

Don looked up and caught his daughter's eye, giving her a false smile as if to say, *'Nothing to worry about, little Dolly Daydream. It's all okay.'*

'In that case, I think I'll have a bath and call it a night.' He made for the bottom of the stairs.

'Good luck with that. There's no hot water,' her mum said with an almost joyful note in her voice. She put a cigarette between her lips and rolled the flint under her thumb.

Don pushed the lounge door to, blocking Jacks' view. But despite his lowered voice, she could still hear him.

'Oh, Ida, and you wonder why . . .'

'No, I don't wonder why! I *know* why! I have all the time in the world to sit and think about why!'

Jacks abandoned the phone, suddenly wanting to be anywhere other than listening to her parents arguing. She retreated to her bedroom. This was not the time to be asking for anything.

CHAPTER 15

Gina gave an elaborate wave as Jacks pushed her mum's wheelchair through the door of the coffee shop on the seafront and snaked round the tables to take up the seat alongside her.

'Cor, it's freezing out there.' Jacks loosened her mum's scarf, unzipped her coat and ordered two hot drinks. The place was busy and the aroma of toast and freshly brewed coffee made it feel cosy and inviting. Customers clustered around the tables with coats and scarves resting on the chairs behind them. No one seemed in any hurry to go back outside.

There was a strong smell of cinnamon, which always made Jacks feel a little nauseous. The ceiling was festooned with twists of red and green crêpe paper and large silver snowflakes had been pasted on to the windows. On the other side of the glass, shoppers dashed madly to and fro, clearly feeling the pressure as December sped by and Christmas Day loomed closer.

'Well, Ida, I heard about your little adventure last night.' Gina smiled at her friend's mum. 'Did

155

you go out dancing? Because next time, take me with you.'

'Oh God, G. We can joke now, but it was the longest hour of my life. It just didn't make sense. I knew she couldn't have gone far, but you know when you can't think straight and your mind runs riot.'

'Yeah, every day.' Gina pulled a face. 'Still, all's well that ends well.'

Jacks tried to laugh but was still haunted by how scared they had all been. The young policeman had sat at the kitchen table, removed his hat and flipped open his notepad. 'So the lady in question is Mrs Ida Morgan and she is eighty-one?'

'Yes.' Jacks had nodded. 'She has dementia and she's very quiet and frail. And now it's getting late and it's dark and cold. Her coat's still in the house.' She shredded the tissue in her hand.

'Does she have a phone?'

'No.' Her mum didn't have the dexterity to open a packet of biscuits, let alone operate a phone. 'No, she doesn't.'

'How mobile is she?' The young policeman sat with pen poised.

'Erm, she can walk, but she's a bit unsteady and she can't go far. So she can manage from the bedroom to the loo and from the kitchen up the hall to get in her stair lift, but for any longer distances, like going to the shops, she's in her chair.'

'Does she have any hobbies, participate in any sports, belong to any clubs?'

Jacks looked first at Pete and then back to the policeman. *Don't be so stupid! What bloody sports could she participate in?* She nibbled her nail. 'No. As I mentioned, she's not that mobile, or that with it really. Shall we go and look for her again?' She pushed back her chair, feeling impatient, wanting to do *something*.

'Nearly done. Does she have friends?'

It was a difficult question for Jacks to answer. She shook her head and cried, 'No! She doesn't have any friends. She has lots of people who care about her, but no friends.'

Pete took her hand and held it beneath his.

'How long was it between the last definite sighting of her and when you first realised she was gone?'

'About an hour.' Jacks shook her head. *Why didn't I check on her sooner? This is all my fault. I'm supposed to be looking after her. I promised.*

'And there was nothing unusual about her? She wasn't upset?'

'No. I got her started with her tea and she told me she was going away on a trip.'

'She did? So she told you she was going away?' The policeman looked confused.

'Well, yes, but she didn't mean it! She doesn't know what she's saying!' Jacks was getting frustrated by the questions and the lack of action. 'We had a guest over for tea, maybe we should talk to him!' She looked at Pete.

'Why would they talk to him?' Pete asked.

'I don't know!' Jacks shouted. 'I just don't know what else to do. Where is she?'

The front doorbell rang. Jacks ran up the hall and flung it open to see her mum on the doorstep, with Angela by her side, holding her arm.

Jacks shivered as she relived the memory. She looked at Gina. 'Apparently Angela nipped out to do the recycling and came back to find Mum rifling through Ivor's desk, flinging invoices left, right and centre, saying she was looking for some-thing we'd stored there. I have no idea what she was doing. The policeman was lovely, but I still feel embarrassed about causing such a fuss.'

Gina pulled a face. 'Weird that she'd go digging around in other people's stuff – that's not like her. Looking for that bloody letter, I bet!'

'Oh God, G, I hadn't thought of that! You might be right. I just feel terrible about it. She said she was going on a trip and I laughed it off, didn't take it seriously.'

'Mate, you can't beat yourself up about it.' Gina sipped her coffee. 'Maybe you should get her chipped.'

'She's not a bloody dog!'

'I know! But you know what I mean, like a homing device!'

'And she's not a pigeon either!' Jacks laughed in spite of her friend's clumsy comment.

'What's in the bag?' Gina asked, changing the subject as she spied the large carrier with a box inside resting on the handle of Ida's wheelchair.

'Well, don't laugh, but I got Martha a sandwich toaster for Christmas. I don't know what the facilities are like at Warwick, but I thought if she gets back to her room after lectures and is a bit hungry, she can always have a toasted sandwich in her room, or make snacks for her friends.'

'That's a nice idea.' Gina popped a square of shortbread in her mouth and turned towards the wheelchair. 'You look well, Ida. Despite your little adventure. Are you looking forward to Christmas?'

'I have treasure!' Ida announced. 'From my dad. I kept it hidden!'

'Oh, how exciting. I love treasure.' Gina patted her hand.

'You mustn't read my letter! You mustn't. Don't do it!' Ida shouted.

'Don't worry, Mum. No one will read it but you, I promise.'

This seemed to placate her. 'Is Don coming here?' she asked anxiously.

'No. No, he's not,' Jacks answered softly.

'I reckon that letter your mum's waiting for has gone second class,' Gina commented.

Jacks giggled. Gina still had the ability to make her laugh like no one else. 'Reckon you might be right.'

'It's true, though, your mum does look well. But you, on the other hand . . .' Gina tutted.

'What?' Jacks sat upright.

'You look terrible!'

'G, you must learn to stop sugar-coating your thoughts.' Jacks laughed.

'I've known you too long to sugar-coat anything. You look knackered.'

'So I've been told. I don't know why everyone seems so keen on pointing it out to me. It's not like I don't know how tired I am. I do. I'm bloody exhausted! And everyone telling me just makes me feel worse.'

'I'm only going to repeat what I've said a million times before, but can't you get some respite care for your mum? Even if it were just for a week, it would make all the difference. She wouldn't know and a rest would do you so much good.'

Jacks shook her head. 'You know what happened when that home help came in – she went berserk, hated it. It's not fair on them or her.'

'So try a different home help.'

'No. I promised my dad and a promise is a promise.'

'Jacks, I knew your dad nearly all my life.' Gina stirred her coffee. 'Don was a lovely, lovely man and he wouldn't want you working yourself into an early grave, he just wouldn't.'

'It's not that straightforward. She gets very flustered if things are new or there are strangers around. Plus it costs money, a lot of money.' Jacks sipped her latte.

'So use some of your inheritance! That's what it's for, to make life easier!'

'Maybe.'

'I know that "maybe" means no,' Gina almost shouted.

Jacks laughed because G was right again.

'I've already told you I'd be happy to have your mum for a weekend or overnight.'

'Thanks, G, but I wouldn't put that on you. Plus she's better off at home, where everything is familiar.'

'Well, the offer is there. Anyway, let's change the subject. Have you thought any more about going to see Sven in the new year?'

Jacks looked around, as though someone might be listening. Of course they weren't. 'No!'

'Well, you should,' Gina urged.

'Are you trying to get me into trouble?' Jacks whispered.

'I just think you've got a little bit of unfinished business. And it'll be a laugh. I saw how you reacted to his photo – it obviously meant a lot to you and this is your chance to put it to bed once and for all. Fnarf!'

The women giggled like they were teenagers again.

'I can't just up and go to London! What would I tell Pete and the kids? I've never lied to them and I'm not about to start now.'

Gina considered this. 'What about if you didn't have to lie to them? What about if I invited you up to the Big Smoke for a day of shopping and it just happened to coincide with a certain event featuring a certain blonde Swedish nerd with terrible taste in jumpers?'

Jacks' stomach flipped at the idea of seeing him again. 'I don't know . . .'

'Well, think about it. Let me know and if you are up for it, I can put things in place. No one would ever know, only you and me! We'll have a laugh!'

'What would I do with Mum for a whole day?'

'Like I said, get a nurse in, a bit of respite care. There are agencies that would send someone to come and spend the day with her. Surely you don't mind leaving her for a day? There must be one person she'd be happy to be left with. She'd probably be glad of the change of company – having to look at your miserable face must drive her loopy. Or loopier!'

'I'll think about it.'

'Ooh, good. "I'll think about it" is usually a yes!'

And Jacks laughed because she was right yet again.

'So,' Gina started, 'Pete told Rob that Martha's got herself a young man!'

'Well, yes, she has. But not so young – he's twenty and works in a garage in town. He's called Gideon.'

'No need to ask if you approve!' Gina laughed. 'The curl of your lip says it all. And your voice! You sound like you're spitting poison, the poor sod. I feel a bit sorry for him and I've never even met him!'

Jacks rubbed her eyes. 'Oh God, it's not that I don't approve of him. I don't approve of anyone here. I want her to go away and make a life, not get stuck in a rut she can't get out of.'

Gina stared at her. 'They're having a cheeky snog

on the Marine Parade, Jacks, not waltzing up the aisle. You need to let it run its course.'

'Did Pete tell you to say that?'

'No, but if he had, I would, because that's right. You're getting your knickers in a twist over nothing. Mark my words, by the new year, Gideon will have moved on and Martha will be lying on her bed, crying over what might have been and rehanging her Justin Bieber poster.'

'I hope you're right.' Jacks polished off the last of her coffee.

'I usually am.' Gina grinned. 'Just ask my husband.'

Ida turned and opened and closed her mouth as if about to speak. She twisted her fingers in agitation. Jacks helped lift her cup of tea to her mouth. Ida took a sip and then spoke with such clarity it took both Jacks and Gina by surprise.

'Such a waste of life, two of us sitting waiting for him night after night. Did it make her happy? I don't think so. I don't think it did.'

Gina and Jacks stared at each other, wondering who Ida was talking about.

'You are not wearing that!' Jacks spoke authoritatively as she turned her attention back to the mound of potatoes that she was peeling.

'What's wrong with it?' Pete crept up behind her and made the nose and antlers on his reindeer flash. 'If you can't wear your Christmas jumper on Christmas Day, then when can you wear it?'

Jacks laughed. 'You look like a right wally.'

'Thought we weren't supposed to call our family members names?' Martha wandered into the kitchen and took a seat at the kitchen table.

'It's Christmas, normal rules don't apply! I can call your dad a wally and you can get me a large glass of wine, which I shall drink while I get the lunch ready.'

'Drinking during the day?' Martha tutted.

'Yep. And I might have two puddings as well, who knows?'

'Can I have two puddings?' Jonty chirped up from the hallway, where he was directing his remote-control car.

'Yes.' Jacks nodded.

'Can I have a glass of wine then, if he's having two puddings?' Martha asked as she poured one for her mum.

'Yes.' Jacks nodded again.

'Can I get a motorbike?' Pete thought he'd try his luck.

'No!' Jacks waved the vegetable knife at her husband.

'But it's not fair!' He slapped the table as his voice went up a couple of octaves. 'I have to share a room with Jackieeeeee and I want to go out with my mates and she won't let meeeeee!' Pete imitated his daughter before falling against the chair opposite her and slumping into it. 'No one understands me and my boyfriend's got a silly naaaaaame!' he wailed.

'Very funny.' Martha pursed her lips but couldn't fight the smile that spread.

Jacks leant against the sink and giggled.

Martha sipped the glass of white wine that she had poured herself. 'He might have a silly name, but he bought me this!' She gathered her hair and pulled it to one side to reveal a silver chain with a delicate filigree heart hanging from it. She was clearly pleased as punch.

'Oh! It's beautiful, love.' Jacks had to admit, it was lovely. The smile her daughter gave her made her almost forget where the gift had come from.

'Can I have some wine?' Jonty stood in the doorway.

'No. You are having two puddings,' Jacks reminded him.

Martha faced her brother and took an elaborate sip. 'Ooh, this is nice, much nicer than two puddings!'

'You've got no boobs!' Jonty shouted at his sister.

Jacks sprayed wine over the potatoes and Pete guffawed loudly.

'Jonty!' Jacks squealed. 'What a thing to say to your sister!'

'I heard her saying to Steph that she wanted bigger boobs and I said she didn't even have any to start with, let alone bigger ones!'

Martha stood from the table and tackled her little brother to the floor, kissing his face and tickling him as he screeched for mercy. Ida rang her bell from the lounge and Pete jumped up. 'I'll go!' He took a moment and looked back into the kitchen at his family. Jacks caught his eye and smiled. This was a good, good day.

The Davies household was full of laughter for the rest of the afternoon. The turkey and all the trimmings were cooked to perfection and there was even a blue flame flickering on top of the Christmas pud. Jonty had two helpings, as agreed. Pete kept his novelty jumper on all day; it flashed while he napped on the sofa, his tummy full of trifle. Ida wore her good jewellery, stretching her fingers and staring at her eternity ring as though it was the first time she had seen it. Jacks looked at Jonty's beaming face as he gazed at the remote-control car that Santa had brought him, mesmerised by the continual whizzing back and forth. She knew they'd been right to dip into their savings. At bedtime, he had to be prised away from it.

Jacks sat on the lounge floor, eating chocolates she didn't really want, just because they were there, and half paying attention to the Christmas movie. She shot the occasional look at Martha, who was a little quieter than usual. She had her phone on the cushion by her side and was regularly sending and receiving texts, alerted by the tiny buzz that saw her fingers dart out and reach for it. Jacks didn't have to ask who they were from.

As Jacks washed the pots at the end of the day, she thought about the year to come, another year without her dad. Pete came and stood next to her, picking up a tea towel to help dry.

'Just think, next Christmas our girl will be home from university and when everyone else is asleep,

I'll sit here with her, glass of wine in my hand, and listen while she tells me all about it.'

'You'll miss her, won't you?' Pete whispered.

'I really will. But I'd never stop her. It's right she goes, goes and lives!'

'You've done us proud today. The food was lovely, it's been great.' Pete pulled his wife towards him and kissed her gently on the mouth.

'Blimey, Pete, reckon that glass of whisky's gone to your head.' She leant into him.

'My head and my toes! It's making me want to dance!' He placed one hand on her waist and raised her hand inside his as he waltzed her in a circle, lifting her off the floor and ignoring her squeals.

'Fancy an early night?' He looked at his wife, his eyes crinkling into a smile.

'Only if you promise to take that bloody jumper off.' She giggled.

'Deal.'

Pete leant in again for a second kiss when Jonty's voice called from the landing.

'Mu-um? Martha's being sick!'

Jacks rested her head on her husband's chest. 'How much wine did she have?'

'I'm guessing too much!' He laughed. 'Let's get her sorted and I'll meet you under the duvet in ten minutes.'

Jacks nodded. She was relaxed and content, emotions that had been absent of late, and it felt good. She got a flash of guilt, remembering her secret dreams. She didn't need adventure, didn't need glass decks and champagne on tap; everything she needed was right there under that cramped little roof. She took a sip from her glass of Baileys – her fourth of the evening, but who was counting? It was Christmas after all.

CHAPTER 16

Nineteen Years Earlier

Jacks hesitated on the wide front step, hating that she felt unworthy to be a guest in such a grand house. And what if, after all the years of wondering what it might be like to live somewhere like that, she was disappointed?

She wasn't.

'Come in. Shut the door!' Sven beckoned her into the vast square hallway.

She looked down at the intricately designed floral pattern of blue, brown and green tiles. 'This floor is beautiful.'

'It's original Edwardian, apparently.'

Staring up at the high, vaulted ceiling, she noted the blue glass chandelier and then the wide staircase and its mini landings, off which she could see doors that led to more rooms than one family could ever need. 'The whole house is beautiful!' The decor was minimalist. No clutter, no fringing, no chintz. Everything was plain and clean looking.

'Well, it's not ours, not really. It's only a rental, but it's our stuff in it.' Sven shrugged and opened

169

the kitchen door. 'You can leave your coat and bag on the floor. Unless you want to do homework?'

She smiled as she shrugged off her coat. 'The International Monetary Fund? Think I'll pass.'

Sven grinned at her as she relaxed and began to enjoy herself.

Everything was in good order: pristine paintwork, swept corners, shiny surfaces and smear-free glass. Large modern paintings, the kind her own mum and dad would mock, took pride of place on the high walls. It was stunning.

The kitchen at the rear of the house was no less impressive. It was the biggest she had ever been in, with white units, shiny white countertops and an enormous double-fronted fridge, an American fridge. She pictured her parents' cramped kitchen, harshly lit and stuffed with blackened saucepans that hung from a rack, jars full of beans, pulses and pasta sitting on dusty shelves and a stack of newspapers, the phonebook and several aged breadboards taking up valuable workspace. That room would fit into this one three times.

A noticeboard was hung with notes and memos written in Swedish. She studied the letters, forming words she couldn't pronounce, the odd O and A with little dots above them. She ran her fingers over the immaculate double sink and tried to imagine standing in front of the sparkling range, cooking a meal and serving it to her family gathered at the long rectangular table. Tall ladder-backed chairs of the palest blue, each with a small navy-and-white gingham ribbon tied to its frame, encircled the table, in the middle of which sat a wicker bowl full of lemons. The room looked like something out of the design pages in her *Marie Claire*.

'Is this where your mum makes her meatballs and pickles?'

'And heats up pizza!' He smiled.

'I can't imagine living anywhere with this much space.' She stretched out her arms and threw her head back. 'I want to live in a house with space, room to breathe, to move! That's my dream.'

'We'll go out to Montana and buy a ranch, with hundreds of thousands of acres that you can roam all day. We'll have so much space, you won't be able to see the boundary, whichever way you look. And we'll sit on our deck at night and listen to the insects and animals, watch fireflies and rock back and forth on our swing-seat. And we'll have dogs, definitely.'

'That sounds nice.' She looked up as Sven walked towards her.

'It will be nice. We'll get old and do crosswords together and take walks and grow our own vegetables and keep horses!'

'Will we have children?' She hardly dared ask, but with all that space and a big house . . .

'No.' His answer was definite. 'They would only distract us. And trust me, I was one once – they're not that appealing.' He smirked.

Jacks swallowed the flicker of disappointment,

but he was probably right, this boy who had seen life and experienced things she could only dream of and whose parents were far from provincial. What did she know?

He walked over to the window, in front of which stood a pale-blue daybed with a button back, facing the garden. Two fat pillows of an oriental design in blue and pale gold sat at the head. Sven pushed off his trainers using the opposite heel and lay on the long couch. He reached up, taking her hand into his, and pulled her down on to the bed.

She shivered, despite the warmth, and knelt by his side. 'Can anyone see?' She pointed towards the window, through which the sunlight poured.

'No. It's just the garden and then a wall.' He paused. 'I have something to tell you.' His tone was earnest.

Jacks hovered on her knees, poised, waiting for his revelation as he massaged the backs of her hands with his thumbs.

'I love you. I loved you the first time I spoke to you and I knew I'd love you before that when I saw you across the hallway.' He shrugged his shoulders. 'That's it! I love you!'

Jacks felt her face break into a wide smile at the same time as tears threatened. 'I love you too, Sven, and I always will.'

He shuffled across the daybed until he was lying in the middle of it. 'Are we safe? Protected?' he asked huskily.

'Yes.' She nodded. 'I feel very safe when I'm with you. And no one knows about us, we are a secret!'

She kissed him as he pulled her leg until she was sitting on top of him. She bent forward, kissing him deeply and with unrestrained passion, which he returned as he arched forward, reaching up under her school shirt and unhooking her bra with dexterity. There was no discussion, no planning, no permission sought or given; what happened next came naturally to them both. It was the perfect and predictable act between two people who were very much in love.

As they lay hand in hand in the aftermath of their union, Sven brushed his fingers through her hair.

'Can we get a couch just like this, when we live in Montana? We could put it on our deck and lie on it while we watch the fireflies.' She smiled against his chest.

'I think that's a very good idea.'

'Promise you'll never leave me,' she whispered.

He kissed her forehead and lay back on the pillow, dozing. She laid her head on his chest, feeling very protected indeed and wanting to stay in that moment forever.

CHAPTER 17

'I can't believe I am doing this!' Jacks practically squealed as they boarded the train and found their allocated seats, laughing like teens at the slightest provocation.

She had spent the previous night and that morning tearing around the house in a tizz, wanting to get everything organised for the twelve hours she would be away from home. It didn't matter that Pete told her he would take care of things. In fact the nicer he was, the worse she felt about nipping off to London. He had given her some spending money, urging her to get herself 'something nice'. She attempted to assuage her guilt by leaving things as ordered as possible. The kids would come downstairs to find cereal in bowls, with spoons by the side, school shirts ironed and hanging on the doorframe of the lounge. She had even made rounds of sandwiches for her mum that were clingfilmed and on a shelf in the fridge, clearly labelled with a Post-it note.

'For God's sake, Jacks!' Pete observed. 'They aren't babies, they can get their own breakfasts. And the lady coming in said she'd do your mum's lunch.

You have to stop making work for yourself. I know you're tired, but you don't help yourself, love. If you eased off a bit and let everyone else do more, things would be easier for you.'

'I like to be in control, I like things to be done properly,' she answered as she wiped down the drainer by the sink.

'I had noticed.' He sat at the table and poured milk on to his cornflakes. 'Just try and forget about us all for a day. Try and relax, have fun!'

She stopped cleaning and looked at her husband. The reason for her trip sat in her throat like a golf ball, the deceit as hard as a lump that she couldn't shift. 'Thanks, Pete. I'll be back tonight. I love you.'

'I know.' He beamed.

'How are you feeling?' Gina asked as she shrugged off her coat, bundled it up and threw it on to the rack above their heads. She adjusted her bra strap and got comfy for the journey.

Jacks blew air from bloated cheeks. 'Like I did when we were fourteen and used to skive swimming and go to the arcade! Excited, nervous, shit scared of getting caught, but like I'm alive. If that makes sense?'

'Perfectly. You okay going backwards? Only it makes me feel sick.' Gina grimaced.

'Sure. I can't remember the last time I was on a train. They are much smarter than they used to be.'

'Yes, this one isn't even steam!' Gina quipped.

'You know what I mean! It's quite luxurious.' Jacks ran her hand over the newly upholstered seat. She stowed her bag on her lap, dipped inside it, found her purse and removed her ticket, which she held in her hand.

'Why are you holding your ticket?'

'I don't want to lose it and if the inspector comes round I'll panic if I didn't know where it is. I don't want to get chucked off.'

Gina laughed.

The train was only half full. There were a number of men in suits, a couple of women with laptops open and the odd student, nose deep in their phones. Jacks smiled, picturing Martha. It had almost been a spur-of-the-moment decision to come. After the magic of Christmas had fizzled, she had felt the familiar low. With all the excitement out of the way and nothing but the credit-card bills and cold weather to look forward to, she agreed with Gina that a bit of adventure might be just what she needed. Ever since seeing Sven in the magazine, she had carried this new image of him around in her head and she had to admit that, like a rotten tooth, she couldn't stop probing, no matter how painful.

'Do you think Mum'll be okay?' Jacks flicked the ticket between her thumb and forefinger.

'You said she was fine when you left?'

'Yes,' Jacks confirmed. 'Very calm. Didn't flinch when I introduced her to the nurse and said I was going out for a bit.'

'And you said the nurse was nice?'

'Oh yes, she's lovely. Seemed really kind, an older lady who said there was nothing she hadn't seen or done. I liked the way she spoke to Mum – respectful, gentle. And she said I could call any time for any reason.'

'Well, that's great then.' Gina looked at her watch. 'Thing is, Jacks, we have been together for forty minutes and that is the sixth time you have asked if Ida will be okay.'

'Sorry.'

'No, no need for sorry. I understand, I do, but you have to try and relax. This is a day of adventure and you have to enjoy it.'

'That's what Pete said, bless him.'

'You mustn't feel guilty, Jacks. This is just a bit of fun and it will do you good. Sven is the distraction you need right now.'

Jacks shrugged. She wasn't very sure of anything.

'When's the last time you had a day that was just yours? When you went out for lunch and mooched the shops, stoked your fire?'

Jacks looked out of the window and thought hard. It was probably when Jonty was tiny and her mum and dad had taken the kids out so she and Pete could have a day. They had gone into Bristol and walked on the harbourside and had lunch at the Mud Dock bike café overlooking the water. 'About six years ago, I think.'

'There you go then. You deserve this.' Gina smiled. 'It's exciting, isn't it? Are you nervous?'

'Oh God, so nervous and guilty all mixed in together. There was Pete waving me off and the kids saying have a great time! I nearly didn't come.'

'Well, I'm glad you did. It's not like you're running off with the bloke, never to return.' Gina rearranged her chunky multi-coloured necklaces over her ample bosom and sat back in her seat. 'You're not planning that, are you?'

'Don't be daft!' Jacks shouted, unable to confess that in her imagination she kept seeing herself either being swept up in Sven's warm, friendly embrace or redecorating two of the bedrooms in a mansion in San Francisco for Martha and Jonty. She shook her head. It was only fantasy, but Pete deserved more. She felt another wave of guilt. 'Do I look okay?'

Gina smiled at her friend. 'You always look okay. You just don't know it. You've got a killer figure.'

Jacks ran her palm over her thighs. Her bootcut jeans were snug. She had carefully chosen a silky white T-shirt with a waterfall neckline; it was flattering and smart but not overdone. She had teamed it with a turquoise pashmina and a large turquoise-coloured ring that she'd found in a charity shop. The inside of it turned her finger green, but she doubted anyone would be examining her fingers that closely. She had put make-up on: peachy blush sat on her cheeks and tinted gloss made her full bottom lip shine.

'I mean it, Jacks. You are one sexy woman.'

Jacks waved her hand as if to shoo away the

178

compliment. 'Must be all that running up and down the stairs!'

'Well, whatever it is, you look fab and you look pretty and happy. You don't always look happy, but you do today.'

Jacks nodded into her lap. 'I still really miss my dad a lot and that's like a sadness that is always there.'

'It'll fade, Jacks.'

She looked out of the window at the trees and hedgerows rushing by. 'He was lovely, wasn't he? More than my dad, he was my mate, the person I called if the washing machine flooded or the car wouldn't start. Even now, I wish I could grab the phone to ask him a question – he just seemed to know stuff. Or to share something that the kids have said. And the shock when I remember that he's not going to answer . . . it leaves me speechless, every time.'

'I know you were close to your dad and I bet you must really miss him. But I think . . .' Gina paused.

'You think what?'

'I think taking on your mum was a noble thing to do.' Gina sighed. 'But I've known you since primary school and you and your mum were never close. She wasn't that type of mum, was she? Not the sort of cuddly, make-it-all-better mum.'

Jacks shook her head. 'I suppose not, no.' Gina was right. Ida had never been the kind of mum to invite Jacks' friends home for tea, or make her room cosy or put her arms around her after a crappy day and tell her everything would be okay.

'And you're being the best daughter you can be, I know that, but you're going above and beyond. You're knocking yourself out every day and it would be better for her and for you if she was somewhere she could get twenty-four-hour care. Then you could get your life back and Martha could get her room back. It's important.'

'I know it's important, G! Do you think I don't?' She sniffed back her tears; she wasn't going to cry, not there on the train, in public, and not after having so carefully put on mascara and eyeliner. She didn't want to arrive at the Boat Show looking like a soggy panda.

'Of course you know, but you're my best mate, Jacks, and watching you run yourself into the ground is horrible. It's like you're serving out a sentence. But it doesn't need to be like that. Ida doesn't know whether it's bed time or the January sales, she is in her own little world. It makes no difference to her who cuts up her food or helps her in the shower, but it would make a huge differ-ence to you and the kids.'

'Actually, G, it makes a huge difference. She can get very flustered if I'm not there.' Jacks hated having to explain.

'But she didn't this morning, did she? Maybe when you tried before, when everything was a bit new and strange, that was the case, but now she's not as with it as she was, maybe things might be different? She's slipped quite a lot in the last eighteen months.'

'I know. But I made a promise, a promise to my dad.'

'Jacks, I've told you what your dad would think. And not only that, he was very poorly, whacked out on painkillers when he died.'

Jacks shook her head, trying to erase those last moments on that dreadful day. She recalled the sound of his laboured breathing, the gap between each breath growing longer and longer, and her sense of confusion as she'd simultaneously prayed it was and wasn't his last.

Gina continued. 'He wouldn't have been too aware of what he was saying. He might have meant look after her that day, or at his funeral. You don't know what he meant, not really, not literally, but you've taken his words as some kind of law and it's ruining your life!'

'It's not only what he said, it was the way he said it. And besides, this is a chance to . . .'

'A chance to what? Get close to your mum?'

Jacks nodded and stared out of the window, hearing her mum's words. *'You can be selfish and selfish people are very hard to love . . .'*

'Can we please change the subject?' she asked.

'Sure. Tell me about Gideon Parks.'

'Oh God, do I have to?' Jacks raised her eyebrows.

'Pete told Rob he was a smasher.'

'Did he now?' Jacks laughed at her husband's summary. She could hear him saying it. 'Truthfully,

G, he is. I know you think I don't like him, but it's not that. He's lovely, but he's not what I want for Martha.'

Gina snorted. 'Well, that might be too bad! What about what Martha wants for Martha?'

'How can she know what she wants? She's a baby! She might make a decision now that'll haunt her for the rest of her life and it'll be too late, she'll be stuck.'

'Are we still talking about Martha?' Gina stared at her friend.

'Tickets, please!'

'Ooh! Here!' Jacks panicked and held hers in the air.

Gina laughed loudly.

The two women wandered along the busy platform at Paddington, marvelling at the station's grand metal roof.

'Isn't this beautiful, G?' Jacks looked skyward.

'Course it is. Designed by old Isambard Kingdom Brunel, who also designed our very own Clifton Suspension Bridge. Come on, West Country!' Gina shouted.

'Did he help design the Leaning Tower of Pisa by any chance?'

'Don't think so. Why?'

'No reason.' Jacks smiled and thought about Jonty. 'Actually, Gina, I could do with nipping to the loo.'

They navigated the crowds, ducking to avoid the

wonky-legged pigeons that homed in on anyone eating food, and made their way to the toilets on the other side of Platform 12. Gina stared at the turnstile barring her entry.

'Thirty pence for a wee? Are you kidding me?' she asked at a volume that caused stares. 'I'd rather wait till we get back to Weston and go for free!'

A businesswoman in a suit walked around the giggling pair and deposited her change in the slot.

'Jeez!' Gina wasn't done. 'This is daylight robbery! I don't earn enough to wee in this city! Come on, you'll just have to cross your legs.' She took Jacks by the arm and marched her away.

'I love London!' Gina shouted as they stepped on to the escalator down to the Tube.

'I'm a bit scared of the Underground,' Jacks confessed as they queued for their one-day travelcards.

'Why?'

'I dunno.' Jacks fidgeted with her scarf. 'Apart from the fact that I might wet myself, I suppose cos it's so busy and I always think I'm going to get lost or pushed on to the track!'

Gina laughed loudly, then removed her friend's pashmina and used it to tie their wrists together. 'There. Now you can't get lost. You are tied to me and if you go over the edge, we go together. Happy?'

Jacks giggled at her mate. 'Happier,' she admitted, raising their joined wrists. 'I feel like a toddler!'

'Don't talk to any strangers!' Gina yelled, much to the amusement of everyone else in the queue.

The two made their way across town from Paddington, first heading east on the District Line and then changing to the Docklands Light Railway. The women were fascinated by the crowds of people huddled together in such an enclosed space; they made a plan in case they got separated.

The closer they got to the exhibition centre, the sicker Jacks felt. She placed her hand on her stomach and exhaled. 'I think I'm going to be sick.'

'No you're not! I will not let you go in there smelling of sick. You are going to be fine and confident and cool and you are going to march up to him and say casually, "Well I never, Brains! Fancy seeing you here!" or something less crap, but make it sound as though you are just bumping into him, okay?'

Jacks giggled. 'As if I'd just bump into him! I never go anywhere like this!'

'But he doesn't know that, does he?' Gina squealed.

'I'm not sure I want to see him, not now. Can we just not go in?'

'No! We are going in. This is one of those things that might make you feel like pants before you do it, but afterwards you'll be really glad you did. You just need to dig deep and find the courage, like diving off the high board.'

'I never dived off the high board. I never got the confidence.' Jacks looked at her friend.

'Well, you should have, it was brilliant. And this is going to be brilliant too. Just go for it. You'll be okay.'

Jacks nodded, feeling far from okay. 'I feel like I did at the school disco, waiting for someone to ask me to dance, clinging to the wall while they played Dr Hook, trying to be invisible while you snogged the face off Richard Frost.'

Gina stared at her friend. 'Are you stark, staring mad? What are you on about? Urgh! Richard Frost? I never did!'

'You did so! I saw you!'

'Have you seen him recently? He runs the arcade on the pier.' Gina shuddered. 'I mean, he's nice looking in an Elvis kind of way, but the worst bloke to get off with in the world! Like snogging a double-mouthed octopus! Not that I would know, because I never kissed him.' She coughed to clear her throat.

'Just think, G, if you'd stuck with him, you could have had free rides on the waltzers whenever you wanted, you'd have saved yourself a fortune!' Jacks laughed, forgetting her guilt, enjoying herself.

They joined the end of a snaking queue.

'Oh God, I mean it, I really don't want to go in!' Jacks gripped Gina's arm.

'Well, you are going in. I shall make you. So that's your choice: you either stroll in and look confident or I'll sling you over my shoulder and deliver you, fat arse first, on to his big posh boat, dumping you like a bag of eels. Which would you prefer?'

Once again Jacks was giggling. 'Stop it, G! You know I need the loo!'

'Anyway, if you feel nervous, just think of those horrible hand-knitted jumpers that he used to wear. He looked like a right plonker!'

'Yeah, a right plonker who left Weston and has this amazing life! Bet he spends hours wishing he'd had a shop-bought jumper like everyone else and was now running the arcade on the pier like Richard Frost who you snogged the face off!'

'Shut up! I never did!' Gina shouted a little too loudly.

Both women collapsed against each other in giggles, for the second time that day, drawing stares from those around them in the queue.

The exhibition hall was much bigger than Jacks had imagined. Vast and echoey, with rows and rows of stands staffed by yachting types who all seemed to be sporting tanned faces and forearms with pale-coloured jumpers draped over their shoulders. They spoke loudly and confidently and seemed to know each other, gesturing and shouting over the heads of the throng. She felt as far out of her depth as it was possible to feel.

'Right, this is where we split up. You go find lover boy.'

'Please don't call him that!' Jacks glanced over

her shoulder, although she had to admit that the chances of bumping into any of Pete's work colleagues from the building site were pretty slim.

Gina laughed. 'I'm only teasing you. You go find Brains and I'll be in the bar in the middle. I'll wait for you, no rush. Come there when you're ready, okay?'

Jacks nodded. She felt sick and scared. Pulling at her T-shirt front, she smoothed invisible creases from it and adjusted her pashmina before wiping the sweat from her hands on the front of her jeans and swiping a finger under her nose.

'You look lovely, mate. You really do. Be confident, be sexy and kick ass!'

'Who do you think I am? Angelina Jolie? I'm Jacqueline Davies from Weston. I don't do sexy or kick ass, I gather up the dirty washing and cook the tea!'

'Go!' Gina patted her friend's bum as she half shoved her into the crowd.

Jacks studied the little map in her hand. 'L34,' she repeated out loud as she wandered up and down the similar-looking aisles. Stalls demonstrating the latest nautical navigation aids and others selling everything from deck shoes to life vests were packed side by side. Jacks wandered aimlessly, trying to get her bearings, only realising she was retracing her steps when something she had already passed caught her eye.

'Shit,' she muttered under her breath.

'Need any help?' A confident-looking boy in a

pale blue Boat Show polo shirt was grinning at her and waving his clipboard.

'Thanks, my love. I'm looking for L34, can't seem to make head nor tail of this little map thing!'

'Ooo arr, me hearties! You sound like a pirate. I love it!'

'Sorry?'

'Your voice! You've got a pirate accent!'

Jacks stared at the boy. It wasn't a plum he had in his gob but rather the whole tree. She thought of what Pete would say: *'And you sound like a proper knob.'* Jacks smiled and marched forward. Confidence stirred in her stomach. Pirate indeed!

With her head held high, she scanned the white signs above each exhibit, eventually reaching a large enclosure housing a vast yacht, marked off with a cordon of thick, royal-blue rope set into shiny chrome stands – the kind she had seen at film premieres on the telly. The whole thing shone under a canopy of twinkling spotlights.

'L34,' she whispered. She folded the map into her handbag and took a deep breath. For the first time she noticed all the pretty girls who were standing around, every one of them with long legs and long hair and wearing matching pink T-shirts and short white shorts. They held little silver trays filled with glasses of sparkling plonk and were handing them with a bobbed curtsey and a cute smile to the crowds of men gathered round the boat, all of whom seemed to be dressed in similar navy blazers and toffee-coloured chinos.

Other girls had stacks of glossy brochures balanced in their arms, which they waved enticingly at visitors carrying plastic bags already straining under the weight of free booty.

Jacks had never been one for boats, despite having lived by the sea her whole life. Her maritime experience was limited to a quick circuit of the Marine Lake in Pete's mate's canoe every once in a while, but that was just to please Pete. Give her solid ground any day. This boat, however, was something else. Its sheer size was breathtaking. Her eyes counted fifteen shiny chrome-edged portholes along the hull and she wondered what lay within. She looked up on to the deck, where a clutch of shiny-haired people with toothpaste-white smiles raised glasses, trilled laughter and chatted. In that instant, something caught her eye. Her stomach dropped. She exhaled, her mouth dry as her hands shook.

It was only a glance, one tiny sighting in the crowd of a shape so familiar that even the glimpse was enough to leave her winded. She had pictured him every day for so many years, held his face and every detail of him in her mind, so much so that after all this time, all it took was a brief sighting of the back of his head, his hand raised, a slight nod, and she knew it was him. She felt quite light-headed until she remembered to breathe.

It didn't matter that it had been nearly two decades since the breath had last caught in her throat like this and her heart had danced such a crazy rhythm; it was as if that time had been erased. Things she had quite forgotten were suddenly crystal clear again. She was once again engulfed in the scent of the cheap white musk perfume that they'd both loved. She was lost in a world of mix tapes and innocence, of school uniforms and rushing home for tea, of hurried, desperate kissing wherever and whenever possible, of lying on a pale-blue daybed with the sun streaming through the vast kitchen window, and of restless nights, beset by whirring thoughts, her mind occupied by the promise of a glittering future, on a ranch in Montana, where the fireflies danced . . . That future had shone like an orb, always slightly out of reach – to her at least. But from what she saw in front of her now – the glamour, the undeniable smell of money – it seemed that Sven had grabbed it and run with it, just like he'd said he would.

Jacks stood still, like prey unsure whether it had been spotted, hoping that if she stayed like that long enough, no one would notice her. Him included. She didn't dare move as she studied the crowd, trying to spot him again.

'Hello.' She looked down towards the man that stood only five feet from her. She hadn't seen him leave the deck, but there he was, in front of her, just as she had imagined him on so many nights. His voice had changed. It was deeper and a Californian drawl now muted his Swedish accent.

Jacks raised her hand; her tongue remained stuck to the roof of her mouth, making speech impossible.

She couldn't speak, let alone kick ass. Definitely more Jacqueline from Weston than Angelina bloody Jolie.

He smiled his easy smile and his eyes crinkled. His clothes looked expensive and he wore them with casual elegance; his shirt buttons were undone at the top and his hands were now pushed into his jeans pockets. His shoulders were raised, his arms straight, emphasising his broad shoulders and slender form. He wore suede Gucci loafers that were old but well looked after, and no socks. Not a hand-knitted jumper in sight. Deeply tanned, he looked like someone who had just come back from a foreign holiday. The scent of good living wafted off him.

Jacks was suddenly aware of her crow's feet, her home-dyed highlights and the cheap wedding ring that felt very heavy on her finger and appeared to pulse with a life of its own. She instinctively covered it with her other hand.

She ran through lines in her head. What should she say? What had she practised? *It's been a long time . . . I found you . . . ! Here we are then . . .'* Jacks drew breath to speak when his voice sliced through the air.

'Welcome to our home for the next few days!' He raised his hands and with his arms outstretched indicated the yacht behind him. 'I'm Sven Lundgren, CEO of Somniorum Yachts. Do you have an appointment?' he asked casually, his eyes wide, his smile warm.

'An . . . an appointment?' she repeated, staring at him. 'No. No I don't. I didn't know I'd need one.' She shook her head, her eyes on the floor.

He looked back at the boat. 'Well, I think you're in luck. We can squeeze you in. Come with me,' he ordered.

Jacks had forgotten that about him, the way he could speak with such authority that others did his bidding. It made her feel a little weak and she liked it.

'Have you come far?' he asked casually over his shoulder, waving to people as he navigated the crowd.

Yes . . . I've travelled for years – nineteen years of my life – to be here today . . . 'Not really. From the West Country. We came on the train, just for the day.'

She felt her cheeks blush. Exchanging small talk as if he was a stranger was excruciating. Jacks wasn't sure what was going on. Was he waiting to greet her somewhere more private? Then something inside her snapped. He wasn't taking her somewhere for a private reunion – he didn't recognise her! Her mouth was dry and the blood seemed to drain from her head, sending an icy cold quiver right through her. She wanted to disappear. Her mind raced as she tried to think of something to say that would break the awkward silence.

'I thought I recognised the accent,' he said. 'I lived there once myself, a long time ago.'

'I doubt it's changed much.' Jacks tried to keep the warble from her voice. *For God's sake, shut up,*

Jacks, you sound pathetic. Of course it hasn't changed. Nothing ever happens there and nothing ever happens to you.

'Are you buying today?' He turned to her, bright voiced and wide eyed.

She twisted her wedding ring with the back of her thumb. *Buying! Me, who trawls the supermarket for bargains and adds up everything in my head before it so much as touches the basket on Mum's lap?* 'No. Just . . . just looking.'

'That's the fun part, yes!' He nodded his head and tapped his chin with his manicured finger. 'Making the decision, thinking about the detail? It's like accessories shopping and I think women enjoy that bit the most, am I right?' He grinned.

Jacks stared at him. She was not enjoying anything, and was unsure if she ever would again. She was broken, distraught, embarrassed beyond belief and wishing that she'd never come. 'Yes.'

'So you live in the West Country?' he asked, sounding more polite than interested.

'Yes.' *Only a few streets from where I grew up, from where we went to school, from where you held me and made me feel alive and told me I would go on a great journey.* She concentrated on making one foot follow the other, following him up a narrow, shiny gangplank when all she really wanted to do was run in the opposite direction.

'Let me show you around.' There was a flash of coolness in his manner.

Jacks followed him down to a kitchen that was

decked out with every conceivable mod con. 'It's a big kitchen for a boat,' she noted, awkwardly, hardly able to think of what to say. *But not as big as the one where we lay together and you made me love you.*

'Yes, it's the biggest galley on any private yacht on the commercial market. But you need something this size when you're entertaining large numbers and the boat sleeps sixteen guests, plus staff.'

'Sixteen? Gosh.' She thought of her little house in Sunnyside Road that had trouble accommodating five. 'How much would a boat like this cost?' She tried to sound interested, wanting to get the exchange over as quickly as possible so she could leave.

Sven shrugged his shoulders. 'Upwards of forty million. Depends on the technology package – you can double that at the top end.'

Jacks shook her head. So much money and yet the words tripped off his tongue with ease. They were from different worlds and always had been. She considered their own nest egg, which had diminished a little because of Christmas, down now to seven thousand pounds. She doubted that would be enough for even one of his fancy chrome portholes. 'I don't get technology. Any technology. It mystifies me.'

He reached for a glossy brochure, flipping it open to show her a diagram. Standing close to him was like torture. She felt her stomach flip.

'We design our systems so they are very intuitive. The panels in each zone are the same, so you only have to learn it once. You can control every element of the boat from the central hub in the main salon, all from the comfort of your armchair. For example, you can alter the deck lighting to suit your mood – there's a rainbow of colours; you can switch on the hot tub, get it warmed up; and you can even programme the sound system in the bathrooms. All with one touch of a button.'

'Don't think I could manage it, no matter how easy you've made it.' She studied his temples where his hair had thinned and noted the weathering of his skin, the result of a life in the sunshine, no doubt.

'I'm sure you could.' He smiled, politely.

Jacks shook her head. 'Don't think so. It took me ages to figure out how to release the arm on my mixer and that's just one button. If there's a power cut, I can't use the cooker as I don't know how to reset the clock and it won't switch on without that. I can't answer the kids' phones, and I don't understand why we have two remote controls for the telly. Sometimes I fancy a bit of *Flog It!* while I'm ironing, but after five minutes of pressing different buttons trying to figure out how to switch it on, I give up and put the radio on.' She was aware she was babbling but couldn't seem to stop, nervous of what might happen if she did.

'You have children?' He blinked quickly, this

clearly the single fact he had taken from her rambling.

'Yep, two. Martha's about to go off to university, she's going to be a lawyer, and my son is only eight. He's hilarious.' She smiled and blushed, ridiculously embarrassed at having to confess she had sex with someone else. Utterly ridiculous. What did it matter? She was a thirty-six-year-old married woman, of course she'd had sex with someone else and what was it to him anyway, some bloody yachting millionaire who didn't even remember her.

'What about you? Any kids?' she asked, cursing the misplaced flash of envy she felt towards the woman who might have borne him a child.

'No!' he said sharply, with something akin to relief. 'I didn't seem to find the time.' He laughed, awkwardly. 'If you get my meaning. I don't mean the actual becoming a dad – that can take seconds, I am reliably informed!'

Twelve minutes, that was all. Twelve minutes that changed a girl's life.

'It never appealed, really. Too much to do, too many places to see and I don't like to be anchored, unless it's with our own patented anchor that comes as standard on this model.' He laughed again.

'Well, yes, they certainly do anchor you. It's a full-time job looking after them, and now I have my mum too . . . I never really have time to do my own thing.' Without warning, tears started to prick behind her eyes. 'I'm sorry I've wasted your time,' she blustered. 'The kitchen is . . .' She ran her eyes over the sleek lines, white leather upholstery and integrated appliances. 'It's lovely.'

They made their way out on to the deck. 'Take care, Sven.'

'Yes, you too.' He raised his hand. His sign-off was impersonal. He turned away immediately and she watched as his shoulders relaxed. Only then did she allow her tears to fall.

She thought of all the times he had spoken her name, all those dark nights, tenderly sounding out the syllables while they held hands under the stars. She wanted to disappear. Better still, she wanted to rewind time and never set foot on his bloody boat. She looked up and he was gone. Swallowed by the crowd of glamorous yachters who vied for his attention.

She jogged along the gangplank, ignoring the stares of the pretty girls with their wine and brochures, unaware that they were wondering why their CEO had taken this particular woman below decks and what had made her cry. She made her way to the middle of the hall, where Gina sat at the bar with a glass of wine.

Gina looked up into the blotchy, make-up-smeared face of her friend. 'What happened? Are you okay?'

'Let's go home, G,' Jacks managed.

'Do you want a drink?'

'No!' she answered, a little more sharply than she'd intended. 'I just want to go home.'

'Has he upset you?' Gina asked protectively.

'Upset me?' She sniffed. 'No. He didn't even remember me!' She made her way towards the nearest exit.

Gina swigged the last of her wine, hurriedly placed the glass on the counter, picked up her bag and followed her mate through the crowds.

They climbed into Gina's Corsa in the car park at Weston-super-Mare train station. The moment they had clicked their seatbelts, Jacks started to cry. Having sat in silence for the entire train journey, it was a relief to finally give vent in the privacy of the little car.

'It's okay.' Gina rubbed her friend's back as she leant with her head on the glove box.

'No. It's not okay. I feel like such an idiot!'

'Well, don't. It's his loss. He's not worth bothering about. Today was only meant to be a bit of fun. I just wanted to get you out of the house. So what if he didn't remember you? I bet you walk past loads of people every day around town who think, "Ooh that's that Jackie Morgan who lied about her friend snogging Richard Frost," and you will have no idea who they are!'

'This was different.' Jacks sat up straight and tried to contain herself.

'No it wasn't!'

'Yes it was, G. You don't understand!' Jacks raised her voice in frustration.

'Tell me then.'

Where to begin? 'It'll sound ridiculous when I say it out loud.'

'That doesn't usually stop you.' Gina smiled.

Jacks drew breath and sniffed. 'I know we were only very young and it was only one summer, really, but it meant a lot to me.'

She paused. *How much to tell?*

'I told you that I think about him a lot, and I do. A lot. Some days I feel so old because I haven't achieved anything and I know exactly where I'm going, I know exactly what my life will be like until I die. I'll never get to live in one of the houses on the front, I'll never see the world and I'll never get my sodding conservatory!'

'So you're upset because you'll never have a conservatory?' Gina tried to understand.

'No!' Jacks shook her head. 'I'm upset because for me Sven has always represented perfection. He's not washing-up or cluttered hallways or uncarpeted stairs or struggling to look after my mum; he is pure, of another time when I was truly happy, with no responsibilities, and I thought . . .'

What did I think? 'I thought that it must have been the same for him. I felt strongly connected to him. And that connection has kept me sane. And today I found out that there is no connection. I'm just some silly cow who has had her head full of crap for all these years. I'm embarrassed and I'm sad, because it's gone now, that little tunnel of hope I used to climb up when things got bad. It's disappeared and I'm truly, truly stuck and I feel lonely.'

'Please don't feel lonely. You've got a lot of people who care about you and you've achieved a lot, Jacks. Two great kids . . .' Being childless, Gina considered this to be her friend's greatest achievement.

'I know. I know. And I love them, you know that.'

Gina nodded.

'But, sometimes, it's not enough.'

'I think we all feel a bit like that sometimes.'

'I've always thought of him as the one that got away.'

'Got away from what?' Gina twisted her body towards her mate.

'From me!' Jacks cried then, gulping down tears laced with embarrassment.

'Oh God, you're really sobbing!'

'Sorry, G.' She sniffed some more.

'I had no idea you felt this way, Jacks. God, if I thought it was going to upset you, I'd never have mentioned the bloody magazine or going to see him. I thought it was just a laugh. I'm sorry.'

'No, don't be sorry. It hasn't upset me.'

'Doesn't look like it!'

'Honestly, G, I'm glad you did. I'm okay. I just think I've got a lot going on at the moment.'

'This isn't like you.' Gina sighed. 'I've never seen you like this.'

Jacks blew her nose into a tissue and wiped her eyes. 'I know it's ridiculous, it's just that . . .'

'Just that what?'

Jacks hesitated, wondering how much to share.

'It's as I said, the thought of him, the idea of him often gets me through difficult days.'

'Blimey, really?'

Jacks smiled, composing herself. 'Yes, really! And I know it's stupid, naive, embarrassing. But you sometimes have those relationships, don't you? Ones that change you, shape you, and that's what we had, even though we were young. It was very special and it opened my eyes.' She looked at her friend.

'Wow. I knew you'd had a fling, but I thought it was a little crush, nothing more. You got together with Pete so soon after he'd left that I forgot you were ever with him. I only ever think of you with Pete, if I'm being honest.'

Jacks sighed. 'I was looking at some of those women at the Boat Show today, with their designer clothes and acrylic nails, and those young girls who jump on boats and sail around the world and I thought, why has nothing great ever happened to me? How do you get to live somewhere fabulous and not have to add your shopping up in your head as you go round the supermarket? How do you get to be like that?'

'Money,' Gina surmised.

'Yes, it is money, but it's something else too, it's like a belief that your life can be like that and so you make it happen. I'm just so glad that Martha's got it. I want her to do it all.' Jacks smiled at Gina; even the thought of her girl was enough to lighten her mood.

Gina started the engine. 'Come on, let's get you home.'

Home, thought Jacks, *where that bloody bell is waiting for me.*

CHAPTER 18

Nineteen Years Earlier

'So, what do you think?' Gina hopped on the spot in her blue Buffalo platform trainers, clearly excited.

'About what?' Jacks smiled at her friend.

'For God's sake! I've been rabbiting on at you all the way along the pier and you haven't even been listening!' Gina tutted.

'I have!' said Jacks, laughing.

'What have I said then?'

'Something about moving to Bristol to go and work at the Thekla and designing T-shirts and starting your own label.'

'I knew you weren't listening, but good guess. Where is your head at today? You are bloody miles away.'

I am. I'm on a deck in our ranch in Montana . . . I'm wandering around the Franklin Park Zoo in Boston. I'm sitting by a lake with my man . . .

She shrugged. 'Just thinking, that's all.'

'Fuck off!' Gina shouted loudly, flapping her arms and trying to scare the seagull that was lunging in for a chip. 'I hate these bloody birds!' She turned back to Jacks. 'I was actually telling you about Pete Davies.'

'Pete who has a trial for Bristol City? Not that he ever mentions it, ever!' She laughed.

'Yeah, well, that's the thing. He's buggered his knee, trial's off. He ain't going nowhere. He did it in training and now won't even make First Team captain, let alone the big time. It's a bit sad, really, isn't it, cos that's like his one thing. He's crap at everything else.'

Jacks nodded. Gina was right, he was crap at everything else and it was a bit sad, but thankfully, nothing to do with her.

'Chip?' Gina held the bag up to her friend.

Jacks waved her hand in front of the bag as though it was offensive. She had no appetite at the moment. Only yesterday she'd had to explain to Sven that she didn't want to eat the sandwich he'd made her because she felt queasy and had this metallic taste in her mouth that she couldn't seem to shift.

The two girls walked arm in arm until they reached the end of the Grand Pier, where they sat down side by side on the bench and looked out across the sea. A large tanker made its way slowly across the horizon, heading for the docks at Avonmouth.

'What is it you're thinking about then?' Gina asked as she folded the hot, salty chips into her mouth.

Jacks pulled her coat around her form and smiled. 'My future, I suppose.'

'I thought we had a plan for our future? To move to Bristol, share a flat, marry members of Take That – bagsy Jason Orange, by the way! – and where I will design T-shirts and get signed by a big fashion label.'

Jacks managed a small smile.

'Oh, I get it, you've changed the plan. *You're* going to work in the Thekla and marry Jason Orange, aren't you? You better not be, cos firstly I'd have to beat you up for stealing my man and secondly, I'd really miss you.'

'No. He's not my type.' *I prefer studious Swedish boys who will sit with me on a deck in a swing-seat that rocks . . .* 'I just think it's funny how you can drift along and then, *click!*, something happens and it's like your life is mapped out.'

'I'd hate that! Hate my life to be mapped out. I like the idea of the unknown, of adventure lurking around the corner, not knowing where I'll go or who I might meet. I think it's the best bit.' Gina scrunched up her remaining chips into the soggy-bottomed bag and hurled them in the bin, before reaching for the fags and lighter that sat in the front pocket of her denim jacket.

'I would have said the same, but now I don't know.' Jacks looked at her friend, already feeling the separation that would see them living on different sides of the Atlantic. 'I feel quite good about knowing my future. I feel calm, happy!'

'Blimey mate, what's clicked for you then? Who are you – Mystic Meg? Where's your crystal ball?'

'It's not that, I don't know . . .' she kicked her toe against the wooden planks, not wanting to give too much away, 'but haven't you ever woken up and not felt afraid of what's around the corner?'

Gina stared at her and drew on her cigarette. 'Can't say I have, mate, reckon I might need a peek in your crystal ball!'

Jacks wrapped her arms around her torso, hugging herself against the breeze. *I haven't got a crystal ball, but I have got a secret . . .*

CHAPTER 19

During the fortnight following her visit to London, it was as if Jacks leaked sadness. She found it harder to paint on her smile and harder still to pretend that all was well. Pete tried his best to make things right, but his inability to fix the issues of which he was unaware only served to irritate Jacks. Martha took full advantage of the lull in her mum's concentration and spent as much time with Gideon as possible. Jonty didn't even notice that anything was amiss, happy in his world of computer games and toy soldiers and enjoying having the room to himself when Martha was absent, giving his remote-control car free rein over the floor.

Two weeks on, Jacks sat at the table listening to Pete's cornflakes hitting the bowl. They sounded to her like tiny stones, loud and intrusive. Then came his noisy crunching and swallowing and the repeated swooping of the spoon back into the bowl to cram in another mouthful even though the last was still lodged in his cheeks. It made her feel sick. Every day it made her feel sick, but today more than ever. As he leant in to kiss her goodbye, she pulled away. She noticed the flash of distress in his eyes, but it was as if she couldn't help it.

'Have I got a shirt, Mum?' The voice floated across the landing and down the stairs.

'In the airing cupboard!'

'Mu-um, is my PE kit clean?' Jonty called.

Shit! No, it wasn't. It was in fact still sitting inside a carrier bag on the back seat of her car. 'I'll fetch it, Jont!' She decided to refold it and spray it with deodorant and hope he didn't notice.

Ida's bell rang out.

'Nan's ringing!' the kids chorused.

Jacks placed her face in her hands and cried.

That afternoon Jacks pushed her mum's wheelchair through the front door, then helped her out of it. It was a beautiful day and they had been for some fresh air. Frost covered the ground, but the sky was big and blue, the kind of day that reminded you what life in the summer felt like, willing you to hang on, to get through the winter. After changing Ida and settling her in bed for an afternoon nap, she folded the wheelchair and squashed it into the space under the stairs.

'I've got that treasure!' Ida called out.

At least she's not going on about that letter any more, thought Jacks. 'Don't worry, Mum, when we find your treasure, I shall bring it straight up.'

Sighing, she took the carrier bag with the double-knotted handles out to the wheelie bin. She wandered into the kitchen and was stunned to see Martha sitting there with her head resting on her fist, her elbow propped up on the table. 'Oh, hello, love. You made me jump! I didn't know you were home. Why aren't you at school?'

Martha looked up and shrugged. Jacks could see she had been crying.

'Are you poorly? Do you want a hot water bottle for your tum?' Jacks went through the familiar routine.

'No. I'm not . . . not ill, Mum.' The breath caught in her throat.

He's dumped her. Jacks felt a small flicker of joy that her daughter's life could now finally get back on track. Gina had been right: it had run its course and Gideon had moved on.

'What's the matter, darling? Talk to me. You know that if I can make it better, I will. Always' Jacks sat next to her girl and placed her hand over the back of Martha's slender palm.

Martha's tears came again. She cradled her head in her arms as her shoulders heaved.

Jacks smoothed her hair. 'It's okay, darling. It's all going to be okay. You are so young, Martha, and there are plenty more fish in the sea, just you wait and see. And as nice as he was, you will meet another Gideon at university – in fact you'll meet an even better Gideon, one with a future, with prospects, and you will be glad that this came to a halt when it did.'

Martha sat up eventually and took some deep breaths. She swiped at her tears with her sleeve, smearing her heavy kohl make-up along her arm in the process. 'We haven't . . .' she stuttered. 'We haven't finished, Mum.'

'Oh. I just thought . . . Is everything all right at school?'

Martha nodded. 'I got a message from UCAS.'

'They haven't taken away your offer from Warwick, have they? Can they do that?' she gasped.

'No.' Martha sniffed. 'It doesn't work like that.'

'Thank God for that!' Jacks exhaled.

'The message was that I've got another offer. From Bristol.' These words made her sob even harder.

'Yes!' Jacks clapped. 'I knew it! That's wonderful! Brilliant! Don't cry, you silly thing. I like the sound of Bristol; I could come and visit you, take you out for lunch and even do your washing if you get stuck. I know I promised your dad I'd let you get on with it, give you independence, but I could have a laundry load collected, washed, dried and back to you within an afternoon. It'd save you the job. You can just concentrate on your studies then. And we're only up the road if there's an emergency, which I'm sure there won't be, but there's no harm in having us close. You might even get those posh halls up on the downs!'

'I won't need you to do that, Mum. It's not going to be an issue.'

'Oh. Okay. So do your own washing!' Jacks gave an awkward laugh.

'This is not about laundry!' Martha shouted.

Jacks thought it might be hormones. Her little girl was probably a bit overwhelmed by the changes about to happen in her life and that was more than understandable – leaving home and moving far afield to live alone was a big deal. Not that she had ever done it herself, not really; she had simply swapped one street for another and instead of waking up and meeting her mum and dad in the kitchen, there'd been Pete there instead.

She paused to let the air settle, then tried again. 'Why are you crying then, love? Do I need to go and find another bottle of Buck's Fizz?'

Martha sat up straight and coughed. She tucked her hair behind her ears, trying to contain herself. 'I'm not going to Bristol.'

'So, Warwick then? That's fine; it was the one you preferred, wasn't it? Did I tell you I went online and had a look at their site; they've got a coffee shop, a supermarket, even a hairdresser's, right there on campus. It's amazing! Don't be sad! It's an easy decision, you funny little thing. Dad and I don't mind where you go, as long it's the right course for you and you are safe, that's all that matters.' Jacks squeezed her hand.

'I'm not going to Warwick either.'

There was a second of silence while Jacks digested her daughter's words, trying to comprehend.

'Don't be daft, of course you are. You can get the grades, I know you can! This is just a pre-exam wobble, but you've had them before and you always come through. Always!'

'I'm not going to university. I'm not going and that's that.' Martha withdrew her fingers from beneath her mum's and folded her hands into her lap.

'What are you talking about? Of course you are! Besides, I've already got you your sandwich toaster!' Jacks felt her heart begin to hammer as a headache thumped behind her eyes.

Martha took a deep breath, looked at her mum and swiped her eyes one more time. 'I'm not! Don't you get it? I'm not going anywhere!'

'You are talking rubbish.'

'I'm pregnant.' Martha's words cut through the air and plunged into Jacks' heart like tiny daggers.

'What?' This had to be some kind of joke; only it wasn't funny, not in the slightest.

'I think you heard me, Mum. I'm pregnant.'

'You can't . . . no . . . I don't . . . Tell me it's not true,' she stammered, aghast.

Martha stood from the table. 'I can't tell you it's not true, because it is.'

There were several seconds of silence while Martha's words bounced from the walls and settled in Jacks' brain. She tried to steady her shaking hands on the tabletop as she heard Martha tread the creaky stairs. She replayed the tutor's words loud and clear in her head. *The sky is the limit for a girl like Martha. With hard work and application, she can pick her path!* No. No. No. No! This couldn't be happening. She wouldn't let it happen!

Gripping the banister, Jacks climbed the stairs, her limbs like lead weights. She paused on the landing at the sound of her mum's bell. Jacks opened Ida's door, poked her head in and raised her finger, speaking a little more sharply than was necessary.

'I'll be one sec, Mum, just give me a minute. I've got to talk to Martha and then I'll be straight in.'

She shut her mum's bedroom door tightly, then leant against the doorframe of the kids' bedroom.

'Are you going to keep it?' she whispered.

Martha nodded, her expression fixed. 'Yes.'

Jacks hovered at the end of her daughter's bed, red mist clouding everything. Her breath came faster and faster as tears of anger and frustration broke the surface. Her limbs shook.

'Are you fucking insane?'

Martha stared wide eyed at her mum, but didn't respond.

Jacks bent low towards her daughter. 'You must be. You must have lost the fucking plot!'

'Mum!' Martha wrapped her arms around her trunk and shrank back against the pillows. 'You are really swearing.'

'That's because now is the time for swearing. It's the right fucking time! Do you hear me?' She spoke through clenched teeth.

Martha closed her eyes, wanting to block out the words.

'Have you any idea what you have done, any idea what you are doing?' Jacks turned and slammed out of the room. The crash made Martha jump and she instinctively placed her hand on her stomach.

Ida's bell rang. Jacks stuck her head round the

door, yelled, 'For Christ's sake, give me a bloody minute!' and withdrew. She stormed back to Martha's room and wrenched the door open again.

'Everyone told me to let things run their course, said that I was overreacting! But I bloody knew, I knew the moment I saw you talking to him that you were going to fuck up your life! I prayed I was wrong – you have no idea how hard I prayed – but no one was listening.'

The sound of Martha's tears broke the silence between her rants.

'Do you have any idea what you have done? Do you? You have put a noose around your neck. In fact, no . . .' Jacks ran her fingers through her hair and turned in a circle. 'A noose would be too quick. You have injected yourself with a slow poison. It'll kill you in the end, but it'll take twenty years. Twenty years of fucking mediocrity that you will have to wade through until you drown in it!' Her face flushed scarlet, her eyes were wild.

Martha cried silently now.

Jacks wasn't done. 'Each year the air will get thinner and your heart heavier, until one day you just won't bother getting up any more. Look at me! Look at my life!' She beat her chest with her fist. 'I have one bra, did you know that? Just one greying bra that I wash, dry, wear, wash, dry, wear. That's it, just one. I have hairy legs to save on razors and waxing. "Why don't you ever get new clothes, Mum? You look like a tramp, Mum!"' She imitated the kids' voices. Martha sobbed. 'Why? Because there isn't the fucking money for clothes, not for me! And there's me dreaming of a bloody conservatory when I can't even buy another bra – how funny is that! And my kids, who have a ten-year age gap, have to share a bedroom. Things are shit.' She clenched her fists. 'Absolute shit and I wanted better for you. I wanted you to travel, to be someone, to move away from here! And you could have, you can! You have the offers and the ability!'

Jacks felt the strength leave her legs as she slumped down on to the worn carpet with her back against the bed frame.

'I will be someone, Mum. I . . .'

'No! No you won't. Don't even say it! You'll be like every other girl who waits at the bus stop, tapping into her fucking pay-as-you-go phone while her baby sleeps in a dirty pushchair. And you could have had it all!'

Martha stood. 'I have got it all! I've got Gideon and I'm having our baby.'

'You don't even *like* babies. Remember what you said about Jayden, next door? "He's a squirmy pink little thing," that's what you called him. You said you couldn't see what was so sweet about him.'

'And you said it's different when it's your own.'

Touché.

Jacks' eyes blazed. 'Listen to yourself, Martha. You sound so stupid! And I never had you down as that. You can pick your path and you are choosing *this*?' Jacks laughed, an unnatural, high-pitched giggle. 'And I know you think that Gideon is the one.' She laughed again. 'I'm sure you see yourselves growing old together with roses around the bloody door. But you won't. It's a trick. It wears off, no one tells you that, and the love you think you've found? Jesus Christ, that person might not even remember you in a few years! No matter how often you think of him, crave him! He'll only have a vague recollection of you, this boy who's stolen your heart.'

'You don't know what it's like for us. Or how we feel about each other!' Martha raised her voice.

'Don't I, Martha?' Jacks scrambled to her feet and clenched her fists. 'Do you think I was born like this?' She plucked at her jumper. 'Born knackered? Of course I wasn't. When I met . . .' She hesitated, checked herself. 'I . . . I was just like you, bathing in the glow of first love, wanting to touch him, wanting him to touch me, constantly. I watched him sleep, drank in his words; he was like a drug and I would have done anything he asked, gone anywhere he wanted, because all that mattered was being with him. It was like an addiction . . .'

Martha looked at the floor. It sounded familiar.

'And do you know what happened? Do you? Suddenly I'm retrieving Pete's dirty socks from the floor, arguing about how and where to save money and climbing over his naked arse in the middle of the night to go and tend to my mother. And it happened in a blink.' She clicked her fingers. 'A blink!'

'That won't happen to us. I rea . . .'

'. . . lly love him!' Jacks finished her daughter's

sentence. 'I know, Martha, and no one has ever loved anyone how you love him and how he loves you and no one else on the planet could possibly understand because what you are feeling is unique. I get it. But what you need to realise is that you are only reciting the lines that every woman comes up with when she meets a Gideon or a George fucking Clooney lookalike with all the chat and a few quid in his pocket. You aren't unique, you're not even right, you are just at that stage.'

'It isn't a stage. It's real!' Martha wailed.

'No it isn't. But part of the trick is that it feels real! And by the time you realise that, it will be too late.'

'I think I know the difference, Mum. You have to give me some credit.'

'Do I?' Jacks snorted. 'This is not why I had you, Martha. Not to lead that life.'

'Not why you *had* me?' Martha stared at her mother. 'It sounds like I was bred for a specific purpose!' She rubbed the tops of arms.

'Maybe you were, maybe I had you to make something of yourself, to live a really great life.'

'Or maybe you had me so I could live out your dreams, do all the things you didn't and couldn't, isn't that more like it?'

'Yes, I suppose so, a bit. But in a good way!'

'What possible good way? What's good about taking all your failings and the gaps in your experience and trying to make me do them? Maybe I don't want what you want.'

'Well, I think we've established that!' Jacks snapped.

'Is this because you don't like Gideon? Is it about him?'

Jacks sighed and rubbed her hands together. 'It's always about him, Martha! And it always will be until you see sense!'

'Or see it how you want me to see it.'

'It's the same thing.'

'No it isn't.'

Jacks looked at her daughter. 'You are only half formed; you're like a cake that's not done in the middle. One that looks lovely on the outside but needs another twenty minutes until it's cooked through. You aren't ready yet!' Jacks was screaming now. She banged the wall with her flattened palm.

'Ready for what?' Martha looked confused.

'For anything! Anything!' Jacks took a deep breath to calm herself. 'You're only eighteen. You think you're grown up, but you're not, you are still so young. Trust me, I know. And nature can be very confusing and a bit cruel, giving you boobs and urges and cleverness. But essentially you are still a young girl and you have to believe me when I tell you that the further you get from eighteen, like when you're thirty, forty, fifty – which, trust me, will start coming round way too soon – you will realise that I am telling you the truth.'

'I don't see what age has got to do with anything! I'm old enough to make decisions and you've always told me to trust the voice in my head and I do! It's you that doesn't trust it.'

Jacks considered this. 'I have a voice in my head too and mine is screaming at me that you are making a big mistake!'

'Well, maybe you should tell your little voice that my mum has raised me right and I trust my own thoughts and decisions!'

Jacks opened her mouth to reply but couldn't think of a single thing to say.

Martha's voice was little more than a whisper. 'I love you, Mum, but you've got to let me live my life. There's the clue, right there. My life. Not yours, mine.'

Jacks looked into the face of her determined child, a girl on the verge of womanhood.

'Martha, please,' she begged, her voice quieter now. 'I know you are smart, smarter than me about nearly everything, but I have lived, I have been through the cycle and I can talk from experience.'

Martha pulled her ponytail tight and hopped off her bed. She dried her tears and picked up her bag.

'I am begging you, begging you. Please don't have this baby. It will be the end of you, the end of everything.'

'You met Dad when you weren't much older than me,' Martha shot back. 'Are you saying that was the end of everything for you?'

There it was, the ace in the pack. The indisputable fact. How was she to answer? How could she use the words that danced on her tongue, words of bitter regret that could never be erased. She and Pete had worked hard to shield Martha all these years; she wasn't going to come clean now. She wanted to say something, wanted to say, 'Yes! I thought it was the end of everything because it meant the end of dreaming, it meant being abandoned by the man I loved!', but she knew she couldn't. She couldn't ruin it all now.

She looked into Martha's eyes, which were brimming with tears, and reached for her hand. 'No. No, my love. Of course it wasn't the end of everything. Because we had you and that was the most precious gift in the world! But it was hard, too hard sometimes, and we had to make a lot of sacrifices. We still do.'

Martha headed for the door. 'If you don't want to wake up next to Dad's arse every day and you hate your life so much, do something about it. But don't confuse your life with mine. We are having this baby and that's that.'

An hour later, Jacks heard the front door slam. The bell rang as if on cue. She made her way into her mum's room.

'I appear to have passed water,' Ida sang.

'Yep, although do you know what? What you mean is no such thing. You mean you've shat yourself again or if we are lucky it's just piss.' She pushed her mum back on the mattress and pulled up her frock. 'Changing you is like being given a raffle ticket, I never know what I'm going to get.'

'I'm expecting a letter.'

'You're not.' Her tone was sharp. 'You're not

expecting a letter. No letter will come. Do you understand?' Jacks shouted as she raced around the bed and threw open the bedroom window.

'Toto?' Ida looked towards the door.

'I'm going mad. I'm going fucking mad.' Jacks breathed deeply as she braced her arms on the windowsill and looked out over the rooftops of Sunnyside Road. The big blue sky had disappeared, giving way to cloud that was grey and miserable. It looked anything but sunny.

Jonty had been given an early tea and was watching telly when Pete came through the door.

'Evening folks!' he called from the hallway.

His jovial tone set Jacks' teeth on edge. He sauntered into the kitchen in his sweatshirt that was covered in mud and dried cement and splotched with pale patches where weedkiller had spilled. He took one look at his wife's face and placed his large hand on her shoulder. 'What's going on?'

He scanned the darkened kitchen; the only light came from the single bulb in the cooker hood. The oven was cool and dark, no tea had been prepared. 'Is your mum okay?'

Jacks nodded, irritated that the only possible reason for their routine being upset would be if Ida had popped her clogs.

'Have you seen Martha?' she asked, checking to see if they had conspired, wondering if she had been the last to know.

'No. What's up? Is she okay?' Concern was creased

across his face as he took the seat next to his wife. 'Jacks, what's going on? You're scaring me.'

'I'm scaring myself, actually.' She gave a small laugh. 'She's pregnant.'

There it was, delivered without preamble or discussion – she was capable of neither.

'What?' Pete squinted as she sat back in his chair.

'You heard. PREG-NANT,' she enunciated.

'Oh, dear God!' Pete ran his dry, cracked fingers over his face. 'You're kidding.'

'Do I look like I'm kidding?' she barked.

'Where is she?' he asked softly.

Jacks shrugged.

'Is she okay?'

Jacks looked up at him, realising that she had forgotten to ask. 'I don't know. I can't believe it, Pete.'

'How far gone is she?'

She hadn't asked that either. 'I don't know. I lost it. Shouted at her. I'm so mad! So angry, I can't think straight. She's messing up her life.'

Pete stood and reached for the car keys on the sideboard. 'Do you think she'll be at Steph's?'

Jacks didn't know how to respond. She had no idea where her daughter was. She'd heard the front door slam while she was dealing with Ida, that was all she knew. Pete's words made her feel bad.

'I'll go and see if I can find her.'

'Yes.' Jacks wanted Martha home; there was still time to make her see sense.

'I can imagine how disappointed you are. Upset.

222

But it'll be okay, Jacks.' He gave a small smile, as usual looking for a way to placate, make things better.

She looked at her husband. 'Will it?'

He smiled. 'It will. It's not the worst thing that can happen, is it?'

'Isn't it?'

'No. No, love, it isn't. You know that.' The two exchanged a long look. 'We need to talk. Later, when Jonty's in bed. I'll go see if I can find her. Shan't be long.'

Jacks sat at the kitchen table, wishing she were able to go and find Martha herself, fearing they were all in conference somewhere. She wanted to intervene, have her say. She was worried that Pete would simply say that things had a way of figuring themselves out and then they'd all sit back and watch another life spiral out of control.

She imagined confronting Gideon, pictured their exchange. Dipping into her mind, she sorted through the fog of anger and upset, plucking phrases that she wanted to launch at him. '*Why do you think you might be good enough for her?*' was one she kept repeating. Along with, '*She had the whole world at her feet and you came along and pulled her off track, so now what? You are destroying her chances and one day she will resent you for it!*' Or maybe she would try a softer tack, try appealing to the kind nature he had displayed when he brought her flowers and chatted to Jonty. '*It's not *too late, Gideon; it's not too late to change the outcome. Everybody makes mistakes.'* Even me, she thought. *'But you are both so young that you can fix things and put it all behind you and have the life you were supposed to have . . .'* The life I was supposed to have . . . This thought caused her tears to spring again.

It was an hour later that she heard the front door close. Pete walked into the kitchen. 'Here she is, safe and sound.' He smiled as he patted his daughter's hair.

Jacks glanced at Martha's complexion, blotchy from sobbing, her lids swollen and her eyes bloodshot. Her heart flipped at the signs of her distress. She was torn between wanting to hold her and wanting to shout some more, trying to make her see sense.

'Do you want anything to eat?' she asked, carefully avoiding eye contact while trying her best to be conciliatory.

Martha shook her head. 'No thanks,' she said, her voice nothing more than an embarrassed whisper. 'I got something at Steph's.'

'Does Steph know?' Jacks fired at her.

Martha nodded.

Then so will the whole of Weston . . . Jacks kept that thought to herself, but it was another blow. She was certain that once people knew, it would be harder to fix and impossible to ignore.

'How far are you?' She looked at her nails, attempting to keep calm.

''Bout ten weeks,' Martha whispered before more tears came.

Jacks thought back. *Christmas, New Year, you were sneaking out, meeting up, probably going to his empty house or his garage. All that covert texting at the table, that bloody buzz that set my teeth on edge because I knew it was him. Can't believe I was so bloody stupid!*

'Get yourself up to bed, love. I'll bring you up a cup of tea.' Pete smiled at his little girl.

Martha hesitated as she walked from the kitchen. She looked at her mum. 'I'm sorry, Mum. I know you think I've let you down, but I didn't plan any of this. It just happened.'

Jacks opened her mouth to comment that these things didn't 'just happen', but no words came out.

Pete stood back to let Martha pass, leant against the sink and waited until she had climbed the stairs. 'You need to stay calm, Jacks, for everyone's sake but especially Martha's. We need to keep her close, to look after her and we can only do that if she feels comfortable here.'

'Oh, well, I'm sorry if it's me that's messed up! Why do I get the feeling that I'm at fault here? As if it's me that's flushed her one chance of happiness down the loo. I might have known it would come back to something that I've done!'

'I'm not saying that. I'm just saying that it's already a difficult time and we know it's going to get a lot harder, so we need to smooth things over. Things have a funny way of working out.'

'Oh, for Christ's sake, Pete, will you listen to

yourself? Do they? Honestly? When are things going to start working out for us, eh? When will our fortunes turn around? I've been listening to you say that for the last nineteen years and I'm still bloody waiting.'

Pete turned his back to the table and stared out of the window into the narrow strip of garden.

'That's the thing, Jacks. My fortunes did turn around, the day I got you and then Martha and Jonty, our little house, everything. I think I'm the richest man alive. I might not have boats and flash watches, but I'm not stupid, Jacks.' He shot her a look. 'In fact, I'm clever enough to know when I've got it good. Things might not be perfect, like having your mum call on you every five minutes, like living without enough space to swing a cat, not being able to afford the luxuries I want to give you all or send Martha to Paris with her mates. But on the whole, things could be a lot, lot worse. So things have worked out for me. I'm just sorry you don't feel the same.'

'Pete . . .' She drew breath, choosing her words carefully. 'I didn't mean it like that. I didn't—'

'It doesn't matter what you meant. It is what it is.' Pete clicked the kettle and concentrated on making a cup of tea for his daughter, who was upstairs crying into her pillow with her heart fit to burst, trying not to wake her little brother on the other side of the room.

CHAPTER 20

Nineteen Years Earlier

Jacks sat in the front room of her mum and dad's terraced house while her mum cried into her handkerchief and her dad nodded quietly by her side. She felt the walls pressing in on her; it was as if the air was being sucked out of the room. She thought she might suffocate.

'And where's the boy now?' her dad asked gently as he calmly set aside his crossword and placed his pencil on the little dictionary that balanced on the arm of the sofa.

'I don't know. America, I think. Possibly Boston, but definitely America. I'm not sure . . .'

'That doesn't narrow it down much; it's quite a big place. Bigger than Weston.' Her dad tried to lighten the moment.

'I know it's bigger than Weston! Everywhere is bigger than Weston!' Uncharacteristically, Jacks flared at her dad, who shrank from her jibe.

'You're a fool if you think you'll ever see him again. I knew it! I said, didn't I?' Ida shook her head as she drew on her cigarette.

'He doesn't know, Mum! He's not like that. It's not his fault – I never got the chance to tell him and then his family had to leave in such a rush. I'm sure that if he did know, he'd be right here.' *And when he contacts me, I will tell him and he will come for me . . .*

Ida tutted. 'But he's not right here, is he?'

Her mum's question caused her hot tears to fall once again.

Ida turned to her husband. 'I said, didn't I? Find a nice local boy, someone who is good to his mum, a family man. But no one listens to me, they never do. I just wanted what was best for her, for her future. I want her to have the best life possible.'

'We both only want what's best for her, Ida.'

Her dad's support and her mum's words of kindness, despite her disappointment, only heightened Jacks' distress. Now she felt guilty as well as everything else. More tears fell. Tears she thought would never stop, clogging her throat and filling her nose and mouth, a river of sadness that she just couldn't stem.

Her dad patted her hand. Her lovely dad, always trying to make things better for her. For the first time she understood what real grief was – all previous little spikes of sadness seemed like mere rehearsals by comparison. Jacks closed her eyes, knowing she would never forget the moment, nor the scent in the room: her mum had been baking and the aroma of cinnamon and mixed spice was strong. Her nausea didn't need much prompting.

'What are you going to do?' Ida asked from the chair in which she was curled, her cigarette extended between two fingers held high, her voice softer now.

Jacks shrugged. The details were sketchy, but she was certain of one thing. 'I'm having this baby and that's that.'

Later, Jacks lay on her little bed staring at the ceiling and thinking. Why had he gone without even saying goodbye? She pictured lying on the grass with her hand inside his, feeling like the whole world was open to her, that she could go anywhere and be anything. It had felt good. *'Meet me on the Lake of Dreams . . .'* She looked up at the moon, which now seemed to haunt her though her bedroom window. She turned and buried her face in her pillow. *I wanted you to take me with you. Take us with you! Oh, Sven, I love you. I really do. I wish I could talk to you . . .*

It was a week later that his note arrived. The reality of her situation hit her with the force of a punch in the gut, making her vomit and leaving her weak. She let the bath run full. It didn't matter that the water was only lukewarm; the purpose was to let the sound of the running water drown out her crying.

'All okay in there, love? Were you being sick?' her mum asked as she passed, knocking twice on the door with the hand that wasn't holding a cigarette.

Leave me alone. Please just leave me alone. 'Yes.

But I'm fine now,' she added, with as much brightness as she could muster. She waited till she heard
Ida's slippers pad down the stairs towards her
comfy chair.

He had gone to America, to live in Boston with
his family in a big house where there was room
to breathe. And he would not be making contact
or coming to fetch her any time soon. She reread
the note in her hand, hoping to find a line that
told her this was all a horrible mistake and he was
on his way, coming to take her hand and tell her
everything was going to be okay. She studied his
spidery writing, his words poetic and meaningless,
muting any sentiment they might have conveyed.
Gone was the roaring passion that had made her
fall into his arms and lie with him under the stars.
Gone was the excitement of planning, the painting
of a future so real she could smell the dusty
Montana dusk beneath its low-hanging moon.
There was no message of hope, no words of
longing. This was his goodbye.

If she were being honest, she'd known this was
how it would end, known he would continue on
his adventure while she remained there, living in
Addicott Road with her mum and dad and hoping
for a place at college. Although even that now
seemed beyond her reach. She placed her hand
on her tummy and read his note once again.

*I think maybe we were right in our assump-
tion that the beginning is the most exciting part.*

*We were just beginning and it was exciting,
wasn't it? The reality is a harsh lesson.
Geography may be our jailer, but time will see
that distance eroded and we must dance beneath
the stars until the day that the miles disappear
and who knows, maybe we can embark upon
a new beginning . . .*

'Who are you trying to kid, dance beneath the fucking stars?' Jacks pressed her hand against the mirror, leaning on it for strength as tears coursed down her face and splashed into the olive-coloured sink. 'It's rubbish, Sven, all of it. I'm not dancing anywhere, just like I'm not gong anywhere. I'm stuck here without you and I'm pregnant!' She howled again as the whisper left her mouth. 'I'm pregnant, Sven, and I don't know what to do . . .'

She pulled the note into shreds and threw it down the loo, instantly regretting its disposal as she watched the waterlogged message sink to the bottom before flushing it away.

CHAPTER 21

The bright, sunny weather was at odds with the mood in the Davies household. It had been a week since Martha had told her mum and dad and the atmosphere was still strained, with every member of the family struggling in their own way to come to terms with the situation. On the drive to school, the car was uncharacteristically quiet. There was no chirpy banter from Jonty in the back seat, no witty exchange with Martha as she applied her make-up and hummed along to a tune on the radio.

'All okay back there, mister?' Jacks asked in as light-hearted a tone as she could muster. 'Are we buckled up?'

Jonty nodded, looking quite forlorn.

She tried again. 'You're very quiet. Got anything good on today?'

Jonty shook his head before piping up, 'Martha was crying in the night. It woke me up and then she was talking to her boyfriend under the duvet. I heard her whispering and then crying again.'

Jacks stared at him in the rear-view mirror, watching as he fidgeted with the zip on his coat.

When would be the right time to tell him? When would she finally have to admit that her family was just like everyone else's and that there would be no graduation ceremony for her clever girl, no cap and gown worn for the formal photo, no letters after her name and no travelling with a little black case on wheels as she attended business meetings in far-flung capitals.

'Sorry if I woke you up, Jont.' Martha turned and smiled at her little brother.

'Are you okay now, Martha?' he asked.

'I will be,' she said, before getting out of the car, her bag of useless textbooks flung over her shoulder.

Jacks spent the return drive chatting out loud to her dad.

'Oh God, Dad, I feel like everything is slipping through my fingers. I've never felt this low. I could run away, I really could. I could just run away. I'm trying, you have got to believe that I am trying, but I don't know how much more I can take. I'm sorry. I don't want to let you down, but I feel like I can't breathe.'

The car behind beeped; she hadn't realised the lights had turned green.

She thought back to her teens, when all she'd wanted was for life to fly by faster, catapulting her into adulthood and all the wondrous things that awaited her. And now she regretted that impatience, understood that she'd been running blind, hurtling towards a future that was nothing like the one she'd hoped for. For years afterwards, she'd drawn comfort from the happy memories and taken refuge in dreams about her life as it might have been had she tried harder to hang on to Sven. If only she had tracked him down and given *him* choices. But the fact was, he didn't even remember her. She was nothing to him.

Sitting in the car, contemplating this, she inhaled sharply as her mobile phone rang on the passenger seat.

'Yes, this is Martha's mum.' Her stomach knotted as it always did when an unfamiliar number came up. Who was this? School? Hospital? Was her daughter okay?

'Hi there, this is Gideon's mum, Allison. I hope you don't mind me calling. I thought it might be a good idea if we met up?' The woman had a Bristol accent and sounded about her age. She also sounded more than a little nervous.

'Yes,' Jacks said, wearily. It probably couldn't be avoided.

A couple of hours later, after she'd completed her chores and got her mum ready, she drove up Grange Road.

'We're off on a little adventure, Mum. Going to meet someone for coffee. Maybe you could have a nice bit of cake. Do you fancy that?' She pulled the car into Weston General Hospital.

Ida looked up at the modern, brown-brick building. 'Harptree.' She stated the word clearly and concisely.

Jacks stared at her mum. 'Yes, that's right.' She walked round to the back of the car to retrieve Ida's wheelchair, feeling quite choked. 'Harptree' was the name of the ward her dad had been in when he died.

The two made their way to the Costa coffee shop just inside the main entrance. Jacks wheeled her mum up to one of the small tables, got three coffees and, as promised, a piece of carrot cake for Ida. She smiled awkwardly at several of the nurses who came in holding purses, walking briskly and ordering hot drinks with no time to waste. And then Allison appeared. Jacks instinctively knew it was her. The way she hovered in the doorway, looking anxious, swallowing and glancing around as if hoping to spot a friendly, supportive face. Jacks could see where Gideon got his good teeth and wide smile. Allison also had great skin; she looked younger than her forty years, with her hair cut into a short bob. She was wearing navy trousers, clogs and a royal blue tunic with short sleeves and white piping on the collar and sleeves. She had a little upside-down watch hanging from the breast pocket and a pair of scissors poked out the top.

'Jackie?'

'Jacks, yes. Hi. I got you a coffee, didn't know how long your break would be or if you were in a rush, so I thought it'd save time. It's a latte, hope that's okay.'

'Any coffee is always good, thank you.' Allison

raised the cardboard cup and sipped. 'And thanks for coming here. It's hard to organise things outside of here, with my rota, but I'm on a break, so . . .'

'This is my Mum – Ida.' Jacks filled the seconds of silence while both wondered how to continue.

'Ah yes. Hello, Ida. Martha has told me all about you.' She smiled.

Jacks felt a churn of unease. She hadn't realised that Martha had met Gideon's mother or that they had exchanged this level of information. She pictured them sitting around Allison's kitchen table, laughing and planning like a family; even the thought of being excluded in this way made her feel sick. But it was her fault, she knew. She had effectively excluded herself.

'It's good to meet you. I haven't much time, so I guess we should cut to the chase, talk about the situation,' Allison prompted.

'Yes,' Jacks sighed. She was quite prepared to cut to the chase. She wanted to be honest, but part of her also wanted to wound this woman who seemed to be better informed and better connected to the young couple than she was. 'I'm not happy about it.'

'Me either.' Allison widened her eyes and pursed her lips.

Well, at least that was something, at least she wasn't planning a baby shower and starting to knit booties. Jacks considered how best to proceed. Everything she wanted to say was cued up on her tongue. First on her list was how Martha was throwing away her chance to go to university. Jacks took a deep breath, but Allison had taken the lead.

'I like Martha very much, I really do. She's a lovely girl. But she's so young and I don't think you can know your mind at that age, not really, and that worries me. Gideon has worked very hard to learn his trade. He has big ambitions to set up on his own and my fear – apart from him getting hurt by someone who is too young to know what she really wants – was always that he might . . . I don't know how to put it.' She bit the inside of her cheek as she looked at the floor. 'I guess I was always worried that he might get saddled with a baby who he will have to spend the next eighteen years paying for.' She shrugged her shoulders.

Jacks stared at Gideon's mum across the table and fought the desire to shout. She had to stay calm, as Pete had reminded her, for everyone's sake. 'So to get this straight, you are worried that Martha has got herself pregnant just so that Gideon has to support her? Is that what you are saying?'

Allison raised her hand as if to ward off any further comments. 'Not exactly. I don't think it was done on purpose – you know what it's like with kids, they confuse sex with love.' She shook her head disapprovingly. 'But I know that for some girls it's quite an attractive option – to not have to work, to have kids, stay at home. Not that that was how Gideon was brought up – I have always worked full time, never relied on anyone but myself, financially. I like being independent.' Allison sipped her coffee.

Jacks felt like crying. She wanted to tell Allison how she used to work in the bank three days a week, before she'd become her mum's full-time carer. She wanted to shout how going out to work was a piece of cake compared with being on call twenty-four/seven, a slave to the sound of her mum's bell. She felt attacked and her instinct was to defend herself. But this wasn't about her or Allison, this was about their children. Plus Jacks knew what a nurse's life was like; during all those long shifts she probably looked after thirty Idas. She determinedly followed Pete's advice, stayed calm and spoke from the heart.

'Martha was all set for university. She's had offers and is very capable of getting the grades and I feel that she is throwing it all away. I'm not just *unhappy* about the situation, I am gutted, absolutely torn apart.' Jacks found it harder to voice this than she'd expected. A lump built in her throat. 'She's not the kind of girl to sit at home and not work.'

'That's what *she* said.' Allison again confirmed the relationship she had with Martha.

'Well she's not a liar either and so if that's what she said . . .' Jacks let this trail.

'Martha said you didn't like Gideon.' Allison's tone was quiet, far from aggressive, but hurt.

God, Martha! Is there anything you are not telling this woman?

'I'm sure that's what she thinks, but it's not true. I haven't had a real opportunity to get to know him, but he seems like a very nice boy and Martha is clearly very fond of him. I suppose I'm angry with him for putting my daughter in this situation. But I'd be angry with whoever it was.'

'He *is* a really nice boy, hard working and genuine. He's had a lot to deal with in his life. He took it very badly when his dad and I split up. His nan pretty much brought him up – I was working all the hours – and to his credit, he's looking forward to having a family of his own, more so than I would have imagined. He came with Martha for her appointment yesterday, took to it like a duck to water. He's always liked the idea of children. I think that comes from feeling quite lonely as he grew up – we don't have a big family, just him and his cousin Tait, and Tait was born and brought up in Sydney; my sister emigrated years ago. But I hear what you are saying about feeling angry. I feel the same.'

Jacks stared at her. *Appointment? What appointment?*

Allison placed a finger under her little upside-down watch and checked the time. 'Look, I've got to get back to the ward, but it's good we've met at least, and had this chat. Whatever happens, I've got a feeling they are going to need us, both of us.' She smiled, bending low and resting her hand on Ida's arm. 'Bye, Ida, it was nice to meet you.'

Jacks watched her stride out of the coffee shop

and towards the lifts. The meeting hadn't exactly gone as she'd planned it.

Back at Sunnyside Road, she pulled the wheelchair from the car.

'Come on, Mum, let's go get some air.'

Jacks wanted to walk, clear her head while she replayed the conversation with Allison. Pushing Ida along the pavement on their way to the shops, she thought about Martha having gone to the appointment without even telling her. Yet Allison, almost a complete stranger, had known all about it. Who were they, this woman and her son, whose lives had suddenly become enmeshed with her own? *Oh God, I'm losing her! I'm losing her, and that woman, with her full-time job and upside-down watch, will just replace me, take over. I'll be squeezed out . . . Please, someone, help me! I don't want to lose my daughter.*

Jacks wheeled her mum around the corner and out towards the Beach Lawns. 'Let's go pick up some bits for tea, shall we?'

As she rounded the bend, she saw Gideon on the opposite side of the street. She looked down, making out she hadn't seen him, but he was clearly heading for her. *Shit!*

'Mrs Davies? Mrs Davies?' he called.

Jacks slowed and waited for him to catch up. 'What, Gideon? What do you want?'

'I don't know.' He looked at the ground.

'You've come after me to tell me you don't know what you want?' she barked.

'Yes. Well, no, not really.' He licked his lips, which were dry with nerves. 'I just think we should talk to each other. I want to talk to you.'

Like Martha does to your mum, you mean? 'Well, go ahead, talk.' She stared at him.

He hesitated. 'I practised what I was going to say to you, but . . .'

Jacks groaned.

'But now I'm here in front of you, I've gone a bit blank.'

Jacks watched him kick the toe of his black Converse sneakers against the pavement. He looked up at the sky as though that might be where his inspiration lay, flicking his long fringe from his eyes. 'The thing is, I know you don't like me.'

Oh God, not you too! 'It's not that I don't like you. As I said to your mum earlier, it's that I don't like you for Martha, don't like how you have come along and messed up her life.'

'Okay.' Gideon was calm. 'I think that's kind of the same thing, but the point is, I love Martha, I really do and she loves me and I won't always be working for no money in some backstreet garage. I'll have my own car business one day. I've got plans.'

'You think this is about money?'

'Isn't it?' He looked confused.

'No, it isn't! It's about Martha achieving her dreams, finishing her exams, going to university and watching the whole world open up in front of her. You are stopping her doing that. *You.*' She ground her teeth. 'My daughter could pick any path, that's what her tutor told me. Those were the actual words. She is so smart, she can pick any path!'

Gideon nodded. 'I know she's smart. But the fact is, she's chosen me. That's the path she picked.' He looked again at the pavement. 'It's happening. We're having a baby and I want you to feel happy about it.'

'Do you, Gideon? You want me to feel happy? Well, there's a coincidence, because I want to feel happy too.' With that she steered her mother along the pavement and didn't look back.

Mid afternoon, Jacks heard the front door close and looked up to see Pete coming into the kitchen.

'You're early,' she observed.

'I finished early so I picked the kids up.' He smiled at her as though expecting praise.

Jacks simply nodded, not willing to thank him for collecting his children, something she had to do most days.

Martha had gone straight up to her room, avoiding her mother, and for this Jacks was grateful. She could delay for a while longer the decision about whether or not to mention her hospital appointment. Jonty trotted into the kitchen with his bag of dirty PE kit in his arms.

'Is that for me?' Jacks asked, as though he had brought her a gift.

'Yes.' He dumped it on the table and without

breaking his stride asked, 'Is Martha going to have a baby?' He was wide eyed. 'Elliot said she was, but I said I didn't think she was because she doesn't even have a husband who could be a daddy.' He wrinkled his nose and waited to see who was right, him or Elliot.

'That's right, Spud, she is going to have a baby.' Pete smiled. 'Exciting, eh? You will be an uncle!'

'I don't think I'm old enough to be an uncle, am I?' Jonty looked quizzical.

'Sweet Jesus,' Jacks muttered under her breath and covered her eyes.

Jonty considered the news as he reached into the biscuit tin for a pre-tea cookie. He stopped midway, with his hand in the tin, and turned to his parents.

'What's up, mate?' Pete was primed for an adverse reaction; he had lots of answers ready.

'Well . . .' Jonty swallowed. 'I was just thinking . . .'

'Thinking what?' Pete urged.

'I don't want to share my room with Martha and a baby. I don't think there will be enough space.'

'Oh, don't you worry about that!' Pete laughed. 'These things have a funny way of working out.'

Jacks stared at her husband. Was that the best he could come up with? She had to admit that she too was curious about how on earth they were all going to fit into their already cramped terrace. Unless . . . *Oh no!* Her blood ran cold at the thought. Martha might go and live with Gideon!

This was the first time she'd considered that. If Martha left, it really would be the end.

Jonty, placated by his dad's stock phrase, grabbed his biscuit, held it in his mouth while he replaced the lid, and went off to slump in front of the television.

Jacks sighed and started to tell Pete about her horrible conversation with Allison, who had made her feel like an outsider in her own family.

'I felt left out,' she admitted. 'Jealous.'

'Well, that's just rubbish. You're her mum!'

The bell rang upstairs.

'Yes, but I don't feel like her mum right now. I feel more like the enemy.'

She hurried out of the kitchen and up the stairs. When she opened her mum's bedroom door, the smell was overpowering. Her eyes watered as she flung open the window.

'Come on, let's get you into the shower.' She pulled her mum up a little more roughly than she'd intended.

'Ow! You are hurting me!' Ida yelled.

Jacks ignored her as she propped open the bathroom door with her foot and slid back the shower door. She stripped her mum and nudged her clothes into a pile with her toes.

'It's too hot!' Ida screamed. 'You are burning me!'

Jacks thrust her own hand under the running water. 'Look! No it's not, it's cool! For God's sake, how many more times do I have to tell you that?' she snapped.

The two tussled in the shower, both soaked and covered in lather. Jacks sniffed back the tears as she wrestled her mum into her clean nappy and clothes.

'Everything okay?' Pete asked from the doorway.

'Oh, everything is peachy!' Jacks said flatly as she gathered up her mum's soiled clothing.

'I'm worried about you.'

'Well, I'd say you've quite a lot to be worried about, wouldn't you? It's been a bit of a time of it, hasn't it? Our eighteen-year-old daughter is up the spout by some bloody lout and my mother goes wandering off into the night so we have to call the police! I expect the *Jeremy Kyle* research team will be on the phone any day, asking if we want to star in a summer special. We might as well – they might pay us enough to afford a crib and it's not as if the whole fucking town doesn't already know all our business!'

'Why are you fighting?' Neither of them had heard Martha approach.

Jacks rounded on her daughter. 'Why do you think, Martha? What could Dad and I possibly have to argue about? As if our life wasn't perfect enough, we now have your baby to consider and as Jonty asked earlier, where exactly will this child sleep? What do you suggest? That we put a cot in the hall? Or maybe give you the lounge and we can all sit on our beds like in a student bedsit! Not that you would know about that, as you are never going to be a student, are you? I forgot!'

Martha started to cry.

'That's great, that's exactly what we need – more tears. Because, trust me, if tears were the answer, Martha, I'd have fixed everything a long time ago! I tell you what, why don't you tell your dad how you got on at the hospital yesterday? I'm sure, like Allison, he'd love all the details.'

'Go easy, Jacks,' Pete interjected.

'Go easy? Oh yes, I forgot it's all my bloody fault. As usual.' She was shaking now. 'Do you know what? I'm sick of it, sick of it all. I'm going out.' She placed her mum in the stair lift and fastened the strap. 'See you down there, Mum!' she yelled.

'Where are you going at this time of day?' Pete said worriedly, not used to such erratic behaviour. 'It's almost dark.'

'Anywhere, it doesn't matter where. Somewhere I can have a little think. And I'm taking her with me.' She pointed at her mother. 'God forbid I should get time off from nursing her for five minutes, that would be too much to ask!'

Pete looked hurt. 'You can leave her here, of course you can.'

'Can I, Pete? I had one day to myself and it was like I was being punished when I got back. It's just not worth it.' She recalled coming back from London, tired and emotionally drained, to be greeted by Ida, clearly out of step, giving her bell even more exercise than normal. She had rung three times that first night. 'I might as well just accept that I'm tethered to her, whether I like it or not!'

'Toto?' Ida called.

'You'll have to shout a bit louder than that,' Jacks yelled. 'He's been six feet under for the last twenty years!' Ida stared at her. 'Come on.' She lifted Ida from the stair lift and put her coat on, then slammed the front door shut behind her.

It was getting dark as they drove through town and out on to the motorway. Jacks gained speed as she gripped the steering wheel, ramming her foot down and pushing the gears through their paces.

'Do you know the worst thing, Mum? It's that you hated my dad. You must have. You made his life a fucking misery and all he ever did was work hard to keep you in fags. He was a wonderful man, what did he do to deserve that treatment? You were so horrible to him so many times and it affected how I loved you and in return how you loved me. I couldn't get close to someone who treated him that way, how could I?' Her eyes welled as she sped down the outside lane.

'Are you capable of loving anyone? Why did you have me? Why did you bother? No one forced you! You'd have thought you might have been happy to have a child after all that time, and yet you shut me and Dad out like we were lepers. Why couldn't you have joined in our laughs, just once, instead of sitting to the side, looking on, judging. My whole life I felt like an inconvenience and isn't

that a turnaround? Now you're the bloody inconvenience!' Jacks glanced at her mum, who stared
out of the window, seemingly oblivious.

'And now Martha . . . She's throwing away her
life. Throwing it away. I can't believe it. I can't!
And who did that bloody woman think she was
today? How dare she tell me what I should be
doing or what my daughter needs!' Jacks shook
her head as she thumped the steering wheel.

Ida didn't stir; she was looking at the pretty
streetlights that lit the way along the wide lanes
as they turned off the motorway at Gordano
Services and headed towards Bristol.

'I thought it was a good idea to give you that
bell in case you fell or got scared or needed something. But instead it's like my remote control: you
ring it and I jump. I hear it all the time. I hear it
over the telly, over the kids' voices, everything. It
rules my life and I fucking hate it!'

Jacks drove with no direction in mind until she
found herself at a turning for the Clifton Suspension
Bridge. She reached into the cubby in front of the
gearstick and selected a pound coin from the little
hoard she kept for emergencies. She tossed it into
the barrier bucket before driving slowly over the
magnificent bridge.

'Lovely!' Ida commented as she looked out to
her left at the wide bend of the river, on its way
through the Avon Gorge.

Jacks drove along the grassy downs and stared
enviously at the grand five-storeyed Georgian

houses lined up like sentinels. They were all beautifully lit from within. She gazed at the tall sash windows, which allowed glimpses of carefully poised lamps and plush curtains. She indicated and slowed as they passed Clifton College, its ancient buildings gathered in front of a pristine playing field, its interior lights sending out a golden glow. 'Looks like bloody Hogwarts,' she observed as they slowed over the bumps in the road.

She stopped by an ancient stone arch to let a boy cross, a tall, dark-haired boy in a fitted blue suit with a burgundy scarf at his neck and a stack of files and textbooks in his arms, a boy who smiled and waved, polite, yet in a hurry to get wherever he was going. The kind of boy who would go to university, where there would be a girl . . .

'She's having a baby. It doesn't matter how often I say it, I feel sick every time. Why did this have to happen?'

They drove past the zoo and up on to Circular Road with its incredible views of the Avon Gorge and the Severn Estuary. Jacks pulled over and parked on the downs, which were deserted at that time of the evening. She sat for a minute before cutting the engine and stepping outside. She hauled the wheelchair from the boot and pulled her mum into it, ignoring Ida's groans as she manhandled her and put her seatbelt on.

She pushed the chair up the path until they reached the high viewing point that looked down over the gorge. It was hard in the dark, navigating the dips where the gravel had been scuffed away to nothing. The wheelchair teetered to the left and right. Ida sat very still as Jacks steered her with determination. The chill breeze whipped their faces as they neared the cliff edge, drying Jacks' tears almost as soon as they fell. They could see the bridge illuminated in the distance. It was stunningly beautiful.

Jacks stood very still, gripping the handles of her mum's wheelchair, her knuckles white. The beeps and revs from the traffic below were the only thing to break the silence. 'I feel like everything is going wrong for me. My heart is beating too quickly, pushing my blood round so fast that I feel like it might burst.' She stared at the top of her mum's head. 'I don't expect you to understand, but to love so deeply makes you vulnerable, makes you weak. And now I know what they say is true: the opposite of love is not hate, it's indifference. The boy I loved, the one I still dream of nearly twenty years on . . . It turns out he's indifferent, and maybe he always was. The idea of him, the memory of what we had and the dreams of what we might have had, kept me going for years, through all the down times, and now that's gone too. Everything I used to rely on is turning to dust.' She released the sob that had been building in her chest. 'I'm tired, so bloody tired.' The lights twinkled far below. 'And poor old Pete, we had so many hopes, thought we were kindred spirits, but were we? Or were we just a couple of bloody rejects making the best of a bad situation? I don't know. And now it's happening all over again with Martha, marching into a life I didn't want for her.' She shook her head. 'I don't know how I can live with all this disappointment, all this bitterness.'

'I need to find my treasure. And that letter. I'm waiting for them.' Ida's voice carried on the breeze.

'You are not!' Jacks screamed. 'You are not! Just like I'm not waiting for a blonde stranger to come and take me away from the shit, you are not waiting for a letter! Do you understand?'

Ida twisted round to face her daughter. She was crying. 'Toto?'

'I can't do this any more. I can't.' Jacks spoke into the darkness. 'I'm so tired and everything feels so hopeless.' She sobbed as she moved the chair forward an inch. Loose stones clattered off the edge of the path and down the cliff face below. 'I've got nothing to cling to. Nothing. It's like I'm floating, rootless, homeless. My life punctuated by that bloody bell! I can't do it any more. I can't. And I don't want to let Dad down. I tried, Dad, I really did.'

Jacks drew back her arm and closed her eyes. With all the force she could muster, she lunged forwards. She stood back and listened to the sound of metal pinging and bashing against the rocks until there was nothing. Silence.

Sinking down on to the damp ground, she breathed deeply and calmly before giving way to tears. She slid further down on to the hard gravel, where she lay in the dark on the cold cliff edge. With her face pressed against the ground, she felt the sharp bite of stones against her cheek. 'What do I do now? What on earth do I do now?' she cried into the darkness.

Nearly two hours later, she opened the front door on Sunnyside Road to find Pete standing in the hall.

'There you are! I was getting really worried. Where on earth have you been? It's late. I kept trying your phone until I realised you'd left it on the kitchen table.'

Jacks shrugged, staring at her husband, unable to find the words and feeling too weak to converse.

'Come on, Ida,' Pete continued. 'Why don't I take you through for your tea? You must be starving. I've made fish fingers. Kitchen looks like an explosion in a food factory, but the food tastes good.'

He took the handles of his mother-in-law's wheelchair and steered her along the hallway. 'I'll see to your mum, Jacks. Why don't you go and have a lie down?'

Jacks stared at him with a blank expression on her face.

'Don't worry, love, it's all okay. All I want to do is help you, look after you. We are on the same team, remember? I'll get Ida settled and she can ring if she needs anything. Take your time.'

'She can't ring, actually.'

'Why not? Where's her bell?'

'At the bottom of the Avon Gorge.'

Jacks climbed wearily up the stairs and col-lapsed into bed. As she pulled the duvet over her head, welcoming the dark escape it offered, she pictured Ida's tear-stained face. 'God, I'm so sorry, Mum,' she whispered, overcome with guilt at the thought that she might have frightened her mum. She decided to try extra hard tomorrow to make it up to her.

CHAPTER 22

Nineteen Years Earlier

'Next!' The receptionist shouted into the crowded room of the Health Centre.

Jacks looked at the number on the board. She'd be the next to go in. She placed her Walkman headphones over her ears and pressed play, letting the soothing sounds of her mix-tape take her away. She smiled as D-Ream's 'Things Can Only Get Better' played loudly in her ears. *Ain't that the truth . . .*

As she sat practising what she needed to say and how she might say it, praying she'd get one of the female doctors, the door opened. She glanced up and was horrified to see Pete Davies limp in, looking nonchalantly around for an empty seat.

'Shit,' she muttered under her breath, sinking down as far as possible into the orange plastic chair and wishing she'd brought a book with her so she could bury her head in it. He did a double-take as he spotted her, lifting his hand in a hesitant wave. She cringed. The last time they'd been alone together was when they'd snogged on the dance-floor of Mr B's.

'All right, Jacks?' He lowered himself into the chair beside her, keeping his right leg straight as though it was splinted. He was as usual wearing a tracksuit.

She pressed pause on her machine and lowered the headphones so they sat round her neck. 'How's your knee? I heard you'd damaged it.' She felt her cheeks colour, unsure if mentioning it was the right or wrong thing to do.

'It's knackered.' He sighed, patting the thigh of his damaged leg.

'Will it get better?'

Pete laughed and shook his head, as though even saying the words required the disguise of humour just to make it bearable. 'Nope. I've done the ligaments and it's a weakness, apparently. I'm having physio, but that's just to get me walking properly.'

'What you gonna do?'

He looked her in the eyes for the first time. 'I don't know, but I know what I'm not gonna do and that's play football, not for Bristol City anyway. I might get a game with a smaller club – it's too soon to tell how my leg'll shape up.'

Jacks searched for the right words. 'It's only a game, though. Right?'

'Next!' The woman's voice boomed from behind the receptionist's desk.

'Oh! That's me. See you, Pete.' She gave a small

255

smile as she stepped over his extended leg and made her way into the doctor's room, trying desperately to look as if she was popping in to discuss a minor ailment and not the fact that her whole world was crashing down around her.

The next day as she walked home along the seafront, taking the long route and enjoying the fresh air, which helped clear her head, she spotted Pete sitting on one of the benches.

'You stalking me?' he asked as she sat down next to him.

She laughed. 'No, although you'd be quite easy to stalk, seeing as you can't run away at the moment.'

'Good point.' He smiled and patted his leg. 'You feeling better now?'

'What?' She looked up.

'You were at the doctor's? I just wondered if you were feeling better?'

'Oh.' She hid her relief: no one was talking, no one knew. 'Yep. Thanks.'

The two sat and stared at the water, strangely comfortable in the silence that cocooned them. Neither of them felt the need to fill the quiet with banal conversation.

It was Pete who eventually broke the silence. 'I was thinking about what you said.'

'When?'

'You said it's just a game. But you were wrong,' he whispered.

'I was?' She tried to find his thread.

'You said it as though it didn't matter – football.' He ran his fingers up and down the open zip of his tracksuit top.

She nodded. 'Oh yes.'

'But it's more than that. More than that for me. It's the one thing that I am better at than anyone else. It's the one thing I love. And it was going to make me enough money to have a really great life. And now it's gone, all of it.'

Jacks twisted her body until she was facing him, sitting sideways on the bench. 'I'm sorry, Pete. I wasn't being funny. I didn't know what to say to you.'

To her horror he started to cry. He pushed his fingers into his eye sockets to try and stem the flow. It didn't work. His tears trickled out regardless. She edged closer to him, placed her hand on his back and patted him as if she were consoling a small child.

'Don't tell anyone,' he mumbled, his voice strained with emotion.

She wasn't sure if he was referring to his injury or his tears. 'I won't. I promise.'

He took a deep breath and threw his head back, trying to compose himself, sniffing and wiping his eyes, mortified by his outburst.

'I've got a secret too,' she whispered.

'What is it?'

'You can't tell anyone.'

'I won't,' he said with sincerity.

'I've got myself into a bit of a mess.'

'What kind of mess?' he asked softly.

She nodded. 'I'm having a baby.'

'Fucking hell!' he gasped.

'Yep, fucking hell.' She sighed. 'I haven't told anyone, not even Gina. I don't know why I told you, but now that I have, I feel a bit better.'

'Who's the dad?' Pete sat up straight.

'Sven.' His name stuck like pins in her throat.

'No way! I didn't know you two were . . .' He shuffled on the bench.

'Well, yes, we were, we did, once or twice, that's all,' she admitted, as if her pregnancy wasn't proof enough.

'Hasn't he moved to America?'

Jacks nodded and it was her turn to cry.

'Jesus, will you look at us, sitting here crying! What are we like!'

'We're a bloody shambles!' Jacks smiled through her tears.

'Don't cry, Jacks,' he said gently. 'These things have a funny way of working out.'

She looked up at him and blew her nose on a tissue. She really, really hoped he was right.

CHAPTER 23

Placing the basket on her mum's lap, Jacks pushed open the doors of the supermarket with the small front wheels of the chair.

'Here we go, Mum. What do you fancy for tea? I was thinking I might do gammon with a pine-apple ring on top – you like that, don't you?' She was determined to make it up to her mum after the scare she'd put her through the night before. 'Used to be Dad's favourite, didn't it? With chips and ketchup on the side. Think I'll do that.'

She slowly perused the aisles, scanning for the red labels indicating that something was heavily discounted or on a two-for-one offer; whatever it was, she would buy it regardless and then find a way to incorporate it into her menu. Over the years this had resulted in some rather interesting combinations: her hot-dog pasta and custard with meringues were both still legendary. On a normal day these recollections would make her laugh, but not today. Not when her heart was still beating too fast for comfort and her whole body seemed suffused with sadness. She couldn't get out of her head the image of Allison's face, chatting merrily about Gideon and his love of kids.

'Jacks?'

She turned to see Lynne walking towards her, with Caitlin-Marie waddling along by her side. The girl wore black leggings that were stretched so thin over her bump and thighs that her knickers and protruding belly button were visible; she looked like she was about to pop.

'How are you?' Lynne was her usual lively self. She turned her attention to Ida. 'Hello, Mrs Morgan!'

Jacks smiled. 'We're great, thanks. Wow, Caitlin, look at you! You look well. How much longer?'

'Any day.' Caitlin-Marie, morose as ever, rubbed at her swollen stomach and sighed. 'Just want it to come out now.'

Lynne giggled. 'I've told her, just you wait till it is out, then you'll be wishing you could pop it back in! You'll never have a moment's peace! Worth it, though. I can't wait.' She bobbed on the spot.

Jacks stared at Caitlin's bump and tried to imagine Martha looking the same way. She swallowed the bile that rose in her throat.

'Our Ashley called last week. She's in the Dominican Republic, wherever that is! Staying with her friends in an all-inclusive resort, on a break from the cruise. I said to her, it must be a hard life, if you need to go to an all-inclusive resort to have a break from a cruise! Half her luck!' Lynne roared.

Jacks stared at Lynne and remembered Ashley

Gilgeddy, who only last year had got into a fight on the pier and been arrested. Who had got an illegal tattoo when she was sixteen; who had fluffed her one line in the Nativity play. This was the girl who was seeing the world.

'You all right, Jacks? You look a bit pale,' Lynne said, sounding concerned. 'Must be the shock.' Lynne hesitated, as if expecting Jacks to say something. 'How is Martha? Is she coping?'

Jacks felt her legs shake as she again pictured Gideon's chirpy mother. Lynne knew, everyone knew. 'She's fine,' she said as her cheeks flamed and her shoulders sagged.

It hit her all of a sudden that she'd always seen her family – her girl – as being a cut above the rest. That knowledge had been like a secret, a secret that allowed her to walk with her head held high, shoulders back and a confident smile on her face. What was the phrase . . . Pride comes before a fall? Well, she had certainly fallen. She was now so low that she didn't know how she was going to get up again. Or even if she could.

'Give her our love, won't you? Tell you what,' Lynne gushed, 'when the babies are here, we can take them for walks on the pier, a couple of grannies together!' She laughed. 'We'll have to get those pack-away plastic hats and sit over a cuppa for hours while we split a tea cake, eh, Jacks?'

Jacks tried to laugh but couldn't. Instead, she turned her mother's chair and walked briskly in the opposite direction, towards the exit, desperate for some fresh air. It was only when a strong, masculine hand gripped the top of her arm that she realised where she was.

The man's voice was loud, threatening. 'Can I ask you to step back inside the store, madam?'

She looked up into the face of the burly security guard with the heavy Eastern European accent and saw him eyeing the basket of shopping that sat on her mother's lap.

'Oh, don't worry, I wasn't going to run off. I just needed some air. I'll come in and pay for it now.'

'So you are aware you left the store without paying?' he asked, unsmilingly. The peak of his cap was pulled low, covering his eyebrows.

'Yes! But I'll be straight back in. I just need a minute.' She smiled, trying to shrug her arm free.

The security guard, whose shiny name badge said 'Mateusz', grabbed his radio and called for back-up.

Jacks snorted her laughter. 'You are not serious? Oh, for God's sake! What do you think I'm going to do? Leg it with my mum in a wheelchair and make off with a tin of pineapple rings and a box of sponge fingers?'

Mateusz didn't appear to be listening. Jacks was rendered speechless as he held her arm and marched her back into the store. She was vaguely aware of Lynne and Caitlin watching, standing next to the guy with the dreadlocks from the fish counter, his mouth agape.

★　　★　　★

262

Gina pulled the car up outside the Davies' house. 'Do you want me to come in with you?'

'No.' Jacks shook her head. 'We'll be fine. Thanks for picking us up.'

'It's okay, mate. Anytime. At least I didn't have to bail you out.'

'Christ, I hope there will never be another time. I'm so embarrassed.' Jacks sniffed.

'It was obvious the manager could see it was just a misunderstanding,' Gina said. 'I once got home and realised I'd left a box of beer in the trolley and hadn't paid for it. I usually get the girl to lean over with her little gun thing if something is too heavy to lift, but I must have forgotten.'

'Did you go back?'

'Did I buggery!' Gina laughed.

'Did you see the way Lynne looked at me?' Jacks stared at her lap. 'Everyone will know.'

'So? Who cares?'

'I care, G. What will I say to Pete?'

'Tell him what happened. It was a stupid mix-up and if old what's-his-name the security guard hadn't been quite so keen to get a merit point, we'd have all got home a lot sooner. Don't worry about it.'

'They asked me to find another store to shop in.' Jacks' lip quivered at the humiliation.

'Well, that's their bloody loss. I shan't be going there again, that's for sure!' Gina sounded indignant. 'That will see their sales of Jaffa Cakes and white wine take a tumble. I shall definitely be stealing my beer from elsewhere and they have no one to blame but themselves!'

Jacks tried to raise a smile. 'Suppose you've heard about Martha?'

'Yep.' Gina nodded. 'This is a small seaside town, where word travels fast due to lack of anything else of interest going on. In fact the word was probably out shortly after he'd rezipped his fly, if that Stephanie Fletcher had anything to do with it.'

'Gina!'

'What? It's the truth.' Gina sighed. 'I'm only trying to cheer you up, mate. Is she okay?'

'I don't know. I think we're all in shock.'

'That's understandable. You know where I am when you want to talk about it.'

'Thanks, G.' Jacks climbed from the car and opened the hatchback to retrieve her mum's wheelchair.

'I will say this, though,' Gina shouted across the back seat. 'If you are planning on upgrading your life of crime to, say, bank robbing, let me know and I'll bake you a cake with a gert big file in it!'

Jacks laughed in spite of the horrible situation. Her laughter quickly turned to tears as she trod the path with her mum and it began to rain.

'Is my letter here?' Ida asked as Jacks fumbled in her pocket for her door key.

Jacks ignored her, unable to find the strength to respond.

★   ★   ★

Jacks sipped warily at her tea as Pete walked into the kitchen. She noted his agitated stance, the way his fingers flexed by his side. He obviously knew.

'Good day?' she asked.

He gave one brief nod. 'Rob called me at work, told me what happened. We went for a beer. I've left you a couple of messages.' He was breathing quickly.

'I haven't checked my phone.' She had been hiding away, not wanting too much contact with the outside world.

'What happened?'

Jacks sighed. 'It was a mix-up. I nipped outside the supermarket to get some air. I wasn't thinking straight.'

Pete sat down. 'I was so worried.'

'Don't worry, no harm done, only to my pride.'

'One good thing, Jacks, at least now you'll have more to talk about on the *Jeremy Kyle Show*!' he said, trying to lighten the mood.

Jacks scraped her chair back from the table. 'Very funny.'

Pete ran his hand over his face and pinched his nose. 'Oh, and before I forget, Gina asked if you could meet her by the pier. It all sounds very mysterious. I said you'd be there by eight. You'd better get going.' He smiled briefly.

Jacks wondered what Gina wanted at that time of night. Especially as they'd seen each other earlier. But she was never one to turn down an opportunity to share what was bothering her with her friend.

She decided to walk to the pier, hoping that ten minutes in the fresh air might help calm her a little. As she stepped out into the evening chill, her hands trembled in her pockets. It had been quite a day.

Wandering along the Marine Parade, beneath the loops of lights hanging lamppost to lamppost, Jacks smiled. She had always loved the place at night. No matter how many times she had seen it over the years, it still felt almost magical as the pier glittered like a Christmas tree in the distance and the Weston Wheel shone against the dark night sky. The raindrops sparkled on the lights and with the fresh, salt-tinged breeze blowing off the sea, Weston held a sense of promise that was lost in the daytime, when the sunlight revealed it to be a damp, decaying resort of faded signs and faded glory that only cheap pints and even cheaper shots could transform into the seaside paradise its visitors had been hoping for.

Jacks recalled the many times she had walked along the prom with her dad when she was little. One day in particular stuck in her memory. She had been wearing her pink padded anorak with the hood and matching mittens on a string that dangled from the cuffs. She had insisted on walking backwards while facing him, trusting him to tell her if she was going to bump into something. He had laughed as she lost her balance once or twice and turned to see what was behind her, fear of the unknown taking her confidence. He had bent down and spoken to her softly. 'Do you know, Jacqueline, people who look backwards can't see where they are going and are liable to get lost. You need to look forwards, look ahead and the path'll be clear. Looking back will only get you into trouble.'

Funny how she still remembered that. 'I miss you, Dad.' She spoke to the horizon. 'Every day I miss you. I'm sorry I lost it with Mum yesterday. I know it's not her fault. And what am I going to do about Martha? How can I make her see what she is throwing away?' She rubbed the side of her face, realising it was streaked with dirt and the sticky residue of mascara.

A snazzy red sports car was parked up. She paid it little attention, used to seeing such vehicles, usually owned by the Bristol elite, who liked to zoom down the motorway, pull over and take in the sea air whilst eating fish and chips in the comfort of their luxury interior. The passenger door opened. Jacks tutted and skirted to the left slightly to avoid it.

'Jacks!' a voice called from within. A voice she recognised instantly.

She stopped in her tracks and listened, staring out to sea, wondering if she had misheard the name called in the wind.

'Jacks!' There it was again and this time she was certain.

What on earth . . .? 'Sven?'

He climbed from the car and leant against the roof. 'Please get in.'

She stood, stunned and squinting, trying to comprehend that he was there and that he recognised her. 'What do you mean, "get in"? Why would I get in your car? I haven't seen you for a lifetime and when I did see you, you clearly didn't recognise me. What d'you want?' she snapped.

'I want to talk to you.'

'You want to talk to me? After all these years, you want to talk to me?'

'Yes.' He nodded.

'What, about your mega-million-bucks boat and how many people you can fit in its kitchen? Cos I couldn't give a shit actually – I've got one or two other things going on right now.'

'Just get in the car. Please!' He tapped the roof and shivered.

'How did you find me? And what's Gina got to do with this? I thought I was supposed to be meeting her.' She looked towards the pier, confused.

'I used her ticket details to track her down. It gave her mobile number and I got her to arrange this. I know it sounds devious and I'm sorry. I didn't know how else to get hold of you.'

'Well, I'm sorry you've had a wasted trip. I haven't got anything to say to you.'

'Please, Jacks.'

'Please what?' she shouted. 'I don't know what you want from me. I don't know why you are here!' She smacked her chest.

'I'm sorry about how I treated you at the Boat Show.' His eyes were wide, lips pressed, palms upturned. He looked sincere.

'What do you mean, "how you treated" me?' She was confused. 'You're not to blame. It was a stupid thing to do, jumping on a bloody train and wasting that whole day. Why did I think you'd remember me? It's not as if we'd kept in touch, and we were just kids, right? It was all a very long time ago. Let's just pretend it never happened.' She turned to walk away.

'I am to blame.' His voice was level. 'And I need to tell you something.'

'What? What do you need to tell me? Tell me quickly because I've got to go.' She stared at him.

'I never forgot you. Not for one second.'

'Why are you saying that? Don't tease me, Sven. I feel humiliated enough as it is.'

Jacks felt her tears threaten once again. She turned and set off at a rapid pace along the sea wall, keeping close to the edge, as far from him and his flash car as she could manage.

Sven ran to catch up with her. She heard the double beep as he locked the car and then the sound of his soft soles treading the pavement.

Oh God! Go away! I can't cope. Don't talk to me, don't touch me!

He caught up, grabbing her by the top of her arm.

'I mean it. I didn't forget you.'

'You didn't?' she whispered.

Sven shook his head. 'I wish I had. I wish I could.'

Jacks suppressed a smile. Her heart swelled with something close to relief, but that quickly turned to anger as she realised what he had done. 'Hang on a minute, so you *pretended* you didn't know me?'

'I know.' He hesitated. 'It looks bad, but I also know that you came all the way to London to find me and that tells me something. Is there any chance you could still maybe have feelings for me? I know it sounds ridiculous, but do you?'

'Feelings for you? Yes, I've got feelings of pure rage right now! How could you do that to me, make me feel like shit! Like I was nothing! How dare you? How could you take the piss out of me like that?'

'Just give me half an hour, Jacks. Let me talk to you and if after that you don't want me to contact you again then I won't, I promise. But just give me half an hour.'

Jacks looked up and down the Marine Parade to make sure she hadn't been seen, then made her way to his car. She slid into the soft leather seat, liking the warmth and quiet it offered; it was a bit different from her little Skoda.

Sven smiled at her and switched the engine on. The car warmed almost instantly.

'You're not kidnapping me, are you?' she asked with a flash of excitement in her eyes.

'No. Gina knows where we are.'

Jacks smirked. 'Mind you, don't think my lot could afford much by way of a ransom.'

Sven laughed. 'You are still funny.'

'Funny weird,' she said, recalling the events of the last thirty-six hours. 'I can't believe you're here. I can't believe I'm in your car! This time last night I was lying at the top of the Avon Gorge with my face in the dirt, wondering why everything has to be so bloody difficult.'

'It doesn't have to be,' he replied.

'Maybe not in your world. But in mine . . .' She felt her lip tremble. 'Oh God, all I seem to do these days is cry. I don't know why. I'm sorry.'

'That's okay. Do you want a tissue?' He produced one from a pocket in the car door.

'Actually, I do know why I'm crying.' She sighed.

He raised his eyebrows in enquiry.

'I'm crying because I know that even if I didn't have my family, even if I had all the time in the world to do my thing, I would be just as stuck as I am now because I don't know what my thing is. I don't.'

'That's sad.' He seemed genuine.

'Yes. It is sad, bloody sad.' She nodded vigorously. 'I can't remember the day I woke up and realised that my life was never going to change. In fact I don't think it was one day, it was more a gradual process, like getting fat or going bald, I imagine, where you get used to the gradual shifts in how you look until it's just how you are. I suppose it was like that. Just like every kid, I used to spend hours dreaming about all the things I might become. But you don't necessarily think about how you'll get there, do you? You just picture yourself having arrived, giving an Oscar speech, chatting to Lorraine about your latest adventure.'

Sven laughed. 'I didn't just picture it. I made it happen. I knew what I wanted to achieve, I visualised it and I went for it.'

Jacks blinked at him. 'Well, good for you! Aren't you the lucky one.'

'I didn't mean it like that. That sounded boastful and I'm not like that.'

'No, it's okay. It's probably true. I didn't make it happen, didn't make anything happen and that's my fault, right?' She sank back into the soft leather, which seemed to cushion every part of her body. It was lovely. 'I have a little life, but it's a good life in a lot of ways. I know that I make everyone else happy. But it's like there's no room for what makes me happy, no time for me.'

'So you are the sacrificial lamb? Giving up on your dreams so your kids can achieve?'

Jacks shook her head. 'Not really, no. That makes it sound terrible and it's not like that.'

'Really? Doesn't sound like it.' He was almost scoffing.

Jacks looked at him and realised, aghast, that she was crying again. 'I have a family. And they're not perfect, but they're all I have.' Without thinking, she reached into her bag and pulled out a photograph of Martha and Jonty, sitting on the sea wall in the summer, Martha looking straight into the lens with her hair plaited on one side and Jonty sticking out his tongue. She handed it to Sven. 'My kids, my heart. I could never do anything that would make them see me in a bad light, do you understand that?'

'I do.' He stared fixedly at the picture before handing it back. 'But they're not babies and you need to think about your life too.'

Jacks shook her head. She was confused enough without adding this to the mix.

'Don't cry, Jacqueline, please.'

Jacks nodded at him. 'I can't help it. My dad died and I still haven't got over it. I've got a lot going on at the moment.' She wiped her runny nose on her damp tissue. 'And I'm crying because you're a let-down, Sven.'

He looked at her. 'Am I?'

She held his stare. 'I wish I'd never come to find you, because after I'd seen you it was like a big wake-up call. You've rubbed out my silver lining, blocked off the light at the end of the tunnel, burst my bubble. And that means that now, when I'm elbow deep in shit-covered laundry and so knackered I can't remember what I climbed the stairs for, I don't have your face, your beautiful boy's face, in my mind any more, willing me on. Instead I have to think of something else to drive me forward. It's not you. Not any more.'

He stared at her quizzically. 'You were pregnant, weren't you?'

A stunned, heavy silence followed. Both of them physically sagged in their seats.

'What?' Her voice quavered.

'When I left with my parents to go to Boston, you were pregnant.' He studied her eyes, looking for a clue.

She stared at him, open mouthed. 'How . . .?'

'I knew it, Jacks. I remember you couldn't eat anything, felt queasy, had that metallic taste thing going on. And you looked different, blooming. I knew.'

'You did?' she gasped. She pictured her eighteen-year-old self, sitting in her parents' lounge. *He doesn't know, Mum! He's not like that. It's not his fault – I never got the chance to tell him. I'm sure that if he did know, he'd be right here . . .'*

'What the fuck!' She placed her head in her hands and leant forward. 'What the fuck! Oh God!'

'And then, a few months after I'd left, I called and spoke to your mum and she told me you were married – to Peter Davies.' He curled his lip as he tapped the steering wheel with his index fingers.

'You spoke to my *mum*?' Her voice had gone up an octave.

He nodded.

'I feel sick. I'm going to be sick!' She fumbled against the door in the half-light, looking for a means to open it.

He pressed a button and the window whirred down.

She gulped deep breaths of the fresh air that

whipped around the car, then turned to face him. 'But . . . but that means you abandoned me! It means you knew and you abandoned me! All that bullshit about coming with you and you just left! You fucking bastard! How could you do that to me?'

'I was so young, too young . . .'

'You were? And what about me? I didn't have the option to bugger off, did I?' She stared at the horizon, thinking about Pete, who had been there, just like he had been there ever since. She fumbled with the door once again, finally locating the handle. 'I've got to get back to my family.'

'I loved you, Jacks.' He reached out to touch her arm.

'Don't you touch me! You don't know the first thing about love. It's when you stick around and show support, not run away at the first hurdle, that's not love! Fuck off, Sven. Go back to your beautiful glass-fronted house in San Francisco and your forty-million-pound yachts. There's nothing here for you, there never was.'

He looked hurt. 'I want to give you this.' He unfurled a rectangle of paper from his top pocket and handed it to her.

She opened it carefully. It was a cheque. A cheque for a quarter of a million pounds. Jacks stared at him, her fingers shaking. She held it in her hands and thought about the motorbike it would buy Pete, the extra bedroom it would mean for Jonty and the crappy lampshade in their bedroom that needed replacing. She then pictured the shreds of a note that she had flushed down her mum and dad's loo all those years ago. She folded the paper and ripped it into tiny pieces that she threw at him like confetti.

'You can't buy me as if I'm one of your fancy accessories, that's not how things work. And you can't make up for being such a shit by giving me this. I don't need your money and I don't need you! I never did. Stay away from us.'

At Sunnyside Road, Jacks put the key in the door and was met by darkness. The only light came from the kitchen. She walked in and found Pete sitting at the table. He was strumming his fingers lightly on the table.

'Everything okay? Mum all right? Kids?' she asked nervously, her face scarlet as if he could sense her deceit.

Pete nodded. 'How was Gina?' he whispered, his voice thick and croaky, as though he hadn't spoken for a while.

Jacks walked straight to the sink and ran the tap, staring at the steady flow, anything other than look him in the eye and lie.

'Good.'

'Yes, I thought she looked good when I nipped round earlier to see if you wanted a lift back. I thought you might appreciate that after your escapade earlier. I was worried about you. So, as I say, she was a bit nervous maybe, surprised to see me, but generally good.'

Jacks tried to interpret the edge in his voice. She turned off the tap and slowly faced her husband, leaning against the sink with her arms folded across her chest. What had Gina told him?

'Look at you, you've been crying. You're all flustered.' Pete looked her up and down. 'What happened?'

Jacks thought about the posh car and its driver, who would now be heading back to a life that was never hers to have. She swallowed and looked at her hands, as if they might be stained with guilt. 'I . . . I let things get a bit messy.'

'So I heard.' He pointed at the chair opposite. 'Sit down.'

She sat. 'Pete, I . . .'

'No. Just listen. How long have you known me, Jacks?' he asked.

'What? Don't be daft! You know how long I've known you.'

'Oh, I'm not daft. Just answer the question.' There was a tone to his voice that she'd rarely heard.

She shook her head and thought. 'Since I was eleven.'

'That's right. Twenty-five years. A long time.'

She nodded. It was.

'And married eighteen years,' he added.

She nodded again.

'In that whole time, Jacks, I have only ever put you and the kids first. I've worked as hard as I could to make a life for us.'

'I know that,' she whispered.

'Do you think I didn't have dreams?' he asked.

She looked at him, unsure of how to answer.

'Do you think when I was younger I saw myself lugging wet turf around on muddy building sites with an aching back?'

She carried on staring at him, her heart pounding.

'Because I can tell you, I didn't. You know I wanted to be a footballer, everyone knows that, but when I knew that wasn't going to work out for me, do you know what I wanted to do?'

She shook her head.

'I wanted to go to college. I fancied the idea of putting a suit on and working in an office. Did you know that?'

'No.' She looked at her hands.

'No,' he repeated. 'But I couldn't go to college, couldn't learn a skill or get trained in computers or anything because I had a wife and a baby, a little girl who was more precious to me than anything and I had to earn money to pay the mortgage to keep a roof over your heads and to put food on the table.'

'I know, Pete, and I'm grateful for how hard you work.' She was sincere.

He raised his finger to quiet her.

'Every day I get in the van, put the radio on and blast my feet with hot air, trying to store up some heat for the day ahead. I hate being cold. I hate it. And every day I drive past men in suits and boys in suits, all reading the paper or watching the world go by with fancy haircuts and clean shoes and I wonder how you get to be one of them blokes who wakes up and puts a suit on and sits behind a desk, shovelling paper instead of soil, answering the phone instead of the yell of a site foreman. I sometimes think that might have been me if things had been different. That's my pipe dream, Jacks, to be a manager. I know how funny that must sound, but who knows, if I hadn't fallen in love with a girl so young . . .' His voice was now thick with emotion. 'And that girl . . . I watch her now, watch her shrink away from me as her jaw tightens every day with irritation if I eat noisily or don't put my boots away or any of the million other things I do to annoy her and I have to stop myself from reminding her that I'm tired too and that I'm only human, I'm going to make mistakes sometimes.'

'I'm sorry.'

He ignored her, maybe he hadn't heard. 'And the thing is, you don't need to tell me how disappointed you are with your lot in life – I know it, I can see it in your face and in your actions and in your constant bloody daydreaming. Your disappointment only makes me feel even more worthless.'

'I never wanted to make you feel like that.'

'Well, you have, you do. I have never refused you anything, never flinched when you brought your mum into our home, knowing it was going to mean upheaval for me and the kids. I haven't even moaned about our crappy sex life. I'm thirty-six, Jacks, not ninety-six! Do you think that it's okay for us to live with no intimacy? Because it's not.'

'I know.' She nodded.

'But all that, everything that has gone on, is now irrelevant because we have a much bigger problem on our hands. A problem you have created.'

She stared at her husband, her knees shaking beneath the table.

'There is a very fine line between being kind and tolerant and being a mug, a pushover, and you are about to find out the difference.'

'Pete, I—'

'I haven't finished.' He again raised his hand, his voice louder now. 'I am frightened. For the first time in my life, I am properly frightened.' He blinked quickly.

'What are you frightened of?' Her voice was soft. She sat back in the chair wide eyed and afraid of what might be coming next.

'I'm frightened of losing my little girl. My little girl who needs me more now than she has ever done before, my little girl who is pregnant and lost.'

'How could you lose her?'

'Did you tell him?' he shot back.

Oh God! He knows! He knows where I was and who I was with! 'No.' She shook her head, her arms flat against the tabletop, fingers splayed. 'I swear to you, I didn't say anything. But he kind of guessed. Swear to you I didn't bring it up! You don't have to worry—'

Pete seemed to crumple on the table, tears of relief streaming down his face. He pinched his nose and wiped his eyes. She had never seen him cry like that before.

'"Don't have to worry"?' he interrupted. 'I'm her dad. I'm her dad, Jacks!' He slapped the table. 'And I love her more than I love anything. All those nights I got up for her when she was tiny, gave her her bottle, held her when she was sick. Every spare minute I wasn't working, I was painting pictures, glueing bloody pasta on to card, playing sharks in the bath. I taught her to swim. We grew vegetables in the garden. I drive her around, like a bloody taxi. I'm her dad!' he cried.

'You are! Of course you are, you always have been. You are her dad!' Jacks was crying too now.

'I don't envy anyone, Jacks. I never have. I don't need millions. All I have ever wanted is this life, our life, here in this town, in these streets, where we all know each other and look out for each other. That's enough for me. All I need is to know that I'm coming home to you and that my kids are happy. That's it.' Pete raised his arms and let them fall. 'That's all I need.' More tears flowed. 'But maybe that's not enough for her – I can't compete with yachts and money and flash cars, how can I? I can't even send her on a bloody school trip or give her a room of her own!'

'She doesn't need any of that. She only needs you. Like I needed my dad. He was never rich, it was always the things he did that were important, not the things he could or couldn't give me. Who else would punch a dent in my pillow every night and say, "There you go, Dolly, a nest for you to sleep in." No one can match that, of course they can't. I used to dream the sweetest dreams, knowing my dad was along the corridor, keeping me safe. And it's the same for Martha, she doesn't need things! And you don't have to compete. That's never going to happen. It's done!'

Pete stood up, scraping the chair back and pointing his finger at his wife. 'It better be. Because, trust me, I'm not putting up with any of that shit. Do you understand me?'

Jacks nodded.

'You make sure, Jacks. You make sure things are sorted properly, cos if you don't, the choice might be taken out of your hands.'

CHAPTER 24

Nineteen Years Earlier

They walked along Bristol's harbourside. It was a grey day and rainwater had gathered in shiny pools in the gaps between the cobbles.

'You fancy going on one of these big boats, sailing away somewhere?' Pete asked, teetering perilously close to the edge of the harbour wall.

'No! I don't like the sea much. And I don't want to have to come and fish you out either, so come back here!' Jacks instructed.

'All right, bossy! Are you worried I'm going to get hurt?' He laughed, edging closer to the wall.

'Yes!' Jacks looked away.

'Because you care about me?' Pete asked, looking up through his eyelashes, nervously.

'Course I care about you. You're my mate.' She smiled at him. Kind Pete, who had been so good to her, keeping her secrets and bringing water biscuits into school to help combat her morning sickness.

'Good, because I care about you.'

Jacks smiled. 'We're lucky, really, Pete. Some people go through their whole lives without anyone caring about them or being kind to them.' She considered this. 'I wish my mum and dad were kinder to each other.'

Pete coughed, embarrassed. 'Are they not?'

'Not always,' she admitted. 'I sometimes feel like my mum doesn't like me. Especially when my dad and I are having a laugh.' It was the first time she had told anyone this, but with Pete it was as if she could share anything.

'Maybe she resented having you in some way. Maybe life was getting easier for them when you came along and then financially things got tough again? Or could she be a bit jealous of you and your dad? Maybe she feels pushed out? After all, they had a lifetime together before you arrived. I don't know.'

So many maybes, but maybe he was right. 'I don't know either,' she said.

'I think this trial with Weston might be a goer,' said Pete, keen to change the subject. 'I mean, okay, it's not big league like City, but if it keeps me playing and means I can work as well, it's like the best of both worlds. I'll be earning *and* playing footie, which is not just a game . . .'

'I know! It is much, much more than that!' She laughed. 'The physio seemed quite hopeful, didn't he?'

'Yep.' Pete gave a small smile. The disappointment of not getting his chance to shine was still acute.

'I don't know what I'd have done without you these last weeks, Pete.' She was sincere.

'Well, I don't want you to have to do without me and I don't want to do without you.'

'Well, that's that then, we are officially stuck with each other. Shall we get a cuppa?'

Pete walked forward and held her arm. 'I love you, Jacks.' His words were delivered without preamble and took her by surprise.

'You do?' She placed her hand on her belly, trying to fathom what kind of man would want to take her on. She had nothing to offer and was pregnant by somebody else.

He nodded.

'Oh God, Pete, I don't know what to say. I've had so much going on in my head . . .' She was flustered.

'I know and I think that love can start in the strangest of ways – things aren't always cut and dried. My mum always told me that being mates was the most important thing.'

'I think your mum's right.' She laughed, trying to ease the tension of the moment.

'And who knows what else we might become. It's not about how we start, Jacks, it's about how we finish up, and I want to finish up with you.'

'Is that a proposal?'

'Do you want it to be?'

She laughed again. Her thoughts turned to the boy who had run out on her. *Maybe the beginning isn't always the best bit* . . . 'I'm scared, Pete, and

I don't want to promise you anything that I can't deliver on.'

'Nothing's certain, Jacks.' He tapped his leg. 'Nothing. But if you think you want to give it a go, I'm up for it.' He smiled.

She smiled back at him. 'I think I do.'

He took a step closer and held her in his arms. 'Are we getting married, then?' he whispered.

'Yes, reckon we are, if we can find a frock to go over my fat stomach!' She giggled before pulling back to kiss him. It was a surprising kiss that left her feeling light-headed and wanting more.

CHAPTER 25

After the argument about Sven and everything, Jacks sat alone in the cold, dark kitchen, thinking things over. She stayed there until the sun crept over the neighbours' plants and into their garden and Jonty appeared in the doorway in search of breakfast cereal. His hair was mussed from sleep and his pyjama bottoms hung off his skinny frame.

'Mrs Palmer says I need to take in photos of my parents when they were babies for our collage project,' he announced as he carried the milk to the table.

'When do you need them by, Jont?' she asked. *Not today, please. Please, not today . . .*

'Today,' he answered as he slopped milk all over the floor.

'Perfect.' She gave a weak smile.

'Toto?' Ida called loudly.

'Nan's shouting!' Jonty yelled, despite sitting only a foot away from her.

'Yep, I heard her, mate. Eat your cereal.'

Jacks made her way up the stairs and walked into Ida's room.

'Morning, Mum.' She dug deep to find a jolly tone, smiling as she drew the curtains and opened the window. Sitting on the side of the mattress, she took her mum's thin hand into her own.

'Mum, I want to apologise. I'm sorry if I scared you the other night. I had no right to take you up to Clifton at that time of night. I should never have shouted at you and I'm very sorry.'

Ida reached out and stroked the hair from her daughter's forehead. It was a gesture so sweet, so touching and unexpected that it took Jacks' breath away. 'Pretty. Always a pretty girl,' she mumbled.

It was one of the only times Jacks could recall her mum giving her a compliment like that. She bent forward and placed her head on her mum's shoulder. 'I love you, Mum.' The words tumbled out, not often spoken aloud and never before as sincerely felt.

'I have some treasure,' her mum responded.

'Yes, I know.'

'I want that letter . . .' Ida whispered.

Jacks laughed and nodded as she stood, pulling back the cover to get the brand-new day started.

Grabbing the car keys from the hall half an hour later, Jacks was startled by the sight of her daughter on the stairs. Martha's complexion was pale and she had large dark circles beneath each eye.

'How are you feeling?' she asked, unable to maintain eye contact with her own daughter, in whose company she now felt a little shy.

Martha shrugged and looked tearful. Jacks didn't

want to argue, she didn't have the energy for it. She took a step towards her. Then Martha spoke.

'Gideon's mum says if it's a problem me being here then we can go to her house.'

'Did she now?' Jacks pictured Allison cleaning the spare room, passing judgement at every opportunity. 'A problem you being here, in the house you grew up in? The house you live in with your family? Don't be so daft.' She was insulted, embarrassed that Martha seemed to have no limits on what she discussed with this stranger. She spoke more sharply than she intended. 'Who does Allison think she is, encouraging you like that? And might I remind you that you are only just eighteen and you have school to attend, exams to take and rules to follow!'

Martha turned to walk back up the stairs. 'I don't think the rules apply any more, Mum. I'm having a baby.'

'And don't I know it!' Jacks snorted. 'You are taking those exams, Martha. At least have the sense to see that they are important!' An image of the coffee shop at Warwick University floated into her head. 'Oh God!' And yet again it hit her like a jolt to the chest, the realisation of how things had changed and how many doors had closed.

Jacks shouted up to her mum and instructed the kids that they needed to get a wiggle on. She went out to the car, switched on the ignition, and sat there and waited, watching as Ivor jumped into his van and roared away. She blushed, feeling like an intruder, as she caught the kiss Angela blew down from the upstairs window to her man.

Jonty jumped into the back seat. 'I don't think these photos are what I'm supposed to be taking.' He thumbed the prints in his hand. 'You and dad are teenagers in these photos and not babies and Mrs Palmer said we had to take pictures of you when you were a baby. These are rubbish.' He sighed.

'Just tell Mrs Palmer that they'll have to do for now and I'll have a search in the loft at the weekend, okay?'

'Be too late at the weekend, I need them now,' he muttered and immediately opened his comic.

Martha seemed to be taking an age and when she did appear, she was carrying a holdall that looked heavy. 'Do you need a hand? What have you got in there?' Jacks asked as she stowed it on the back seat next to her little brother.

'Just some of my stuff.' Martha spoke to the window as she buckled up her seatbelt.

'What do you mean, "some of your stuff"?'

Martha pulled back her shoulders as though this more determined stance might give her the confidence she was looking for. 'I just told you five minutes ago! I've decided I'm going to stay with Gideon and his mum for a bit.'

Jacks laughed, a sharp snort of shock. 'Don't be so silly, Martha! Of course you're not. Put your bag back in the house!'

Martha shook her head and adjusted her seatbelt.

'I'm not being silly. And if you don't want to take me to school, I understand. I'll get Gideon to pick me up.'

Jacks twisted so her back was against the driver's side window; she wanted to face her daughter. 'What are you playing at? There's no need for dramatics. You can't be serious. You think I'm going to let you go and shack up with your boyfriend and his mother, God knows where, so you can do God knows what? Of course I'm not! You're a child! You're still at school!' The last words came out more as a squeak.

'Mum, I'm going. I need a break.'

'*You* need a break?' Jacks didn't know what to say, she felt completely numb.

'Yes, I do! Every time you look at me, I feel guilty, sick and I don't want to feel like that.' She ran her hand over her stomach. 'I know you are angry and hurt, but you can't punish me every day, it's not fair and it's making me feel ill and anxious and I can't go on like that.'

'No, it's not like that, Martha! I love you. And I want to be there for you and the baby. You need your mum!' Even to her own ears she sounded desperate.

'Oh God!' Martha ran her hands over her face in exasperation. 'That's a new one! That's not what you've said so far and I'm not falling for it now just so you can keep an eye on me all the time and stop me going to see Gideon. Who, by the way, is not the enemy, he's my boyfriend and he's

291

sweet, which you'd realise if you bothered to get to know him, which you haven't. He's reading a baby book and every night he phones me before I go to sleep and tells me what he's learnt and what's happening to the baby and what we can expect. But instead of being with him, looking at the pictures and asking questions, I'm lying there, whispering, in a cramped room opposite my little brother, who's got Spiderman posters on the wall!'

'I can take them down if you want me to.' Jonty's small voice came from the back seat. Jacks had quite forgotten he was there.

Martha was crying now, hot, angry tears, but she smiled back at her brother. 'No, you don't have to do that, Jont. They're fine. I was just saying it's a bit too squashy for both of us.'

'I could go in with Mum and Dad?' he suggested.

Jacks felt her lip tremble, overwhelmed by her son's kindness. She indicated and pulled away, not wanting to make him late for school.

When they got to the school gates, Jonty ran inside with the comic in his hand. Martha hesitated in the passenger seat, slowly releasing her seatbelt.

'I don't want this to be any harder than it has to be. But honestly, Mum, this is the toughest, scariest thing I have ever done. And it's as if you don't even understand that.'

There was a moment of silence.

'I went for my first scan – it was incredible! I got a picture of this perfect little baby. But I couldn't share it with you. Can you imagine what that's like?'

'Yes.' Jacks heard the catch to her voice. 'I can. And I am so, so sorry. Please, can I see the picture?'

Martha got out of the car and retrieved her bag from the back seat. She was crying openly now. She unzipped the bag and threw a crumpled, grainy, black-and-white image on to the front passenger seat. 'Have it. There's another one at Gideon's house.'

The words twisted like a knife in Jacks' heart. 'When are you coming home?' She fought her tears, not wanting to cry there.

Martha stuck her head through the back door. 'I guess when it feels like home.'

Jacks watched as Martha made her way along the main walkway into the upper school, lugging her bag as she went. Stephanie Fletcher seemed to appear from nowhere, linking her arms with Martha and walking tall as if her friend was the trophy everyone wanted.

She unrolled the crumpled scan and traced her fingers over the tiny white shape.

Jacks changed her route halfway home, replaying conversations in her head with Sven, Pete and now Martha. The information and words exchanged swirled in her head like a badly tuned radio with all three voices fighting to be heard. She wanted a little clarity and thought a bit of straight-talking with a certain mechanic might help.

She pulled into the road where Gideon worked. She cut the engine, walked up the driveway and was hovering by the wall, wondering if she should go in and what she should say, when she heard his ready laugh and then his words, loud and clear.

'So it's all good. All good, Dad. She's lovely, I know you'll love her.'

'Well, I can't wait to meet her.'

'Shit!' Jacks murmured. The man sounded like his son: affable, confident and calm.

'This is a big step, son.'

Big step? That's an understatement! Jacks had to stop herself from jumping in and shrieking at them both.

'Having a baby isn't something you do on the spur of the moment, it's a lifetime of commitment.'

'I know. I know that.' Gideon's tone was firm. 'But I love her, Dad. She's incredible. She's smart and I can't believe she'd love someone like me, but she does and I'm never going to let her go. I want to give her a good life. I want to look after her and our baby. She makes me want to be a better person, if that makes sense.'

'It does. I'm proud of you, Gideon. I always worried that because things didn't work out with your mum and me, it might put you off becoming a dad and settling down. I'm glad it hasn't. And I know you've had a rough ride. But you're a great kid, a great man.'

Gideon laughed. 'That's the thing, Dad. I'm not having a go at you or Mum, but I know what it feels like to be in the middle when it goes wrong and I'm never going to put our little one in that situation. I'll work at it. If I can make Martha happy, then everything else should follow, shouldn't it? And I know we probably haven't had the best start, but it's not about that, is it? It's about the finish, about how we end up that matters.'

The man chuckled. 'Tell you what, son, you seem to have it a lot more figured out than I have and I'm twice your age!'

'I have got it figured out, Dad. I want to open my first garage in the next year. Start small, but I've done the projections and I reckon we could expand quite quickly. Then in a couple of years, when the brand is up and running, offer it as a franchise.'

'Wow! You've obviously given it a lot of thought.' His dad sounded impressed. As was Jacks, if reluctantly.

'I have. I can't wait to get started, to be my own boss. I've come up with a whole range of services and I want to run a training programme for people who have the interest but not the qualifications, help get them started too and tie them into my business so I keep the skills.'

'And you can do all that?' His dad sounded a little sceptical.

'All that and more. I've got mates who would love the jobs. I mean, we could do high end as well, total van refits for the surfies, conversions with living quarters, you name it!'

'How much do you need to get started, properly started?'

'I've found the perfect premises and the bank said they'd lend me some money, but they want a massive deposit and that's where we come unstuck. I mean, what do they think, that I've got cash stuffed under a mattress? I'm putting every penny I can away for the baby.' Gideon sighed.

'I wish I could help . . .'

'No, Dad, don't be daft. Who has that kind of cash? It's a shame, though. It would have been perfect. It's an old lock-up with a workshop on the ground floor, a nice space and a flat above – smart, you know, like an American loft. I took Martha to see it and she got it, instantly. She's got great vision. She wanted to put old tin garage signs on the walls and a big retro fridge in the corner and a football table—'

'They're all good ideas,' his dad agreed.

'Yeah, but pointless, cos I haven't got a deposit and I can't see how we can get one. It's gutting. I just want to do right for Martha and the little 'un.'

'You will, son. You'll see.'

Jacks fastened her coat and walked slowly back down the drive to her car. She drove home, her appetite for tearing a strip off her daughter's boyfriend somewhat abated. It wasn't that she was happy about the situation, far from it; she was now more confused than ever. He clearly wasn't some shyster about to run out on Martha and if anything this only irritated Jacks even more. She thought about Gideon calling Martha every night and relaying what he had learnt. This boy was making it very hard for her to hate him. She sighed as she thought about the cheque she had so readily destroyed and the difference that money would have made to the young couple. 'You can be stupid sometimes, Jacks,' she whispered to herself. 'Why don't you think before you act?' As she uttered the words, her dad's image floated to the front of her mind; she had to duck round it to check the rear-view mirror before turning right.

CHAPTER 26

Gina scooted to the end of her friend's bed, flung open the window and pulled out her cigarettes.

'You can't smoke in here, G!' Jacks had taken her pillow from beneath the duvet and placed it behind her back to make a seat.

'Why not? Your mum and dad smoke – they're not going to smell it. And if they come in, I'll lob it out the window.' She sparked the flint and took a drag, letting the wisps of smoke fill her mouth and stream out through her nostrils.

'I'd just rather you didn't,' Jacks pressed.

'What's wrong with you? You've been right moody all day and now I can't have a fag in your room, which I've done a million times before!'

Jacks retched and placed her hand over her mouth.

Gina stared at her mate. 'Are you going to be sick?' She glanced round the room, looking for a suitable receptacle, then took a final drag before flicking the butt out of the window and blowing the last of the smoke outside.

'Are you all right?' Gina crossed her legs and sat in the lotus position as she pondered her ashen-faced friend.

Jacks nodded. 'I've got something to tell you.'

'What?' Gina flicked through her notebook, scanning her homework tasks.

'I'm pregnant.'

Gina sprayed laughter over her friend and leant back against the wall. 'No you're not, you silly moo!'

'I am.' Jacks stared at her friend.

Gina sat up straight and shook her head, as if trying to fathom which question to ask first. 'Are you winding me up? You can't be!'

Jacks shook her head. 'I'm not joking. I am, G.'

'Who's the dad?'

'Pete.'

'*What?*' Gina squealed.

Jacks nodded. 'Pete Davies.'

'But . . . Pete Davies? He can't be! I knew you had that snog at Mr B's, but you've always gone on about what a waste of space he is and now you're telling me you've been shagging him?' Gina's mouth hung open.

Again, Jacks nodded.

The two girls sat in silence for some seconds. There was an awkwardness between them that they'd never felt before.

'I thought you told me everything?' Gina's voice was soft, hurt.

'I did! I do!' Jacks pleaded.

'Clearly not.' Gina gathered up her books and placed them in her oversized satchel.

'Don't go, G! Please!'

Gina ignored her request. 'I honestly don't know what to say to you. I feel like I've been punched. You and I don't have secrets. I can't believe it!' She shook her head.

'It just kind of happened.' Jacks sat with her eyes downcast.

'These things don't just "kind of happen". You make them happen.' Gina paused. 'Do your mum and dad know?'

Jacks nodded.

'Do you love him?'

Jacks gave a small shrug and nodded again.

'Fucking hell.' Gina picked up her bag and slung it over her shoulder. 'Fucking hell! Are you going to finish school?'

Jacks nodded for the third time.

Gina stared at a spot on the wallpaper, her thoughts far away. 'I feel like I've lost my dream. I thought we'd go to Bristol like we agreed, get a flat, get jobs. That's how I saw it happening. I figured that if we did it together, it would be possible, we'd look after each other. I really wanted that.' Gina left the room without looking back.

'I really wanted that too,' Jacks whispered as she slithered down her bed and buried her face in her pillow.

CHAPTER 27

Jacks drove straight back to Sunnyside Road after her aborted attempt to have a go at Gideon. As she pulled up outside her house she spotted Gina's Corsa parked further down the road. They met on the pavement.

'Oh God, Jacks, are you okay? Last night was a complete nightmare. I'm so sorry!' She looked at her friend, her usual smile replaced now by an expression of concern. 'Pete turned up at our house and I didn't know what to do! I couldn't lie to him, I didn't know what you'd said or whether you were home already from seeing Sven. I thought you'd probably had a row and he'd come to see Rob. I'm so sorry if I dropped you in it.'

'It wasn't your fault. You were in a horrible position. Sorry you got dragged into it.' Jacks opened the front door and shouted up the stairs. 'Home, Mum! Be up in a second!'

'It is my fault, kind of. I'm the one that suggested we go up to London. I should never have brought that bloody magazine over. I started all this!' Gina sighed.

'No, G, you didn't. It started years ago, long

before you saw him in a magazine. Don't worry about it.' Jacks was sincere. She made her way to the kitchen and filled a bowl with instant porridge oats, ready for the microwave.

'Is Pete okay? He seemed really mad last night.'

'He is mad and he has every right to be. He left early this morning without having breakfast. I didn't see him. But we needed to talk and clearing the air like that has to have been a good thing. It was long overdue.'

'There's something else.' Gina chewed her lip as her eyes darted from Jacks to the floor.

'What?'

Gina let out a long sigh. 'I googled Sven last night, had a good root around.'

'Well, hey, Miss Marple! What did you discover? Anything juicy?' She tried to keep the mood light, masking her fury at him having tried to buy her forgiveness.

'I printed this out.' Gina removed a sheet of A4 paper from her bag and unfolded it. 'Here.' She pointed at the top of a paragraph. 'Read that bit.' She took a seat at the table.

'Sven Lundgren blah blah blah . . .' Jacks scanned the words. 'Whose first super-yacht was called . . .'

Gina smiled. 'Yep. That's the bit.'

Jacks reread the line. 'Was called *Lady Jacqueline*.'

'How about that! He named his bloody boat after you!'

Jacks nodded but wasn't really paying attention. She was busy studying the following paragraph:

The Lady Jacqueline *was the first of the fleet for Somniorum Yachts, which takes its name from the Latin,* Lacus Somniorum, *meaning 'Lake of Dreams'.*

Jacks felt conflicted. A small part of her wanted to whoop with joy at this revelation, but it didn't change the fact that he had left her. He had known she was pregnant and he had abandoned her, leaving her alone to pick up the pieces of her broken life.

'And there's something else – this is the last thing, I promise!' Gina squirmed.

Jacks looked at her mate. 'What else did you discover?'

'Nothing. I didn't discover anything, but I did speak to him.'

'To Sven?'

'Yes. He called me this morning.' Gina tapped the table.

Jacks wished her stomach didn't keep jumping at the sound of his name.

Gina continued. 'He stayed in town last night and is heading back to London today. He flies back to San Francisco tomorrow, but he asked if you would go and meet him.'

'Why would he want to meet me? I thought I was pretty clear where we stood last night.' Jacks stirred her mum's porridge and then filled the kettle for her tea, thinking about how he had let her down.

'I'm just the messenger.' Gina held up her palms. 'But he sounded pretty desperate. He's going to

303

be on the Marine Parade, where he was parked last night.'

'When?'

Gina looked over her friend's shoulder at the kitchen clock. 'Now. He said he'd wait for an hour and then he'd be off.'

Jacks recalled Pete's words. *'You make sure, Jacks. You make sure things are sorted properly.'* She had to put the lid on this once and for all.

'I'll just run this up to Mum. Do you mind sitting with her for half an hour, G?'

'Course I will. Take your time.' She squeezed Jacks' arm.

Jacks drove to the Marine Parade and parked her Skoda behind his flash car, which she could see in the daylight was a Ferrari. She checked her face in the mirror and ran her fingers through her fringe before furtively walking round and climbing into his front seat.

'Thank you for coming to meet me,' he whispered, sounding relieved.

'Gina said you were heading off, so I thought it best we didn't leave anything unsaid.' She nodded, not wanting to give him the satisfaction of a smile.

'I couldn't sleep last night.'

'Me either. Seeing you unsettled me. And it upset Pete.'

'I'm sorry.' He pushed a button on the dashboard. The engine roared.

'Where are we going, Sven? I've got things to

do. Just say what you need to and then we can go our separate ways.'

'Please, Jacks, drive with me for a bit. For old times' sake.'

Jacks sighed and shook her head. 'Okay, but make it quick.'

He indicated and pulled out into the morning sun, pointing the car away from the seafront. The car was very low to the ground and seemed to glide along the roads, which were clearly still familiar to Sven. Jacks thought how much Jonty would love a ride in this snazzy sporty number. She felt guilty as she pictured her family, only a couple of miles from them but a whole world away. She was looking at streets that she strolled daily, but it felt different, seeing them from inside the tinted windows of such a beautiful vehicle.

Sven pulled up by the path that led to the playing field.

'Oh no!' Jacks laughed, in spite of herself. 'What are we doing here?' She shook her head.

'Come on, humour me.' Sven jumped from the car and opened the boot, from where he pulled two very puffy, silky soft, silver jackets. 'Put this on,' he instructed.

Jacks took the coat, which was as light as a feather, and did as she was told. It was surprisingly warm.

They sidled through the open gates. Sven marched ahead as they tramped across the playing field, tripping in the dips and stumbling over the uneven tufts. Their clumsiness, and their nerves, made them laugh.

'This is the spot!' he announced, before sitting down on the wet grass. 'Come on.' He patted the ground by his side.

'I can't. I'm too old for mucking about like this, Sven.'

'Come on! Just sit down!'

Jacks lowered herself on to the grass and sat, hugging her knees and feeling awkward. They sat in silence for a while, neither wanting to break the magic that had transported them back across time.

Eventually, when their breathing was in sync, Sven whispered, 'When I picture you, it's here, in this field. I still find it amazing that we are so minuscule, so tiny in this great big universe!'

She smiled ruefully. 'I remember you telling me how to spot the Pole Star. I still look for it regularly and even now, every time I stare up at that big old star, I think of you.'

'I thought we were going to conquer the world,' he said quietly. 'Together.'

'Looks like you didn't need me after all,' she retorted. 'You seem to have done all right.' Her tone was clipped, laced with sarcasm. 'One thing I just can't understand: why did you make out you didn't recognise me at the Boat Show? I was so hurt, Sven. Embarrassed.'

'I wanted to hurt you. God, it sounds so childish. I'm such an idiot and I'm sorry, really sorry. But I wanted to hurt you for not having waited for me.

I swore I would never come to you, you would have to come to me, to want me.'

'But it was you that buggered off, not me,' she said evenly.

They were silent for some seconds until he shrugged and turned towards her. 'Thing is, Jacks, I was just a kid. A frightened kid with this big future ahead of me, a future my parents had plotted out for me. And I didn't know I had options. I may have been acting like the big man, but I was only just eighteen and I was scared.'

'And so was I!' she said heatedly. 'Left to literally carry the baby all by myself.' She clenched her jaw, pictured the schoolboy Sven, tried to put herself in his young head. She softened her tone. 'And let me ask you one thing, if you had had options, Sven,' she asked, 'would you still have gone?' She held his eye.

He took a deep breath and nodded at the ground. 'Probably.' Shaking his head, he carried on, hesitantly. 'When I found the courage and called your mum, I couldn't believe you were already married to one of the sheep-boys. I just couldn't believe it! I've thought about it a lot over the years. I have everything I ever wanted, you know, but last night I could taste that jealousy again, the rawness of it – you picking one of the football team over me . . .' He gave a small laugh.

'You might have had options, Sven, but what were mine? Pregnant and single at eighteen – what were my prospects? And don't you dare call

Pete names! He did an amazing thing. He rescued me, gave me a home and a family life. He's a good man. He was wonderful, did all he could to make things better for me. He was more than I deserved.' She looked Sven full in the face. 'He has loved me and your daughter ever since, been the best dad any girl could hope for. We are both lucky to have him.'

Sven winced and turned away. 'Did you love him?'

Jacks shook her head. 'No. Not then, not immediately. I almost played at it at first. It came later, when we had the baby. And now I do. I love him very much.' She pictured her husband wheeling her mum down the hallway to eat the tea he had cooked, heard his voice offering to fetch her glasses for her. A kind man, a good man, with whom she shared a life, a family.

'I see.'

'Don't get me wrong, I was devastated when you went.' She stared at the horizon. 'And I think I've spun that over the years, made you into my knight in shining armour, fantasising that with you my life would have been perfect.'

'Life's never perfect,' he said.

'I think I've figured that out. I've also realised that it doesn't have to be perfect – you just have to be happy.' She laughed as though this was a revelation. Her mum's words floated into her head: *'Selfish people are very hard to love.'* She looked at Sven, realising how easy it was to love Pete, the least selfish man she had ever met.

'I agree and I've nearly got my perfect formula for happiness.' He moved a little closer towards her.

'You have?' she asked suspiciously.

'I have. I'm happy as long as the adrenalin is pumping, things are moving quickly and I have a large bed and a glass of chilled champagne waiting for me, wherever I decide to lay my head. No burdens, no ties.' Sven ran a finger over the sleeve of her jacket. 'Come with me, Jacks. Just you and me, no distractions. Let's go chase adventure!'

Jacks stared at him, this stranger, who was looking at her so eagerly. 'Have you not understood anything of what I've been saying, Sven? My life is all the adventure I need. My perfect formula is lying next to Pete, looking up at our ugly lampshade and knowing my kids are safely asleep in the room next door.'

She realised the truth of her words as she spoke them. 'He was there when I needed someone and he didn't abandon me. He stuck by me, always has.'

'And I didn't.'

'No, Sven, you didn't. You went to America. You kept telling me how easy it would be for me to pack a bag and go, but I can see now that it would have been just as easy for you to unpack your bag and stay.'

Sven looked across the field with an expression of resignation. 'I loved you, Jackie Morgan. I really loved you. What we had was real, forever real. It was magical. And I thought you felt the same.'

'I did,' she whispered.

'But not now?' It was the last throw of the dice.

'Not now.' She shook her head, resigned. There was just one final thing that needed clearing up. She took a big breath, steeling herself. She knew she had to ask, it was only fair, no matter how painful.

'Do you want to see Martha? Know anything about her?' Her heart hammered in anticipation of his answer. She dreaded the prospect of having to confess everything to her little girl when she was at her most vulnerable and she hated the thought of how much Pete would be hurt in the process.

Sven shook his head.

Jacks exhaled slowly and felt a tumble of giddy relief. 'I guess that's what "no burdens, no ties" means?'

'I guess so. It would all be too complicated,' he murmured.

She stood, unzipped the silver jacket and handed it to Sven. 'I won't ever forget you, Sven. But it's time I moved on. We aren't kids any more. I have a family, kids of my own and a husband who has given up so much for our happiness. He's my real knight in shining armour.'

Sven's mouth narrowed; he looked hurt. He remained where he was as Jacks started to walk towards the gate. 'Can I give you a lift?' he called.

Jacks pictured climbing into her dad's little Skoda back on the Marine Parade, feeling something close to happiness. She laughed out loud. 'I don't think so.'

'Jacks?' he shouted.

'What?'

He twisted round. 'My first yacht in the group, she was called *Lady Jacqueline* and she was beautiful – different, unique, unlike any other. She was ready to take to the high seas and conquer the world.'

Oh she was, Sven, she was.

'I never thought she'd become washed up, stranded in the place she was supposed to sail away from . . .' His words were cutting.

Jacks turned, wrapped her arms around her cheap cardigan and stared at the forlorn figure in the middle of the school playing field. When she spoke, her voice was firm.

'No, Sven, that's not what happened. She decided to stay put and let the world come to her. And it did. And you were wrong, you know: home is not a state or a feeling, it's a place. And for me, it's here. I'm home.'

Jacks couldn't see Gina's Corsa as she pulled up, but she did spot Pete's van. It was unusual for him not to be on site at that time of day, especially as it wasn't a cricket day. She poked her head into the empty kitchen and then crept up the stairs and hovered by Ida's bedroom door.

Her mum was under the covers with her fussy bed jacket on and her head propped against her favourite pillow. Pete was sitting in the chair to the side of the bed, still wearing his heavy work

311

boots. He was leaning forward with his elbows on his knees and in his hands was a sheet of paper. Ida was staring at him intently. Her gnarled fingers gripped the edge of her pink candlewick bedspread. Jacks leant against the doorframe and listened. Pete's voice was low and gentle.

'And so, my darling, that is all my news. I remember the day we met – you looked so pretty. Do you remember that day?' Pete paused and looked up at Ida, who had a flicker of a smile around her lips. He coughed and went back to his sheet of paper. 'It was the best day of my life and I will never forget a moment of it. Take care of yourself, Ida. I will miss you every single day. Keep this letter safe and know that I will be thinking about you even if I can't be with you. I love you forever and ever. Your loving husband, Don.'

Jacks felt the tears pool as she watched her kind man reading to her mum. Her wonderful man, who worked hard for his family and had been by her side in sickness and in health, for richer and for poorer. She knew she was lucky to have him.

Pete folded the sheet and placed it in the drawer of Ida's bedside cabinet. 'If you need me to read it to you again, then just shout.'

'Dear, dear Toto.' Ida smiled and closed her eyes.

Pete pulled the cover up to her chin and patted her arm. 'That's it, Ida, you have a bit of a nap.' He crept backwards from the room and turned to find his wife crying in the hallway.

'I had a great idea as I was driving in,' he said.

'It suddenly struck me, why make her wait for her letter, why not just make the letter arrive? And it did the trick. She seems settled.'

'Thank you. Thank you, Pete.'

He pulled her to him and held her in his strong arms. They stood for a few minutes, feeling the solidity of each other beneath their palms.

'Why are you crying? Don't tell me you just saw the post-match analysis for City at the weekend? We've had a bloody shocker!' He kissed her head as she leant into him.

'I love you, Pete. I really love you.'

'I know.' He squeezed her tight.

Jacks stood back and looked up at her husband. 'I am sorry. I'm sorry!'

Pete nodded, keeping his eyes fixed on hers. 'Are we all right now? All sorted, girl?'

Jacks smiled and nodded. 'Yep.'

'Good.' Pete sighed. 'Then let that be the end of it. Cup of tea?'

'Yes, please. Cup of tea would be lovely.' She touched his arm. 'I heard you reading to my mum. That was a lovely thing to do.'

'Well, as I say, I figured if she actually got what she wanted, then she might stop fretting about it.'

'You are very wise.'

'Don't know about that. Reckon if I was a bit wiser I'd have kept old Giddyup away from Martha.'

Jacks knew they had to broach the subject. 'She's gone to stay at his house, with his mum.'

Pete nodded. 'I know. She sent me a text.'

'She told me a few things this morning about how she's been feeling and it's made me think—'

'Let's chat downstairs.' He reached out and held her hand as they made their way slowly down the bare, creaking stairs to the kitchen.

Jacks lowered herself into a chair. 'I think you're right. It's not the worst thing that could happen, Pete, is it? Not really.'

Pete placed the mug in front of her as he spoke. 'It's not, love. There's many a bloke that would have done a runner, but not him. He proper loves her and she loves him. And when you proper love someone, that's what you do, you stick around no matter how hard the going gets.'

Jacks took his hand, thinking of her earlier encounter. 'I know. It's just not what I wanted for her. She's so smart!'

'Yes she is and that's why we have to trust her to make her own life.'

'I know, I know,' Jacks conceded, staring into her tea as though that was where the answer might lie.

Pete's voice was steady. 'I was thinking about how your mum and dad reacted. After the initial upset, they were lovely, accepting, and it made everything easier, didn't it? And then I came along and they were good about that too. Imagine if we'd had to deal with hostility from them as well. That would have been tough. As I see it, we've got two choices: we either support her, help her, love her, like we have done since the day she was born, or we lose her. And that would be the worst thing. It's that simple.'

'I don't want to lose her! I really don't,' Jacks cried.

'Then it's an easy choice, love.' Pete rubbed his palms together. 'We know, don't we, that you have to stick together, work things through.'

'Yes we do.'

'And you're sure we're okay?' He looked at her, his words heavy with meaning.

Jacks held his gaze. 'I saw him again, just to say goodbye.' She sniffed.

'Still have one of his mum's old jumpers on, did he?'

Jacks laughed and shook her head. 'I feel like I've put a few ghosts to bed.'

'Good.' He was firm. 'All I want is to make you all happy. That's all I ever wanted.'

Jacks stood and wrapped her arms around his neck. 'And you do, my lover, you do.' She kissed him hard on the cheek. 'He offered us money, said he wanted to help. I told him we didn't want it, we didn't need anything.'

Pete nodded. 'We don't miss what we've never had, eh, girl?'

Jacks sighed and sat down next to him.

There was a banging noise overhead. 'What in God's name is that?'

'Ah, yes, I gave your mum a stick, told her to bang on the floor if she needed anything.'

'Think I preferred the bloody bell!' Jacks stood.

'Coming, Mum!' she shouted as she trotted up the stairs.

Later that night, Jacks sat in the car with the engine off and stared up at the windows of the Parks' house in Alfred Street. Not that there was anything to see. It was an inky blue night and the lights inside were on and the curtains drawn. She imagined Martha indoors with Allison and Gideon, eating her tea, watching TV, lying around in her pyjamas, living in this house to which she had no connection. Picturing the scenes of domesticity was like sticking a knife into her gut. Half an hour passed and then her mobile buzzed on the dashboard, making her jump.

'Where are you, love?' Pete's voice was soft.

'I'm in Alfred Street,' she admitted, 'just sitting outside their house.'

'What are you doing that for?'

Jacks shrugged. 'I just want to see her.'

'Do you want me to come and sit with you?' he offered.

'No. But thank you. It's best you're there in case Mum wakes up. And Jonty's asleep.'

'Have you seen anything yet?' Pete hated the thought of his daughter being away as much as Jacks did. Jacks had spied him earlier on, laying a palm against Martha's pillow and arranging her soft toys on the end of her bed, like he used to when she was little.

'No.'

'Are you going to knock on the door?'

'No.'

'Oh, Jacks, is this what you're reduced to? Sitting in the street trying to catch a glimpse of her? It's not going to help, you know.'

She felt the familiar hot trickle of tears. 'I miss her. I miss my daughter and I feel like everything is falling apart, Pete. I keep thinking about when I was little and my dad built me a Wendy house on the grass round the back. I loved it. I used to sit in it and make out I was cooking the tea and expecting visitors. But we left it outside, uncovered, all winter and the glue got wet and the plywood rotted. It collapsed and lay on the lawn in bits. It wasn't my house any more, just these flat, useless panels, no longer fit for purpose. And that's like my life. Everything has gone flat, fallen apart and I don't know how to put it all back together again. I don't know where to start.'

'You can start by coming home. Sitting in the street by yourself will do you no good at all.'

'She said she'd come back when it felt like home. But it won't ever feel like home, not while she's not in it and not talking to me.'

'She'll come back, Jacks, I promise.'

Jacks started the engine. 'God, I hope you're right.'

'Come home, Jacks, and have an early night. You're tired.'

She took one last look up at the windows before reluctantly pulling out of Alfred Street.

CHAPTER 28

Eighteen Years Earlier

It was early evening at Weston-super-Mare General Hospital when Ida drew her eyes away from the little telly that was mounted high on the wall in the corner of the waiting room. The local news was on, but with the sound muted she could only guess at the stories from the pictures and the smiles or frowns of the presenters. She watched as Don came back through the swing doors and into the room, shrugging his shoulders and wringing his hands as if the outside cold still clung to him.

'Where have you been?' she snapped, her voice full of mistrust. Twenty minutes was plenty enough time for him to have been up to something.

He turned to look at her, removed his coat and placed it on the empty chair alongside. 'To make a phone call.' His tone was level. He hitched his trousers, sat down and rested his ankle on his opposite knee.

Ida shook her head.

'Oh, the head shaking now? Even here, today?'

318

Don swirled his hand in the air, as if she might be unaware of where they were.

'Do you think I want to be that person?' she whispered, rearranging her handbag on her lap, grateful for the prop.

He folded his arms across his chest. 'I don't think you know how to be anything else any more.'

'And whose fault is that?' She stared at him.

'Mine.' He closed his eyes and bowed his head. 'Everything is always my fault. I think we established that a long time ago.'

'Do you know, you are right.' She sighed. 'I don't know how to be any other person and that's the worst part of it for me.' Her lower lip trembled. 'I never wanted to be like this, to live like this!'

Don snapped the newspaper, opening it wide and lifting it to cover his upper body and face. There was a brief pause in their bickering, then Ida broke the silence again.

'It doesn't feel like eighteen years ago that *I* was giving birth. I remember every second of that day like it was yesterday. Every single second.' She smiled at the memory.

'Ah yes.' His voice floated from behind the red-top. 'You had a go at me then as well, I recall.'

'And do you remember why?'

He laughed loudly and let one side of his newspaper fall, freeing a hand so that he could rub his tired eyes. 'As if I could for one second forget.'

There was another moment or two of silence.

'Do you think . . .' She hesitated. 'Do you think,

if things had been different for us, if we'd been different parents, given a better example maybe, we'd still be sitting here now?'

Before Don had a chance to answer, the nurse popped her head round the door. 'Just to let you know, your daughter's doing great. No news yet, but shouldn't be too much longer!' She smiled and retreated, eager to get back to wherever she was needed.

'Come on, push!' Pete shouted, gripping Jacks' hand inside his.

Jacks screwed her eyes shut and tried, really tried. Her face was contorted and scarlet, her head bent down to her chest. Then she gasped and lay back against the pillow, suddenly limp and breathless. 'I'm too tired. I can't . . . I can't do this any more.'

It had been seven hours of hard work. Her muscles were tired, her will was waning and she desperately wanted to sleep. The gas and air were now proving ineffective and they were too far into proceedings for an epidural to be of any real use.

Pete leant forward and placed his hand on her back, talking directly into her face. 'Yes, you can, Jacks! You can do anything. Anything. And you are nearly done. Nearly there, love. Isn't that right, Cath?' He looked across at the midwife, who was sitting on a stool with his wife's feet by her ears, her head bobbing between the stirrups.

'Yep, he's right. One or two big pushes and

we are going to have ourselves a little bibber babber!'

Jacks threw her head back and smiled in spite of her exhaustion, picturing her baby, who very soon she would be meeting. Her long fringe was stuck to her face with sweat; she was thirsty but wary of drinking as she didn't want to complicate matters by needing to pee.

'Just think, years ago, you'd have simply dropped your little one behind a bush and carried on working in the fields!' Pete grinned.

'Not sure that's helpful.' Cath smiled curtly at the nervous dad-in-waiting, who so far had been doing a grand job of supporting his young wife.

'I'm just saying it's the most natural thing in the world, isn't it?' He repositioned his gown, which had slipped down his arms.

'Doesn't feel natural right now.' His wife sighed. 'It feels like hard bloody work! Don't reckon I could go back to work in the fields!' She puffed.

'You don't have to worry about that, girl. You've got me.' He beamed. 'I'll go to work and bring you whatever you need. That's my job, to look after you, and I always will, always.' He squeezed her hand. 'I'm a footballer.' Pete beamed with pride at the midwife. The novelty of talking about his new role as the star striker for Weston-super-Mare AFC still hadn't worn off.

'Oh God, here we go, I can feel it coming again!' Jacks pushed her bottom down into the mattress and leant forward. With her teeth gritted and her eyes once again tightly closed, her face got redder and redder with the exertion. 'Oh! Oh shit!' she managed, breathless now.

'That's it! Breathe, my love! You are doing great, Jacks! Breathe!' Pete puffed with bloated cheeks and lips pursed. All inhibitions now gone, he was lost in the moment. As he gripped her hand and squeezed her shoulder in support, he wasn't thinking about his footballing career; he was her husband, about to become a dad. The two of them weren't simply recent school-leavers now; they were grown-ups, new parents.

'Don't leave me!' she shrieked.

'I won't! I'm not going anywhere. I'll be right here. We're a team, you and me.'

'Not just now, we're not.' She sighed. 'Don't leave me! Not ever!'

He looked her in the eye. 'I won't. Ever. I love you.'

She stared at her husband. 'And I love you, Pete, I really, really do! I love you!' She sobbed.

'You do?' he asked, beaming with joy.

She nodded. 'I do! Oh God! Oh God!' She panted the words. 'It's really happening. I can feel it!'

'This is it!' Cath said. 'The head is crowning. Nearly there! Come on, one big push for me, Jackie! Nearly there!'

And then, in a matter of seconds, after a guttural shout that seemed to come from deep inside, they heard the sound of crying. It was a stuttering call from new lungs. Cath lifted the baby girl and placed her on her mum's chest, still attached by the umbilical cord that had been her lifeline for the last thirty-nine weeks.

Jacks lay back against the pillow with her small, wet child on her chest, kissing her damp head as her little fingers flexed in the air and her tiny mouth sought her mother's skin.

'She's . . . she's so beautiful!' Pete managed through his tears. 'Hello! Hello, my little girl,' he whispered as he kissed her head with its soft covering of down.

'Can someone go and tell my mum and dad?' Jacks asked.

'Sure.' Cath smiled. She walked down the corridor and into the waiting room. Ida and Don both stood up, side by side, desperate for news. 'Hello, Granny and Grandpa! You have a beautiful granddaughter. Mum and baby are both doing well.'

Don turned to his wife and pulled her towards him. Reaching up, she held him close, enjoying the moment as she inhaled the scent of the man she loved, the man she had always loved.

'Fancy that! Our clever girl, eh?' Don whispered into her hair, kissing her scalp.

Meanwhile, the cord had been cut and the baby had been checked. She was perfect.

The obstetrician washed his hands in the little sink at the side of the room. 'Have we got any names yet?' he asked.

'Yes.' Jacks nuzzled her new daughter with her mouth and nose. 'This is Martha.'

The doctor wandered over as he dried his hands, smiling at the little family who were huddled together, staring at each other in wonder. 'Well, hello there, Miss Martha. Welcome to this funny old world!'

Jacks felt her tears flow again at his words. 'Hey, Martha, I'm your mum. Yes I am, I'm your mum and I am so pleased to meet you. We've been waiting for you, your dad and me, and we already love you so, so much.'

'We do,' Pete confirmed. 'We really do.'

He beamed at his wife. 'You are the cleverest woman in the whole wide world!' He kissed her firmly on the cheek. 'That was amazing. Just amazing. I can't believe we did it, can't believe what you did! You were brilliant.' He kissed her again. 'I'm a dad, Jacks! Can you believe it? I'm a dad!'

'You are, Pete. You're Miss Martha's dad.' She smiled at her husband.

Don sat forward in the lounge chair, rubbing his hands. 'Shall I make a fire? Is she warm enough?' He bent over the carrycot and stared at his sleeping granddaughter. 'Will you look at her? One week old and already a proper bobby-dazzler!'

Jacks smiled at her dad, unsure if being a bobby-dazzler was a good thing. 'No! It's not cold, she's fine, Dad.' She grinned, happy in the afterglow of childbirth and feeling very clever at having produced such a beautiful child. As if on cue, Martha lifted her fists and with a red angry face let out a little cry.

'Someone knows it's teatime,' Pete commented from the table, where he was studying the back pages of the newspaper.

Jacks felt her nipples tighten and her milk begin to trickle. 'Yep, come on, let's get you fed.' She carefully lifted her baby girl from the cot and carried her upstairs to her old room.

Her mum scurried ahead of her and placed two extra pillows by the headboard. 'Do you want a blanket?' she asked, hands clasped at her chest, desperate to help in some way.

'If you like, Mum. Then come and chat to me if you want?'

Ida nodded and reappeared with the pink candlewick bedspread, which she tucked over her daughter's legs. She perched awkwardly on the end of the bed, looking away as Jacks pulled the press studs on her maternity top and released the flap of her nursing bra. Jacks noted the way her mum kept her body turned until Martha was latched on and the muslin covered most of her breast. It made her smile that her mum and dad were so prudish, even when it came to feeding the baby. She suspected it was an age thing. It suited her fine; she didn't particularly want them seeing her body and had absolutely no interest in seeing theirs.

'She's adorable, Jackie.'

'She is.' When it came to her little girl, there was no room for modesty; Martha was, in her opinion, the most perfect child ever created.

'And Pete seems to have taken to it.'

'He has, he's wonderful. I express milk and he does the night feeds, everything. Don't know what I'd do without him.'

'Well, doesn't look like you will have to do without him. He's not about to go gallivanting off anywhere.' Ida shook her head, her tone and choice of words as close as she could get to mentioning Sven's name and what he'd done.

'Martha's lucky,' Jacks said. 'She's got the best dad in the world.'

Ida raised an eyebrow. 'I thought you had?' she said, her tone clipped.

'Well, yes, of course, but I reckon Pete will shape up to be as good as my dad.' Jacks stroked her daughter's head as she guzzled.

'We can only hope!' Ida clenched her teeth.

'It takes a lot to be a good dad. I think support is the most important thing,' Jacks said. 'Don't you?'

Ida considered this. 'I think a happy mum makes a happy dad, a good dad. A dad that considers the family unit as a whole, doesn't exclude anyone.'

'Or maybe it's a mum that doesn't let herself be excluded.' Jacks held her mum's eye.

Ida stood and arranged the curtains before walking to the door. 'If only it were that easy.' She smiled and left Jacks alone to feed her baby girl.

Ida heard Don and Pete shouting at the TV as they watched the match together; they were making a racket. She trod the last step as the telephone in the hallway rang.

'Hello?'

There was a beep before she heard the voice and when it came through, the voice had a faint echo, as though it was a long, long way away.

'Mrs Morgan?'

'Yes?'

'This is Sven . . .' She heard him swallow. 'I'm—'

'I know who you are.'

There was a pause. 'Can I speak to Jacks? It's important.' He sounded in a rush.

'No, you listen to me, this is important. Jacqueline doesn't want to talk to you. She is with her husband at the moment—'

'Her husband?'

'Yes, that's right. Didn't you know? She married Pete Davies, a lovely, lovely boy.'

CHAPTER 29

Jacks woke as the sun crept through the gap at the top of the curtains, a full twenty minutes before her alarm. She tussled with her dressing gown in the dark, alerted by the sound of vomiting that was coming from the bathroom. Was Jonty not well?

She hurried across the landing and stopped at the open door. There, sitting on the floor, was Martha! Back home after two months away that had felt like a lifetime! The poor girl was retching and groaning as she vomited into the toilet bowl, but Jacks could only feel a swell of happiness at the sight of her. *My little girl. She's here, she's home!*

'Oh, Martha!' she gasped. 'Are you okay, love?'

Martha shook her head. 'Mum . . .' was all she managed before the next bout hit.

Jacks sat on the floor behind her daughter, resting against the bathtub as she rubbed her back, just as she had over the years whenever she was ill. She pictured Martha as a little girl, her knobbly spine inside a nylon nightie with a Disney princess on the front.

'Do you remember when you wanted to be called

Kida after the girl from that Disney *Atlantis* movie?' she asked.

Martha nodded.

'And you wouldn't answer to anything else for weeks. I'd stand there yelling up the stairs, "Kida, your tea's ready!" Neighbours must have thought I was mad.'

'Thank you for not changing my name like I asked you to,' Martha mumbled between groans.

'That's okay.'

Martha leant forward, propelled by the violent sickness that gripped her. Jacks scooped her daughter's long hair into a ponytail and held it in her palm while nature took its course. Finally, Martha rocked back on her haunches and Jacks handed her some loo roll to wipe her mouth with. She threw a towel over her trembling legs. Martha's bump was impossible to ignore now.

'I feel horrible. My boobs hurt and I'm still really sick.' Martha turned and placed her head on her mum's lap. It was as if she had forgotten they were warring.

Jacks stroked her hair away from her face and cooed soothingly.

'It's so tough, Mum. I know I need to study, but I feel so sick.'

'It usually passes, love, and they say it can be a sign of a good strong pregnancy.' She remembered her own bouts of morning sickness, trying to be ill in silence, not wanting to alert anyone into thinking that something was amiss. And Pete turning up at school and giving her a packet of water biscuits. He had smiled at her as they'd whispered in the corridor; Martha at that point was still their little secret. That was what they had agreed, until he could book the Register Office and silence the gossips.

'Dad said I should come back, that it was making you sad, and I don't want that.'

'I didn't hear you come back. I'd have stayed up if I'd known.'

'Dad said Gideon can stay on the sofa some nights and that I can go to his when I want. And I do want to be with him all the time,' Martha mumbled, 'but I can't because I'm still at school and I don't want to upset you and I know you don't want me to see him. But he's this baby's dad and I don't want him to miss out on anything and I love him. I need him, Mum. I really do.'

Jacks closed her eyes and whispered to her little girl. 'I know. And it will all be okay.' She thought of how much harder things would have been without Pete's strong arms and kind words to soothe her every night. 'These things have a funny way of working out.'

She heard a short laugh from the landing and looked behind her to see Pete standing in his pyjama bottoms and his vest. 'Now you know my secret. It's what you say when you can't think of a solution.'

She smiled at her husband. 'I bloody can't.'

'We'll do it together.' He smoothed her head.

Jacks reached up and kissed his calloused palm. 'Like always.'

Jonty appeared and sat on the floor behind his dad and closed the door behind him. It was a second or two before he asked, 'Why are we all in the bathroom?'

And they all laughed, even Martha, who managed a giggle despite her nausea.

Jacks dropped the kids at school, happy to learn that Martha had not missed a day in the last few weeks. There was a lively atmosphere in the car, everyone clearly enjoying the return to normality. She watched how Martha placed her school bag over her neat little bump. Her daughter's embarrassment made her sad.

'Only me, Mum!' she yelled as soon as she got back home. 'Up in a sec!'

She was grateful that Ida had slept in, giving her and the kids time to chat. Even Pete seemed his old self. In fact, no, better than that; he seemed happier than he had in an age.

She placed the bowl of porridge on her mum's tray and climbed the stairs.

'Morning! It's a lovely brand-new day! Martha is home. Can you believe that? She's finally home.' She delivered the tray and drew the curtains. 'Thought we'd go for a wander today, what do you think? A nice stroll and a bit of fresh air, do us the world of good.'

Jacks showered and changed her mum, wrapped

a soft blanket around her legs and pushed her mottled feet into her shoes that fastened with Velcro. As she pushed Ida out on to the street and popped the double-knotted carrier bag into the wheelie bin on the way out, Angela from next door was coming through her gate.

'Morning, Ange.'

'Morning, ladies. How are you, Ida?'

'She's great.' Jacks answered on her mum's behalf. 'How's Jayden doing?'

'Getting big! He managed to sit up last night. You probably heard the champagne corks popping and the trumpet fanfare – Ivor went nuts! You'd have thought that child had won an Olympic gold from watching his dad.'

'Ah, bless.' Jacks laughed. 'Maybe he will one day, who knows!'

'God, you sound like Ivor. He's already googled flights to all the major capitals of the world and tried to work out how much it might cost for us to get to them in 2032!'

'That's hilarious! What's Jayden getting a medal in?'

Angela tutted. 'The hundred-metre sprint, of course.'

'Of course!' Jacks laughed. 'I like his confidence and his planning. And why not? Who knows what course his little life might take?'

There was an awkward silence while both women considered Martha's altered course, how excited they had been when she got her offer from Warwick.

'Jacks, I hope it's okay, but I wanted to drop these off for Martha.' Angela lifted her arms to reveal a Moses basket, a stack of white vests and tiny babygrows and a couple of sleep suits.

'Oh, Ange!' Jacks stared at the paraphernalia. It made it real, this was stuff for a baby. Martha's baby. 'That's so kind of you. She's busy at school, her exams kick off next week.' She took the items into her outstretched arms.

'Oh God, rather her than me. Tell her good luck in case we don't see her.' She pointed at the Moses basket. 'Jayden's grown out of so much stuff, but if Martha doesn't want any of it, no biggie, just tell her to pass it on or give it to the charity shop, whatever. Just thought she might be able to make use of it.'

'Thank you, Ange. She'll be touched.'

'No worries! Better get back, his lordship's in his high chair in the kitchen, probably redecorating the walls and ceiling with his juice cup!'

Jacks returned inside and stashed the basket and clothes on top of the cardboard boxes in the hallway.

As she pushed the wheelchair to the seafront, she shared her thoughts with her mum. 'That was nice of Ange to bring those things in for the baby, wasn't it? Makes it quite real, though, the fact that a little girl or boy is going to fill out those clothes,' she said. 'I don't know, Mum, you think you know where you are headed and then something comes along and the rug is pulled out from under you. Things change so quickly. That's what I've struggled with.' She swivelled the chair round a corner, avoiding a pothole. 'I thought Martha's path was set – I thought mine was. And I suppose, if I'm being honest, one of the reasons I'm so hurt is that I saw my life improving too. I loved the idea of going to stay with her while she was at uni, seeing her with her gang of new mates. I was excited. But what she says is right – it's her life, isn't it, not mine. And Gideon does seem sound, supportive. What you'd call a lovely boy!'

Ida raised her left hand and pointed forwards.

'Oh, giving me directions now? I see!' Jacks laughed. 'Okay, let's wander up the pier. We haven't done that for a while, have we?'

Jacks pushed her mum's chair up on to the wooden planks of the Grand Pier and trundled slowly down the iconic walkway. Ahead of them, the island of Steep Holm glistened in the sun, and with Worlebury Hill to the right, it was a beautiful sight. Lovers walked arm in arm on the flat sands, and further along at Uphill Beach dogs yapped and fetched sticks and balls in the distance.

'You warm enough, Mum?' Jacks bent forward and retucked the blanket over Ida's arms. They carried on, past the funfair, where she caught sight of Richard Frost at work with a spanner on one of the machines. She chortled to herself.

She parked Ida's chair next to a bench and sat looking out over the vast expanse of water, breathing deeply and enjoying the peace and quiet, which was broken only by the shrill screech of scrounging seagulls.

'This is where you used to come with Dad, isn't it? After dancing the night away at the Grand Atlantic all those years ago. I used to love looking at the pictures of you both all done up, you in your red lipstick, looking like a proper film star! And Dad in a bow tie.' Jacks tutted. 'Those were the days, eh? I bet you miss him. I know you must. I do, still, every day.'

Jacks looked over at her mum. She thought they might do exactly as Lynne Gilgeddy had suggested: have a nice cup of tea and split a tea cake.

Ida's head was resting on her chest. 'You okay, Mum? You don't look too comfy.'

Jacks reached out to touch her mother's cheek, worried that if she slept in that position, she'd wake with a crick in her neck. She pulled her hand back and yelped. Ida's skin was cool to the touch and her face no longer wore a frown or the contortion of fear; instead, it seemed smooth, younger, rested. Her mum looked calm, peaceful, even happy, as though she had been set free.

'Oh, Mum! Oh no!' Jacks sank down on to her knees at the end of the Grand Pier and placed her head on Ida's lap, gripping the soft blanket between her fists. 'Don't you leave me too, Mum. There's so much we need to say to each other. Please, Mum, don't leave me! I love you. I really do.'

★   ★   ★

For the next five days, Jacks felt like she was wading uphill through treacle. She was exhausted, every action stalled by her grief, meaning she got nowhere fast.

The house was eerily quiet. She trod the stairs and put the clean laundry on the kids' beds, then stood outside her mum's bedroom. She hesitated as she turned the handle. The room needed airing; it still smelt of her mum and all her old-lady ailments.

Jacks flung open the window and studied the framed photos on the windowsill, snapshots of a life now done. Sinking down on to the candlewick bedspread, she ran her fingers over the undulating lines of the pattern, stumbling across the bald patch where her childhood fingers had plucked the cotton bare. Fresh tears sprang as another mouthful of guilt slipped down her throat. The times she had snapped in frustration at her mum were at the front of her mind, along with the look of fear on Ida's face as she had wheeled her to the edge of Avon Gorge.

'Oh, Mum, I am so sorry. I was just tired.' She ran her hand over her eyes, removing it to stare at the stack of nappies and baby wipes that were piled on top of the dresser. She considered the fact that she'd never again have to carry another one of those soiled nappies down the stairs or have to shower her mum in the early hours. Her shoulders sagged with relief, which fuelled the next mouthful of guilt.

Pete knocked on the door as he entered. 'Can I come in?'

'You're already in,' Jacks mumbled from her mum's bed, where she now lay face down, her face buried in the pillow.

'Cooksleys just called to see if you'd had any more thoughts about the music.'

'Anything'll do – it doesn't really matter.'

'It can't be *anything*, Jacks. Let's have a think about what your mum would have wanted, songs that meant something to her. What's that one she liked . . .?' He snapped his fingers. 'You know the one – she used to smile when it came on.' Pete tapped the doorframe, as though the annoying rhythm might help his thought process. 'I can't think what it's called. It'd come on the radio and she'd smile and nod a bit.'

Jacks lifted her head and stared at her husband. 'You mean "Happy", the Pharrell Williams song?'

'Is that what it's called?' He hummed the tune.

Jacks sat up. 'You want them to play Pharrell Williams' "Happy" at my mother's funeral?'

'Well, I can tell by your tone that it's a no, but at least we're talking about it.' He smiled.

Jacks felt a small smile form on her lips too, more out of habit than any real cheeriness. 'I don't want to leave this room and I don't want to see anyone. I just want to stay here, where she was.'

'That's okay, love, you don't have to. The kids are fine. There's nothing that needs doing. You can sit up here for as long as you like.'

'Are you sure Jonty's all right?'

'Yes, he's fine. After more cuddles than usual, but that's to be expected.'

'I feel empty,' she whispered. 'Like I'm hungry. But not just that, like I've been hollowed out.'

'You're in shock. It will get easier, I promise.'

She looked at her husband. 'After Dad died, I concentrated on looking after Mum. It took up all my time. I was so busy that I didn't have time to really think about losing him. But also, while she was here, it was as if he was too, in a way. One half of my mum and dad – does that make sense?'

Pete nodded and sat on the side of the bed. 'Yes, it does.'

'And now they've both gone and I feel lost. I'm an orphan, Pete, and even though I'm grown up, that thought makes me so sad.'

'You're not alone, Jacks. You've got us and we're not going anywhere. And you're right, you did give your mum all your time, but now we can have some time together, like we used to. And not only will we have more time, but you'll be less tired, so the time we do get together will be better.'

'I suppose so.' She nodded.

'I was happy to have Ida here, you know that, and you made things the best they could be, but she didn't really have a life. It can't have been great for her. She didn't know what was going on most of the time.'

'I know that, but what about me? What about

338

my life? I miss her! I wanted my mum and dad around me for as long as possible.'

Pete gave a short laugh. 'I know, but that's not how it works, is it?'

'No. It's not.' Jacks sank back down on the pillow. The two sat in silence for some minutes.

'What about the song she and your dad danced to at our wedding? Your dad brought it along, the old smoothie – what was that one?'

Jacks smiled and pictured her parents waltzing cheek to cheek. 'It was Nat King Cole, "Unforgettable". He loved it.'

'How about I tell them to play that?' Pete coaxed. The funeral parlour needed an answer.

Jacks nodded and slipped further down the mattress, burying her head and closing her eyes.

CHAPTER 30

Thirteen Years Earlier

Jacks switched on the radio and hummed along to Kylie's 'Can't Get You Out of My Head' as she wiped the work surface for the fourth time and refilled and boiled the kettle. She put her hair into a ponytail and took it down again, irritated.

'What time did you get up, missus?' Pete asked from the hallway.

'Five.' Jacks wrinkled her nose.

'What are you like? It's going to be fine. Don't forget, if she sees you in a tizz, she'll know something is up and she'll get jittery. We have to keep calm, remember?'

'I do remember, but I can't say I'm finding it easy.'

'I'll take her. I've told the lads I'll be in late. You'll only blub and it will throw her off balance. I can keep my cool and make it a great adventure, okay?'

'Well, let's both go, but I'll stay in the car. Deal?' She wasn't about to miss out on this monumental moment.

'Deal.'

Pete walked over and took his wife into his arms, holding her tightly and kissing her forehead then her nose before progressing to her mouth. She kissed him back eagerly, enjoying the flood of desire that raced through her veins. Pulling away suddenly, she giggled. 'This is not the time or the place, Pete! We've got too much going on this morning.'

He growled at his wife as he reached for her waist. 'I only need five minutes. Four, even . . .'

She slapped his hand away and tutted playfully. 'Make yourself useful and get her shoes and bag ready.'

'I hope it doesn't rain today. Wouldn't it be terrible if I got sent home and had to spend the afternoon holed up in here with you, under the duvet.'

'What's got into you?' She laughed as she handed him a mug of tea. 'One spoonful of bromide or two, sir?'

'For God's sake, don't call me sir, you're making it worse!'

'Perv.' She threw the tea towel at him.

They heard their daughter tread the stairs and both stopped to stare at her as she stood in the doorway, her long hair mussed and her Little Mermaid pyjamas all crumpled. Jacks felt her bottom lip tremble and turned her attention to making the porridge.

An hour later, Pete pulled the van into the lay-by

and cut the engine. Martha sat up front between her parents, her little legs swinging back and forth in her new shoes and her hair pulled into two neat bunches. Her royal-blue cardigan was too big and it was the first time she had worn a tie.

'You look so grown-up, baby. I'm so proud of you!' Jacks kissed her face. 'Have a great day and don't forget to remember every detail and tell me all about it! See you later!'

She reached over, lifted her daughter down to the pavement and handed her to Pete, who was in position on the kerb. She watched him walk Martha to the school's front gate, then slid down, making sure she was out of sight, and felt in her bag for a tissue.

Martha gripped her dad's hand. 'I'm scared, Daddy,' she whispered.

He bent low until their faces were level. 'What? Are you kidding me? My girl, who jumps in the deep end without armbands, who has got rid of her stabilisers? What could you possibly be scared of?' He kissed her little nose.

'I'm scared I won't know where to go.' She looked down at her shiny new shoes.

'Then you just ask someone. And you won't be on your own, there are lots of people starting school today.' He swallowed the lump in his throat.

'My tummy's a bit flippy.' Her voice was small.

'So's mine,' he confessed.

'Will you miss me today?' She gazed up at him forlornly.

Pete took a deep breath as the tears rolled down his cheeks. He struggled to get his words out. 'I . . . I miss you every minute that I'm not with you, Miss Martha. Every minute, every d . . . day.' He felt a reassuring hand on his shoulder and turned to see Jacks smiling at him.

Martha looked up at her mum. 'Look after my daddy today. He's going to miss me!'

She leant forward on tiptoes and kissed his cheek, before turning and skipping across the playground and into school, as if she had done it a million times before.

Pete stood and fought to regain his composure as his wife rubbed his back and walked him back to the van. 'There, there,' she cooed. 'It'll soon be home time.'

CHAPTER 31

A fine rain fell on the June day as Gina stood with Jacks' cousin under the covered walkway by the door to the crematorium and ushered people inside. Jacks was at that moment standing outside the house on Sunnyside Road admiring the shiny black hearse that would take Ida on her final journey. She looked at the beautiful flowers that graced the top of her mum's coffin and the wreaths and bouquets that sat around it. It was a riot of colour – Ida would have been very chuffed. Many of the neighbours had drawn their curtains as a mark of respect for the family that had lived on Sunnyside for the last nineteen years.

Pete came out and stood in front of his wife. 'How you feeling?'

Jacks shrugged as she buttoned the black mackintosh up to her neck and adjusted the black-and-white chiffon scarf that she had tied in a bow at her throat. 'Bit numb really. My head's too messed up for me to feel sad – does that make sense?'

'Yep.'

'I haven't even cried, Pete, not really. I mean the odd tear yes, but not proper crying, because it doesn't feel real.'

'I know, love.'

'It was different when Dad died. Because he was ill, I knew it was going to happen. I was waiting for it almost. But I didn't think my mum would die. I know that sounds stupid, but I just didn't consider it, I thought she'd get ill or just gradually go downhill, but I thought it would be slow and not for ages. I didn't think she would go just like that.' She shook her head and looked once again at the coffin.

'We'll just get through the service and then the wake,' Pete said. 'And then we'll come back and hunker down. We'll shut the world out and you can sleep and rest without interruption, okay?'

Jacks nodded. *Okay.*

'So sorry, Jackie, really am.' Mrs Dodds, their old neighbour from Addicott Road, hovered in front of her.

'Thank you.' Jacks nodded. She looked around the small crowd that had gathered in the front bar of the Grand Atlantic and searched for Pete. He was bending down, chatting to Jonty, who looked a little lost but otherwise fine.

'She was a good age, mind,' Mrs Dodds continued, through the mouthful of crisps she had grabbed from one of the plates of food that had been laid out on the bar.

'Yes, she was.' Jacks nodded again, as though on automatic pilot. There were only so many different words she could summon to respond to the same regrets and condolences offered in muted tones as distant relatives, friends and neighbours showered her with puff-pastry crumbs from the sausage rolls or breathed sherry fumes in her direction.

The door of the bar opened and in walked Martha, with Gideon by her side. Jacks noted the swivel-eyed stares of the mourners, all of them looking at her and Martha and wondering for a heartbeat whether there would be any more dramas in the Davies clan.

Jacks reached out and pulled her daughter towards her. They stood in a hug. Finally Martha pulled away. 'I brought Gideon.'

'So I see.' Jacks glanced at the boy over her shoulder. He had clearly made an effort. He'd put his long hair into a ponytail and was wearing a white shirt and black tie with his jeans.

'Sorry about your mum.'

'Thank you, Gideon.' Her tone was formal; it was almost automatic when she addressed him.

'When my nan died, it didn't feel real. Not for years. She practically brought me up after my mum and dad split up and I kept going to call her. I really wanted to see her, every day. It was horrible. Still is, really.'

Jacks nodded and thought about her dad. She knew how that felt.

Martha took a deep breath and tried to stem

her tears. Gideon placed his arm around her shoulders and whispered into her scalp. 'We'll just get through this and then you can get some rest, okay?'

Martha rallied slightly and smiled up at her man, who had the ability to make everything feel a little bit better. Jacks watched as they sloped off to find a seat.

Gina sidled up to her friend. 'How you doing?'

'Not sure. I want to go home now – well, I do and I don't.'

'Not too much longer.' Gina smiled. 'By the way, I've still got the storage boxes of Ida's stuff in my garage. Let me know when you want them and I'll drop it all by. No rush, of course.'

'Thanks.'

When the last of the mourners had left and Jonty, Martha and Gideon were heading back to Sunnyside Road, Jacks walked to the car with Pete. 'Gina's still got boxes of Mum's stuff in her garage.'

'Do you want to go and get them now?'

Jacks nodded. 'May as well.' She wanted to delay going home to the house with the redundant stair lift and the bath hoist they'd never used.

Pete carried the large square cardboard boxes up the stairs and placed them on the floor. Jacks lifted the top one and put it in the middle of Ida's bed. She ran her fingers over the photos on the windowsill and picked up her mum's bed jacket that lay in wait on the pillow.

'What do we do with all her stuff?' she asked.

'Nothing. Not until you're ready. But when you are ready, some will go to charity, some we'll keep and some we'll throw away. Don't worry about it now, though. It can wait.'

'What's that?' Jonty asked from the doorway, pointing at the box on the bed.

'Some of Nan's stuff from the move, bits and bobs we left at Aunty Gina's. Just going to have a sort through.'

'I was a bit scared of her,' he whispered.

'Who, love? Aunty Gina?' Jacks asked.

Jonty shook his head. 'No Nan.'

Jacks sat on the bed and beckoned her boy into her arms. 'Why on earth were you scared of her? She was just a little old lady.'

'She used to be quiet and then suddenly shout things and call me Don or Toto and it used to make me jump.'

'She was a bit confused, love. She wouldn't have wanted to scare you. She loved you.'

'And sometimes she was a bit smelly and I didn't like that.'

'She couldn't help it, Jont. She was old, but she was like a big baby in a lot of ways.'

'Is that why she had food on her face?' He blinked.

'Yes.' Jacks imagined seeing Ida through his eyes and understood that she probably hadn't seemed all that appealing.

'Is she with Grandad now?'

'I think so.' She hugged him tight. 'They are

probably dancing on a pier somewhere, having a jolly old time.'

'Is she still confused, do you think?' Jonty had obviously been giving it some thought.

'No.' Jacks smiled. 'I don't think she is. I think, wherever she is, she's happy and not confused any more.'

'That's a good thing then.'

'It is, mate,' Pete interjected.

'Can I go and watch telly with Martha and Gideon now?'

Jacks nodded and he padded down the stairs in his socks, avoiding the tacks.

'Do you think he's okay, Pete?'

'Yes, love. It's a period of adjustment for us all, but it's like anything, isn't it? As long we all keep talking, we'll be fine.'

She ignored the lesson.

'Let's see what we've got here.' Pete opened up the box and pulled out a neat stack of folded pillowcases.

'Charity shop,' Jacks said decisively.

'You sure you want to do this now?' he asked as he placed them in a pile. He reached in again and brought out a geometry set, intact and unopened.

'Jonty might be able to use that,' she said.

'Doubt it.' Pete sighed as he lifted out an empty Nike trainers box. This made them smile – the idea of wrinkly, creaky Ida owning a pair of hi-tops and going running. They wondered who'd given her the box.

Pete handed it to Jacks, who carefully lifted the lid to reveal a bundle of paperwork, all tied up in a piece of lilac ribbon. Jacks loosened the ribbon and let the bundle fall apart on the bed. She raked through it, selecting a photo of herself with her dad in front of the Winter Gardens. She remembered it being taken. She was nine. They had been about to go inside and watch the Gang Show when her mum had pulled out the camera and snapped away. Jacks laughed into her palm. 'Oh God! What am I wearing?'

Pete took the photo and studied the image. 'Dungarees! Nice!'

'I loved them. I wore them all the time. And please note the stripey socks, which were a carefully thought-out accessory.'

'Your dad looks so young,' Pete observed.

'He was fifty-four, so quite old to have a nine-year-old, at least among my friends.' Jacks nodded as she rummaged through the pile. 'Look at this!' She held up a piece of card with two tiny milk teeth sellotaped to it. 'These were the first ones I lost. Mum must have got them back from the tooth fairy!'

'She must have!' Pete laughed.

A yellowing piece of paper caught her eye. She removed it from between the coach tickets, a memento from her parents' trip to France and a birthday card Ida had received from her sister, whose pink glitter stuck to her fingers. Jacks unfolded the single sheet and instantly recognised her mother's beautiful penmanship.

350

'I'd forgotten what lovely writing she had.' She turned the page to show Pete, then started to read it.

Pete watched as her face crumpled and her mouth twisted.

'Oh, Pete!' Jacks placed her palm on her chest and handed the sheet to her husband. 'Oh God! I don't know what to think.'

Pete read the letter addressed to his father-in-law out loud.

'In response, Don, I watched you with Jackie tonight and my heart sank. She thinks the world of her dad and yet you calmly lie and tell her you've been working, when I know you were with Joan. Mr Wievelmore told me he saw you again. The pleasure he takes in keeping me informed makes everything even harder, but I understand, she is his wife and he really doesn't know what to do either. That makes two of us. Your lies are making me ill, making me angry and making my home feel like a prison. I love you. All I've ever done is love you, and Jackie made us complete. I thought we would have been enough. To find out you and Joan have been carrying on all that time, behind my back, even through my pregnancy, is more than I can bear. My heart is broken, but I will try, I will try to carry on for the sake of our little girl. Please give her up. Tell me what I can do to make you give her up. I can't share you. I won't. Ida.'

Pete glanced up at his wife, who looked horrified.

She shook her head. 'I can't believe it.'

Pete reread the detail. 'Who's Joan Wievelmore?'

'I don't know. I've never heard the name before. Do you think it's true?'

Pete nodded. 'I do, Jacks. I don't know why she'd keep the letter all these years if it wasn't. And it certainly sounds true.' He scanned the words again. 'It says "in response" – do you think your dad might have written to her?'

Jacks grabbed the pile and sifted through the sheets and envelopes, sorting though postcards and photographs until she found it. The envelope was blank and unstuck. She pulled out the two sheets and flattened them with her palm against her thigh before lifting them towards the light and reading out loud. She wanted Pete to hear it too.

'I have thought long and hard, Ida. Living with a secret is a very hard thing to do. I agree that Jackie should not be lied to; she's my daughter and as far as I am concerned deserves to be given the facts. Joan and I fell in love. It was simple, it happened. She made me happy. She makes me happy. I cannot give her up. I simply ask that you let me go, then there will be no more lies. I sometimes think my punishment for having fallen in love is the way you refuse to release me, wanting me to spend my days apart from her, with you reminding me of my many failings. It's a hard lesson for me to learn and a rotten way for us both to live. Surely you can see that you would benefit from the freedom too? You are a wonderful woman, Ida, and I want you to be free to go and live your own life in your own way, so I can do the same. I stay for Jackie. But that doesn't mean I don't want to be elsewhere. I do. I love you too, in my own way, but as we know, that's not always enough, is it? Whoever said life was easy? Don.'

Jacks slumped on the bed and shook her head. 'He wanted to leave us. I can't believe it. Not my dad!'

Pete lay next to her. 'It was a long, long time ago and nothing to do with you. Your dad loved you very much, you know that.'

'These must have been the letters Mum wanted to find, the ones she was waiting for, the ones she kept asking about. Do you remember, she said once that I mustn't read her letter. She shouted it. "You mustn't! Don't do it!" And then when she went AWOL at Ange and Ivor's, she said she was looking for something we'd stored there. This is what she was looking for.' Jacks fanned the papers against her palm. 'She wanted to keep this from me. Oh, Mum!'

She started to cry, properly cry, for the first time since Ida's death.

'I shouted at her,' she sobbed. 'I should never have shouted at her. I just lost my patience sometimes and I was a bit rough with her once or twice when she was in the shower. I didn't mean it. I was just tired. So tired. And . . . and I scared her, took her to the Avon Gorge in the dark. I should never have done that. I wasn't thinking straight.' She sobbed harder, almost hysterical.

353

'Don't cry, love. Don't cry. Calm down, Jacks.' Pete held her tight. 'You did everything for your mum. She was happy and she knew she was loved.'

'Oh, Pete . . . Pete . . .' She gulped, trying to speak through her tears. 'I miss her, I miss her being here and I thought my dad was perfect! I did! I thought he was the most perfect man!'

Pete thought back to the night a few months ago when he'd sat at the kitchen table and watched the hands on the clock turn so slowly he was convinced time was going backwards. 'No one's perfect,' he whispered.

'I thought Dad was. But the worst thing is that I hated the way Mum treated him – it made me feel angry with her, I despised her at times, but all that time she was heart-broken. Imagine her having to live like that! He had done that to her and I didn't know!' Jacks let her tears fall as she buried her head in the candlewick bedspread. 'Oh, Mum! I'm so sorry. My mum! And now it's too late. I'm so sorry!'

Pete held her even tighter.

'I can't believe it, Pete. Why did he do that to us? Hurt her and lie to me? I can't believe they had this secret.'

'Everyone has secrets, Jacks. And you mustn't let this change things. You adored your dad and he you. What went on between him and your mum is a whole separate thing. They were grown-ups and it's to their credit that they kept it from you.'

Jacks shrugged free from his grip and sat up,

trying to catch her breath. 'Since Dad died, I've had a little picture of him in my mind all the time. His face has just sat there, in the middle of everything I look at. But now it's gone. It's just disappeared.'

Pete took her hand inside his. 'Maybe that's a good thing. Maybe you'll be able to see your own family a bit more clearly now.'

'You mean Martha, don't you?' Jacks started crying again and collapsed against her husband's chest.

'Yes I do,' he whispered. 'And remember what we agreed, Jacks, about telling her. That time is getting close now, you know that, don't you?'

Jacks nodded, how could she forget? They sat together in silence, both digesting the facts of the letter and its implications. It was Jacks that spoke first. 'I need to re-evaluate, Pete, need to get my mind straight and think about life going forward. My dad was right, I need to look forwards, look ahead and the path'll be clear. Looking back will only get me into trouble.' She had a sudden flashback to the day her mum died and the way Ida had gestured at her to carry on straight ahead. She smiled through her tears. 'Even Mum was telling me to go forwards, I think, in her own way. You know, Pete, I don't think she was always quite so out of it as we thought.'

Pete was only half listening as he picked up an A4 envelope and flipped it open. He held the contents up to his face. 'Jesus Christ!'

'What is it?' Jacks shrank back. 'I don't know if I can cope with more bad news.'

'It's not bad news, love. It's a certificate and a letter signed by your mum and her solicitor, and a note for us, from Ida.'

Jacks took the piece of paper and swallowed as she spoke the sum aloud. 'Thirty-five thousand pounds in Premium Bonds!'

She read the letter through. 'Inherited from her father . . . Now I come to think of it, when I was little she used to talk about Granddad being good with money. Used to irritate the hell out of Dad when she mentioned it, he thought it was made up!'

Pete stared at her. It was some seconds before he spoke. 'I don't know what to say.'

'Oh, Pete, this must have been the treasure! I thought it was just her mind playing up, I never dreamt . . .'

The two sat in silence for some minutes, until Jacks spoke. She sat up straight and coughed. 'I've got an idea, Pete, but only if you agree . . .'

'Try me.' Pete leant back against the headboard of Ida's bed and listened to his wife.

CHAPTER 32

Thirteen Years Earlier

Pete and Jacks stood by the side of the pond and watched as Martha put the bread bag on the ground and instead pulled her bag of Twiglets from her pocket.

'Martha, darling, the bread is for the birdies and the Twiglets are for your lunch!'

'But I don't like Twiglets, so I'm swapping!' she stated matter-of-factly.

Jacks turned to her husband and leant on his arm, laughing. Pete patted her hand. 'She is so like her mum.'

'Yes, she is.' Jacks shook her head, picturing herself at five years old.

The gaggle of birds gathered around Martha's feet. She squealed and jumped backwards. 'Daddy! I don't like them!' She ran back to the protection of her parents, burying her head in her mum's lap.

'Oh, Martha, they won't hurt you. You were doing a great job of feeding the ducks – good job you were on hand to give them some lunch.'

'They're not ducks, they're geese.'

Pete nodded, looking again at the cluster of birds. 'Yes, of course they are. Silly me!'

Martha stared at her dad. 'You can tell the difference because ducks have pretty babies and geese have ugly babies.'

'Ah, yes, you're right. Now you come to mention it, there's a very famous story about an ugly duckling who is in fact no such thing. He grows up to discover he is actually a beautiful swan. D'you know that one?'

'No.' Martha screwed up her nose.

'Was I an ugly baby or a pretty baby?' she asked.

'Oh, you were the most beautiful baby in the whole wide world! The most amazing baby Weston General has ever seen! In fact they are going to put a little blue plaque on the wall saying, Martha Davies was born here!' Pete answered truthfully.

'Are they really?' Martha took this quite literally.

'Absolutely.' Pete nodded.

'Don't you fib to me, Daddy!' Martha waggled her finger at him, learning this action from when she had been similarly reprimanded.

'I never would. Would you like me to tell you the story about the ugly duckling?' he asked, bending down towards his daughter.

Martha considered his offer. 'No,' she replied and she ran back to the path for another lap around the pond.

Jacks roared with laughter. 'Well, that told you, Dad!'

Pete placed his wife's arm through his. 'Must be losing my touch.'

'Doubt that, you old charmer.' She sighed.

'Do you remember when we used to come here courting? We'd park the bikes and lie on the grass, looking up at the sky?'

Jacks smiled. 'I do. And you used to give me a load of old baloney about how you nearly got the big call from the premier league! You could charm the birds out of the trees.'

'I only wanted to charm you.' He came to a standstill.

'Well, it worked. You got me.' She looked up, watching Martha on the path.

'Yep, I was punching above my weight on that day.' Pete bent forward and kissed his wife.

Jacks leant back and let herself be kissed. She felt her spirits lift; he still had the power to make that happen.

'I love you, Jacks.'

She nodded. 'And I love you too. And that's enough, isn't it? You don't need no fancy football lifestyle?'

'It's enough today.' He smiled. 'It really is.'

'She's right, though, Pete . . .' Jacks let this trail.

'Who is?'

'Martha. We shouldn't lie to her, ever. We need to be straight about everything.' She looked at the floor, avoiding his gaze. Pete sighed loudly. 'I know, but the idea of it. It kills me.' He spoke through gritted teeth.

Jacks heard the catch in his throat and nestled against his chest. 'I think we should tell her when she's older. Old enough to make sense of it all.'

'When will she be old enough, Jacks?' he said, his perplexed tone genuine.

'I don't know. Maybe when she becomes a mum?' she suggested.

It was a few seconds before Pete answered, as the two stood watching their little girl, jumping on the water's edge, chatting to the ducks as she dropped bread and Twiglets into their greedy beaks. 'Okay. We'll tell her when she becomes a mum, that's only fair, isn't it?'

Jacks hugged him tight. 'It is, my love.'

CHAPTER 33

The summer had come and gone, but it still felt strange to Jacks to be able to walk at her leisure along the Marine Parade without a wheelchair to push. Weston-super-Mare had as ever put on one hell of a show for the holiday-makers, but now September had arrived the place felt like a hall the day after a party. Everyone was taking stock, cleaning up and preparing for things to get back to normal after all the excitement. Jacks looked out over the pier and smiled; her hometown had never looked lovelier.

She breathed in the sea air and thought about how much had changed in the couple of months since Ida's passing. The day of the funeral had been a day of revelations and new beginnings. She remembered how, after finding her mum's 'treasure' that evening, she'd desperately tried to make things normal. While Pete had tucked Jonty into bed, she'd filled the kettle and made four cups of tea. She chortled to herself, recalling how, when she'd pushed open the lounge door with her foot, bringing in the tea, Martha had quickly pulled her legs off Gideon's lap at the sight of her and sat up straight, and Gideon had smoothed his hair, reminding her that they were both still kids.

Jacks handed out the mugs and took a seat in one of the empty chairs. 'Your dad'll be down in a minute. We need to have a family chat.'

Gideon stood up and hovered awkwardly. 'I'll leave you to it, then, Mrs Davies. I hope you're feeling okay. I thought today went well – I mean, funerals are never nice, but it was the best it could be.'

'Sit down, Gideon, you're family now. And for God's sake, call me Jacks.'

Gideon sat. Martha gave him a quizzical look; she was as much in the dark as he was.

Pete came in and grabbed his tea from the tray. 'So . . .' He took a sip of his drink. 'It's been quite a day.' He smiled at his wife. 'Jacks and I have been talking and we want to get things straight. Don't we?'

Jacks nodded. *I really do. Life is too short – I've learnt that. I wasn't the perfect daughter, but I can be a great mum and a bloody brilliant grandma.*

'Thing is, Gideon, this is not what we planned for our daughter.'

'I know, I know, but—'

'Let me finish.' Pete cut him off mid sentence. 'But you're a decent lad.'

'He really is, Dad.' Martha grabbed Gideon's spare hand and held it tight.

'We are trusting you with the most precious thing we have. I have loved that girl since she took her first breath and I shall love her until my last.' Pete was visibly choked.

Jacks swallowed the tears that gathered at the back of her throat. *You are her dad, Pete, and you always will be.*

'I won't let you down.' Gideon sat straight-backed and spoke sincerely.

Pete looked at his wife, who gave an almost imperceptible nod. 'A little bird tells me you have plans to open your own garage, doing modifications and stuff.'

'Yes!' Gideon's face lit up with equal measures of surprise and enthusiasm. 'I know I can make a go of it. I've done the business plan, it's flawless.'

'We even found a premises.' Martha looked at her parents. 'Gideon went to the bank and everything. We can't do it now, but we will do it one day, won't we?' She looked at her man.

He nodded. 'We will.'

'Why can't you do it now?' Pete asked.

Gideon shrugged. 'We need a big deposit – silly money, really. So I have to earn more first and then see where we are.'

'There's a way we can get you started, Gideon.' Jacks spoke directly to him.

'What?' He looked from Jacks to Martha and back again.

'Pete and I are going to give you some money to get your new business off the ground, to give you and Martha the right start.'

Gideon stared at her, dumbstruck.

'We want you to show Pete your business plan, let him get it checked over, and if it's as sound as you think it is, he'll go back to the bank with you. There's equity in this house and we have some money. And if it all works out, who knows . . .?' She smiled.

'But . . . but . . . How? Mum? I . . . I don't . . .' Martha couldn't speak through the tears that stopped the words in her throat.

Gideon stood and walked over to Pete. He reached out and shook his hand. 'I don't know how I can ever thank you. I don't. No one has ever helped me out, never. And you're doing this?'

'You don't have to thank us, just look after our little girl.' Pete held his eye.

'I will. I promise. I love her.' Gideon beamed.

Jacks stood and walked over to the sofa, sitting down in the spot vacated by Gideon. Martha threw her arms around her mum's neck. 'Thank you, Mum. I don't understand how, but thank you! I love you. I really do.'

'I love you too, always have and always will, no matter what.' Jacks kissed her girl. 'God, it's been some day today. I am exhausted.'

'Me too!' Martha stretched.

'Angela dropped off some bits and bobs for the baby the other day, did you see?'

'No!' Martha sat up, excited, free at last to mention the child that was growing inside her.

Jacks jumped up and came back with the Moses

basket and the vests and clothes donated from next door. Martha held up a little vest and placed it on her chest. 'It's tiny!'

None of them heard Jonty enter the room; he couldn't get off to sleep with the loud voices and what sounded like celebrations coming from below. He looked over at his big sister. 'I don't think that's going to fit you.'

'It's not for me, you doughnut!' Martha yelled.

'Don't call your brother a doughnut!' Pete and Jacks chorused in unison.

Jacks smiled as she replayed the happy scene in her mind and crossed the road to the supermarket. She wandered the aisles, muttering to herself, trying to think what to make for tea. 'Chicken? No, we had that last night. Pork chops? No, Jonty won't eat them. I could make a fish pie. Does Gideon like prawns? I don't bloody know . . .'

'Jacks?' a voice called from behind.

'Lynne! Ah, lovely to see you. How are you?' She beamed.

'I'm great! Ashley's home for a week or two. I love having her here, hearing all about her adventures and it's good for her to spend time with Molly, Caitlin-Marie's little girl.'

'Ah, Molly, that's a lovely name. How's she doing, she must be getting big?'

'Yes, she's cute. Nearly seven months old now, if you can believe it! Goes so quickly. And how's Martha doing?'

'Oh, due any day now. She's got her bag packed

by the front door and her dad's sitting with the car keys in his hand day and night, just in case! Gideon's mum works at Weston General and is already giving firm instructions about how this baby'll be born!'

She and Allison had silently reached an understanding that they both only wanted what was best for their kids and that they were powerless to change things anyway. Jacks had decided she rather liked Allison's forthright nature and thought it highly possible that they might become friends.

'You seem quite calm, considering,' Lynne noted.

'Do you know, I am. It's funny, Lynne, but when I was looking after my mum, I didn't have time to think. I was on autopilot, but for the last few months I've had time back and it's helped me take stock. I've kind of slowed down and it's good, like I can see things a lot more clearly.' *Poor Mum.* She pictured pushing her mum around with the basket on her lap. 'I miss her, though, really do.'

Lynne rubbed her friend's arm. 'Course you do and I was very sorry to hear she'd passed on. But you were wonderful to look after her for as long as you did. She was always beautifully turned out and I always thought she looked very happy, just to be with you.'

'Thank you, Lynne.' Jacks felt a little overcome by the compliment. 'Right, suppose I better get on and get home.'

'Good luck!' Lynne shouted as the two headed off in different directions. 'Ooh,' she called over her shoulder, 'forgot to ask, how did Martha get on in her exams?'

Jacks stopped and turned. 'Her exams?'

'Yeah.' Lynne nodded.

'Oh, she got three As!'

'Bloody hell!' Lynne laughed.

Jacks smiled as she reached for a tin of pears, which she would serve with custard. *Yep, you said it. Bloody hell!*

Two days later, Jacks was making tea for the builders, workmates of Pete's who were doing their new loft conversion – or 'Jonty's floor', as it was now known. She walked past Ida's old room, unrecognisable since Martha and Gideon had moved into it. With all the clutter removed, it was quite spacious and it was amazing what a lick of paint and some new carpet had done. The cot was assembled in the corner and a nursing chair sat under the window in preparation, with Ida's favourite soft blanket folded over the arm.

'Mum?'

'Yes, love?' Jacks popped her head inside the door.

'Can you call Gideon for me?' Martha asked.

'Sure, where is he?'

'He's at the garage, the new tenants are moving in upstairs.'

Gideon had decided, much to Jacks and Pete's relief, that the sensible thing would be to rent out the flat above his business premises. The income it would bring would be far more beneficial than the privacy it would give them. And he figured that when the baby came along, Martha would need her mum on hand.

'Are you all right, love?' Jacks looked at her daughter, who was sitting on top of her duvet with her arms braced behind her and her bump filling her pyjama top.

'I think something might be happening, Mum!'

'Really?'

Martha nodded, smiling and calm.

'Oh God, right! I'll go call him. You stay there!' Jacks pointed at the bed.

Martha laughed. 'Where do you think I'm going to go in this state?'

She ran to the kitchen and grabbed her phone. 'Goodeon? Gid, I mean Gideon, good, you need to come home. Martha thinks something's happening!' she shouted.

'Oh, okay, Jacks, I'll just finish up here and come back.'

'No! Don't just finish up there, come straight back now!' she yelled. 'I don't understand how you two are so calm!' she shrieked.

'All right.' He laughed. 'I'm on my way. Do you want anything picking up from the shop?'

'The shop?' she squealed, almost breathless. 'Don't stop at the shop! Come back now! Come straight home!'

Gideon snorted down the line. 'Only kidding. I'm not going to stop anywhere. I'll be back soon.'

'And drive carefully!' she managed before ending the call and immediately dialling Pete's number.

'Mum?' Martha called loudly.

'Hang on, Pete!' Jacks shouted, covering the mouthpiece and running to the bottom of the stairs. 'What is it, love? Are you okay? I'm just updating Dad and then I'll be up!'

'Yeah, I'm fine. I was just wondering, have I got a clean shirt?'

Jacks leant on the banister and laughed. 'Yes, in the bloody airing cupboard!'

Jacks fidgeted in her uncomfortable vinyl chair in the waiting room while Pete and Jonty crowded round Pete's phone screen, watching a cartoon.

'I hope it's a boy!' Jonty looked up.

'Well . . .' Jacks looked at her watch. 'Not too much longer to wait and you'll find out.' She smiled at Pete.

'I think I'm too young to be a grandad!' he moaned.

'Bit late for that,' she responded. 'Fancy a breath of fresh air, Jont?' She could see he was getting a bit antsy.

'Sure.' He followed his mum out into the cool night.

They rested on the low wall by the entrance and looked up at the sky. 'Did you know, Jonty, the moon is about a quarter of a million miles away.'

He looked at his mum. 'No, I didn't know that.'

'And what's even more amazing is that, despite

being just over two thousand miles wide, you can fit the whole thing behind your thumbnail. Look!' She held her thumb up in the air and closed one eye, watching as her son did the same.

'You're right, Mum. That's amazing!'

Jacks smiled.

'Mu-um?'

'Yes, love.'

'We're doing show and tell in school and Mrs Palmer says I have to take in a pet. I said we didn't have one, but she said we can bring in anyone's pet, so I have to borrow one.'

'Are you kidding? That's a big ask. When do you need a pet by, Jonty?' *Please not tomorrow. Please, please not tomorrow . . .*

'Tomorrow,' he said.

'How did I know you were going to say that?' She gathered her son into her chest. 'Come on, let's get back inside. We don't want to miss anything, do we?'

Allison came hurtling through the swing doors and plonked herself down next to Jacks. 'They won't tell me anything,' she said huffily. 'I know some of the nurses up there and even they won't tell me a bloody thing!'

'This is the hardest bit, isn't it? The waiting.' Jacks smiled at her and reached into her bag for the sweets she had been saving for when they needed a lift. 'Who wants a sucking sweet?' she asked, holding the open tin in her outstretched hand.

'Ooh, me!' Gina shouted as she swept into the room, holding a large bunch of flowers. 'What did we get?'

'Nothing yet, G. Still waiting.' Jacks grinned at her friend.

'Damn. I was hoping for a quick cuddle and then to get home in time for *Corrie*!' Gina tutted.

'Jonty likes a cuddle, G! Will he do?' Pete teased.

'No way! I don't!' Jonty squirmed and punched his dad on the arm.

'I've got a cuddle waiting for me at home,' Allison whispered.

'Ooh, Allison, you dark horse. Who's the lucky man?' Jacks asked.

'Well . . .' Allison reached for the edges of her cardigan and pulled them around her bust. 'It's early days, but I must admit I'm quite keen.' She smiled.

'Where did you meet?' Gina asked, loving the gossip.

'On the pier. He works up there. He's lovely, his name's Richard, Richard Frost.'

'You all right, Gina?' Pete asked as Gina leant forward, apparently choking on her sweetie.

Jacks jumped up and with her shoulders shaking in silent giggles, she rubbed her friend's back. 'Oh, she's just a bit overwhelmed, what with the baby coming and everything.'

The two friends caught each other's eye as they swallowed their hysterics.

It was an hour later, when things had calmed

slightly, that Gideon walked into the waiting room, pushing Martha in a wheelchair. 'Sorry, people! False alarm!' Martha shouted, her arms above her head.

'Oh no!' Jonty yelled.

Pete groaned and Gina stared at the bouquet she had spent fifteen quid on. 'You may as well take these.' She handed Martha the flowers. 'And try and keep them fresh till the baby comes, I can't be getting you any more!'

Martha inhaled the scent of the white flowers. 'Aww, thank you, Aunty G. I can appreciate them now. They're lovely.'

Gideon drove Martha and Jonty home while Jacks and Pete ambled across the car park and climbed into the van.

'Thought we'd be coming home with a baby,' Pete said. 'It feels a bit flat after all that excitement.'

Jacks laughed. 'Tell you what, it was a good dry run and personally I've had enough excitement for one day. A bit of flat suits me just fine. Shall we get everyone chips?'

'That's the best idea you've had all day. I'm bloody starving!' He kissed his wife.

Pete pulled into Sunnyside Road and shunted the back end of the van into a space, grinding the gears into reverse repeatedly before jumping forward inch by inch, until finally he got the thing parked, even if it was at an untidy angle. Jacks waited for him on the pavement, her arms full of hot bags of chips slathered in salt and vinegar. Pete jumped down from the cab and they trotted down the road side by side.

'False bloody alarm, I still can't get over it. That's a few hours of my life I'm never getting back.' Pete chuckled as he put his arm around Jacks' shoulders. 'She's late and unprepared for everything, that girl. Having this baby is going to be no different.' They laughed.

Pete's phone beeped in his pocket. He glanced at the screen and pulled his arm from his wife's shoulders. 'Ah, God, it's work.'

'At this time of night? Can't you tell them you're busy?'

'I can't, love. I'm going to have to go and sort it out. We've got a big job on and there's been a mix-up with the slabs. Shan't be too long. You get them chips inside before they go cold.' He kissed her cheek and climbed back into the van.

A few minutes later, Pete drew up on the seafront and sat waiting, trying to still his heart, which was beating a little too fast for comfort. A pair of headlights swooped into the space behind him and he heard the roar of an engine revving loudly, the bass reverberating in his rib cage. He got out of his van, conscious of his work attire with its splashes of cement and mud. He should have shaved. Cursing himself for his misplaced vanity, he wished he didn't feel so nervous.

Sven slid out of the red Ferrari and stood on the pavement. 'Hello, Pete. How are you?' He walked confidently towards Pete, as though it had been months and not almost two decades since their paths had last crossed. He nodded at him with his arm outstretched, but Pete declined to shake Sven's hand. Instead, he stared at him, his gaze unwavering, his stance challenging.

'What do you want?' Pete asked.

'I was in London on business and thought I'd come down. It's only a couple of hours in that.' He pointed to the car. 'I got your number from Gina.'

'I said, what do you want?' Pete concentrated on keeping his voice steady.

'To talk to you,' Sven answered, standing with his legs slightly apart and his palms splayed, trying to look unthreatening.

'You've got two minutes,' Pete said curtly.

'Is that right?' Sven asked with a hint of amusement in his voice, unused to taking orders from anyone. He looked over Pete's shoulder into the dark space beyond the sea wall. 'This might take a little longer than two minutes.'

Sven's tone infuriated Pete. He rushed forward, grabbed Sven's lapels and pushed him against the Ferrari, pinning him to the car. 'I said two minutes – you just wasted ten seconds!' he almost whispered.

Sven gave a small laugh. 'I can see you are still of the view that a quick flex of your muscles will solve anything. I remember you and your flailing fists.'

It took all of Pete's strength not to rise to the jibe. His voice was level but he spoke through gritted teeth. 'I don't like you. I don't like anything about you and I wouldn't hold back in showing you just how much.' He didn't notice Mr Vickers from the hardware store strolling along the pavement with his scruffy dog.

'All right, Pete?' Mr Vickers said as he passed, as though it was quite normal for Pete to be pinning a man against the side of a Ferrari.

'All right?' Pete responded, never taking his eyes from Sven's face.

Mr Vickers whistled and called his dog to heel. He turned his head to call over his shoulder. 'Oh, by the way, Pete, can you tell Ivor I've got his paint in?'

'Will do.' Pete nodded.

'You always thought you were such a big shot,' Sven snarled, 'you and your football mates, all laughing at me. You were so small-town it was funny, but you had such big ideas!'

'Don't tell me this is about school, me laughing at your bloody jumper?' Pete pulled away as the strength left his wrists.

Sven stood straight, smoothing his white shirt and tailored jacket back down over his jeans. He coughed and pushed his fingers through his blonde hair, but he didn't say anything.

'That's pathetic! Don't you see? You won!' Pete laughed. 'You've got the flash car, the big boat, the bloody platinum credit card. You got the works, mate. Me? I have to scrabble down the back of the sofa to find the price of a pint. So piss off back to wherever it is you've come from and enjoy your life. And leave me to get on with mine.'

'Ah, but I didn't win, did I? You got Jacks and you got my daughter.'

Pete froze, the words hovered in his throat and his head swam.

'Martha is my daughter!' Sven said it loudly this time, as though it might be news to Pete.

Pete's face crumpled. With his eyes screwed tightly shut, he winced as if in extreme pain. When he opened his eyes again, he tried to control his shaking limbs and calm the tremor in his voice. 'I'm afraid you've got the wrong end of the stick, sunshine. She is not yours. I am her dad and that is that. Now just do as I've asked and leave, leave us alone.'

Sven flipped his car keys in his palm. 'I want to be reasonable, but you think I can't take steps? Make things official? It would take days, that's all.'

'And what would that serve? What the fuck is this all about?' Pete thought about where they had been only hours earlier. It had been such a lovely day. But now the excitement of becoming a grandad had been wiped out by this and he was scared, the most scared he'd ever been.

'Clarity. I think it's important we all know where we stand.' Sven gave a faint smile.

Pete took a deep breath, delivering his words carefully. 'I was a kid when I fell in love with Jacks, without the first clue about life, and there I was, responsible for a baby! Most blokes would have done a runner, but not me. And here's the thing. It takes a lot more than a quick shag to make a dad. I have been there since that little girl took her first breath, held her hand on her first day of school and read her stories before she fell asleep. I'm her dad.' He pointed at his chest. 'And there ain't nobody in the world going to take that away from me.'

The two men stood face to face. Pete took a step closer towards Sven. 'I am not a proud man and so I am going to beg you. My daughter is about to have a baby. There's no way she could deal with you turning up, neither could my wife. And quite frankly, neither can I.'

He turned, walked across the pavement and sat on the sea wall, staring out towards Steep Holm. He felt numb as he imagined Martha running into Sven's arms as they were reunited. Pictured Jonty eager for a ride in the flash car. It caused him physical pain, the thought of losing his daughter and not being able to provide what this man could. He'd never felt so powerless in his life.

Sven sidled over and sat on the wall beside him. He raised his hands. 'Don't punch me!'

Pete shook his head. 'I haven't punched anyone since I was at school.' He saw Sven's shoulders relax. The two sat side by side in silence for some seconds.

'I don't know why I'm here really.' Sven sighed. 'My life can feel empty at times. I sometimes wonder what it would be like to have a family and I thought I could just . . . I don't know . . .'

'Take mine?' Pete asked. He rubbed his hands together. Even after years of working outside, he still hated the cold.

'No. Not take yours, but be involved somehow. That doesn't seem like such a good idea now.'

'It isn't.' Pete looked at his adversary. 'I've dreaded you coming here. Dreaded it since the day she was born. For her whole life it's hung over me like a recurring nightmare. You're the only thing in the world I'm afraid of. Because you can fuck up my family, the people I love more than anything.'

'I'm not going to do that.' Sven spoke clearly. 'But I did want to give you this, a letter.' He pulled a cream envelope from his inside pocket. Pete took it into his palm and turned it over. It lay there, balanced. 'Is there anything in here that could hurt her?' Pete's voice was quiet.

'No.' Sven shook his head. 'It's an apology. I have told her that I'm sorry I walked out on her before she was born and I've said how lucky she has been to have a dad like you, one that has always been there for her and always will be . . .'

Pete nodded.

'I've also said that I won't make contact with her, but if at any point she wanted to come and see me in San Francisco, then she would be very welcome. That's it.' He shrugged, clasping his hands in his lap. 'Only give it to her if you think it's the right thing to do, Pete. But I hope you do.'

Pete carried on as though Sven hadn't said anything. 'I've always had this little nagging voice at the back of my mind that my daughter's love would come at a price, that I'd have to pay. I hated that feeling. I still do.'

Sven shook his head. 'You know, Pete, there are some people in this world who would have named me and taken millions. You could have and I would have given it willingly.'

'I never wanted your millions, just wanted my family.'

Sven nodded. 'I don't really know how to say this, but thank you for looking after her.'

Pete stared at him, unsure if he was referring to Jacks or Martha. Part of him wanted to rage at this stranger who had the nerve to thank him, but there was also a tiny flicker of compassion, gratitude that he recognised the part Pete had played. He stood up.

'Do me a favour, Sven. If you ever cared about Jacks and if you have a shred of interest in what's best for Martha, then please stay away. I don't want to see you again.' Pete strode back to his van and jumped in, placing the letter on the back seat.

'You won't,' Sven whispered as he stared out to sea.

'Mum?' Martha called from the hallway.

'What, love?' Jacks stirred the milk into her coffee.

'I think I've started for real. I want to go back

to the hospital!' Martha sounded anxious as she placed her hands on her stomach.

Pete came through the front door and took one look at his little girl. 'What's up, love?'

'Ooh, Dad, I've got these little shooting pains travelling from my spine across my tummy and down the tops of my legs.'

Pete stared at her, feeling helpless, remembering the day he'd watched her being born. He wished he could take the pain for her.

Martha started to cry. 'I don't feel too good.'

'Oh, love! It's okay, I promise, it will all be okay.' Jacks wrapped her arms around her daughter, rocking her as best she could.

Martha bent forward. 'I'm a bit scared.'

'Course you are, but there's no need to be, you're going to be in the very best hands.'

'Martha?' Gideon called from the bathroom doorway, bare chested and with a towel wrapped round his waist. 'Where are you? You okay?'

'I think I've started properly now. This feels different. We need to get going!' She leant against the stack of boxes in the hallway.

'I'll grab the bag.' Gideon raced into their bedroom, threw on his jeans and a T-shirt and hurtled down the stairs with Martha's overnight bag and the car keys. 'Come on, babe, let's get you back to the hospital. It'll be okay, don't worry. Jacks, you and Pete meet us there. Ivor said to pop Jonty in with him and Ange if the baby came at night. Can you do that?' he asked as he ushered his girlfriend out of the front door and into the car, fastening the seatbelt over her bump.

Jacks nodded from the doorstep, admiring the way the boy was taking care of his family. 'We'll be there as soon as we can.'

'Please hurry!' Martha shouted through the window as the car pulled away.

'Will she be okay?' Pete asked.

Jacks took a deep breath. 'Yes, of course. But seeing her like that makes me realise she's only a little girl, really, isn't she?' She shoved the remnants of a bag of chips into Pete's hands and ran into the house to shepherd Jonty next door.

Jacks and Pete sat in the waiting room, which was a lot quieter than it had been earlier.

'Get everything sorted for work?'

Pete paused. 'It wasn't work, love.'

'Oh?' Jacks looked at him quizzically.

'I went to see Sven.'

'Oh god, Pete! I . . .'

'No. There's no need to say anything,' he interrupted her. 'It's all sorted.' He nodded. 'All sorted.'

'I love you Pete.' She squeezed his hand.

'Me too. Our first grandchild, eh?' He shook his head.

'Funny, isn't it, that this is where Martha was born. And me! It makes me think about my mum.'

Jacks rested her head on his shoulder and he inhaled the scent of her. 'Ah Ida, bless her.'

He whispered as he held her. 'I feel quite sorry for Sven, actually.'

'You do? Why?' Jacks looked up at her husband.

'Because for a simple twist in fate and timing, he could have had you. He's got everything, Jacks, all that money, flash car, boats, but I tell you what, he's got nothing. Absolutely nothing.'

'Sure you wouldn't like to swap me for a motorbike and a new van?'

'No!' He laughed. 'Well, it depends. What capacity is this new van?'

'Bloody charming!' She laughed as he reached over to kiss her.

The swing doors flew open and in rushed Allison. 'Have I missed anything?' she panted.

'No. It's all good. They've taken her through to the delivery suite and Gideon's with her. Guess we just wait.'

'Got any more of them sucking sweets, Jacks?' Pete asked as he rubbed his stomach.

''Fraid not.' She laughed, knowing he was reminding her about Richard Frost.

What seemed like hours later, Jacks gave a start and shook her head vigorously. There was a fraction of a second when she didn't know where she was and she thought she'd heard her mum's bell.

'It's okay,' Pete reassured her. 'You nodded off.'

Gideon was standing in front of them wearing a blue hat that looked like it had been made out of a Jeyes cloth and a green hospital gown. He surveyed the small group of family that now crowded round him. Unable to draw breath as the tears coursed down his face, he said, 'Oh God, Martha is so amazing. I knew I loved her before . . .' He sniffed. 'But I never knew I could love her as much as I do now. She's amazing. She worked so hard. I'm so proud of her. She did brilliantly, she really did.'

Jacks and Pete both got tearful too as they held each other tight. *Clever, clever Martha!*

'Oh, Gideon, that's wonderful! I'm so proud of you both. What is it?' Allison chipped in, beaming, her hands clasped in anticipation under her chin.

'A baby! A beautiful baby!' Gideon gave in to the next wave of tears that swamped him. Pete slapped his back and fought his own emotion.

'Gideon?' Jacks asked firmly.

'Yes?' he said, looking slightly bewildered.

'This baby that Martha has just had.'

'Yes, Jacks?' he sobbed.

'Is it a boy or a girl?'

He stood tall, and announced with pride, 'It's a girl, a little girl.'

All four stood crying and drawing breath, letting this wonderful fact sink in.

'You go first.' Allison placed her hand on Jacks' back, urging her forward.

'Are you sure?'

'Yes, of course. She'll be wanting to see her mum.' Allison nodded.

Jacks followed Gideon into the small anteroom off the delivery suite where Martha lay. She gulped, feeling quite overcome with emotion as she saw her little girl, who beamed despite her obvious fatigue, cradling her daughter.

'Oh, Mum!' Martha cooed. 'Look at her! She's so beautiful!'

Jacks bent down and placed her finger in her granddaughter's tiny palm. 'Oh, Martha! She's amazing. Hello! Hello, darling girl!' The little girl curled her long fingers around her nan's, holding on for all she was worth. 'Look at that! She's so strong and so clever! She's holding my hand and she's got quite a grip!' *She's going to be a piano player, I can see it now! She'll play at the Albert Hall in a long taffeta gown and the posters will all have 'Sold Out!' pasted over them as all the tickets will have been snapped up. Pete and I can sit in a box and watch everyone watching her!*

'What's her name?' Jacks asked, unable to tear her gaze from her granddaughter.

'Maggie. Meet Miss Maggie Ida Parks.'

'Oh, that's lovely! Hello, Maggie. Hello, my clever, clever girl! You are so beautiful and clever, just like your mum. You are perfect.'

EPILOGUE

'Pete?' Jacks shouted up the stairs. There was no answer. 'Pete!' she yelled again, louder.

'What, woman? For God's sake! I was in the bathroom!' he shouted from the landing.

'Are you ready? I do not want to be late!' she hollered.

'Not quite, no, but if you hadn't called me, I would be!'

Jacks tutted.

'Thought we weren't meant to shout up and down the stairs!' Jonty yelled from the top floor.

'Very funny, mister. You get down here now too. Say goodbye to your mates. We've got a very important birthday party to get to.'

Jacks put her lipstick on in the hall mirror while three pairs of feet hammered their way down the stairs, shaking the rafters.

'Thanks for having me!' Milo shouted as he sat on the floor by the front door to put his trainers on. Jacks was very strict on her no-shoes policy, wanting to preserve the carpet in its pristine state for as long as possible. Milo made for the street, where his mum sat in the car, waiting to give him and Elliot a lift home.

'You're welcome, love.' Jacks smiled at him, waving her hand at his mum through the open door.

'It was a great sleepover!' Elliot offered as he followed Milo.

'Good. No doubt Jonty will be having another one very soon.'

She waved the boys off and went to collect the cake. It sat on the shiny worktop in the new kitchen she had helped Pete design. She knew she would never get sick of walking into the big open-plan space and seeing her clutter-free surfaces and shiny chrome cooker. And of course her beloved conservatory, which spanned the width of their house in Sunnyside Road. Gideon and Pete's business was going from strength to strength.

Pete walked in behind her. 'Ooh, you smell nice,' she said as she inhaled his lemony scent. 'What do you think, Pete? Does this cake look okay? I'm a bit worried about it; maybe I should have bought one instead? Shall I nip up the shop and get one? There's still time.'

Pete knew how many hours she had spent baking and icing Maggie's fifth birthday cake and the time she had taken to mix just the right shade of pink icing. He squinted at it as he slipped on his smart trainers and decided not to mention that the wording looked very much like 'Happy Birthday Moggie'.

'It's perfect, love. You've done a great job. You could rival that Mary Berry.'

'I doubt that!' she scoffed, secretly delighted by his compliment.

The three of them piled into the car and Jacks held the cake on her lap. 'Go steady, Pete!' she yelped as he drove round the one-way system and on to Gideon and Martha's beautiful Victorian villa on the seafront.

Gideon opened the wide front door and stood back. 'Blimey, didn't recognise you in your jeans, Pete!' He smiled.

'You can laugh, but putting on a suit each day makes me feel the part,' Pete replied. 'It's all right for the lads to be in their scruffs on the forecourts, but when I turn up, at whichever branch, they expect their business manager to be dressed accordingly!'

'Yes, boss. Anyway, let's see this cake we've heard so much about!' Gideon clapped his hands as he bent down to kiss Jacks and peek at the cake. 'Why have you made a cake for the cat?'

Pete stood behind his wife making hand gestures at Gideon.

'It says "Maggie"!' Jacks answered firmly.

'Oh, right. My mistake.' Gideon grimaced and led the procession into the vast kitchen, winking at Pete.

Maggie was sitting on the floor, with Aunty Gina, Allison and Richard all watching her and oohing and clapping as she tore the paper from her presents.

'Thank you! Mummy, look!' she shouted as she added a tiara and a backpack to the pile of many similarly princess-themed items.

'There she is, the most beautiful girl in the whole wide world!' Jacks gushed. *My little concert pianist!*

'Nanny! I got a new tiara!' Maggie clapped and waved at her favourite person.

'Hello, my darling. How lovely! I'm coming for a cuddle in a minute. I'll just put your cake down.'

'I need you now, Nanny! I need to sit on your lap, I've been waiting for you all day!' she whined.

'Oi, missus, birthday or not, we'll have less of the dramatics.' Martha rolled her eyes.

Martha had strung some of Jacks' homemade bunting from the fireplace to the fridge; it spanned the whole room and Jacks thought it made the place feel homey. Martha stood at the sink, draining pasta while trying to chop an onion; she was as ever running hopelessly late and in a bit of a muddle, despite having had all day to prepare.

'Oh, that's lovely, Mum!' She grinned as she looked at the cake. 'Don't know what you were on about, Dad. It definitely says "Maggie", not "Moggie"!'

'What do you mean?' Jacks looked at her daughter.

'Oh, Dad sent a text saying don't say it looks like "Moggie" as you'd spent an age on it. But it doesn't, so no need to worry!'

Pete hid behind Rob and Gideon's dad, who stood nursing beers by the French doors and admiring the walled garden.

'In fact, Mum, lunch is going to be a bit late. Would it be okay if we had cake first?' Martha asked as she scuttled from drawer to drawer and back to the hob.

'Yes, of course!' Jacks couldn't wait to get it cut, to avoid further ribbing.

'We can sing to her later, pop a candle in what's left, she won't mind!' Martha winked.

'No cake for me.' Jonty rubbed his stomach.

'Why's that, mate? Have you got period pains?' Gideon shouted as he came in with a bucket of cold beers.

'Very funny!' Jonty was used to the family joke, which seemed to run and run.

Jacks was concentrating on cutting the cake into slices when Martha put down her chopping board and looked over at her. 'Can I ask you a favour, Mum?'

'Course, love.' Jacks fetched the side plates from the cupboard.

'I was wondering if you'd mind picking Maggie up from school on Tuesday? I'm in court, don't know how long the case will run. You don't mind, do you?' She twisted her hair into a ponytail and laid it on her shoulder.

'Of course I don't mind – you know I'll have her any time. I love having her.' Jacks smiled. It was true, she was completely smitten. As Gina had pointed out, her whole face changed when she mentioned her grandchild.

Jacks looked at the photograph on the mantelpiece

of Martha on her graduation day, standing proudly in her cap and gown and holding her scroll. She remembered the conversation they'd had when Maggie was six months old, offered casually while Jacks was bathing the baby.

'Mum?'

'What?' Jacks turned to her daughter, giving her her full attention.

'I've got something to tell you.'

'What?' Jacks' heart sank in readiness for whatever bad news was lurking.

'I've been offered a place at Bristol Uni.'

'You . . . you have?'

'Yep.'

'To study what?'

'I'm going to read law. I want to be a lawyer.' Martha's words hung in the air. 'What do you think?'

Jacks stared at her daughter and was for once speechless.

'What do you think, Mum?' Martha repeated.

Jacks stared at Maggie, who looked blurred through her tears. 'I think . . . I think you can do anything you put your mind to, my clever girl.'

'Why are you crying then?' Martha laughed.

'Because I'm happy.' Jacks sobbed.

'Blimey, I'd hate to see you when you were upset.' Martha placed her arms around her mum and hugged her tight.

Pete's reaction to his daughter's plan had been less emotional. 'Have you still got that sandwich toaster?' he quipped.

For Jacks, the double bonus was that she got to see a lot more of her tiny granddaughter while Martha was studying. It was amazing how Martha managed to juggle everything so well, but she still needed her own mum's help, which made Jacks' heart sing. Between her duties as a grandma and looking after the books for Pete and Gideon, she was busier than ever and loving it.

Martha's graduation was a day Jacks would never forget. She laughed to herself, remembering how, even though they'd zipped up the motorway in Pete's shiny blue BMW, they'd still cut it fine. The traffic had been heavy and they'd found themselves running up the steps of the Wills Tower just as the ceremony began. Jacks had fidgeted throughout the rather long roll call and then suddenly it was their turn. When Martha's name was read out, along with a special mention for her first, Jacks stood among the sea of faces clapping loudly and caring little whether it was the right thing to do. She had waited her whole life for that moment. She stared as her little girl walked calmly in her cap and gown up to the podium to be handed her scroll. Tears streamed down Jacks' face and her chest swelled with pride. *She did it! She bloody did it! My girl, my daughter. She has picked her path; she's going to be a bloody lawyer.*

'Nanny! Look what I got!' Maggie pulled Jacks from her memories as she called out, swirling round in a long, pale blue dress with what looked like a bridal train, and her matching tiara.

'Ooh, you look beautiful, Mags!' She laughed.

Jacks went out into the garden to give Pete some cake. 'What you doing out here on your own?' she asked.

'I was just thinking about your mum and dad actually. What would they have made of all this, eh?' He gestured at Gideon and Martha's house. 'They'd be so proud, wouldn't they?'

'They would, love.' Her mind turned to her poor old mum and her imperfect dad; two normal parents.

Pete smiled as he bit into the pink-topped sponge. 'This tastes lovely and I think Moggie'll love it!' He stood behind her and cupped her bottom in his hand as he kissed the back of her neck.

'Pete!' She shrank away from him. 'Jonty's around!'

'Can't wait till tonight when he's on his own floor, miles away . . .' He kissed her again and she giggled.

'What's miles away?' Jonty asked. Neither of them had heard him approach.

'The moon,' Pete answered, quick as a flash.

'I know. About a quarter of a million miles, in fact. But you can still fit it behind your thumbnail, can't you, Mum?'

Jacks looked at her son as he held up his thumb and closed one eye.

'Yes, yes you can.' She nodded, thinking for the

first time in a long time about Sven and feeling . . . nothing but a warm glow as she pictured her old friend. She pictured the moment they had told Martha and handed her the letter. She had surprised them both with her stoicism, her maturity. 'I have the best dad in the world, that's all I need,' she commented, as she folded the paper back into its envelope and threw herself into Pete's arms.

'And I ain't never going anywhere Miss Martha,' he had managed to say through his tears. That had been quite a day, when Martha finally understood Jacks' need for her to succeed and her desire to try and stop history repeating itself.

Jonty ambled back inside the house.

'I wonder what else she'll do, that girl of ours,' Pete said. 'She's having one hell of a journey.'

'She is,' Jacks agreed. 'Bit like us. We did it all so young, so now we're like an old couple even though we're only just in our forties!'

'Yep, that's our one good thing, girl – our history, what we've been through. I wouldn't change a single thing. And we've still got a lot of living to do.' He smiled at his wife.

'You're right, Pete. One thing I know for sure is that life is what you make it. No one can make it for you. You have to grab it and run with it or you'll sink, and sinking is the easy option. You have to work hard and fight for better. That's the truth, isn't it?'

'It is, girl. It is.'